KATHY STROBOS

Copyright © 2023 by Katharine Strobos

All rights reserved.

This is a work of fiction. Names, characters, places and incidents are products of the author's imagination or are used fictitiously and are not to be construed as real. Any resemblance to actual events, organizations, places or persons, living or dead, is entirely coincidental.

No portion of this book may be reproduced in any form without written permission from the publisher or author, except as permitted by U.S. copyright law.

ISBN: 9781958894033 (EBook)
ISBN: 9781958894040 (Paperback)

Cover Design: Cover Ever After

www.kathystrobos.com
www.kathystrobosbooks.com

Published by Strawbundle Publishing
New York, New York

To my readers.

Also By Kathy Strobos

New York Friendship Series
A Scavenger Hunt for Hearts
Partner Pursuit
Is This for Real?
Caper Crush

New York Spark Series
My Book Boyfriend
Love Is an Art
My Secret Snowflake
My Rock Star Neighbor

For giveaways, updates on new releases, behind-the-scene news and what's going on in my life, please subscribe to my mailing list at https://kathystrobos.com/sign-up-for-my-newsletter/
For translations, please also visit my website.

Chapter One

Tessa

I EAT MY CUBE of cheddar cheese off its toothpick, even though my black shirt hardly allows my arm to bend at the elbow because the dried paint there has hardened. But although the lime-green paint blob audibly cracked, no flecks dot the worn, wood floor of this gallery. My best friend, Miranda, in her typical, emotionally exuberant fashion, went a bit overboard with this costume. Last night's idea to dress up as an artist to be the bait to catch a scammer conning artists seems a lot less brilliant now.

Miranda and I huddle in the very back corner of this white-walled space, now converted into a hip art gallery on the Lower East Side. Bright-neon abstract paintings dot the walls, while metal sculptures command the floor space. The one closest to us looks like a robot made out of a car door, with metal tubes for legs and arms. His head is a paint bucket. It's not bad, but it would be cooler if it were an actual robot—preferably one that did housecleaning and delivered trays full of cups of coffee, the rocket fuel that sustains me through my crazy, New York City lawyer workload.

"Tessa, why are you dressed as an artist who hasn't washed her clothes in days?" William Matsumura, Miranda's boyfriend, asks as he joins us. He laces his fingers through Miranda's, pulling her closer to him.

"That scammer guy is supposed to be here—the one who ripped off Yvette, that emerging artist I just met," Miranda says.

"I'm supposed to be a struggling artist. We're hoping I will look like a good target and he'll try to scam me," I say. I'd suggested I be the bait last night when Miranda had been pacing about our living room, outraged about how this guy, Jurgen, had made all these false promises to Yvette and tricked her into paying him so much money.

Scammers who prey on vulnerable women are *the worst*. Or maybe the ones who prey on old people or children are the worst. But they're all bad. Foiling them gives me great pleasure.

"Yvette said he'd picked her up at an opening here," Miranda says. "If he tries to scam Tessa, then we can build a case against him."

"Isn't it unlikely this scammer is going to pick up Tessa?" William asks.

"It's still a chance. Doesn't she look like a passionate artist who is on the verge of being discovered?" Miranda asks.

"She looks like she's given up hope and was unable to even dress up for this show," William says, earning an elbow in his ribs from Miranda.

"I should look like I'm here to fill up on the free food." I gesture with my fork to my paper plate, filled with cheese cubes and bread.

On the west side of the room is a long bar manned by three bartenders, a crowd clustered around it. I haven't even attempted to try to battle to get a drink.

"Do you see him?" I ask.

"No." Miranda shakes her head. "Wait. Yes. There he is. He just walked in."

At the entrance stands a tall guy in a green, velvet jacket with wavy, brown hair in a ponytail. He's channeling a romantic poet aesthetic.

"He's good-looking, objectively speaking," I say.

"Undoubtedly helps his scam." Miranda frowns. "Yvette said he has this whole 'I wasn't good enough to make it, but you've got what it takes. I can teach you' spiel. He's despicable. What kind of person would take advantage of all that hope and vulnerability and promise them connections and art shows—the whole inside scoop? She paid him thousands of dollars."

"You have to know who to trust," I say.

Miranda's glance meets mine in silent acknowledgment of that truth.

"Ready, set, action," Miranda says.

Miranda and William walk over to the metal sculpture near Scammer Guy. Like a besotted puppy, I eagerly tail after my supposed artist idol, Miranda.

"I've followed your career from the beginning." I say my well-rehearsed lines as we maneuver in earshot of Scammer Guy. "You're such an inspiration to me, especially because you didn't succeed at first and kept trying."

"Thank you so much," Miranda says. "That means the world to me. It's hard. I wasn't sure I was going to make it either. You have to believe in yourself and know what you want."

"Do you have any tips for an aspiring artist like me?" I ask.

Miranda gives her standard advice and a pat on my shoulder. And then she gently disentangles herself from me, saying she and William are going to get some food. Given my still-full plate, I can't really follow them. I'm left standing alone by Mr. Alleged Scammer.

Perfect.

I let my shoulders droop and eat some more cheese. Like a tentative mouse.

But he doesn't take the bait.

He walks away and joins another group of black-clad artistic types.

So frickin' frustrating.

I wander around, studying the art. Bunches of people cluster here and there around the sculptures.

It would appear suspicious if I approached Scammer Guy dressed like this.

Miranda and William are so cute together. She's laughing. William looks at her like he adores her and can't believe he's lucky enough to be with her. That's relationship goals right there.

It's crowded now. I eat the last of my cheese and crackers and throw away the plate in a silver garbage can by the refreshments table. Miranda and William are talking to a columnist who gave her last art show a glowing review. I check out the other people in the room.

A blond guy, tall, lean, and lanky, stands near this metal sculpture in the middle of the room, grinning and chatting with two other guys. He's gorgeous. That tousled hair. Defined cheekbones. Strong jaw. Fit. A fitted, white, button-down shirt slightly open at the collar. He throws his head back, laughing at whatever his friend said. I feel a tug in my chest. *And with a zest for life.* He leans in to listen to his friend, who looks like he could star in a Korean drama. Also incredibly good-looking. But his friend keeps checking his phone and smiling, like he's having a secret conversation with someone special—like a girlfriend.

My phone beeps.

Miranda: *Scammer Guy left. We can hang out again.*

Miranda joins me. "William is getting me some fruit."

"I'm sorry it didn't work," I say.

Miranda whistles through her teeth. "It happens. It still gave us some intelligence. I thought for sure he would approach you, but he didn't. We'll have to try a different tactic at the next art opening." She glances around. "There are a lot of good-looking guys here. Maybe we should focus on that instead. Are you sure there are no prospects here?"

"I can't date now," I say. "It will be the Wyatt scenario all over again, where I get dumped because I'm working all the time. I need to focus on work and earning the summer bonus."

"We just have to find someone else who works all the time. Then he can't complain about your hours." Miranda scans the room. "Surely there must be someone here you find attractive. You can at least start up a conversation and decide if it's worth pursuing."

"That's true." I look again for the blond guy and find him almost immediately by the bar. We're about ten feet away in the middle of the room by a sculpture of a metal spider; a car tire is the body, and the legs are made out of soup cans stuck together.

"That guy." I tip my head toward him.

"I've been watching him," Miranda says. "I thought he was your type. But he blew off two different women. I think he wants to hang out with his friends. Or maybe he has a girlfriend."

I feel a pang. He probably has a girlfriend. Lucky woman. But if he doesn't …

We watch as another woman—this one wearing a stylish skirt suit with lawyer vibes—approaches him, smiling flirtatiously. A brief conversation ensues. He smiles but, gesturing to his friends, tips his head down as if saying no. She retreats, rebuffed. She pouts as she rejoins her friends.

"You never go for the easy one, do you?" Miranda asks.

"No," I say. "Unfortunately."

His dark-haired friend pats him on the back. He shakes his head, his hair falling forward over his forehead. I want to smooth it back.

He also appears to be close to these friends, so that's a good sign.

"But I do like a challenge," I say. "It might be time for *The Lady Eve* approach. At least that way, he can take the initiative to pick me up if he wants, and he doesn't have to reject me outright."

"What's *The Lady Eve* approach?" William asks as he rejoins us, handing Miranda a plate of strawberries, grapes, and cantaloupe chunks.

"It's a 1940s film," I say. "All these women are unsuccessfully hitting on this millionaire at a restaurant. And Eve, played by Barbara Stanwyck, is giving her dad a play-by-play of their failed approaches. Both she and her father are con artists. Then when the millionaire leaves, she trips him and then berates him for breaking her shoe. She insists he accompany her to her cabin for a replacement. So, she successfully picks him up."

"You're going to trip that guy?" William asks.

"No." I shake my head. "But he's going to think he picked me up." I roll my shoulders and stretch, playing it up. "But I need your help. All you have to do is cut in front of me at the bar and order a drink. But do it aggressively. And then leave."

"It's amazing that it works." Miranda shakes her head in disbelief.

It doesn't *always* work. The guy has to be a nice guy, somewhat observant, and not totally engrossed with his friends. *And someone who cares about fairness.*

It's not risk-free.

"Can't you just go up to him?" William asks.

"Normally, I would," I say. "But as you said, I'm dressed like I haven't washed my clothes in days. If I walked up to you looking like this, when you were single, would you chat with me?"

"No." William frowns. "I mean, I might."

Another woman in a suit walks right up to Hot Guy and does the hair flip. He chats with her for a moment and then turns back to his friends.

"He does appear to be rejecting all the women who approach him," Miranda says.

"Let's try it," I say. "If it doesn't work, it doesn't work."

Here goes. I swish over to stand near Hot Guy. Our glances meet, and a definite awareness of each other shimmers across. He smiles. I look away. Even that brief glance ... My pulse races.

But I ignore him. Luckily, there's still a crowd two-people deep around the bar. I try to order a beer, but the bartender is busy and doesn't see me. Granted, I'm only trying when the bartender isn't looking.

I also don't exactly look like someone who is going to tip.

William walks up and cuts right in front of me, grabbing the female bartender's attention and ordering two drinks. I try to peer around William's broad back to place my order, but it's as if he's blocking me out. The bartender shifts to the other side of the bar. William leaves with his beers.

The blond guy leans over to me and says, "That wasn't fair. You were here first."

And he's a good guy—at least as far as this test shows. I shrug as if I don't care. "It's okay. I'll get the bartender the next time around."

"I'll help," he says.

The bartender returns, and I signal more vigorously this time. Hot Guy also raises his hand to help. She takes my order for a beer.

"Let me at least pay for it so you don't think all guys are assholes," he says.

He probably thinks I can't afford it.

"I'm not that judgmental. I'm not going to discredit an entire sex based on one bad apple." I bite my lip. Is that absolutely true? Some bad apples can really leave a sour taste. "I like to give each person a chance to prove himself. But I do appreciate the offer."

I face him, and my heart flutters as our glances meet.

Why does he have to be so attractive? And why do I have to be wearing this paint-splattered shirt?

The bartender hands me my beer. I pay and leave a large tip in the cup.

Hot Guy smiles at me. "Well, I just wanted to help you out." He turns around as if to return to his friends.

Not interested. At least I tried. And it's not like I want to chase after someone who's not interested. I turn to retreat to my friends.

His friend, a few feet away, is giving him a thumbs-up and has a huge, goofy grin on his face.

He sighs.

"Your friend seems incredibly happy that you're chatting with a woman," I say.

"He's completely in love with his new girlfriend and wants everyone to experience the same bliss. Especially me." Hot Guy smiles wryly and faces me.

"That's a good friend," I say.

"The best." His eyes soften. "Are you here alone?"

"No. I'm here with my best friend and her boyfriend." I have to raise my voice a bit to be heard above the din of the conversations. "She's an artist and a lead singer for the band, The Tempest." *That was stupid.* I wanted to impress him, since he's now been compelled to stay with me to make his friend happy. But if he saw me with Miranda earlier, and now sees William with her, he's going to wonder if we're connected. I shift so I'm facing Miranda and William, forcing him to move so that his back is to them.

Hot Guy tilts his head. "That's cool."

"I am, unfortunately, not as cool and can't sing." This paint-covered getup also doesn't look remotely cool.

He leans closer and whispers, "I can't sing either." My heart flutters as his breath grazes my ear.

"Let's agree to never do karaoke with them."

"You still seem pretty cool to me." He smiles crookedly. He has a very small chip in an otherwise perfect set of teeth. He has such chiseled cheekbones. Our glances meet. *Zing.* A zippy feeling races through me. *Wasn't quite expecting that.*

"I'm Tessa." I put out my hand to shake his. His grip is warm and firm.

"Zeke." He doesn't let go of my hand. He looks surprised too.

We stand there, gazing at each other, acknowledging this attraction.

"I'm also here with friends. And work colleagues. We all work together." He takes back his hand. "My friend went to college with the sculptor. It's his first major show."

"That's cool," I say. "It seems impossible to break out if you're an aspiring artist, so this is huge."

Mr. Scammer is next to me. He's back.

"You must be an artist." Hot Guy gestures to my clothes.

Oh no. Scammer Guy is just standing there. Not moving up to order. He's listening in. But I don't want to *lie* to Hot Guy. But this is also my chance to hook Scammer Guy.

"Yes," I say. "But very much a struggling one." I'll explain to Hot Guy later.

"What kind of artist are you?"

"A painter."

"Any upcoming shows where I can see your work?" he asks.

"No." I let my shoulders drop. "I'm not at that level yet."

Ugh. I need to be pathetic for Scammer Guy, but I hate being incompetent. I handle multibillion-dollar lawsuits for Fortune 500 companies—and win. I'll never attract Hot Guy like this. And if I do, do I want him?

Chapter Two

Zeke

She's not a lawyer. Phew. Dylan thinks I'm crazy with my "never date a lawyer" stance. Given that he was "no women, love doesn't exist" after his last breakup, before he met his fiancée, he has no right to talk. "No lawyers" is targeted. Feasible.

Not that her occupation wasn't clear from her paint-bespeckled shirt. Odd choice for a night out. But preferable to pearls and suits.

She has mesmerizing, blue eyes and wavy, blonde hair. *What am I doing?*

I came here to hang out with Ben and Dylan—definitely not to pick up women. I'm on a break. But no harm in making a female friend and chatting about what it's like to be an artist. Something that I at least have peripheral experience with.

"My dad is a writer," I say. "There's so much rejection. I wouldn't be able to take it."

"Art has so much rejection." Tessa sighs. "Is he published? What does he write?"

"Yes. Mysteries."

"That's amazing. I love a good mystery, deciphering the clues to figure out who did it."

"It is cool," I say. "Especially when he's in the middle of plotting, and Post-it notes are all over the wall of his office. It looks like a crime scene board."

A few feet away, the sculptor waves his hands, explaining his metal sculpture, composed of tubes and car parts, as some critique of capitalism. Three finance guys are clearly not his target audience, although he did try to sell us one work.

"Can you usually guess the murderer when you read it?" she asks.

"No. You'd think I'd have some insight as his son, right?"

"Not necessarily. I mean, he has to deceive his faithful readers."

"Deceive?"

"Leave them guessing. That's a better way to phrase it." Her brow furrows.

"But I do try to figure it out. I'm one of his beta readers, and that's one thing he always wants to know: Who do I think did it?"

"You must be close if he allows you to beta-read his manuscripts. Did you ever want to be a writer?" She tucks her blonde hair behind her ear.

"Never."

"That's very definite."

"Math and history were my favorite subjects. English, art ..." I shake my head. "Torture."

"I'm surprised you still want to talk to me, then." She crosses her arms.

"I said the wrong thing, didn't I?" I ask. My face warms.

She laughs. And I feel a burst of pride that I made her look so delighted. I like her smile. It's open and playful. And that she's casually dressed—that messy, painted top and a short miniskirt. Not that I'm checking her out. Or in the market. Even if I did just help her out. And even if there was that flare of attraction.

I'm not in any place to be dating anyone. I have to impress my boss, Charles. My fund was recently sued, and the litigation is taking up all my extra time. I can't lose focus again by dating and getting my heart stomped on. Especially someone without any references. Not that common friends did me any good when I was dating Paisley. Except that they seemed as shocked by her betrayal as I was.

But I also haven't felt that electricity with anyone since Paisley.

It's not like I want to be some monk. Ben is right that I should get back out there.

She shakes her head, still smiling. "Actually, I think you said the right thing. Brownie points for self-deprecating honesty. But I'd recommend against saying that to any other artists you meet."

"Point taken. I'll stick to saying I've wanted to work for a company ever since I was a kid and used to have to hang out after school with my mom at her office. She's an accountant. My mom framed a photo of me organizing my desk at home like her office desk."

"Aww. That's definitely a better story. I want to see that picture," she says. "You don't have a copy on your phone?"

"Definitely not. But I'm sure my mom will be happy to show you."

She sips her drink, peering at me over the rim, and then tilts her head. "Are we already discussing meeting mothers?"

I laugh. "For a swap of embarrassing childhood photos? I'm in."

She leans back and narrows her eyes. "It's the stories that accompany the photos that I'm more worried about."

I step a bit closer. "Now that's a tease if I ever heard one. Any you want to share?"

"Not at our first meeting." She lifts her chin primly.

"We'll have to schedule a second, then. Can I have your number?"

"Smooth," she says.

"Too smooth?" Even I think it was too smooth. Or desperate-sounding. I'm rusty.

"Maybe," she says. "But I'll give you my number."

I unlock my phone and hand it to her.

She types in her number. "Still, I'm not promising that I'll share any embarrassing childhood stories."

"Holding out 'til the third date?"

"At least." She raises her eyebrows.

"Maybe we'll even have to have a fourth date. It can take a while to build up that level of trust. But I promise not to share them with anyone." A drunk guy careens toward her, and I pull her out of harm's way. Closer to me. She looks up, surprised. She's inches away. I swallow. "That guy seemed a bit out of control." Her hair has an apple-y, clean scent.

"Thanks." She looks around, and then the corner of her mouth tilts up. She doesn't step back.

That's fine with me. I'm all for sharing the same air space.

She tilts toward me like we're magnets drawn closer.

"Fourth date. Things are getting serious." She winks. "What do you usually do on a date?"

"Good question," I say and look away to think of a coherent response. I glance at her again. "I haven't dated in a while. I guess it depends on what you like to do."

"Good answer." Her jaunty grin makes me smile in return.

I step back. I've forgotten that I'm in a no-speeding zone. And a no-parking zone. I'm not out here to meet anyone.

"But I should probably get going," she says. "I need some more substantive food."

"I saw a burger place next door. Can I treat you to dinner? I don't think it's fancy, but it was crowded." I finish my beer. I did come here straight after work, and I am hungry. It will just be some more talking. Talking while eating is totally safe.

She looks around the room, clearly hesitating.

I wait. I'm surprised by how much I want her to say yes.

She turns back to me. "Sure. But I can't stay out late. I have to work tomorrow, so I need to be fresh. Let me tell my friends."

I exhale, as if I've been holding my breath. "Okay. I'll get a table."

"I'll meet you there."

As I walk toward the door, this guy in a green, velvet jacket waylays me. He has ARTIST written all over him. But not in the positive sense—like I'm trying to make sense of the world, or create something that inspires emotion, or make the world a better place, like the vibe that Tessa was giving off. *No.* More in the pretentious, stuck-up, I'm superior because I don't traffic in the means of commerce sense. I've met types like these before when my dad has book talks, only they're aspiring to write the next great American novel. They're even more horrified when they find out I'm his son and I work in finance.

"What did you think of the show?" the guy asks.

Maybe he's one of the artists.

"I don't know much about art, but I was impressed," I say.

His eyebrows raise. "You're not an art collector or connoisseur?"

"No." Connoisseur looks like the type of word he'd use.

"What do you do?" he asks.

"I'm in finance."

"If you're interested in any of the artwork, I can facilitate an introduction and negotiate a good price," he says. "I'm Jurgen."

I was wrong. He's still pretentious, but definitely all about trafficking in the commerce of art.

"No, thanks. If you'll excuse me, I'm on my way out." I brush past him.

I hand Tessa a menu as she takes a seat at the small, round table across from me in the outdoor section. We're the only couple out here. Most people chose to sit inside, but the night air is warm, and I like sitting outside. This up-and-coming neighborhood is good for people-watching. A light, wooden trough with fake, green plants shields us from passersby on the sidewalk.

Ben looked happy when I told him we were going next door for dinner. And the thing is, I feel good about this. I want to be here with her. She has this certain assurance. She'd have to ... to wear that shirt to an art opening.

We order hamburgers, two glasses of beer, and a plate of fries to share. The waiter comes back with our two beers immediately.

"*Proost,*" Tessa says. We clink glasses.

"You know Dutch?" I ask.

"My roommate is half Dutch, so that's how we toast. *You* know Dutch?"

"I'm of Dutch descent," I say.

"I'm a mutt. I'm a mix of Polish, German, Irish, and English."

"I've always been partial to mutts. I adopted my dog from the ASPCA. She's a sweetheart." I sip my beer.

She wrinkles up her face. "I don't think people usually describe me as a sweetheart."

"No?" I raise an eyebrow. "How do people usually describe you?"

She looks away. "Loyal, a good friend, tenacious, hard-working, competitive. A bit too willing to take risks. Not risk-averse enough. How would your friends describe you?"

"Similar. But maybe too risk-averse. Now." *Since Paisley cheated on me.*

"Now?"

I shrug and look away. "I'm trying to transfer to a different department at work. I don't want to take any risks that might mess that up."

She raises her glass. "Yes. That's exactly the definition of risk-averse. Whereas I sometimes take risks that I probably shouldn't."

"Why? For the thrill?" *Is she another Paisley? Unable to commit because of a fear of missing out on other choices?*

She frowns.

Yeah. My tone was probably a bit bitter, derisive.

"No," she says. "The reward. I'm betting on myself. In my own calculus, I still think that the risk is worth the reward."

"Have you ever been wrong about the risk?"

She smiles cheekily. "Not recently."

Our waiter serves us our burgers and a plateful of fries. She takes a bite of her burger. The burgers are good with slightly toasted whole wheat rolls. She hums as she eats the fries. I almost feel bad taking any.

"That's impressive." I raise my beer to her. I think back to what she said earlier. "But loyal, a good friend ... Why not a sweetheart? Because you're competitive and take risks?"

"Sometimes those risks skirt the line of what could be considered the sweet thing to do. You should definitely not consider me a sweetheart."

"Are you warning me?"

"I am."

"Isn't that kind of a sweet thing to do?"

She laughs and shakes her head, framing her face in her hands. "You're the sweetheart here. Because I'm warning you, and you still want to believe I'm sweet."

"I'm fine with being a sweetheart. I have no problem with that characterization. The question is ... why do you?" I lean forward, closer to her, across the table.

She rests her head on crossed hands, her elbows on the table. "Because I'm a woman and don't want to look like an easy mark?"

The slight breeze blows her hair around her face.

"Because being labeled a sweetheart sounds like a weakness?" I ask.

"Yes."

I stop to consider this. She waits, watching me. It feels like it's just the two of us in the night. "That's true. You can be taken advantage of"—I take a deep breath—"because you're not on guard." *I never suspected a thing with Paisley.* "But don't you think it takes a certain strength too? To not let others' betrayals change you. I don't want to go through life suspecting people of bad intentions. Although that's a lot easier said than done."

We both concentrate on eating for a few minutes, finishing our burgers.

"That's true. I also want to state, for the record, that my intentions toward you are good." She says this with an intense seriousness but then waves a fry at me.

"Do you have intentions toward me?"

"I wouldn't be sitting here if I didn't."

Direct. I salute her with my beer and then finish it. "Do you want to take a walk to Pier 35? Have you been? It's great at night with the view of the bridges and the city lights."

"No, I've never been there. Is it safe at night?" She sips the last of her beer.

"Yes, it's well lit."

"Okay. Let me run to the bathroom, and then I'll meet you out here."

"Okay," I say.

She gets up and disappears inside.

I text Dylan and Ben that I'm leaving with her. I've barely hit Send before Ben is there.

"Did she leave?" Ben asks. "It looked like it was going well." Dylan tries to shush him.

"We're going for a walk along the pier. She went to the bathroom."

"Dude still has moves." Dylan punches me in the shoulder. Ben rolls his eyes.

"It's not moves." I shake my head. "The pier has a great view."

"Sure, it does," Dylan says. "I'll talk to you later this week. And don't forget, if it all goes well, you can always bring her as a date to my wedding."

I shake my head. "I just met her."

"C'mon," Ben says to Dylan. "Let's leave the guy alone. This is a good first step. Good way to get back out there. And she looks like a lot more fun than Paisley."

Once you break up with your girlfriend, that's when all your close friends finally tell you that they never liked her. Never thought she was good enough for you. Worked too much and had no sense of humor.

It's understandable. But not reassuring. Because, before that, they'd said she's great. Although Ben had asked, "Do you know what you're getting into?" I guess Ben was trying to hint at something with that comment. Apparently, Paisley and I had been in two different schools of thought about relationships and fidelity.

They near the corner, even though Ben can't resist turning around and giving me a thumbs-up.

Tessa comes back out and smiles. "Shall we go? You don't need to check back in with your friends?" She waves at the art gallery as we pass it. "Did you come with a lot of friends?"

"I did, but they just stopped by our table on their way home while you were in the bathroom."

We wander past the lit bars and closed stores of the Lower East Side, across Delancey Street. People mill about on the streets, chatting and joking on their way to check out the next bar. Colorful graffiti decorates the closed, metal, roll-up storefronts.

"Where did you grow up?" I ask.

"Manhattan."

"Same. But I spent summers in Holland," I say. We're in a wide-open space, tall apartment buildings on the periphery.

"That's so cool. Where did you go to high school?" she asks.

I was about to ask her that same question. High school is so defining in New York that anytime one born-and-bred New Yorker meets another, that question invariably is asked.

"Bronx Science," I say. "Where did you go?"

"Stuyvesant."

"Ah, so we're rivals." And she's also the product of gifted public high school.

"Not exactly. Stuy is so clearly superior that ..." She shrugs and then pats me on the back. "But Bronx Science is good too."

I snort. "I always found that Stuy students were good at trash-talking but couldn't measure up to their words."

"Those are fighting words, my friend." She side-eyes me. "We'll see."

"Hold on for a sec. I need to figure out where we are." I've lost my bearings talking to her. Signs in Chinese dot the stores. We're near Chinatown, so we're going in the right direction.

We pass the East Broadway subway station and stroll down Rutgers Street. A metal fence cordons off a community garden. Small buildings with fire escapes line this street, but as we reach the end, the view opens up to reveal the brick public housing towers. A breeze carries the smell of salt air; we're close to the East River. As we walk down this open boulevard, a bunch of senior citizens sit on metal, folding chairs outside their red-bricked building, a CD player playing a Chinese ballad.

We wait at the red light to cross the street and then go under the metal overpass of FDR Drive. And then we're right next to the river, the waves lapping softly against the pier.

The Manhattan Bridge towers over the scenery.

A train passes over the Manhattan Bridge, and the rumbling roars through the air. It's much louder than I remember.

"It always shocks me how close you can get to the river," she says after it passes. "And you're right. This is a great view of the Manhattan Bridge and the Brooklyn Bridge."

We walk out on the pier, down the pathway, past the greenery and trees and flowers, toward the giant swings. One is empty, while couples occupy the three other ones.

"Should we swing?"

She nods. We sit next to each other on the metal slats. It's oddly intimate, even though four people could probably fit on each. In the swing next to us, a couple cuddles. I don't feel like I can do that yet. Not after the good guy remark and her trusting me enough to come with me to this pier at night. She pushes off with her feet, and we rock up and down.

"It gives a great view of the bridge and Brooklyn," she says.

"Does it make you want to paint it?" I ask.

She glances at me sharply, and then she frowns. "It should, shouldn't it?" She turns to face me. "Look, I'm not—"

My phone rings. I glance down at my screen. "Sorry, it's the company's lawyer. I have to take this. Unfortunately." I pick it up and say hello to Brooke.

"I'm sorry to bother you this late," Brooke says.

"I hate lawyers," I say. I stand up from the swing, trot down the few steps, and move off to the side where my conversation can't be heard. I lean against the railing next to the river. If Brooke is calling at this hour, it has to be confidential.

"We're not all bad," she says.

"You're the best of the bunch," I say. "I'm only kidding that you need to work all the time on my case and not date Ben. He just left the bar. I thought he was heading home to you." I turn around to look at Tessa. She's pushing off with one foot, frowning.

"Ben says hello. But seriously, Arthur is holding a meeting tomorrow at eight a.m. for pitching potential investments to the various portfolio managers. I just received an email invite and you were not included, even though you should be. Winthrop is."

"Thanks for the heads-up. I'll be there."

Arthur strikes again. Time to call it a night. I walk back over. The light illuminates her face and blonde hair. Her forehead is creased as if she's deep in thought.

She stands. "I should get going. I have to work on my portfolio tomorrow. It was nice meeting you." She puts out her hand to shake.

Like we've met at a business function.

We walk back toward the highway. She's walking fast—not that ambling pace as we strolled over here. We cross over FDR Drive to South Street.

"I hope we can see each other again soon," I say.

What am I doing? Usually, I'm the one hit on. I'm not the smooth operator hitting on random women. And I'm already discussing a fourth date. I run my hand through my hair. What am I thinking? Am I ready to have a new girlfriend?

A taxi is idling there, its small sign on the roof lit, indicating it's free.

She tilts her head. "I hope so." And with that, she waves goodbye and jumps into the cab.

Without even an invitation to share. She did warn me she wasn't sweet.

I look at what she wrote in my phone. No last name. Did she even give me her real number?

And why did my stomach suddenly drop at the thought that she didn't?

Chapter Three

Tessa

Instead of reliving meeting Zeke last night, I *should* get back to work reading the "private" emails of our clients. My office-mate Lakshmi is clicking away at her computer at her desk next to me.

Recruiting ads for lawyers may explain that, in every litigation, the emails of the plaintiff and the employees of the defendant are gathered and reviewed by teams of young lawyers like me to determine whether either side said anything relevant to the lawsuit, with the hope that the other side wrote something that will hurt their case. But what those ads should really highlight is that this is a chance to read the inner thoughts of two guys discussing who they want to date. Figuring out their love lives, which is what I'm now doing, is definitely not included in the position description. People reveal surprisingly personal secrets in corporate emails. It's a cautionary reminder not to mix business with personal.

"Didn't you bet Stuffed Shirt that our team would finish the document review first, before his team did?" Lakshmi asks.

"Yes." I turn back to my monitor, which displays the text of the email I'm supposed to be reading. But where's the fun if I let a little competition stress me out? *No risk, no reward.*

Outside, above the New York City skyline, the blue sky is fading into dusk. Across the way, the lit windows frame other individuals, all similarly staring at screens. Lakshmi glances at me and raises an eyebrow. My distraction must be obvious.

Lakshmi's desk is closer to the door, whereas mine is next to the window because I'm a year senior. We both have L-shaped, white desks, with our computers on a tabletop against the east wall.

I stare at the screen, but instead, I see Zeke's tousled, blond hair that made me want to mess it up even more. That zippy feeling. He was sweet. And the way he'd listened, his head tilted, seeming to want to know me.

Could this be the start of something? It's been so long.

But why does he hate lawyers? He was so adamant.

That was bizarre.

I'd been about to tell him I was a lawyer. I'd forgotten I'd said I'm an artist until he asked me if I wanted to paint the Manhattan Bridge.

No. Not at all.

And I'd also completely forgotten that Miranda and I saw him talking to Jurgen, aka Scammer Guy.

I hope he was able to find a cab. I was so flustered that I left him there. And it's not easy to find a taxi in that neighborhood. And when I arrived home, Miranda was horrified. "Struggling artists take the subway."

But why was he talking to Scammer Guy? Zeke said he was there with a bunch of friends. *Is Jurgen one of his friends?* I should have asked him more about his friends, but I was so caught up in the moment. It's good I didn't reveal I was a lawyer. He lulled me into a false sense of security. Unbelievable.

I check my list of Capital Management employees whom Brooke Smith, the in-house counsel and my company contact, provided:

Zeger van der Zee—fund manager.
Arthur Ross—boss of Zeger van der Zee.
Ben Kim—another employee at Capital Manage-
ment—not involved in this fund.

I turn back to the document review to determine if the employees at this fund I'm defending wrote anything related to the fund or its risk. I open up the next email.

To: Zeger van der Zee
From: Ben Kim
Date: April 12

Is Brooke in Toronto with you?

To: Ben Kim
From: Zeger van der Zee
Date: April 12

No. But she is working on the North American Fund

litigation. If you really want to spend time with her, persuade some plaintiff's lawyer to file some bogus fraud suit alleging your fund misrepresented its risk. I spent all day with her yesterday discussing documents, including whether I store any off the main server. Quality time, my friend. She mentioned she was meeting our outside counsel today.

To: Zeger van der Zee
From: Ben Kim
Date: April 12

I want to date her—not discuss work.

Twenty-five more emails to read, and then I'm done with this batch. I open up the next one.

"This guy, Ben, really likes Brooke," I say. "He wrote Zeger asking if she was traveling because he hadn't seen her around. And Brooke clearly likes him back. She invites him for coffee every day." I mark these emails as irrelevant to the litigation.

"Are they allowed to date?" Lakshmi asks. "Wouldn't that be problematic if she had to defend his fund?"

"Maybe. Optically, it wouldn't look good. But it would depend on Capital Management's company fraternization policy. The client is the fund, not Ben."

I mark this next batch as irrelevant as well. "I hope they're already together by now. These emails are from last month. Ben is so open about his feelings for her, so he must have told her." I click on another email. "Here it is. He wrote Zeger that he's going to ask her out for dinner. What? Wow. Zeger's response is unbelievable."

"Let me see." Lakshmi scoots her chair over to my desk and leans over to see my screen. I tilt it toward her to read the reply email.

To: Ben Kim
From: Zeger van der Zee
Date: April 12
Re: Don't

Don't date a lawyer. Too competitive. And they work all the time. Date an artist. Someone who's creative. Someone who is emotionally open. Not someone who is arguing over commas. And twisting the truth to fit their own reality. I would never date a lawyer again. Learn from my mistake. Brooke seems great, and I highly respect her as a lawyer, but don't date her.

"What the heck? What a jerk!" Lakshmi says.

"Like lawyers can't be creative," I say.

"We do work all the time, though."

"So do artists," I say. "Anyway, Ben put Zeger in his place. Lucky Brooke." I show Ben's reply email to Lakshmi.

> To: Zeger van der Zee
> From: Ben Kim
> Re: April 12
>
> Brooke IS great. And I want to date Brooke for herself. Her career doesn't define her. And I work all the time too.

Exactly. *My career doesn't define me.* I find it weird when friends introduce me as a lawyer because I'm so much more than that.

Lakshmi sighs. "And here I thought that finance guys weren't romantic."

"He's probably the exception. I wish I'd done some sort of litmus test on Wyatt before he dumped me for working too much." To the right of my computer monitor hangs a framed picture of two kids hugging their grandparents and a handwritten letter thanking me for helping with their adoption. That was my pro bono case I was doing after hours instead of going on dates with Wyatt. I don't regret it. What I regret is that *he* dumped me.

Not that I'm bitter. We dated for eight months and broke up about eighteen months ago. On November 1. The date of the New York City Ballet Gala, which I was unable to attend as his date because I got staffed on a hostile takeover case.

He said our relationship clearly wasn't working for him anymore.

Because relationships should be *working* for you.

What kills me is that there were red flags. I liked him, so I let my emotions cloud my rational judgment. So much for lawyers not being "emotionally open," Mr. van der Zee. But maybe he has a point. I know how to protect my heart. But that's not from being a lawyer.

"You should look at it as being a lawyer saved you from Wyatt," Lakshmi says. "Now you can find someone who appreciates you for who you are."

"A competitive, workaholic lawyer?" I ask.

"It looks like there's a market for them. Ask Brooke if Ben has any friends."

"Other than Zeger van der Zee."

"Other than him."

"That's this bunch of emails. How's your batch going?"

"Almost finished," Lakshmi says.

"Anyway, I met someone last night."

"You've been glowing all day. I was beginning to wonder. Did you hook up?"

"We exchanged numbers. But then he said he hated lawyers, so I got flustered and left. But before that, there was definitely chemistry." I open up the folder of documents marked by my team as relevant to study them.

"That's fabulous." Lakshmi clicks on her mouse.

"Dangerous."

"Much better than Wyatt, then. If I recall correctly, you weren't sure you were attracted to him initially."

"Your memory is correct as always, counselor," I say. "I should search up this guy Zeger and see what he looks like."

"You should focus on beating Stuffed Shirt first," Lakshmi says.

I salute her and call the document review room to check how my team is doing. Almost done. I hang up as Stuffed Shirt—today's sartorial selection is a blue, pinstripe suit with a crisply ironed, white shirt—knocks on the door and then sticks his head into our office.

"My team is almost done reviewing their half of the document production." Tom aka Stuffed Shirt steps farther into our office and leans against the wall, one hand on his waist, surveying us. "I hope you're not slowing us down."

"It won't be my team slowing us down," I say. The smirk on his face makes me want to pour a bucket of cold water over his head.

"Did you hear that I won the City banking case?" he asks. "See if you can top that, Jackowski."

"I heard." My tone is purposefully flat. "Congratulations."

He waits for a moment, as if expecting more.

My assistant appears at the door. "Ken from FLAFL is on the line. He has a new case he thought you might want."

FLAFL is the acronym for the Free Legal Advocacy For Liberty, an organization that provides legal services to low-income New Yorkers. White & Gilman has an agreement with FLAFL that it will screen and refer individual cases for White & Gilman associates, like me, to serve as co-counsel with a FLAFL attorney. Usually, our pro bono coordinator posts the cases on our internal website, but Ken and I have worked together for several years now, so he calls me directly with any cases of possible interest to me after clearing it with the firm's pro bono coordinator.

If all goes well—and I get the summer bonus—I plan to quit my job as a corporate lawyer in six months to work for FLAFL.

"I have to take this," I say.

"Still doing all that pro bono?" Stuffed Shirt asks. "That's not going to increase your billables."

"It's not all about billable hours." Did he become a lawyer solely for the money? Not that I don't like the pay … and the security it provides.

"It is for the extra summer bonus." And on that grim reminder, he leaves.

And he's right. I'm going to have to turn Ken down and focus on my billable cases for the bonus. Every summer, our law firm rewards one top-tier associate in each class with an extra bonus. And hours worked for paying clients is one of the main determinants. I pick up the phone.

"This is a compelling housing case for you," Ken says. "She's fighting for the succession rights to her grandmother's rent-controlled Harlem apartment. Her grandmother raised her, and she's lived in the apartment the whole time—until she left to serve in the military. But her grandmother died while she was away, and some man is claiming he's the successor as a 'common law spouse' of her grandmother."

I bite my nail.

No.

I can't say no. Not to this type of case. My best friend's tear-stained face saying she and her mom were going to lose their apartment. That's why I became a lawyer.

"I'm in," I say. "I'll email you with times when I can meet her."

As I hang up, Lakshmi says, "I thought you were not going to take any more pro bono cases so you can get the bonus and pay off your law school debt."

"I couldn't turn this down."

"You could have. Especially since the sooner you pay off your law school debt and quit to work for FLAFL—"

"Shh." Lakshmi knows my plan to quit to work for FLAFL, but she's the only one at the firm. I enjoy corporate law more than expected, but if I work for FLAFL, I can literally change lives. Like how FLAFL saved my best friend, Tara, and her mom from eviction when we were in high school. But I'm still torn because giving up my current salary is hard. This case can be one last chance to make sure that I truly want to quit White & Gilman. Maybe representing pro bono clients as part of my caseload here is enough.

"The sooner all your cases will be those types of cases," Lakshmi continues. "But if you don't get the bonus ..."

"I'm going to get the bonus."

"All I'm saying is at this point in time, your focus should be on increasing your hours working on billable cases—not pro bono."

I nod, acknowledging her point, and refresh my email. And there it is. My team of associates emailed that the document review is complete on their end.

I grab my legal pad and run in as dignified a manner as I can down the hallway to the partner's office at the corner, the carpeting muffling my heels, stopping to walk each time I pass a partner's open office door. So not so dignified. I probably look more like a squirrel scampering, pausing to stick its head up to check for danger. Only a new assistant looks up from her cubicle outside the lawyers' offices. The others are used to my mad dashes.

No Tom.

I knock on the partner's door, and Paul, a distinguished-looking, gray-haired man in his fifties, waves me in. Bird prints line the wall. There's a heron. That's about what I can identify. None of the typical New York City species line the walls. Illustrations of pigeons, cardinals, crows, seagulls, sparrows, and bluebirds wouldn't quite convey the same gravitas, I presume.

"We finished," I say.

"Great job. So, now, we're waiting for Tom's team to finish." He straightens a stack of papers on his desk. "And thank you for working late these past few nights preparing that client memo of our best legal arguments. I appreciate that you went the extra mile to ensure that it was done. Jack was also extolling your work in your recent M&A case with him at the partner lunch yesterday. I hope you get to enjoy your weekend."

Jack is the best. I adopted him as my mentor, even though he's a corporate partner and I'm a litigator, after we'd met at a firm cocktail party in my first year, and he was hilarious.

I sit in the armchair in front of Paul's massive, cherry wood desk. "Did you see my email? Plaintiff admitted the fund was risky but worth it. He wrote "No Risk, No Return" in an email and a Facebook post. That should help us win this case."

"I shared it with Brooke," Paul says.

"But Mr. van der Zee also wrote an email worrying that one of the investments was too risky, given that they had so many retirees investing in the fund," I say. "Plaintiffs are going to love that email."

"That's for the plaintiffs to find. They argue their case. We argue ours. But make sure to prepare a rebuttal."

"Will do." I stand. "The investment was within the parameters of the fund's investment criteria, so legally, he's fine."

Tom knocks on the door.

"Shouldn't you be reviewing your documents?" he asks, that self-satisfied smirk back on his face.

I stare at him. "We finished."

He waves his phone and smiles. Then he shakes his head and sighs. "The paralegal just emailed that she forgot to send over a batch of emails—in your range."

I narrow my eyes. Do I suspect he had something to do with this being "forgotten"?

Yes. Yes, I do.

I hadn't trusted Tom from the get-go when we met as first-year associates at the law firm, but I hadn't been cautious enough. We'd worked together that fall on a case. Tom had told me that he didn't need help one weekend—he had the matter well in hand. I was in the middle of an all-hands-on-deck M&A litigation, so that worked for me. But then Tom complained to the partner about my not helping him. That partner then gave me a critical review that I wasn't a team player.

"Congratulations on getting the job done, Tom," Paul says.

"I'll get right on it." I walk toward the door. As I brush by Tom, he leans in and whispers, "You're slipping, Jackowski. Too much pro bono."

I keep my face blank. It annoys him when he doesn't get a reaction out of me. He tilts his head to peer more closely at me.

"Have a great weekend," I say. And he frowns.

Ha.

But then he smiles and says, "Cheers! I won our bet."

I wince. That means my team is reviewing the documents arriving on Monday.

"Hurry," Paul says. "Time is of the essence, and now we're behind."

"Yes, I will." The door closes behind me as I leave.

I murmur hello to the executive assistants sitting in cubicles lining the hallway outside the closed doors of the lawyers. The grunt of printers printing, a telephone ringing, and a hushed tone asking, "How can I help you?" form the background noise to my thoughts.

I hate losing. Especially in front of a partner.

I slip back into our empty office. Lakshmi must be at her team meeting. Tom is back to his dirty tricks again. Twenty emails still to go.

I click on the folder to pull up the first email. It's another bunch of Zeger emails.

To: Zeger van der Zee
From: Ben Kim
Date: April 14

Do you think Arthur is purposefully setting you up
to fail?

Hmm. So all is not smooth sailing in the Zeger van der Zee world.

To: Ben Kim
From: Zeger van der Zee

I'm not ready to go that far yet. I'd say that Arthur
will not be unhappy if I do. And FWIW, I also don't
recommend dating an office colleague.

No office colleague romance either. Has Mr. van der Zee ever thought that maybe he's too straitlaced to date an artist?

And this one is to his boss. It's a follow-up to his previous email, worrying that the Mexico investment was too risky for their investors. Kudos to him for raising that, even if his boss definitely did not appreciate his concern.

> To: Arthur Ross
> From: Zeger van der Zee
>
> I've looked further into the Mexico investment. The upside is good, and I think we can mitigate the risk.

Good job at backtracking, Zeger.

I finish this batch of emails and notify Paul. I click on the documents Ken sent over about the housing case and review them.

And now I can finally check out what this Mr. van der Zee looks like. Probably looks like a clone of Stuffed Shirt. A starched shirt that can probably stand up by itself. Good-looking if you don't need some humanity.

I do a Google search of Zeger van der Zee. His picture pops up on my monitor. And my mouth drops open.

It's Zeke from last night.

No.

Chapter Four

Tessa

I STARE AT THE photograph of Zeger van der Zee on my monitor, my thoughts completely jumbled.

How could it be the same guy?

"I'm so screwed," I say as Lakshmi walks back into our office, dropping a legal pad on her desk.

"What's wrong?" She plops down in her chair and turns her computer on.

"The guy I met last night."

"The one you really liked?"

"It's Zeger van der Zee, but I guess he goes by the nickname Zeke." My shoulders drop, and I sink into the back of my chair.

"The guy managing the fund we're defending?"

"The very same. What are the chances?"

Lakshmi shakes her head. "You really know how to pick guys who don't like workaholic lawyers."

"Right?" I stare in disbelief at his photo on the Capital Management website.

"Didn't you discuss your jobs?"

I put my head in my hands, wincing. "I was pretending to be an artist to be the bait for this scammer guy."

"Of course you were."

At least Lakshmi is no longer shocked by Miranda's and my crazy schemes. Nope. Now she looks forward to hearing about our escapades. She's swiveled her chair to face me straight on, one side of my L-shaped desk between us.

"There's some guy scamming struggling female artists. He pretends he has all these connections. He also sells them painting lessons. Miranda met someone who'd paid him thousands of dollars. He'd said he needed it to frame her work properly to show this dealer."

"Did he frame them?"

"Yes, but he did such a crap job, they had to be reframed." I sigh. "Anyway, so because Scammer Guy was in earshot, I said I was an artist. And then we were discussing other stuff. And I was about to tell Zeke the truth when he said he hates lawyers."

"He said that?"

"Yes."

Lakshmi leans her elbow on my desk and rests her chin in her hand. "That's not good. What are you doing to do?"

I lean forward over my desk, meeting her gaze. "I don't know. I have to tell him I'm a lawyer, obviously—but in person so I can gauge his reaction. The problem is that we saw him talking to Scammer Guy, so I have to figure out first if Zeke's somehow connected to him. But Zeke seemed like a good guy." But bad guys are supposed to seem like good guys. "Anyway, I read your memo last night. You need more case support in sections four and five. I'll email my comments to you."

"Thanks. I appreciate your feedback," she says. "And especially because I know how busy you are."

My cell phone rings. Capital Management. But not Brooke's number. I pick it up.

"Hey, it's Zeke. I thought I better call, in case you were worried about whether I got home safely."

I laugh. *He's calling the next day!*

Bold. No "wait at least two days" games here.

I motion to Lakshmi that it's him, pointing at his picture on my screen.

"I respect that you're giving me a hard time for taking the cab and not sharing," I say. "I'm sorry about that."

"No worries. There was another cab right behind. But I couldn't *not* give you some flak about it." His deep chuckle does things to my stomach. "Are you free for a date on Thursday?"

I can't go out on a date yet. Not while I'm working on this litigation. And not while he thinks dating an artist is all fun and games and dating a lawyer is some sort of purgatory. I spin my chair around to face the window, my back to Lakshmi.

"I can't. I have to work." That sounds too vague. *Embellish.* "I'm bartending that night." I do sometimes pick up Miranda's bartending shifts when she has a deadline and my schedule is free. It's oddly relaxing. It's like being at a party but with no pressure to make small talk.

"Any other days you're free?"

"My schedule is crazy right now." I wish I could go out on a date with him. The guy in the window across the street is packing up his stuff to go home. He turns off the light. Most of the rooms in that office building are now dark. They must look at ours blazing away at all hours and congratulate themselves for not being lawyers at White & Gilman.

"Where are you bartending? I can keep you company." His voice is deep and confident.

"You'd be way too distracting."

"Distracting?"

"Yes," I say.

"And here I was beginning to think you weren't interested. Especially after the way you left last night."

He is up front. I like that. Ironic if my appeal is I'm not falling over myself for him. With my law firm schedule, this playing-hard-to-get thing could be easy for me.

"Is that a new feeling for you?" I ask, a teasing inflection in my voice.

"Do you think it would be?"

"Possibly." I can't help smiling. "Anyway, I'm definitely interested. Just busy next week." I prefer being up front as well, despite my current lie that I'm an artist.

"Shall I leave the ball in your court, then?" he asks. "You have my number now. If you free up and you'd like to hang out, call me."

"Let me see what I can do about my schedule. I would like to see you. I'm just swamped right now." Piles of paper tower on my credenza in front of the window. And this weekend is going to be a crash course in housing law.

"Okay," he says.

I hang up and turn to Lakshmi. "Let the record reflect that artists work all the time."

"Is that Miranda's schedule this weekend?"

"Pretty much. Except she's performing instead of bartending. But I can't sing, so I'm not going to go there."

"You're not exactly an artist, either, if I remember correctly from that one art class we took with the summer associates at that firm event," Lakshmi says.

"Details." I wave my hand. "It's not like I'm going to paint in front of him. Right now, I have to call Paul and see if I can get authority to try to settle this Capital Management case. I don't want to meet Zeke as his lawyer. And I do have a lot of work this weekend, especially with this succession case. I can't mess it up."

"I still think you should have turned Ken's case down." Lakshmi swivels around to face me.

"I couldn't. My best friend in high school and her mom were almost kicked out of their rent-controlled home by an unscrupulous landlord who'd denied them heat and water. Her mom's boyfriend advised her mom to move out, and the landlord then sent them a notice they'd vacated the premises. The lease was almost termi-nated, but FLAFL saved them—and then her mom found out her boyfriend was being paid off by the landlord."

"Oh." Lakshmi tilts her head. "Is that why you became a lawyer?"

"Basically, yes. I wanted to make sure I knew the laws and how to protect myself and the people I cared about. And, you know, uphold justice and all those good things. Why'd you become a lawyer?"

"My parents gave me a choice: lawyer or doctor. And I took one semester of biology and was like, law it is."

I laugh. Lakshmi asks what Ken's case is about, and I explain it.

"Wow. I see why you couldn't say no." Lakshmi leans forward. "But I thought you had to live in the apartment for two years prior to the death of the primary resident to have succession rights. Isn't she already out because she hasn't lived there?"

"No. Active military service isn't considered a relocation."

"Did the grandmother marry this guy?"

"No. But he is able to show all these other factors to demonstrate an emotional and financial commitment and interdependence. He shared a bank account with her, depositing his check, and took care of her when she was ill. She even gave him power of attorney. He has a compelling case, objectively." *He has more support for his case than I expected.*

"Well, especially if he took care of her." Lakshmi clicks off her computer.

"She met him because he was the assigned healthcare assistant. I think he found an elderly, frail woman with a rent-stabilized apartment and used her."

"Sometimes I think you're a little too cynical for your own good. Although, I guess it helps you as a lawyer."

"If not, wouldn't the grandmother have said she'd met someone? My client Taylor Robinson says she only referred to him as the caretaker."

"Maybe she didn't want to share her love life with her granddaughter."

"Maybe. But I think it's suspicious."

"No faith in true love?" Lakshmi asks.

"Not when there's a rent-stabilized apartment at stake," I say.

"I hope you win." Lakshmi packs up her bag to leave.

"I plan to." My stomach tightens. *I have to win this case for Taylor.*

Paul agreed with my suggestion to propose settling the Capital Management litigation. Thus, it's Monday morning, and I'm sitting next to Paul at a wide conference table. Across from us are the opposing counsel representing the plaintiffs in the litigation suing Capital Management. The three plaintiffs' lawyers all have poker faces and don't look inclined to give me the time of day, never mind agree to settle a lawsuit, as they read my settlement proposal.

We're in our largest conference room to remind them they're up against White & Gilman. The wall of windows has a view of the gleaming, midtown skyline. Stuffed Shirt had another commitment so he couldn't join us. He'd asked Paul to find another date, but Paul said, "This is Tessa's move." Paul is one of my favorite partners to work for because he gives so much responsibility to associates. He only steps in if he needs to. His face right now could be captioned, *This is a waste of my time. Clearly, you should settle.*

I wish I had that kind of dismissiveness. My face is probably more, *Please, please.* I sit upright, my hands in my lap, and try to look like they'd be idiots not to settle.

The most senior partner of the opposing trio places my settlement proposal facedown and steeples his fingers.

"We don't see any reason to agree to this proposal," he says. "The jury will love our plaintiffs. Our plaintiffs are grandparents who were led to believe that this was a safe investment for their retirement income."

"That's exactly why your plaintiff wrote this email to his friend, encouraging him to invest in the North American Capital Management Fund. He wrote: 'It may seem risky, but don't forget—no risk, no return,'" I say, pushing a copy of the email across the table to them. "Not to mention the plaintiff created a Facebook post saying the same thing." I hand over my screenshot of that.

The senior partner's face falls. The three of them huddle to look at the two documents.

There's nothing like that gotcha *moment.*

But I keep my face blank and lean back in my chair. As does Paul.

The senior partner looks up. "We'll talk to our clients and get back to you."

I stand. "Please do."

They agreed to settle. It's a huge win for our client, especially because of Zeke's email questioning whether the investment was too risky. To be fair to him, a fund manager *should* ask those questions. And given that the investment was within the risk parameters disclosed, it shouldn't be considered a harmful email. But you never know how a jury will interpret it, especially with whatever negative spin a plaintiff's attorney glosses on it.

And it's a huge win for me and my quest to merit the extraordinary bonus.

I'm in shock because I wouldn't have been quite as inspired to seek a settlement if I hadn't wanted to stop representing Capital Management before I went on a date with Zeke.

It's the first time I've ever felt that electric spark with someone. If I'm honest, I thought that phrase in romance novels was exaggerated. And I know he seems to hate lawyers, but it's not like that should be a deal breaker. Who picks their partner based on their career? That's ridiculous.

I'll explain in person that I'm not an artist once I figure out how he knows Jurgen. I only said that because Scammer Guy was next to me. He should understand.

Chapter Five

Zeke

I KNOCK ON BROOKE'S door. This lawsuit is a frickin' headache. I should be spending this time deciphering financials and visiting companies to check them out as potential investments for either my North American Fund or for the new venture capital portfolio we're developing. There's enough on my plate with trying to keep two bosses happy. Or rather, impress Charles and keep Arthur content—he's never going to be happy—so he doesn't make my life complete hell. Then Charles can decide he needs me *solely* on the venture capital side of Capital's businesses, and I can say goodbye to Arthur. Instead, my days are filled with meetings with legal about millions of emails written months ago that I don't recall. I don't write them to be parsed word by word.

Charles still hasn't replied to my proposal to include Comidas en Canasta, a company that provides a food delivery app in Mexico City, as one of the investments in our next venture capital portfolio. Last week's visit to their headquarters convinced me. I'll stop by his office after this meeting and follow up. Unless this "interrogation" session runs late into the night. Like the last few times.

"Come in," Brooke says.

"Thanks again for warning me about Arthur holding that meeting without me." I close the door behind me.

She narrows her eyes at me. "It was weird that both you and Winthrop recommended including that up-and-coming Canadian bank in the North American Fund."

I shake my head. "I guess we both read the data the same way."

Do I believe that? No. Arthur must have told Winthrop I was crunching the numbers on that bank. It's small and not likely to be on anyone's radar. Except I'd been in Canada looking at another company for the North American Fund, and the guys I met had been discussing the bank's latest marketing campaign and its subsequent increase in market share. I'd immediately emailed my analysis to Arthur and my junior associate, Ming. But if Brooke hadn't told me about the meeting, Winthrop, with his bow tie, would have been the one recommending the bank as an investment and taking the credit.

I sit in the chair in front of Brooke's desk. A stack of papers rests on a credenza by the window, but her desk is clear. Not even a folder. That doesn't seem good. At least with a pile of email printouts, there's an end in sight.

"The lawsuit settled," she says.

I start. "Are you serious?"

"Dead serious. You can thank our outside counsel."

"But last time, you said my email about the risk profile was going to hurt us."

Brooke shrugs. "They had worse documents. And our outside lawyer showed them those, and that was enough to convince them they didn't want to fight us in court."

Unbelievable. I can breathe again. I lean back in the chair.

Ben knocks on the door and enters. "Lunch? Oh, you're meeting with this guy. Brooke should label that chair with your name. You're here every time I come by. You're lucky I'm not a jealous guy."

"It's all yours." I stand and wave toward the chair. The office is narrow, about eight feet by twelve feet.

"His case just settled," Brooke says.

"I thought you were expecting this to be a long, drawn-out battle?" Ben commandeers the chair. I stand by the wall as Ben stretches out his legs.

Brooke nods. "I was."

"You need to bow down to Brooke now," Ben says. "You can stop complaining about this lawsuit and focus on impressing Charles so you can move away from Arthur and be solely on the venture capital side."

"Thank you so much." I bow my head to Brooke. *Sincerely.* I'm so frickin' relieved the lawsuit settled.

"It wasn't me. It was our outside counsel. She negotiated it." Brooke spins her pen. "I thought it was risky, but I agreed we might as well try."

"This is huge. I have my schedule back." I lean against the wall.

Brooke says, "Maybe we should host the outside lawyers for a congratulatory dinner. They seem like a fun group."

"Done. I'll even cover the costs from our budget," I say.

"Dinner tonight, Brooke? We can have our own celebration." Ben leans forward. "Now that we don't have to sneak out to avoid the death stare from Zeke."

I snort and push off the wall. "I didn't think you should be distracting our esteemed counsel when she could be working on my case."

"We should do a double date this weekend or next with that artist you met," Ben says.

Double dates. Hanging out with a girlfriend and friends. It's been a long time since that's even seemed like a possibility. *But ... Tessa's grin and her eyes twinkling up at me.* Maybe it is.

"She's too busy to go out this weekend." I open Brooke's office door, ready to make my escape. "And I'd like to have a date with her myself before I introduce you two."

As I leave Brooke's office, I run right into Arthur. I step back because I don't want to tower over him. That clearly annoys him.

Arthur is wiry, like his body is a physical manifestation of how tightly wound he is. I'm surprised he's up here in legal. He tends to insist anyone junior come to his office. Brooke may be a vice president, but he's a managing director.

"Congratulations on your case settling." Arthur frowns. "That was a bit unexpected."

It's like Arthur's bugged my life. I just found out, and yet he knows already.

I raise my eyebrow. "You're well informed."

"I wanted to make sure Winthrop's case was a top priority, and Brooke said she would have more time to devote to it because the North American Fund case settled. By the way, I scheduled our next department meeting for Friday at ten." He darts past me and into Brooke's office.

Poor Brooke and Ben.

Friday. At ten. My assistant just scheduled the venture capital portfolio update meeting with Charles to Friday at ten. I'd told Ming, my junior associate, to pull together the first draft of our presentation. It's not going to look professional to reschedule that.

Did Arthur do it on purpose so that there's a conflict with my meeting with Charles? Isn't that too petty even for him? *Stop being paranoid.*

I need to get out, away from Arthur, and report solely to Charles. Running the North American Fund is a satisfying challenge, but not with Arthur monitoring my every move.

But Arthur refuses to give me up. Even though his favorite is clearly Winthrop—and Winthrop's well-connected father. It's because I know what I'm doing. And the returns of the North American Fund show that. A sense of pride fills me. My North American Fund returns beat the market and some funds managed by far more experienced managers.

I head back to my desk on the trading floor but stop by my assistant's desk and ask her to plan the dinner with the lawyers.

She hands me a message. "Charles called about Comidas en Canasta. I'll organize the dinner. Is your schedule currently up to date?"

"Yes. I'll let you know if that changes after I talk to Charles." Or if a certain blonde artist calls me back for a date.

I take the stairs to the floor above us, knock on Charles's door, and then enter.

"Zeke. Thanks for stopping by." Charles swivels around in his chair, away from the three monitors that line his desk. "I'm not sure about investing in Comidas en Canasta. Why do you think this one will succeed and the other food apps won't?"

"The management of this one. The CEO went to Harvard Business School with the CFO and then worked his way up at Seamless in the US. He knows the Mexico City market because that's where he grew up."

Charles nods as I explain further why I think Comidas en Canasta is the right investment for this portfolio. That's one of the qualities I admire about Charles. He's tough but fair.

"Okay. You get returns like your last two investments, and I can make the case that we need your talents *solely* on the venture capital side," Charles says. "Keep it up."

Yes. I'm back in the game. The Paisley breakup derailed me, but I'm back now.

Chapter Six

Tessa

MIRANDA DECIDED THAT WE need reinforcements to brainstorm about how to catch Scammer Guy and has called in our group of friends to meet with Yvette. As I wait for the gang to join me outside Banter & Books on Amsterdam Avenue, I call Zeke. I'm excited that we can now go on a date. *Was I just imagining that electricity? He can't really be friends with Jurgen.* He picks up immediately.

"Hi," I say. "I cleared up my schedule, and Thursday now works. Are you free to hang out?"

"Definitely. Hold on." There's a pause. "Sorry. I'm still at work."

"Oh, you also work late a lot?"

"Yes, unfortunately," he says. "But Thursday is great. I thought you might want to go to this event. Let me find it." The clicking of a keyboard comes through the phone. "It's the Dumbo Arts Center Auction. Would you like to go?"

"Yes." That's such a good choice for a date with an artist. Impressive. "My roommate, Miranda, donated a piece to it." Miranda's latest painting is spotlighted in the window of Banter & Books. It's a mesmerizing pink and yellow—the feeling of joy practically jumps out of it.

"Did you?"

"I wasn't asked."

"Here's your chance to have artwork in it. You can paint something there, and then it will be auctioned off to benefit selected charities, right alongside works by some famous artists."

No.

How am I going to get out of painting in front of him? I can't tell him *now* I'm not an artist. I need to be able to see his face when I ask him how he knows Jurgen. "But won't you be bored if I'm off painting something? I—"

"I definitely won't be bored. I'd love to see you paint. Plus, this would be great for your career."

I clear my throat. "Oh well, then. It would be great for my career." If I was an artist.

"Maybe you can even provoke a bidding war."

If I hire people to bid.

"Let's hope," I say. We set the details and hang up.

It's fine. I'll ask Zeke how he knows Jurgen when we meet. If it seems like he's not going to reveal anything to Jurgen, I'll tell Zeke that I'm not an artist and that I'm actually a lawyer, and then I won't have to paint anything.

I should have confessed over the phone. *No.* The mission is what's important here. Not dating some guy.

Miranda waves from down the street, her red hair vivid against the green jacket she's wearing. We hug hello.

"I asked Zeke out," I say.

She high-fives me. "But you need to make sure he's not good friends with Scammer Guy. You can't risk our scheme to catch Jurgen."

"I know." I can't disappoint Miranda.

"I've found your next chance to trap Scammer Guy. Yvette said he's going to be at the Dumbo Arts Center Auction."

I stare at her. "So am I."

"Exactly. You can pick him up. I've thought about it some more, and the problem was that last time you looked like you had *no* money. This time, you should dress up to look like a good target. And we shouldn't take any chances. You should engage him in conversation. Discuss whatever artwork he's looking at."

"That's a good plan, but I'm going with Zeke. Who wants me to paint. I'm going to tell him I'm a lawyer before I have to paint," I say. "But I'm afraid he'll dump me the minute he finds out."

"Then you should tell him so you don't waste your time. He's not worth it if he doesn't like you for yourself. But first, we need to figure out how Zeke knows Scammer Guy. What if they're buddies or fraternity brothers from college and he feels some loyalty to Jurgen and blows our cover? He said he was there with friends. Jurgen may be a friend. I definitely saw them talking before Zeke left."

Miranda opens the door to Banter & Books, and it smells of chocolate chip cookies. A batch must have just come out of the oven. Miranda walks over to claim our usual cluster of distressed arm, cabriole-legged chairs with these egg-blue pillows by the window, a prime spot that offers either a great view of the street or the other occupants of the café. *Pick your poison.* Our other favorite place is the table in the back conservatory, but that looks like it's been reserved for a private party.

"With the both of them there together, I definitely should be able to get a feel for if Jurgen and Zeke are friends," I say.

"It will also be an opportunity for Zeke to get to know you," Miranda says. "Once he gets to know you, I'm sure he won't care if you're a lawyer, although he doesn't seem entirely rational about that."

"I'll try to determine if they are friends, find an opportunity to chat with Scammer Guy, and then I'll tell Zeke at the end of our date?" I muse.

"He should understand that you were on a mission to foil some scammer dude. And you could always be a lawyer—and an artist in your spare time. Like Bella works full-time as an assistant to make money but is also a published author."

"Except that I can't paint."

"I'm sure you can paint something," Miranda says. "Maybe not when you're tipsy, but if you're focused on it. You must have some artistic genes, given how successful Kiara is. Her last art show received so many rave reviews."

"I think she inherited all the painting genes." My sister would die laughing if she heard I was pretending to be an artist. "YouTube must have some tutorials. If I could fix a toilet following a YouTube tutorial, I should be able to paint something."

"It doesn't have to be good. It's even better if it's bad because if Scammer Guy then shows interest in mentoring you, we'll know it's not genuine. But it can't be so bad that he suspects he's being set up. I can give you some pointers tonight." Miranda's phone rings, and she answers it.

I join the line at the counter to order our drinks. Banter & Books is a bookstore café with an appealing French country decor. White bookcases line the two side walls. Throughout the café are round, worn, wooden tables, surrounded by various tallish, green plants, creating little privacy screens. I take a deep breath. It's definitely eclectic but soothing.

After I order our usual drinks at the counter and take a stand with a number, I pull over a rattan chair from another table since we'll be five in total. Miranda is already seated, typing on her phone.

"Yvette said she's on her way," Miranda says. "Maddie can't make it because she's got a story deadline."

The bell clangs as Lily and Iris come through the door of Banter & Books. We hug hello. I feel like I haven't seen them in ages.

Lily places a pile of books on the center table as she says, "I just have to reply to Rupert's text." She smiles as she always does when texting Rupert, her boyfriend.

"How's work?" I ask Iris as she removes her wide-brimmed hat.

"Busy. What about you?" Iris takes the seat across from me.

"Same," I say.

"Rupert said he feels a little bit sorry for whatever poor guy we have in our sights now because that guy has no idea what he's up against." Lily runs her hand through her blonde hair, smoothing it back. "But not that sorry. He's happy to help in whatever way he can."

Rupert is the co-CEO of Strive Developers, a well-known real estate development firm, but I can't think of any way he can help.

Iris laughs. "We should have had Rupert dress up as the struggling artist."

I snort. "Yes, next time, we definitely need to come up with a role for Rupert."

"He'd probably be recognized," Lily says as she scoops the books off the table and into her backpack.

Yvette comes in next. Yvette is skinny, with almost translucent, white skin, her straight, pale-blonde hair framing her face. She looks at Miranda like she's a goddess. Which Miranda is.

Once we are all settled with drinks, Miranda makes the introductions.

"Yvette, meet the team. Iris and Lily are our research wizards. Iris works in cybersecurity, and Lily is a librarian at the New York Public Library," Miranda says. "And my roommate, Tessa, is a lawyer."

Miranda continues, "As I mentioned, this guy, Jurgen, scammed Yvette. He said he wanted to help her as an aspiring artist but took her money. She paid him to frame her paintings for a show, but there was no show and the framing job was slapshot. She had to reframe them. She paid him three thousand dollars."

Lily drops the book she was holding. "Sorry. Wow. That's crazy." She picks it up off the floor.

"Thank you guys so much," Yvette says. "I feel bad taking up your time. But if Jurgen is doing this to other women, then he needs to be stopped."

"We could sue him for the poor framing job in small claims court," I say. "Did you get a receipt or a contract?"

"No," Yvette says. "It seemed too churlish to ask for that when we were friends, and I thought he was doing me a huge favor by finding this gallery show."

"Without any documents as evidence, that would be hard to win," I say. Yvette's face falls. Miranda shakes her head at me. I get it. *Too harshly said.*

Iris raises an eyebrow at me. We're on the same page. Sympathetic but not exactly sure we have a case here.

"Did you go to the gallery?" Iris asks.

"He said it was a pop-up gallery run by this dealer named Misty Morano. They had a website with a list of shows." She shows Iris the website on her phone.

"It looks like that website hasn't been updated recently," Iris says. "I'll look into it."

"If it is even connected," Lily adds. "Maybe he just picked a gallery website. Did you ever talk to them?"

"No. Jurgen said it was best to let him handle everything."

"And what did he say happened with the show?" I ask.

"He said they couldn't get the funding and it folded." Yvette bites her nail.

"I talked to Officer Johnson," Miranda says. "I met him when my painting was stolen, and he helped me, so I thought he might be able to take Yvette's case. But he would like more to go on."

So would I. This Jurgen guy could just be a crappy framer. But if I play bad cop, Miranda will kill me. She said Yvette was embarrassed enough and initially didn't want to pursue it.

The server deposits a trayful of hot drinks on our table, and we each take ours.

I ask some background questions, such as how she met Jurgen and what he told her, to try to put Yvette at ease. Her leg is bopping up and down. She would *not* be a good witness on the stand. Her hands cradle her mug of hot chocolate as if gaining strength from it.

Really. She's a perfect target. So tentative and unsure. Scammer Guy definitely knows his mark.

That's *not* me.

Should Lily or Iris try to be his mark? They don't convey that either. Especially Iris. She can slay you with a glance. Even with her shiny, dark-brown hair in a ponytail, she radiates confidence. Her parents own a bar downtown, and in college, she bartended there to help out and make money. She doesn't put up with any crap.

And Lily is too busy right now with the community garden that she helps run. It's practically another job on top of her full-time librarian position.

"What happened after the Misty Morano show fell through?" I ask.

"He helped me sell one of my grad school paintings to a collector he knew. That was my first sale to a stranger. I was so thrilled. And after that, he sold another painting to this couple in Brazil. That was super exciting, but we both got conned with that."

"*Conned*?" I ask.

Iris leans in.

"This Brazilian man contacted him. He'd seen the painting on Jurgen's Instagram and wanted to know if we could ship it to him in Brazil so he could give it to his wife for her birthday. My first international sale. I couldn't believe it. And I shouldn't have."

Yvette sighs, sips her coffee, and continues. "Anyway, Jurgen gave me the guy's check when he came to pick up the painting. But the check was for far more than the price of the painting. So right there, he called the Brazilian guy. The guy said he included the price of the shipping and Jurgen's commission, and I should give the difference to Jurgen because Jurgen would ship the painting. I Venmoed Jurgen the difference. Jurgen left with the painting. The Brazilian guy said he wanted confirmation of the freighting before we cashed his check. We also had to use his freighting company."

"The Brazilian check was fake," Iris says.

Yvette nods. "The check was fake."

Lily and Miranda also lean forward now, and we're all silent. Other conversations buzz around us, but we're slowly absorbing this loss.

"I was out one thousand dollars, which was the cost to ship it, and the painting was gone. Jurgen paid me back his two-hundred-dollar commission. He'd already shipped the painting, so that was lost. He was so apologetic and guilt-ridden. I felt so bad for him."

"Did you ever see the confirmation of freighting?" I ask. "Do you know for sure Jurgen shipped it?"

"No."

"Did you ever talk to the Brazilian guy?"

"Yes. That night in my apartment. He spoke Brazilian Portuguese and some English." She stares at us. "You don't think…? No. Jurgen couldn't have been in on the scam. You don't understand. He was really upset. He offered to pay for half of the shipping. I don't—" She stops and her face falls. "Maybe he was. Maybe that was the start of it all. I'm such an idiot."

She puts her empty mug down on the table.

"I read a *New York Times* article recently about fraudsters taking advantage of artists and contacting them via social media with this exact scam," Miranda says.

"But we don't know if Jurgen is involved in this," I say. "This is all conjecture until we have evidence. We need to do our own investigation and figure out Jurgen's role."

"But if he was involved, then he possesses her painting. Plus, he made one thousand dollars," Miranda says. "And now that painting could be worth something. You recently signed with a dealer, right?"

"Yes," Yvette says. "Once I stopped relying on Jurgen to find me a dealer and said we were done, I started hustling on my own to get my work in shows, and I found one. The painting for that Brazilian guy was actually pretty good. It could eventually be worth several thousand."

Some more customers come in from outside. The three new people sit at the table next to us.

"Do you have a copy of the check in your bank statements?" Iris asks.

"I closed that account, but I can try to get that."

"If he's doing fake-check scams, that has some serious penalties," I say. "If we can prove it, Officer Johnson will definitely be interested. And various other agencies. What do you think made him interested in you?"

"I was so enthusiastic and believed everything he told me. I'd just nod. You know. Even when he's blowing his own horn and sounding like a pompous ass and treating me like I'd never done a degree in art, I'd look at him like he was my hero. He laps that up."

She does have a bit of spunk, then.

"Thank you again for taking your time to help me get justice," Yvette says. "I wanted to drop it. I'm afraid this will ruin my reputation in the art world. I'll be looked at as an idiot."

"I doubt it," I say. "I think most creatives are aware that they're swimming in shark-infested waters."

"I'm sure most artists have been scammed at one point or another and in a much less personal context," Miranda says. "And anyway, you should use the feelings you have and put them into your art. That's what I do."

That's one of the things I most admire about Miranda. She takes her most vulnerable moments and makes them public. I shiver. It's so bold.

"I know. I followed your advice, Miranda, and look." Yvette holds up her phone to show us a photo. "My dealer says it's my best painting yet. If I didn't dislike Jurgen so much, I'd dedicate it to him. But he'd definitely take that only in a positive way."

"At that opening, he definitely gave off the vibe that he thought he was great," I say.

Yvette nods. "And I don't want other women to get scammed like I did."

"We'll catch him," Lily says. "We weren't sure we'd be able to save the local community garden, but we did." She and Miranda clink cups.

"I hope so. Paying Jurgen three thousand dollars for that crap framing job made me so upset. I'm working so hard to make money so I can paint. I waitress. I tutor. I don't want to bore you with the odd jobs I've done. Three thousand is a lot for me. That's why I told him we were done."

"Did he acknowledge that the framing was terrible?" Lily asks.

"No. He said it was fine. And it was my choice to have the paintings re-framed." She takes a deep breath. "When I paid the thousand dollars for shipping and lost that painting that I spent months working on ... I almost gave up then. I didn't tell Jurgen. I didn't want him to think that I didn't have the stamina for an art career. But it was soul-destroying. If he was involved in that and the check scam, he's ..." She shakes her head. "He knew how hard I worked. He often called to remind me to eat." Yvette looks like she is going to cry and excuses herself to go to the bathroom.

This is why doing pro bono legal work is important to me. What's at stake is not usually just money. It's a person's life and ability to pursue their dreams.

"Do you think he might be involved in the check scams too?" Miranda asks.

"That's a lot of coincidences if he's not," Iris says.

"I'll approach him at the Dumbo Arts Center," I say. "Let's hope he tries this same foreign collector scam on me. But should I cancel my date with Zeke that night?" I catch everyone up on the Zeke situation.

"You should go on the Zeke date," Iris says. "But isn't it weird that he suggested the Dumbo Arts Center, and that's where Jurgen is going to be?"

"He's a banker. How could he be involved in the scam?" I ask.

"Aren't you defending his fund for fraud? This is just fraud on a small scale," Lily says.

"His fund did not commit fraud," I say.

"I doubt he's in on the scam," Iris says. "But if they're good friends, he might warn Jurgen. It's not like he's going to believe Tessa over some strong friendship. I wouldn't."

This is all a murky mess.

"I'm worried I won't be a good mark because I'm not that good an actress. She seems so unsure, and I don't think I give off that vibe."

"You should paint," Lily says.

"But I can't paint."

"Exactly," Lily says. "You'll give off that unsure vibe."

That's for sure.

"But I also need Zeke to think I'm a painter unless I tell him beforehand."

"That works well. You need to paint something good enough that both Zeke and Scammer Guy think you're an artist," Lily says. "And you can tell Zeke afterward. Give him a chance to get to know you as a person so he can get over his prejudice against lawyers."

"I'm not sure this is going to work." *This is definitely not going to work.*

Chapter Seven

Tessa

"I'LL GET YOU SOME stuff so you can practice painting." Miranda pulls a small canvas out of her stash and finds some brushes and paint. "I'll give you some lessons once I finish this art show application. It's due today, and I want to look it over one more time before I submit it."

Miranda sets me up at an easel and disappears to her bedroom in the back. I rest my iPad on an easel next to mine and read through the YouTube video's instructions meticulously. I squeeze out dabs of purple and blue paint on the canvas and then brush the paints exactly as the video shows. Somehow, the artist in the video creates this feeling of an early evening sky full of possibility, but my attempt resembles a big, purple-and-blue blob.

It's a good thing I'm a lawyer.

Miranda emerges out of our hallway kitchen and comes over to where I'm standing in front of the easel.

"Oh no," she says.

"It's bad, isn't it?" I put my brush into the can of water. *It's a disaster.*

"Yes. I'd recommend a diversion, like bringing a painting you can switch with the empty canvas." She laughs.

"Yes," I say. "You could create a diversion, and William can switch the paintings."

She shakes her head. "I'm working that night, unfortunately. You'll be fine."

"Way to rally to the occasion," I say. "Still, I'll ask Iris to bid on my painting at the auction. I'll buy it back from her. I'm happy to support these not-for-profits."

Miranda waves her hand. "Anyway, being a bad painter will lend credence to our belief that he's scamming artists."

"But if I'm terrible, will Jurgen actually think I'm a good mark?" I ask. "Yvette clearly has talent."

"Yvette is talented. Just too tentative."

I shake my head. "He has no shame. Maybe I should try to reschedule Zeke so I can focus on hooking Scammer Guy." Except that I'm supposed to be focusing on work, and going out two nights this week might be hard. My phone beeps.

Zeke: *I bought the tickets.*

All right. Date night with Zeke is definitely on. And hooking Scammer Guy. I can work late the other nights.

"The video made this painting look doable—at least to create that." I show her the video. "I wasn't aiming for a masterpiece, but I was hoping I could create something worthy of motel art. What am I going to do now?"

"I can give you some tips. I think your strategy of mastering this one painting can still work. And like you said, you're not aiming to look like a successful artist," Miranda says. "Maybe it's even better to test Zeke's desire to date someone creative by portraying an aspiring artist with all the rejection rather than some glamorous world of art openings."

Does Zeke want to date an artist for the social cachet? Ugh. I'm definitely not about that. Wyatt wanted someone who could accompany him to society events.

No. Zeke couldn't. Not with the way I was dressed at the art opening. That outfit definitely did not radiate glamour. I chuckle.

"Oh no. What if Zeke has dated a string of accomplished artists?" I rub my hands on my smock. "I didn't think this through. I hate looking incompetent."

Miranda shows me how to hold the brush properly and how to sweep the paint to get the effect shown in the YouTube video. She pulls her red hair back into a messy bun, slides over another easel next to mine, and works on her painting while I try again. We paint in a comfortable silence. My second attempt looks a bit better.

"This one seems too difficult," I say. "Maybe I should just paint the background and put some stick figures on it. Remember that lecture we went to that linked the cave painters with today's modernists? I can make stick figures. Or make some scribbles."

"You could try that," Miranda says. "I doubt drawing a stick figure will seem credible. Keep working on this one. Remember the rule of thirds."

"Are there rules? Good. I can learn rules."

"You divide the canvas into thirds, vertically and horizontally. And then you place focal points within that, so that you are leading the viewer around the composition. See what I did with this painting?" Miranda points to one of her paintings on the wall. "What do you see first?"

"The blue dot."

"Exactly. Okay, for blue, you should say, 'ultramarine.' You should at least memorize the names of the paint colors." She gives me a box of paint tubes. I put them on our oak dining room table to memorize later and return to stand next to her at my easel.

"And then what do you see?" she asks.

"The thick, orange line."

"Right. That's intentional. Because that gives a feeling of balance. I lead the viewer kind of like the way you lead a witness to admit the truth."

I nod. We discuss the composition some more. The concepts are not completely foreign. Between Miranda and my sister, Kiara, I've gone to enough art exhibits that I know the language. Maybe this is doable.

Watching Miranda painting is very soothing.

"How's work going?" she asks. "Still in the running for the bonus?"

"As far as I know," I say.

The light from the streetlamp outside filters in through the crack in the curtains. Our track lighting spotlights the three easels we set up.

"You must like Zeke," Miranda says. "I thought you couldn't date and work at the same time."

"It's definitely not easy. And I actually thought he might be that unicorn who doesn't mind dating a workaholic. After all, he received a work call and had to cut our evening short. But then he advised his friend *not* to date a workaholic. I don't know. I had fun that night."

Miranda says, "You're usually quite good at compartmentalizing. Saying something like, 'See you in two months after I've received my bonus.'"

"Yes. But there was definite chemistry." That look he gave me by the East River ... mmm. "And I should be able to date and work. You always tell me that."

"You definitely should," Miranda says.

"And given all the women hitting on him, I don't think he'll be around in two months."

"You looked happy when you were with Zeke. Happier than I ever saw you with Wyatt. But." Miranda's brow wrinkles and she looks down. "This is it. This is your chance to get the bonus and the FLAFL job. You've said yourself that the position doesn't open up that often."

"I'm going to get the bonus." My mess of a canvas mocks me. "Last time, with Wyatt, you were worried that I wasn't allowing myself to get too emotionally attached—that I was holding back too much. And now, I actually like Zeke, and you're telling me I should put him on hold?"

"I'm just concerned that he won't be supportive if he doesn't like lawyers," Miranda says. "And it's the timing. Especially when I know how much you've always wanted to work for FLAFL. You've always been so clear on your goals."

Except that I enrolled in law school intending to work for FLAFL, and instead, I went to a corporate firm so I could pay off my grad school debt and benefit from law firm training.

"You do want to work for FLAFL, right?" Miranda puts down her paintbrush and faces me, her gaze serious.

"I do. I really do." I stare off at our wall, filled with Miranda's art, including some paintings that she was never able to sell, even though we both loved them. "As much as I hate the politics of corporate law life, if I get any more used to this salary, I'm not sure I will be able to give it up. Some would say I have the best of both now. I can do some pro bono and also cases covered by *The New York Times*."

"Those are all valid thoughts and feelings," Miranda says. "But give yourself the choice. Make sure your priority is the bonus."

"Don't worry. My priority is still my career before a guy. If anything, the possibility of dating Zeke helped my career because I settled his fund's case and won huge brownie points."

Miranda turns back to her painting and picks up her brush. I dab a few more strokes.

"Then you should go for it," Miranda says. "Your painting doesn't look that bad."

My painting is a little better. The blue-green color matches Zeke's eyes. Oh no. *I'm already in too deep.*

Okay.

One more chance to make him like me for myself. One fun date before I tell him I'm a lawyer. Hopefully, he's not good friends with Jurgen, and he'll understand about our attempt to entrap Scammer Guy when I tell him the truth. So, I guess that's my plan.

And if he doesn't want to date a workaholic lawyer, better to know now. Before I fall any harder.

Chapter Eight

Tessa

Time to trap Scammer Guy and persuade Zeke that I'm creative and fun. Right now, I'm sitting at my desk, meticulously adding paint under my nails with a toothpick. Miranda comes into my bedroom.

"What are you doing?" she asks.

"Have you ever looked at your hands?" I ask. "You always have paint somewhere."

Miranda looks at her nails and acknowledges this. She shows me some announcement on her phone. "If you really want to persuade Zeke that dating an artist is not all fun and games, you should invite him to this MoMA brush technique lecture. I once went with a friend, and she fell asleep."

"I'll keep it in mind. We'll see how this date goes. But lying is too stressful for me. I'm not planning to pretend to be an artist on another date. How do I look?" I'm wearing a black T-shirt, blue jeans, boots, and a chunky, gold bracelet.

"Good. Artsy. Ready for a painting party." Miranda types on her phone. "Anyway, I emailed the info about the lecture to you."

The doorbell rings. I check the video monitor and buzz Zeke in. I open the door and wait on the landing as he comes up the stairs.

"I'm on the third floor," I yell down, peering over the balustrade. He looks good. He's wearing a white, button-up shirt with the sleeves rolled up, jeans, and sneakers.

Upon reaching our floor, he sports a huge grin, and butterflies flutter in my stomach. I smile back.

As he enters our apartment, his eyes widen. Our living room is basically Miranda's art studio. Three floor-to-ceiling windows with indigo curtains, currently tied back, frame the south wall. In the middle is our long, oak table, an oasis amidst the easels, drying canvases, metal cans of paintbrushes, and plastic pots of paint. Our walls are covered with Miranda's canvases of vibrant colors—blue, yellow, pink, purple. It has this wonderful, zippy, crazy vibe.

"Wow." He steps inside and stares at the art. "These paintings are amazing."

"They're not mine," I say. "My roommate, Miranda Langbroek, is a well-known artist. Most of these are hers. She's much better than me."

"The one who is the female lead singer of The Tempest?"

"Yes."

"She's multi-talented," he says.

"She is."

"Where are yours?"

"Oh. Mine. I have a long way to go." Miranda insisted on hanging my six attempts in the corner to "inspire" me. *As if.* My third sky-scape is the best of all my practice ones. It's much improved from the first blue-purple blob painting—excuse me, ultramarine and violet work. I also tried twice to create an abstract composition in case that was easier. The first resembles the test sheet of paper when someone wants to see what each color looks like before actually using it. The second looks like throw-up—not the vibe I want on my date. There's also my tree in a rain-drenched background. I used crinkled-up aluminum foil like the video recommended. A bare tree is recognizable. I think.

His mouth opens a bit. He presses his lips together, and his brow furrows.

I would laugh if I wasn't actually trying to pretend to be an artist. But this is good for figuring out what attracts him to dating an artist.

Zeke clears his throat. "They're …"

He seems at a loss. It is difficult to find the right words to describe my masterpieces.

"Interesting," I say.

"Or evocative." Miranda enters the room, dressed in a 1950s party dress for her concert tonight. "Hi. I'm Miranda, Tessa's roommate." She puts out her hand to shake Zeke's. "I'm sorry I can't join you guys tonight. My band has a gig."

"Good to meet you." He shakes Miranda's hand. "I'm Zeke. I'm looking forward to checking out your music."

"Thank you."

"We should go," I say. We've spent enough time with my "art." Zeke is still looking around our living room as if trying to take everything in.

"Hey, do you bike?" He points at the helmets hanging on hooks next to the door.

"Yes. After the subway, it's my main method of getting around." If I don't count the car service home from the law firm when I work late. "Do you?"

"Yes. We should go for a bike ride sometime," Zeke says.

"We can bike back," I say. "We have an extra helmet. They were handing out free bike helmets at some city event." I disappear into our closet to retrieve it from a shelf and then shove it into a backpack with my own. I grab my jacket.

"At least this time, I know we'll be coming back together," Zeke says.

"If you can keep up the pace," I say.

He grins at me. "Challenge accepted."

Zeke holds the door open for me, and we jog down the steps together.

Outside, the sky is this mixture of blue and purple, zipping with electricity—basically, the blue-hour vibe I'm trying to convey in my paintings. Couples stroll down the sidewalk, chatting about their evening plans.

We amble side by side down the street. His hand brushes mine as we walk closer together to pass another couple on the narrow sidewalk space between the flower enclosure and the brownstone stoop. We turn left on Central Park West to head for the C subway entrance. The light from a black lamppost outlines the silhouettes of the trees in Central Park.

We jog down the steps of the subway entrance, tap our credit cards, and slide through the turnstiles. Another set of stairs, and we're on the downtown platform below. The clock shows two minutes until our train arrives.

A subway poster advertises the Whitney Biennial. "Have you seen that show?" I ask. "It's good." Thankfully, because of Miranda, attending art shows is not out of the ordinary for me.

"No. I should see it. Work has been crazy lately."

"Is it constant, or are there times when it's less busy?" It's weird he doesn't want to date a workaholic if he is one.

The subway arrives, and we get seats.

"It's particularly busy now. I work for Capital Management. I manage our North American Fund, but I'm hoping to move to the venture capital side of the business. The guy who runs it is great. My other boss ..." He shakes his head. "He's difficult."

"Do you think you'll be able to move?"

"I think so. The venture capital boss has more power. I have to prove I'm worth it for him to use his political capital to make it happen."

"Difficult bosses can make your life hell. I hate office politics," I say. Office politics is one of the reasons why I want to leave White & Gilman.

"I didn't think artists dealt much with office politics."

I wince. I forgot I was pretending to be an artist.

"There's lots of politics in general in the artist world. Who's hot/who's not/who's the reviewer who matters/which art galleries will pick up what artists." I know that much from my sister and Miranda, but I can't think of any details. "Since you manage the North American Fund, do you get to travel to Mexico and Canada a lot, then?"

He smiles at me. "That's not the usual question I get."

"What question do you usually get?"

"What do you recommend I invest in? But yes. Mexico City last week, and Toronto a few weeks ago. It's one of my favorite parts of the job."

"I love traveling and experiencing a different culture."

"Same. And even though it's work, it's also getting to meet people in a more substantive context than as a tourist."

I nod.

The subway stops at West 4th Street, and several passengers get off while more come on. Two people squish in next to me, pushing me closer to Zeke. His muscular thigh touches mine. A group of friends hang on to the bar in front of us. A woman pushing a cart manages to squeeze in as the doors close. The guy next to Zeke is wearing headphones, but the music is so loud that I can hear the bass one seat over. Snippets of conversation float over—"I'd never do that" ... "But he was so stressed"—as the train rumbles along the tracks.

I turn to Zeke. "What do you do to de-stress when the office politics are too much?"

He tilts his head and looks at me. "Run, or bike along the Hudson River. I play basketball in Riverside Park on weekends when I have the time. I definitely miss all the sports I played in school. Hang out with friends. The usual things."

His eyes are this very deep blue with flecks of green. And the way he looks at me, it's as if he's fully focused on me.

I nod. His broad shoulders touch mine.

"You said it seemed impossible to break out as an artist," he says. "It must be hard to know how to make it. There doesn't appear to be a linear path."

That's so sweet and supportive.

"It's definitely daunting. I work all the time, and I don't even know if I'm going to succeed." It's easy to channel my feelings about my dream to work for FLAFL to answer his question because most people think I'm insane to give up my corporate legal job. "Most people would think I'm crazy for pursuing my dream."

"Do you care what people think?" he asks.

"I seem to care more than I thought I did." I bite my lip. "But it's not only what strangers think. It's me too. A good income—it's a type of security." *When I say I'm a corporate lawyer, that garners a certain respect—a "don't mess with me" safety.* What if my career *does* define me? I shake my head. "I'm not usually this tentative about my career choice."

The subway swerves, and the people holding on to the handrail in front of us tip forward into our space. One woman apologizes.

"Thanks for taking tonight off," he says.

"I wanted to see you again," I say.

"Do you usually work weekends?"

"I pretty much work all the time." I can at least be honest about that.

"Me too."

He doesn't seem to be ruling me out because I'm a workaholic. That's good.

The train speeds up, and the rattling of the tracks overwhelms the low murmur of conversation in our car.

"What do you do to de-stress?" he asks.

"I hang out with friends," I say. "And watch movies and read books."

The subway stations zip by. We're going under the East River now, and a cool air filters through the train.

"What's your favorite movie?" He turns slightly to look at me.

"*How to Lose a Guy in 10 Days*. Whenever I feel sad and want a pick-me-up, I watch it again."

"That's a good one." He leans back against the seat.

"You've seen it?" Color me impressed.

"What do you take me for?"

"Were you on a date?" I ask.

"I suggested it," he says.

He chose my favorite movie. "I hope that earned you a lot of points," I say.

He side-eyes me. "Should you be hoping that?"

My heart flutters when he looks at me like that.

"Maybe not." Definitely not. I don't want to imagine him in any Netflix and Chill scenarios—with anyone other than me. "Was this someone you broke up with recently?"

"About six months ago." He stares off at a subway poster advertising mattresses. A couple is cozied up on a bed. He looks down.

That's still pretty recent if it was serious. "And you haven't dated anyone since? Is that why your friend was so thrilled to see you talking to a woman?"

"Exactly," he says. "I've been focused on work. You? When was your last relationship?"

"About eighteen months ago," I say.

"I'm surprised you're not dating anyone."

"That was my first serious relationship," I say. "Miranda set me up with this Dutch guy Thijs last spring, but he was moving back to Holland, so we decided to be friends." I fiddle with my backpack on my lap. "So, you liked *How to Lose a Guy in 10 Days*. Would you have been able to forgive Andie for lying to you if you were Benjamin?"

"They were both lying to each other, so both were at fault." He stares off at a subway poster in the corner. "Once someone lies to you, it can be hard to trust them again."

I bite my lip. I wish I'd never said I was an artist.

"What if there were extenuating circumstances?" I ask.

"So she had to lie?" His brow furrows. "It's our stop."

Chapter Nine

Tessa

THE REGISTRATION TABLE IS piled high with paddles for bidding (hopefully on my painting). Two women check off guests. Zeke gives our names.

The Dumbo Arts Center is a very open, white space with high ceilings, columns interspersed throughout. Track lights spotlight the art. A red-and-blue, wooden sculpture practically leaps off the wall to our right. Miranda's abstract color field painting to the left grabs my attention immediately. Next to it is a cool sculpture made out of Tonka trucks. Rows of folding chairs and a small, wooden, raised platform stage announce the auction later this evening.

Scammer Guy is nowhere to be seen. I hope he shows up soon so I can see if he and Zeke talk again and if they appear to be good friends.

I register for a blank canvas and a paddle number. Zeke also registers to bid.

"Do you collect art?" I ask.

"I do have one painting," he says.

"From a previous girlfriend?"

"No," he says. "I haven't dated a painter before."

That's a relief. My lack of talent would not fare well if I was being compared to someone who was actually pursuing that career.

But "a painter" is weirdly specific. "Have you dated another type of artist?"

"I dated a writer when I was in B-school."

Interesting. My friend Bella, who is a writer, works as much as I do. In fact, she's away right now at a writing retreat.

My assigned easel is off in the corner behind a screen separating the participant painting section from the rest of the room. A smock hangs next to it. I put that on and then suggest that I pick out colors. We walk over to the table where plastic bottles and half-rolled, metal tubes of paint lay scattered about.

"Have you done something like this before?" he asks.

"No," I say. "I have to admit, I'm a little nervous. It usually takes me a long time to perfect a picture—not to mention to even know where to begin. Are you sure you don't want to paint? Maybe you will find it less torturous as an adult."

He shakes his head. "I'll leave it to the experts."

"It's definitely something best left to experts. Why do you like math?" I grab a plastic palette. The woman in front of me is methodically picking out her colors.

"Black and white answers."

"No gray zones?" I ask.

"I leave the gray zones to my lawyers," he says.

Will he consider my telling him I'm an artist because I'm trying to hook Scammer Guy a typical lawyer gray zone?

"Do you deal with lawyers a lot?" I ask.

"More than I'd like."

My being a lawyer may be a tough sell. Most bankers aren't keen to deal with lawyers, but they appreciate what we bring to the table. Was his ex-girlfriend an attorney? And if so, how could that factor into their breakup? Unless she sued him afterward for a share of possessions or something, but that seems extreme.

The colors on the table are not quite the same hues as the ones at home. I should've brought my own set. That would've looked so professional. I choose my palette, and we walk back to my easel.

And there looms the blank canvas. Now I know why Miranda sometimes hesitates to start.

All right, let's do this. I lightly brush my first outlines of the tops of the buildings as instructed in the YouTube video. Miranda did reassure me that mistakes in oil paint can be fixed. This is acrylic paint, but let's hope that still holds true.

"What do you like about math?" I should distract him from my painting.

"You can usually figure out the answer."

"That's what I like about—" I catch myself before I say law. "But when it's not black and white, the gray can be where the challenge is ... where it's up to your skills of persuasion."

"Are we still talking about art? Are there rules in art?"

"Of course." I explain about the rule of thirds. "Do you ever break your rules?"

"How do you know I have rules?"

"You like sports and math." I glance at him. "Both have pretty defined rules."

Zeke tilts his head. "Perceptive. I hadn't thought of it like that. I thought I was more of a risk-taker—until recently. If you don't consider yourself risk-averse, do you consider yourself a rule-breaker?"

"No. More willing to take risks within the confines of the rules."

He is standing very close to me, and my pheromones seem to be kicking into high gear. I'm very conscious of being right next to an attractive guy. My heart seems to be beating twice as fast.

I shake my head and try to create that feel of an evening full of possibility with the deep purples and blues.

The brushwork looks like lines of paint. It doesn't carry any emotional feeling. One "ultramarine" stroke is particularly thick. I try to smooth it out. My "sky" is a large rectangle with a stepped edge for the buildings.

"Same," he says. "I have to take calculated risks when picking stocks for my funds."

"No risk, no reward," I say. My brushstrokes do not look quite as good as they did at home. The canvas resembles my earlier versions. *Nerves.* I take a deep breath and breathe out.

"That's funny," Zeke says. "A lawsuit against my fund settled because the plaintiff used a similar expression to acknowledge the risk."

"You must be happy," I mutter. I put that brush down and pick up another one with a different color to make the apartment buildings.

They don't have any depth. They look like squares on the canvas. *Focus, Tessa. Remember what Miranda showed you.*

I should've practiced painting while trying to hold up a conversation. Zeke says something more about the lawsuit, but I miss it because I'm trying so hard to fix my structures.

"Anyway, it's a huge relief," he says. "I'm grateful to the lawyer who settled it. I thought it was going to be a long, drawn-out fight, and it's really freed up my schedule."

"I'm sure they're grateful the case settled as well." *How can my painting look this bad?* "One less thing on their docket."

"Sounds like you know some lawyers."

"I have a close friend who is a lawyer." I glance at him. "She likes law because it's like a puzzle that she has to figure out."

"Interesting. You've learned a lot about being a lawyer from her."

"We're practically inseparable." I pick up my brush again and stare at the canvas. Three squares on top of a purple-and-blue background.

I dab at it some more.

The squares now have big blobs of paint within them.

They look more like some sort of raised relief topographical map of mountain terrain. But square mountains. In the middle of a purple-and-blue paint spill.

With my brush, I try to smooth one out so it looks more like the facade of a building.

My brush goes outside the line, so now it's no longer a straight line but a slightly curvy … no, not curvy, it's a zigzagged line.

Maybe it could be a very modern structure?

I don't know how to fix it.

Do I make the building bigger?

What was I thinking, pretending to be an artist? And worse yet, to have a date where I paint in front of Zeke?

"Would you mind giving me a few minutes alone here?" I ask. "I'm having a hard time concentrating while talking to you. I'm not used to talking and painting at the same time."

Not ideal, but maybe that will show the anti-social aspect of being an artist.

"I need to get in touch with my emotions to convey them on the canvas." I close my eyes and tap my chest. *Miranda would kill me if she saw me doing this.* "Maybe you'd like to get a drink?"

"Oh. Sure," Zeke says. "I'm sorry. Is there something you'd like to drink?"

"A glass of water." Wine did not help my painting at the "Sip and Create" law firm function.

He leaves.

I stare at my canvas to see if there is any way to fix it.

The works of art on the easels near me are all compelling. The woman next to me is concentrating fiercely, her brow furrowed. She's doing a self-portrait (she even brought a mirror), and her charcoal-shaded eyes peer out at me from the canvas.

I bite my lip.

I surreptitiously text a photo to Miranda in case she has any tips. A five-year-old would do a better job. I sigh. I should have never agreed to this.

What am I doing? Now, instead of having fun flirting on my date, I'm telling him to leave so I can paint. When my painting is not going to look like anything spectacular anyway. My goal today was to get Zeke to like me, but instead, I'm focusing on creating some masterpiece. I'm an overly competitive idiot who is trying to make a credible piece of art, even though that's impossible.

And I'm supposed to be figuring out his relationship with Jurgen. But Zeke grins at me, and all thoughts of Scammer Guy and the mission disappear. It's embarrassing.

Whatever. I finish mine up. It is much worse than I expected. I frantically wave at an employee to tell her I'm done. Hopefully, she can remove it before Zeke sees it. I still don't see Scammer Guy anywhere. My phone beeps.

> Iris: *I can't make it. We have a cybersecurity incident. I'm sure someone will bid on your painting. It's for a good cause.*

My stomach clenches. *No.*

An employee with a shirt announcing that she works for the Dumbo Arts Center comes by and takes it. "Do you want to do another? We don't have that many participants, and we have a lot of extra canvases."

"No." I wave at my canvas. "I don't think I should be allowed to do another."

"It's for a good cause." She gives me a pleading look.

I hate when people do that to me.

"Okay." I pay another twenty dollars as Zeke returns. He hands me my water.

I drink it quickly.

"You're done?" He motions to my painting, now being held arms-length away by the auction assistant, as if it's contaminated.

I nod. Time to switch to Plan B and show him that lawyers can be fun.

"We're doing this one together." I grab an extra smock from the empty easel behind mine. "C'mon. Let's go pick out some more colors and dab some dots on the canvas. It'll be fun." I give him that pleading look that worked on me.

He looks at me and chuckles. "Okay."

I add a whole rainbow of colors to my palette, as does Zeke, and we return to our canvas.

"You go first," I say. "You can't mess it up. Dab it on."

Zeke puts a big, black dot in the middle of the canvas. I add a pink circle next to it. He paints a green stripe next to that. I start to paint a red stripe, but someone knocks into me. A huge, zigzag line cuts across the canvas, intersecting the black dot.

"Sorry. I'm so sorry," the guy who bumped me says.

"No, it looks great," I say.

Zeke snorts.

We each take turns adding dots of paint.

"It looks like a Dalmatian gone wild," I say.

Zeke laughs. "Should we name it that?"

"Yes. We should try a splatter technique," I say. "Let's see what happens when we shake the brush at it."

Zeke shakes his brush. Nothing comes off it onto the canvas.

"Harder," I say and demonstrate. Paint splatters the canvas and my smock. "It looks cool."

This one is coming out so much better than my solo.

"You have paint on your nose," he says. I look up at him. He reaches out with a napkin to wipe it away. I stand still. His touch is gentle, and he's biting his lip as if he's concentrating hard. He smells of soap. My heart flutters. He has such long lashes for a guy.

"Thirty minutes until the auction starts!" The announcement breaks this ... whatever this is.

"All gone," he says.

"At least it's washable." I turn to face the easel. "It looks good, right? Maybe I need to relax more when painting."

"It's great," he says.

We flag down the help person and give her our latest masterpiece, *Dalmatians Gone Wild*, for the auction.

"Should we check out the other artwork?" he asks.

"Let's." And I can look for Scammer Guy. Maybe he's hiding among all these black-clad people. But he was quite tall. "I hope Miranda's painting sells for a lot."

We grab two glasses of wine from a passing waiter and join the flow of people checking out the artwork on display. In front of us is a pink, plastic cube. The neighboring piece is that sculpture made out of Tonka trucks. We wait for the people in front of us to finish looking at it.

"I had a Tonka truck as a little boy," Zeke says. "I remember one time when I was five, and I wanted to sleep over at my friend's house. My parents said no, so I was planning to go anyway, and I packed up a pillowcase with my pajamas and put it all in my Tonka truck."

"Did you get far?"

"As far as the front door."

"What happened?" We pause in front of a painting of a field of impressionistic flowers.

"They said I could watch a movie with my older sister instead, and I agreed that was a good substitute. I considered it a win–win for me and my parents. I negotiated for a better option than if I had conceded no sleepover."

"You were that devious at five?"

"I'm afraid so. At least subconsciously. My parents always said I was pretty good at getting my way." He smiles at me. With that dimple, I understand why.

There's Scammer Guy. In front of my work. Here's my chance.

"Do you mind if I go speak to Jurgen, that guy?" I ask Zeke, pointing at Jurgen. I watch Zeke's face for his reaction. *Will Zeke reveal that he knows him? Are they friends?* "He was pointed out to me as someone I should talk to about my career. And he appears to be looking at my painting."

"That guy?" He frowns.

A frown. As if he doesn't want me to go talk to Jurgen. But that could also be because I'm suggesting I go talk to another guy while we're on a date. But it is for work.

Zeke's forehead clears. "No problem. You do what you have to do. My boss texted me while I was getting the drinks. I responded, but I should check if he has any follow-up. I'll grab that chair over there." He points at a chair set up for the auction.

That's definitely supportive of my artist career. I feel touched. And it's so handy to date a workaholic because they can amuse themselves. I don't understand why more people don't see the appeal. But the "that guy?" was weird.

"Are you friends with that guy?" I ask.

"No."

His reply is decisive. Not sure what that vibe was. But he definitely talked to Jurgen at the art opening. I walk over to Scammer Guy.

"I see you're looking at my painting," I say to Jurgen. Most people have given it wide berth. He's wearing a purple, velvet smoking jacket today. He appears to want to draw attention to himself, which seems odd for someone scamming others.

"Is this yours?" he asks.

"Yes." I look eagerly at him to hear what he's going to say. I'm genuinely curious. Is he a scammer? Is he going to say it's good?

"You have a lot of potential. So much emotion already in this."

My eyes widen. "What emotion do you see?"

"Frustration. Passion. Who represents you?"

There was definitely frustration. "Nobody yet."

"I'm surprised," he says. "I think if you brushed up on a few techniques, you'd get an agent."

No way. My sister, Kiara, studied art for years and didn't immediately get an agent upon graduation.

"I could show you." He launches into some technical discussion that makes no sense to me, but maybe an artist would understand it. "Anyway, perhaps we can meet sometime, and I can introduce you to some friends who are art dealers." He hands me his card.

Yes. The scam is on.

"I consider myself a connoisseur of undiscovered, hidden talent," he says. "I couldn't make it myself, but I hope to help others succeed. But I've taken up enough of your time. Your boyfriend is looking impatient over there."

Nice way to see if I have a boyfriend. I glance over to where Zeke is sitting in the second row. Zeke looks totally engrossed in whatever he's reading on his phone.

"It's too early to call him my boyfriend, but hopefully," I say. Amorous interactions with Scammer Guy are definitely off the table.

Scammer Guy walks away, disappearing out the front door.

I take a photograph of his card and text Miranda an update. He seems shady to me.

Someone taps the microphone on the stage set up for the auction. "Everyone, please take your seats. It's time for our auction."

The auctioneer stands behind a podium on the stage next to an easel. I join Zeke in the audience. The auctioneer reminds the crowd that this is for a good cause, supporting Sanctuary for Families, Groundswell, and The Fresh Air Fund. A high school student who participated in a Groundswell project talks about her experience painting a mural on her local school wall and learning art techniques.

I wipe my hands on my pants. Zeke gives me a reassuring glance. They put up two paintings, and the auctioneer announces that they were finished on the spot here. These were clearly painted by actual artists. They may not have dealers, but they are talented. Several people bid.

The auctioneer brings down the gavel at *three hundred dollars* for the two paintings.

Next up are some works by well-known artists. Miranda's painting goes for several thousand. My days of bidding on Miranda's art, to make sure it sold, are definitely over. It's way out of my budget now. Luckily, I have my own collection of Miranda Langbroek paintings—all my birthday gifts and some more I bought because I loved them. My bedroom is like a shrine to the art of Miranda and my sister, Kiara.

And then my "cityscape" is up. *All by itself.* I shift in my chair. This is more nerve-racking than an oral argument in front of a judge.

"We'll start this out at fifty dollars. Anyone?"

Silence. I squirm in my seat.

Can I bid on my own painting?

If only Iris had been able to come and bid.

It's too bad Scammer Guy left. He could have bid on my painting with all its "potential."

"Anyone? It's for a good cause. Giving families a sanctuary from domestic violence. Anyone?"

Chapter Ten

Tessa

THE SILENCE IN THE room is deafening as the auctioneer calls again for a bid and reminds everyone that the money raised supports the Fresh Air Fund. My cheeks flush, and my body seems to be heating up all over—not in a good way. It could not be more obvious that I am a failure as an artist.

Zeke raises his paddle. High. Confidently.

"You don't have to." I pull down his arm.

"I think we have a bid," the auctioneer says. "No?"

"Yes," Zeke yells out. He switches his paddle to his other hand, holding me back, and wildly waves his paddle.

"We have a bid at fifty dollars to the guy in the white. Any others? Going once, Going twice. Sold to Paddle 32." The auctioneer can't say it fast enough. A volunteer hustles my painting off the stage.

I hang my head. "You didn't have to bid. I'll pay you back." I glance at his profile. I'm touched, and my chest expands like a balloon filling up with air.

"Definitely not. It's a good memento." Zeke grins at me.

"Or fuel for a fire." At least he can burn it in retribution and without any guilt when he finds out I'm lying to him. My chest tightens as if that balloon popped. I look down at my lap.

An assistant carries out *Dalmatians Gone Wild* and places it on the easel next to the auctioneer. It looks like an actual piece of art. *We created that.* The bright, primary colors, the composition—it radiates fun.

"*Dalmatians Gone Wild.* A great title. Starting this at fifty dollars," the auctioneer says. "And we have fifty up front here with the woman in the purple turban. Do I have sixty?"

Zeke bids.

"You're bidding on this too?" I ask.

"I definitely want this," he says. "Not that my friends will ever believe I helped paint it."

"We have seventy-five dollars from Paddle 32. Eighty? I have eighty dollars from Paddle 56 in the back. Do I have a bid for ninety dollars?"

Not sure this bodes well for my solo art career.

Zeke shoots his arm up again. The bid jumps from paddle to paddle, the price rising.

"One hundred fifty dollars to Paddle 32. One hundred seventy-five? Do I have any takers? Going once, going twice. Sold to Paddle 32 for one hundred fifty dollars."

Zeke grins at me and high-fives me. "To our future partnership."

I hope so. I want to believe that we have a future.

People smile at us. The lady next to me claps.

The auctioneer puts up the next item for auction.

Zeke leans back and places his arm on the back of my chair, not quite touching me. I relax my shoulders and sink into him. His hand curves around to touch my shoulder. I glance at him. The corners of his mouth kick up. *He bought both paintings.* I cuddle into him happily.

The auction ends about an hour later, and we stand in line to pick up Zeke's purchases. Conversations buzz around us. Next to the line, in a cordoned-off area, volunteers pack the art in bubble wrap for transport home. I look up at Zeke, and he smiles down at me—a grin like we're in this together. My body fizzes.

"Tessa!"

It's my ex, Wyatt. *Why is this happening to me?* The game may be up.

"I thought that was you, but I wasn't sure," Wyatt says, his arm around his girlfriend. The one who replaced me—the same day he dumped me. I've met her before, but usually at Museum of Modern Art events.

"This is Zeke. Zeke, this is Wyatt, my ex-boyfriend," I say.

Wyatt introduces his girlfriend, Marla.

"I just joined the board of the Fresh Air Fund, so that's why I'm here. I thought you might attend. Is Miranda here?" Wyatt cranes his head around me as if to find her. "She's really taken off. I should've bought her paintings when they were at bargain-basement prices in your living room. The ones you have must be worth so much now."

As if Miranda's artworks are objects of commerce and not filled with memories and meaning to me—like the yellow-and-pink color field one that Miranda painted after we had one of our best parties ever in our new apartment. Or her blue, black, and pink shimmery one that reminds me of a rainy New York night after clubbing.

Wyatt sips his wine. His girlfriend scans the crowd, as if looking for someone far more interesting to talk to than me.

"Miranda couldn't come," I say. We've stalled in this line. The same couple is still at the front, paying for their purchases.

It is clear now that Wyatt and I were *not* the best match. I had so looked forward to seeing him when I could and doing whatever fun activity he had planned as a welcome respite from the pressure of my job. Or maybe he's changed. I'm disappointed in myself that we'd dated as long as we did.

He pulls his girlfriend closer. "I'm surprised you're not selling your collection to pay off—"

"I'm not going to sell Miranda's paintings," I interject before he reveals anything. "Those mean a lot to me."

"My love, I see Jain over there," Marla says. "I'm going to catch up with her. It was nice to see you again, Tessa, and meet you, Zeke."

Wyatt's face shuts down as she pulls away.

"Tell her I say hi." Wyatt kisses her on the cheek and watches her leave. She's very confident and clearly does not view our past relationship as a threat. Not that she should.

But Wyatt is still staring at her disappearing back, frowning.

"Shouldn't you catch up with Jain too?" I ask. *Please leave before you reveal my job.*

"They'll want some girl talk time." Wyatt shakes his head and focuses on me, his easy smile returning. "Was that *Dalmatians* your effort?"

"With Zeke," I say.

"That was pretty good," Wyatt says. "Better than your usual attempts." Wyatt was my date at the law firm painting event.

Zeke starts. "That's a little harsh."

"Have you seen her previous paintings?" Wyatt asks.

"Yes," Zeke says.

"Really?" Wyatt's brow creases. "You've been dating for a while, then?"

"This is our first date," I say.

Wyatt smiles again and steps closer to me. "It's not her forte, but she can't be good at everything." He pats my shoulder.

Zeke straightens and looks at Wyatt like he can't believe Wyatt's saying I stink at my career.

Oh no. How slow is this line to pay for our paintings? What is that couple up there doing? It seems the credit card machine isn't working.

"I've improved since then," I say. "How's your work going lately?"

"Keeping me out of trouble." Wyatt looks at Zeke. "What do you do?"

"I work for Capital Management."

We move up a space. Only three more people in front of us.

"Then you probably work a lot too?" Wyatt asks. "You guys might have a chance, then. Tessa works all the time."

"I work a fair amount too. I'm grateful she made the time." Zeke puts his arm around me. The warmth of his arm around me and his shoulder next to mine makes me stand a little taller.

Wyatt stares at Zeke's hand, rubbing my upper arm. "I think that's my cue to leave. It was good talking to you both. I'm in real estate, so if you're ever looking for commercial or residential real estate, ask Tessa for my details," Wyatt says. "Tell Miranda I said congratulations. And thanks for the donation."

He finally leaves.

"Wow, your ex was harsh," Zeke says.

"He was just being honest," I say. "I do need to improve."

Zeke tries to school his face as if my painting isn't terrible.

Poor guy.

There's another holdup at the checkout table. They can't find the painting. Someone forgot to label a painting after they bubble-wrapped it.

"Tessa!"

I turn, and it's a managing director from Morgan Bank. I represented Morgan in an internal investigation involving kickbacks, and he was my client contact. That's the thing about New York City. I'd think I would never run into anyone I know because it's so big. But it is such a small village sometimes.

I am so dead.

"Jim. So good to see you," I say.

"I was just telling my wife here about how impressed I was by your work," Jim says.

That could be interpreted as my artwork. If he has terrible taste.

"Thank you." I shake his wife's hand. "It's nice to meet you."

"This is Zeke, Jim," I say.

"I told her that figuring it all out was like a multi-layered puzzle, boosted by flashes of intuition," Jim says. "It definitely makes sense to look at the big picture and then get down to the nitty gritty of the fine details."

"Yes. Jim is one of my biggest supporters," I say to Zeke. It's true. He wrote the firm a lovely recommendation for my personnel file that should help me get the bonus.

"Knock on wood we don't have that situation again. But if we do, you're the first person I'd call."

I cough. My throat has closed up. I can't stop coughing.

"Are you okay?" Jim asks.

"I'll get you a glass of water," Zeke says.

I nod, still unable to talk, as Zeke leaves.

Phew.

I move up one space in the line.

I manage to stop coughing. "Thanks so much again for the rec-ommendation. That was amazing."

"Of course. Have you decided to apply yet for the FLAFL job? I'll tailor my previous recommendation for it."

"Thank you. I appreciate that." Check that outside reference off—along with the one from the grandparents in the adoption case. Now I need one more for the FLAFL application. And that will be Jack Miller, my mentor. "I haven't applied yet. I'm still learning so much at White & Gilman." The line moves another space, and I step forward to stand next to one of the metal columns interspersed throughout the white space.

"Well, for my own self-interest, I hope you stay. But let me know when you need it. I can't imagine they'd turn you down." He and his wife leave.

I breathe a sigh of relief. Lying is hard. How do people who commit fraud do it? I couldn't live with the fear of discovery.

Zeke returns, and I sip the cup of water gratefully.

"What situation did you help with?" he asks.

"I'm sorry. It's confidential." That's one of the best excuses for avoiding conversation about work as a lawyer. And I have no idea if an art project would be confidential, but then again, neither does Zeke. Or even if he does, it's not exactly a statement he can challenge. "Thanks for the water."

He nods.

It's finally our turn to check out. Volunteers wrap the two paint-ings in bubble wrap and place them in a Fresh Direct shopping bag.

I excuse myself to go to the bathroom. The line is ten-women deep. I should've gone when we were waiting to pay. Wyatt comes out of the men's room.

"Hey," he says.

"Hey," I say. And there's a pause. There was a time when I called him first to tell him that I won a case or thought of a good argument, and now I have nothing to say to him.

He leans in. "There's another bathroom around the corner, downstairs, next to the offices. When we had a meeting to discuss this event, the director showed it to me. Do you want me to take you there?"

"Sure."

He waves to follow him. We walk past the two lines of people through a metal door and down a short staircase to a lower level where some glass-partitioned offices sit.

"Here it is." He gestures at the door marked bathroom at the end.

"Thanks." The ceiling is low down here, and the space feels constricted compared to the high ceilings of the art gallery.

He steps closer to me. "Do you like this guy Zeke?"

He looks so intent and serious, as if my answer matters.

I back up. "It's our first date."

His posture relaxes. "Look, I know I was kind of a jerk in how I broke up with you, but honestly, I was surprised by how upset you were. You gave the impression I was a fun way to spend the time when you didn't have to work."

I stare at him. "I could always be working. I dated you because I liked you."

"I realized that when we broke up." His face crinkles up. "You never shared your feelings—except about your cases, particularly your pro bono ones. In those, you got so involved that I didn't feel like there was any room for me. I didn't seem like a priority compared to your career."

Of course, my career came first. My job is what supports me. I'm not about to rely on a man for that. "You put your career first too. You wanted to break up because you didn't like going to all these functions—which are part of your work—*alone*. I don't remember you making any passionate declarations."

"Fair enough," he says. "I felt like you didn't trust me ... that you were afraid that if you showed any vulnerability, shared any of your feelings, you couldn't trust that I wouldn't hurt you."

Like you did, I'm tempted to say. But I've moved past that.

His eyes soften. "I guess what I'm trying to say, badly, is that we both didn't particularly share our emotions, and I recommend doing that."

"Okay. Thanks for the advice. I guess." I push the bathroom door open.

"Because he looks like he likes you. And if I had known what you felt ..." He pauses as the door closes. I stop and hold it open.

My glance meets Wyatt's, and it's as if regret lingers in his eyes. I did really like him at one point. "Okay. I'll try to be more open about my feelings."

The bathroom is thankfully empty, but not my head.

Just someone to hang out with ...

He didn't know that I cared about him.

It still isn't an excuse to dump me out of the blue and immediately date someone new.

And what was that look of regret? Is he not happy with Marla? Is he regretting breaking up with me?

That ship has sailed.

But good for him if he's opening up more. Uh oh. I better get back up there in case Wyatt decides to talk again to Zeke. Oh no. I wash my hands hurriedly, forgo drying, and race back up the stairs.

Zeke is talking to Jurgen.

I stop short.

Mr. He-is-not-my-friend is definitely conversing with Scammer Guy.

The body language isn't best friends, though. Jurgen has his arms crossed in a defensive posture.

Should I join them? Or try to eavesdrop?

Chapter Eleven

Zeke

"DID YOU LIKE THE art show? I'm Zeke," I say to that guy Tessa talked to. He's definitely bad news. He gave me a weird "salesman" vibe when he stopped me at that last opening. If there's one thing I've learned in business, it's how to spot the sales guy who's hawking empty promises. I doubt he can help Tessa with her career. And I don't want to see her taken advantage of by some unscrupulous con artist.

"Jurgen," he says as he loads up a plate from the paltry, picked-over leftovers at the small cheese and bread appetizer table. I didn't even see this spread earlier.

"I like the show very much." He looks at me, holding his full plate. "Your girlfriend did well. It looks like both her pieces sold." He gestures expansively to a wall where three paintings that didn't sell still hang, not having been removed to be packed up.

Did Tessa say she was *my girlfriend*?

It doesn't seem like he knows that I'm the one who bought them. I shift the Fresh Direct bag on my shoulder that holds our two bubble-wrapped paintings.

"There was even a bidding war," I say.

"Was there?" He cocks his head, like an animal that's caught scent of prey.

I shouldn't have said that. But if he is influential, then I want to support Tessa.

"She heard you have quite a few connections in the art world. Do you?" I ask.

"You're very direct." He crosses his arms.

And he doesn't answer the question.

"I find being direct is best in business," I say.

All of a sudden, Tessa pops up and says, "Hi."

I was so focused on Jurgen, I didn't even see her walking over.

Uh oh. It doesn't look good that I'm talking to this guy because I don't want her to think I'm questioning her judgment (even if I am) or presuming I know better how she should handle her own art career. Paisley used to complain for hours about Arthur mansplaining some concept to her.

Tessa looks at both of us, her head tilted, as if to figure out why we are together.

How can I explain why I'm talking to Jurgen?

"I know most everyone. I've been doing this for many years." Jurgen smiles. Sort of. It's kind of a condescending curve of his lips. "I've never seen you before, so maybe you're the one who's new to the scene? Like in the business world, connections help. You should trust what your girlfriend says."

I do trust Tessa. I don't trust you.

"I'm not his girlfriend, actually," Tessa says. "We're on a date."

I reach out to hold Tessa's hand and pull her gently to stand next to me.

"He seems very protective of you," Jurgen says.

At least he got that message.

Tessa glances at me, her brow wrinkled. The hard clack-clack of the volunteers stacking the chairs sounds behind us.

"But you're no longer making your own art?" I ask. "Don't you want to use those connections for yourself?"

"If I could, I would have. But sometimes you have to realize you don't have enough talent. Better to find that out sooner, right?" he asks. "But I still love art, and my talent is finding other people who are going to make it."

He sounds persuasive. I'll give him that. Maybe I'm being overly paranoid again. Thanks, Paisley.

"Like Tessa here." He smiles at her.

Nope. I don't trust him. Tessa beams at him.

"Good to talk to you both. My friend is calling me." Jurgen gestures to a pale, thin guy who looks like he hasn't seen sun in days and departs.

"How did you hear that he was someone helpful?" I ask.

"He helped another artist I know sell her first painting to a collector."

"I see." That sounds legitimate.

"I thought you said you didn't know him?" she asks.

"I don't know him. He approached me randomly at the show we met at and started talking to me. I just dismissed him." I turn to Tessa. "But when you mentioned you'd heard he was someone to talk to, I thought I might as well talk to him and see what his deal is. You never know if he's a scam artist."

She stares at me, biting her lip. "And what did you conclude?"

"I don't know." *Not for sure.* I think he's a con artist, but I have no proof.

We walk outside. The night air is warm for May, and the street-lamps create puddles of light in the deepening dusk. People mingle on the cobblestoned street outside with red, plastic cups of wine.

Loft apartments and fancy stores now occupy the converted brick warehouses of DUMBO, short for Down Under the Manhattan Bridge Overpass. Metal staircases and cement ramps lead up to the entrances, giving it an industrial feel. The bridge, framed by the brick buildings on either side, dominates the view as we amble toward the river.

We turn left to stroll along the sidewalk nearest the East River. The roar of the subway passing overhead on the bridge rumbles throughout the neighborhood. A breeze wafts over, the smell of sea salt inspiring that lazy, happy vacation feeling. A pathway beckons off to the right, leafy, green trees and bushes held back by curving dune fencing, giving it a beachy feel. I reach out and hold Tessa's hand.

All of a sudden, the skyline opens up. Ahead of us is the Brooklyn Bridge and the East River, its waves lapping against the rocks separating the pathway from the river. Underneath the Brooklyn Bridge is Jane's Carousel, enclosed in a glass building, the bright colors of the playful, metal horses visible even here.

Tessa squeezes my hand.

To the left is a large, Dutch, architecture-style building that is the Time Out Market. Black, wooden shades punctuate each brick-curved window. People dine outside at tables under beige umbrellas at Ciccarelli's as waiters pass through, carrying and clearing plates.

A Roof Deck sign is ahead.

I glance at her as she looks at me, and we both turn to head there. We climb up a metal staircase that clings to the former warehouse wall built by the Dutch in the 1600s. A large, curved window frame—now without any glass—gives a view of the East River.

"I love how they kept the facade," she says.

"I like that the Dutch architecture is still here. Have you been to Red Hook?" I ask. "That really feels like you've stepped back in time to an early Amsterdam."

"Yes. That's exactly what I thought. I took a weekend sailing class in the Hudson, and we docked there to have our picnic lunch. It was so cool. And it totally felt like we'd sailed to Holland."

At the very top, we emerge to breathtaking views of the East River, Manhattan, and the two bridges—the Manhattan Bridge to our right and the Brooklyn Bridge to our left. The island curves a little so that we are in a tiny inlet. Boats motor by in the blue waters below.

"Should we eat here?" I ask. A wooden, lounging bench filled with people is off to one side, and tables are scattered around. Under a metal canopy is a billiard table.

"That sounds good," she says.

I suggest she grab a spot while I pick up our food. She gives me her ramen order and sits on a bench, placing the Fresh Direct bag with our paintings next to her. All around, couples enjoy take-out dinners. There's a shout from a group of friends playing billiards, followed by lots of laughing.

I join her on the bench and take off the lid of my ramen bowl as she does the same.

She turns toward me. "Thank you for buying my painting. I was embarrassed no one bid, so I appreciated it."

I wave her gratitude off. "I'm sorry I didn't bid sooner. I didn't want to stop a collector from picking it up." I just highlighted that one didn't. *Idiot.*

"Is Wyatt the guy you broke up with eighteen months ago?" I ask. "How long did you date?"

She separates her chopsticks. "Eight months. I worked all the time, and he attended all the society events. They're important for his career. The Central Park Zoo party and all the different not-for-profit benefits. I could never make them. We had different priorities, among other things. Not that I don't enjoy going to those events. He found Marla and ended things with me."

"It sounds like those are work events for him."

She nods. "Exactly. I always found that rather ironic. He could combine work and play. I couldn't. How long did you date your ex?"

"Two years."

"That's ... a long time. Much longer than I've ever dated anyone. It must have been serious."

I shrug and look away. *Yes.* I don't want to talk about my ex.

"What's a priority for you in a relationship?" she asks.

"Loyalty," I say without hesitating. "I need to know someone has my back and I can trust them."

Her eyes widen.

"What about you?" I ask.

She purses her lips as she takes her time considering my question. "Loyalty, of course, but also understanding. Someone who understands me and supports me."

I nod.

We both dig into our dishes, and there's a comfortable silence as we savor our dinner.

"Yummy," she says.

"So have you been painting for long?"

"I started painting in kindergarten."

"As one does," I say.

She smiles at me.

The air is balmy, and everyone sitting around appears to be enjoying the night out, excited for summer weather to begin.

"Do you usually date artists?" I ask.

"No," she says. "I'm not hung up on occupation. Why? Do you only date artists?"

"No."

"I would think people in finance would tend to date other people in finance ... or maybe lawyers," she says.

"I dated a lawyer once." I frown.

"And never again?"

"Something like that."

"But it's not like all lawyers are the same."

"Are you trying to persuade me to date a lawyer?" I ask, my eyebrow raised. "Is that in your interest?"

"I have a lot of lawyer friends," she says weakly.

I slurp the last of my ramen. "What made you want to be an artist?"

"It wasn't so much a want, as a calling. But I have a long way to go. I look at this as a marathon."

"I hope you're not going to give up."

"Because my painting was so terrible?" she asks.

"No. No. I didn't mean that at all. I mean, the first one was ..." *Terrible.* I flush and wave my hand. "*Dalmatians Gone Wild* was all you—all your ideas and your inspiration. And there was a bidding war."

She stares at me, her gaze soft.

And I want to kiss her. But ... A baby cries out as his mom puts him in a stroller next to us.

"Mostly, I think you'll succeed because you're so committed," I say. "You can't fail when you're that determined."

"It turns out you're not so bad at artistic endeavors yourself," she says. "I think more color is good for you—not just black and white."

I shake my head.

She pokes me. "Look at that sunset and the vibrant streaks of pink and purple, with yellow and orange burning at the bottom."

People all around us take pictures of the sky.

"Anyway, I'd rather not talk about work," she says. "I feel bad that you had to buy my painting."

"I'm happy I bought it cheap and it didn't get bid up like *Dalmatians Gone Wild.*"

She laughs. "That's one way to spin it."

We finish our bowls. Her phone beeps, and she checks it. Her brow furrows.

"What?"

"It's nothing," she says. "Wyatt asked me out to some event. Weird. We haven't gone out since we broke up. And now is not the time to start."

My take is that Wyatt wants her back. But that's probably my mistrust stemming from what happened with Paisley.

"Do you want to play billiards?" I gesture to the billiard table behind us. The group that was playing is leaving. "I can teach you."

"I can play."

"Are you good?"

"Do you need to ask?" she asks with a mischievous grin.

Chapter Twelve

Tessa

I BEAT HIM. IT was close, but I did a behind-the-back shot and won.

He looks stunned.

Finally. Something I am good at.

"Did you want to say anything more about Stuy grads being good at trash-talking but their actions not measuring up?" I ask.

He shakes his head. "No. No. I take it back."

I pat his back.

Zeke is a good guy. In so many ways. But especially when he was encouraging me to be an artist—to pursue what he thinks is my dream, even though I'm talentless.

I definitely misjudged him, comparing him to Stuffed Shirt. Painting together was fun, and he was very protective when Wyatt was disparaging my artistic ability (even if Wyatt was right). I passed as an artist because I could create art when having fun—when I wasn't following someone else's instructions.

I should give up on this whole artist pretense.

I want to tell him, but I also don't want to. He doesn't seem like he'll forgive my lying to him.

He didn't appear to be friends with Jurgen, based on that conversation. But that could have been staged. And Zeke wondering whether Jurgen is a scam artist, to eventually say that he doesn't think so, in the role of a "neutral third party," could be part of the ploy.

He looked like he'd been caught doing something he shouldn't when I first popped up next to them. I shake my head. I don't know what to think. Zeke couldn't be part of the scam, could he? But why did he have that guilty expression?

I don't know. I'm going to enjoy this date for now and then make the decision as to whether I can trust him to tell him the truth at the end.

I *did* share my feelings with Wyatt—my desire to work for FLAFL and my fears about leaving White & Gilman. But maybe not all my fears. I was afraid to look too vulnerable. Because those vulnerabilities can be taken advantage of by someone you love, like what happened to my friend's mom.

"Let's find the nearest Citi Bike station," Zeke says.

I give him the extra bicycle helmet from my backpack and clip on my own. I often bicycle home from work for exercise and as a good way to clear my head. But Miranda was also adamant that an unsuccessful artist cannot take cabs.

"Biking across the Brooklyn Bridge should be cool," I say.

Zeke takes the helmet and looks at me. He clips it on. "But what about the paintings?"

"We have to get one of the bikes with the wide baskets. They'll fit. I've carried paintings in Citi Bikes before. One of our friends held a show of Miranda's art in her apartment, and we biked the paintings over."

I have a Citi Bike membership, so I wait for Zeke to pay for his rental.

He clicks on the app. "Or should I buy a membership if we're going to be hanging out a lot?"

I blink. I love how up front he is. It's so Dutch. Thijs was like that. "I feel I've made you spend enough money on this date."

I put the paintings in my basket as he pulls out a bicycle and adjusts the seat to his height.

"How did you learn to play billiards so well?" he asks.

"I bartended at a bar with a billiards table one summer during college, and when it wasn't busy, the staff played billiards. And Miranda now bartends at a bar with billiards tables, so I play often when waiting for her to get off work."

He shakes his head. "I don't usually lose."

"How'd you get so good?"

"I studied at the University of Amsterdam as part of a semester abroad program—you know, looking for my roots and meeting extended family over there," he says. "I spent a lot of time in bars playing billiards with some Dutch friends I made there."

"That sounds like a fun semester."

"It was." He smiles. "Do you know how to get to the Brooklyn Bridge bike path?"

"No. I haven't been there in years. Have you?"

"I've never biked over the Brooklyn Bridge. I'm excited. We need to take a picture of us in the middle with the view."

I nod. It's dusk now, and the sky has turned an amazing deep blue.

Suddenly, he leans over and adjusts my helmet so it's covering my forehead. His face is close to mine, and my heart pounds. His fingers graze my cheeks gently as he tightens the strap on my helmet. I think I've stopped breathing.

"Your helmet is too far back. It's not protecting your forehead." He leans back to check, and his gaze feels like a physical caress. He gets on his bike.

"Thanks." I breathe again. "The strap gets loose, and then I forget to tighten it."

I look down at Google maps to collect myself and check the route. It looks complicated, with a circular loop in a park. I show it to Zeke. His phone shows a different route, more like a Z.

"Let's go and ask some other bikers on the way," I say.

"Or we make a left and then a right here."

"All right, you lead. I'll follow."

On the bike path, we cycle under an overpass, then cross a highway. Zeke's ahead. He turns to give me a thumbs-up and waves his hand to indicate we're taking a left turn. I do like a man who can decipher a map.

We stop at a red light. Next to us is another couple, their baskets filled with grocery bags, strawberries and fresh carrots peeking out. We smile at each other.

The light turns green, and we're off again. Zeke signals right. Up ahead, an arrow sign announces the Brooklyn Bridge with an illustration of a bicycle. We cycle on a green-painted, two-lane bike path, me behind Zeke. The wide, green path suddenly narrows into two east–west lanes. A curving, cement barrier with a wire fence on top separates us from the speeding cars.

That cement barrier kills any romantic vibe. Not to mention the cars stampeding past us.

An e-bike passes us, zooming along, while we push uphill.

We're finally on the bridge, but there's no way to stop. Other cyclists are racing toward us in the lane going east, the headlights announcing their arrival, while a few follow behind us in the lane going west. Above us to the left side is the leisurely, wooden pathway for pedestrians. The blue of the river is a distant backdrop through the wire fencing.

But people smile as they pass us, going in the opposite direction. We're in this together. Or maybe I look sweaty and like I'm struggling. Citi Bikes are heavy.

And suddenly, it's downhill. Whoo-hoo! We speed down the road. Zeke looks back quickly, grinning.

And then we're out of the narrow, tunnel-like pathway. In front of us is City Hall Park. Tall, leafy trees hide the stately, white, government buildings, while the lighted display stands selling brightly colored goods for tourists pop out against the foliage.

"That was *not* romantic at all," Zeke says.

"Nope," I say. "Maybe it's the Manhattan Bridge that has the better bike route?"

"But the end was fun."

"Super fun," I say.

We dismount and walk our bikes across the street to City Hall Park.

"When did you last bike across the bridge?" he asks.

"In law school ..." I stop. "My friend went to Columbia Law School, and they did an all-night biking trip around Manhattan, so I went with them. There's something about biking at night. As long as it's safe. But I guess since it was at 3 a.m., we went on the pedestrian pathway. Should we take a picture now?" We pull off our helmets and take a selfie, our heads close together.

We look cute, almost like an ad for a happy, blonde couple.

"We're not done yet." I kick up my kickstand. "Next up is Wall Street. It's cool at night because it's empty, and it feels like biking through cavernous tunnels. You can almost imagine the buildings are mountains." I discovered this after a late meeting with a Wall Street client when I decided to bike back home.

We get back on our bikes. We turn left on Park Row and then turn left again on Spruce Street, then right on Gold Street. The streets are nearly empty, with very few cars or people. This part of the city shuts down at night.

Now in the Wall Street area, we swoop through the narrow streets. Zeke turns his head to grin at me. The air rushes by my face. I feel a flash of pleasure that he likes this too. This has to count more than my saying I'm an artist.

"It does have a canyon feel. It's cool," he says.

We have to switch bikes to avoid the fee for exceeding the rental time limit, so Zeke searches for the nearest Citi Bike station on the app. After forty minutes, Citi Bike charges per minute, so we need to start the clock running again. We cycle to the nearest station at Hanover Square, return our bikes, and take out new ones.

"I love checking out the different neighborhoods of New York," Zeke says.

"Me too. Whenever I feel a craving for travel but can't, I take a trip to a different part. There's so much to see—and feel."

We're at the very bottom tip of Manhattan. The vast expanse of water greets us with the low-lying islands of the other boroughs. The Statue of Liberty beckons from its separate island. We cycle toward the Hudson River to find a bike path. Passing by both the Staten Island terminal and another terminal I don't know the name of, the wide expanse of the Hudson behind us, we continue on through a two-way path surrounded by leafy willow trees, their branches curving over, creating a little oasis. Off in the distance, jazz music plays, but it's muffled by the leaves. A trumpet cries out, its longing reverberating through the hush. Some birds chirp to each other. We slow down to bike side by side.

And I need to put a brake on my feelings. I'm falling for him. But I fear that when I reveal that I lied to him, it will be over.

We reach the horseshoe-shaped boat dock where the yachts moor. People dine outside; I catch a whiff of French fries, lobsters, and fried fish as we cycle by.

Then we find the Hudson River bike pathway. The river glistens in the dark, the lights glowing on the New Jersey side. The night breeze is like a caress. We pass by someone playing electric rock music on their boombox. The music catches that popping excitement, that beat, the zip I feel when our glances catch—a sense of possibility that Zeke and I could work if he can forgive that I lied to him, and if he's not connected to Jurgen, and if he's okay with dating a lawyer.

We turn off at 72nd Street and return the bikes. Then we walk very slowly in the direction of my apartment. I glance at him as he turns his head away. Was he looking at me? I don't want the night to end. And I definitely don't want to tell him I'm actually a lawyer and ruin the mood of this date. Let me have one more nice memory to counter the reveal.

His hand brushes mine. The couple ahead of us stops to kiss. We both stare straight ahead and skirt around them. The air feels heavier now.

We stop at the corner. Mostly taxis and black cars race down West End Avenue, bringing the late-night revelers home. Do I believe him that he doesn't know Jurgen? Do I tell him now?

Chapter Thirteen

Tessa

My phone beeps.

> Miranda: *Great job on scammer dude. Hope date is going well! Sorry I didn't see earlier text about painting. Walked home past salsa night at Lincoln Center! U guys should go if u like him.*

"Lincoln Center is having a salsa night. Do you want to go?" I check my watch. "It's probably ending soon, though."

"That sounds great."

"We can drop off the paintings at my apartment building and then pick them up after."

Zeke glances at me. Does he think that's an invitation to come over later?

I haven't decided what I feel about that yet. Or rather, I'd like him to come over, but I have to tell him I'm a lawyer first. And I don't have sex on the first date. But he must realize that. If I'm not about to share a silly picture of myself, I'm not about to get fully naked. No matter how tempting Zeke is.

We cross the street, pass the still-open deli, and walk down the wide avenue of 72nd Street. At Broadway, we stroll south to Lincoln Center. We take a slight detour to drop off the paintings in my apartment building lobby for pick up later.

On Columbus Avenue, tables are set outside with diners conversing, lingering over dessert. We saunter past the people lined up for the Italian gelato place and the shuttered stores, the mannequins in the window flaunting flowery, summer fashions.

Lincoln Center is lit up, the flags announcing performances blowing in the breeze. A live band is playing salsa music. We jog up the steps, join the line, pass through the metal detectors, and we're in. Zeke takes my hand, and we mingle with the crowds on the outskirts of the dance floor.

"You know that guy in the purple jacket that you talked to?" he asks.

"Yes."

"I know art is your thing and not mine," he says. "But that guy seemed like a pretentious prick. When he approached me at that art reception we met at, he was so full of himself. He asked me if I was interested in any of the art and suggested he could negotiate a discount. I thought he seemed slimy, like he wanted to insert himself into the process and get a cut. I didn't want to say anything at first if he's someone influential. But I don't trust him. Even if he comes recommended, you don't need him."

I squeeze his hand. "I don't think I do."

Yes! Zeke is not in cahoots. I believe him.

One hurdle down. I will tell him when we return to my apartment to pick up the paintings.

The three buildings that frame Lincoln Center are all aglow with a warm, yellow light. Red, blue, yellow, and purple lights tinge the sprays of the water fountain. The crowd is a huge New York melting pot, with everyone enjoying themselves, beaming at each other. That sense of community and esprit de corps is one of the things that I love most about New York City.

"Can you dance salsa?" I ask.

"I took ballroom dancing in college but haven't danced since then."

"It looks like there are lessons in that corner." I point over to where an instructor with a headset stands in front of a line of people.

We join the class of about twenty people, ages ranging from six to seventy.

"Switch your weight when you step. It's not a tap," the instructor says.

We practice the steps in a line with the other students. Zeke is much better than me, but I'm getting the rhythm. The instructor waves his hands. "Go forth!"

Zeke taps me. "Should we try it out now?"

He takes my hand, placing his other hand on my back just below my shoulder blades. His touch is warm and sure. I curl my other hand on his shoulder, my forearm resting on his upper arm, as directed by the instructor. He's so close and so masculine. My heart pounds.

We look at each other, waiting, and he nods his head to the beat. One, two, three, and we're dancing.

Our glances meet as we move to the music, step back in tandem, swing our hips, step forward. My shoulder leans toward his. He swings me around. And then the music slows down. He tightens his grip on my back and pulls me slightly closer. I can feel the muscles in his shoulders working, tightening and releasing. My head is next to his. I look up, and we're so close. The mint of his breath mixes with mine. He closes his eyes, pulling me closer, the side of his head inches away from mine. We sway there, breathing in the moment. My pulse races.

The next song is slower, and we dance cheek to cheek. My fingers curl around his neck into the short hair at the nape. I'm definitely melting.

And then the tempo picks up in the next song. We step apart.

He gestures toward a couple next to us doing way fancier moves. "Let's try that." He spins me around, and his back is against my front. Another twirl and a dip. And then suspended. Our noses almost touch. He holds me firmly, like we fit together. I stare into his eyes. His gaze back is searching, questioning, holding mine.

The trumpets sing their own siren spell.

He switches hand positions so we're holding hands and swinging them in time to the beat. And twirls me once again. There's something so feminine-feeling about spinning. I smile, feeling free—and desired. He pulls me back in. Our lips are so close we could kiss. I glance at him. His shirt is warm under my hand, the cotton soft under my touch. He pauses, waiting, asking. I think I nod.

Yes, we're about to kiss. He angles his head, and his breath grazes mine. My heart flutters. We're barely apart.

And then his lips meet mine in a firm but gentle kiss. I close my eyes and focus solely on this. His fingers reach up to thread through my hair, to hold me tight. We taste each other, tentatively, our lips slanting as we try to get closer, our tongues teasing and tangling. He tastes of mint gum. Everything else fades away as he pulls me in closer, my softness to his firm chest. I slide my hand through his silky, wavy hair while my other hand presses against his hard back. I'm lost in the sensations, in another dimension of pure feeling.

"And that's it." The announcer's microphone crackles. "Let's give a big hand of applause to our band, Orquesto La 18."

We break apart. Clapping erupts around us. We join in, shoulder to shoulder, not looking at each other.

"We hope you enjoyed this night at Lincoln Center. Remember that silent disco dancing night is next week. See you then."

I blink, confused, readjusting to the moment. That was an *amazing* kiss. Zeke also appears disoriented. But then he gazes intently at me, and that electric current pulsates between us.

Zeke pulls me in again and kisses me quickly. I kiss him back, sliding my hands around his back to hold him tight. He chuckles against my mouth and says, "Your hand tickles." We break apart, smiling.

All around us, people disperse to the exits. Zeke holds my hand as we join the crowd leaving. We walk down the steps of Lincoln Center and wait at the corner of 64th Street.

The streetlight turns white, and we cross the wide boulevard to reach Columbus Avenue.

"Can I see you again?" Zeke asks.

"I'd like that very much." Four more blocks, and then I'll tell him. And hope he still wants to see me.

But I'm happy to plan another date now.

"I'm going to an art brush lecture at the MoMA around five on Thursday, if you want to join me," I say. That lecture should persuade him that dating an artist is not all that he envisions. We walk by the closed stores of Columbus Avenue.

"That sounds interesting," he says.

I raise my eyebrow. "Does it?"

"Maybe not, but I'd like to see you again."

He is so up front.

If I tell him now, he still has to come back to retrieve the paintings. He'll probably abandon them instead.

"I'm not sure I'll be able to get out so early, but I'd definitely like to go." He squeezes my hand. "I have to ask my assistant. She is going to schedule a celebration dinner with our law firm who won the case, and I told her my schedule was free that night."

What? No. "That's nice of you. Do they want a dinner?"

"You think they don't? I've never met them. The lawyers settled it before we even did client interviews. It's a huge relief."

"They'd probably prefer their free time rather than having an awkward formal dinner with some clients they've never met before and will never meet again. At least, I think that's what my friend, who is a lawyer, would say." We pause as a dog darts toward the curb, his leash blocking the sidewalk. The woman walking him scurries after him, apologizing for cutting us off, and we pass them.

"Then she's not thinking very long term. It's good for her to build her client relationships for business development."

"Maybe." That was true enough. If I intended to stay, I should build client relationships. "But would the dinner hold that much sway in developing a client relationship? You said they settled the case quickly. Shouldn't their ability alone be the critical factor as to whether you hire them again or not?"

Paul hasn't mentioned that dinner. Maybe it's just him as the partner.

"I may have to hang out with my lawyer a significant amount while working on a case, especially if we have to travel," he says. "It's a lot easier if I get along with him or her."

His hand tightens on mine as he stops short.

"What's wrong?" I ask.

He shakes his head. "I thought I saw my ex."

He drops my hand and stares straight ahead.

I glance at him. *Why did he just drop my hand? Did he see his ex? Does he not want her to see him holding hands with someone else?*

The streetlights glow up ahead as we turn to walk down my street. It's quiet now, just the breeze rustling the leaves of the trees.

He's biting his lip, as if deep in thought.

What happened?

That kiss ... that kiss was *so good.*

We reach the front door of my brownstone building, and I unlock the door, holding it open for him to pass in front of me to grab the paintings. I follow him, letting the door close behind me.

"Look, I have to admit something," I say, then realize I'm talking to the back of his head.

He picks up the paintings, scoots past me, and pulls the front door back open.

He turns to face me. "I have to admit something too. I like you, but I'm still messed up from my last relationship. I'm going to call it a night. I had fun. I hope I can see you Thursday, but if not, another day soon." He smiles, a bit crookedly.

"Oh. I see. Of course. I had fun too." *What happened in his last relationship?*

No upstairs. I feel bereft.

Wait.

I was worried about what to do when he kissed me goodbye, but he isn't going to kiss me at all?

He steps out into the foyer, the Fresh Direct bag on his shoulder. He waves goodbye.

Are we done? Are we going to be just friends? That kiss was amazing. What happened? Did he *not* think that kiss was amazing?

He's out the front door and gone. Like he's running for his dear life.

And I didn't get a chance to tell him I'm a lawyer.

Chapter Fourteen

Zeke

I CLICK TO LEAVE the Zoom meeting where three marketing companies made their pitch for Comidas en Canasta's business. The team is going out to lunch now in Mexico City. I'll check in later to see which one they decided to hire.

I put down my headphones and stare at my screen. My two monitors light up with data flows. Around me, the trading floor is humming. I quickly eat a sandwich I picked up on my way in.

I regret not kissing Tessa again. But that last kiss was so hot, it wouldn't have ended there. *When she relaxed and melted against me ... to pull back was hard.*

I'm glad we were out in public.

And not kissing her goodbye seemed like the right way to go. Not to push it. To keep a distance until I am sure.

Sure of what?

That I wouldn't get my heart crushed again?

As if I had some way to tell.

When I froze when I thought I saw Paisley ahead of us ... That was a grim reminder I'm *not* ready to jump into another relationship.

I hate that Paisley has made me question my instincts. But I can't help it. Tessa seems totally cool, but ...

Plus, I didn't want to look like a jerk who expected more than a kiss on a first date.

"How was your date?" Ben asks, peering around the divider that separates our desks. On the other side of me, Anthony is barking buy orders into the phone.

"Date was great." I check the latest market figures. The fund's returns are on track.

"And was dating an artist everything you imagined?"

I'm going to ignore that slight mocking tone.

"She's terrible." I lean back in my chair, scooting it out a bit so I face Ben.

"A terrible person?"

"A terrible artist—at least at first. Unbelievably bad."

"What do you mean?"

I show him a photo of her painting from the auction. "This is what she painted at the auction event last night."

Ben's brow creases. He's silent, staring at my photo.

"Is it supposed to represent something?" he asks. "Or is it supposed to be abstract?"

"It's not abstract—at least not intentionally," I say. "Guess what it is."

He looks pained. "Is it a submarine under water? A castle wall? It's a castle wall, right?"

"It's a skyline. Those flat, gray boxes—shapes—are the buildings. And this is a window. I'm not sure why there's only one window."

Ben nods slowly. A flurry of activity erupts to our left as one of the traders bids up some stock.

"There's no depth." I shake my head and gesture with my head at the framed, hand-drawn picture on Ben's desk. "Your niece's drawing over there is better."

Ben emits a sigh through his teeth as if perplexed. "Huh."

"So bad," I say. "And now I own it."

"You bought it?"

"I had to support her."

"Where are you going to put it?"

"I don't know yet," I say. "I have to hang it up somewhere in case she comes over."

"You can put it in the bedroom, and then you have an excuse."

"I don't need an excuse." I punch him lightly on the shoulder. Conversations buzz all around us.

"But the rest of the date was great?"

"Great." *Until I freaked out and ran away. But I'm not sharing that with Ben.* "We also painted this one together." I show him a photo of *Dalmations Gone Wild.*

"You painted that?" Ben asks, not even hiding the surprise in his voice. "Mr. Let's-Check-The-Data painted?"

"With her."

"She got you to paint." Ben tilts his head. "And it's such a happy painting."

"She's fun," I say and meet Ben's glance as he takes this in. "And this one was mostly her, so she does have talent."

"That's good to hear."

I nod, but then I shake my head. "Still, it doesn't quite make sense."

"What doesn't make sense?"

"That she's such a bad artist."

"Do you think she was pretending to be bad?"

"You can't fake that." I shake my head. "But it doesn't make sense because she's super cool and amazing at other things. She slaughtered me in billiards. And she definitely enjoyed wiping the floor with me. It doesn't quite square with her personality—that she would want to pursue something that she's terrible at. She looked more tortured than happy when she was painting. I'm sure she'll succeed because she is so determined, but still."

"She beat you at billiards?" Ben asks. "You're like a pro."

"She's a pro. Apparently, she picked it up while bartending."

"Well, that supports her story that she's an artist and bartending to support herself," he says.

I stare at my screen, thinking back to last night.

"Does she think she's a good artist?" Ben asks.

"No. She admits she's not good."

"Well, wouldn't that be hard to be that open about? It seems doubtful that she'd lie about being an artist if she knows she's terrible."

"I'm probably extra suspicious after Paisley." And that's another thing I hate Paisley for ... that now I feel I have to be extra suspicious.

"Who wouldn't be?" Ben pats me awkwardly on the shoulder. "But you shouldn't taint all women—or lawyers—with the same brush."

I change the topic. "How's Brooke? Are you still distracting her from work?"

"I'm doing my best." Ben grins.

I wave. "Distract away. Now that my case is settled, she's working on some cases for Winthrop."

"Sorry, but Brooke can date me and still excel at work."

"I figured as much."

Ben turns back to his work. I click on a new email and read it.

My phone beeps.

I pick it up. Tessa sent a text with a photo attached. Of a drawing. Of two stick figures holding hands.

Tessa: *Had fun last night. I like holding your hand.*

"Did she text you?" Ben asks. "You're smiling."

I nod. The drawing is sweet ... but not for his view.

"We should get back to work." I face my computer screen and scoot my chair up to my desk. I quickly sketch a Dalmatian—or something that could resemble a dog with spots—and text her a photo of it. I check my watch and call Roberto, the CEO of Comidas en Canasta. He picks up on the first ring.

"We loved the marketing company you recommended," Roberto says. "I had my doubts because I'd never heard of them, but the work they've already done in Mexico City is impressive. So yes, we're going to go with them. Thank you for finding them."

Roberto and I talk in some detail about proposed marketing strategy. We're totally on the same page. This company, Comidas en Canasta, is going to be a success. I'm sure of it.

As I hang up the phone, Ben asks, "When are you seeing her again?"

"Thursday. We're going to an art lecture at the MoMA."

"Did you set that up last night?"

"Confirmed this morning."

"So not playing it cool?"

"As if you're one to talk. You definitely didn't play it cool when you were pursuing Brooke, Mr. Can-you-check-out-Brooke's-garbage-can-and-see-if-she-frequents-Starbucks-or-Joe's?"

Ben chuckles. "But I wasn't the one checking out her garbage can."

"You were the one hanging around Joe's waiting for her to show up."

Ben shrugs. "She was worth the wait." He punches me lightly on the arm. "Let me know if you want me to do any reconnaissance for you."

"I'm good." I can trust Tessa. I might as well announce our relationship has no future if I need to spy on her.

Chapter Fifteen

Tessa

ZEKE SHIFTS NEXT TO me in the hard, wooden auditorium seating. Now that I've made the decision to tell Zeke the truth, I want to get it over with. But I was late to meet him at the MoMA, and he went in and held our seats. I couldn't exactly whisper "I'm a lawyer" to Zeke when the lecturer had started holding forth, and I was sliding into the spot he saved for me. So frustrating. On the way over, I'd been all prepared to blurt it out the minute I saw him.

The penalty is sitting through this boring lecture. My huge yawn a minute ago probably belied my trying to appear fascinated. This is excruciating. It doesn't help that the lecturer dimmed the lighting in this lecture hall so his slides can be seen. Nor does the fact that I worked until midnight last night to free up this evening. And I still barely made it out of the office at five.

The head of the person in front of us falls forward and jolts back up.

Zeke catches my glance. His mouth tips up.

If he does think I'm an artist, now he has yet another clue as to my lack of success. The fine details of brushwork bore me.

"In conclusion, the brushstroke is the physical manifestation of the painter. It imparts texture and color, but also emotion. Remember to also ask yourself: What emotion do I feel when I see this painting?" The lecturer points at the last slide of his presentation. "Questions?"

The guy next to us asks a barrage of questions.

As we all file out of the room, he turns to us. "Great lecture, right?"

We both nod.

"Oh, look at this painting here," he says. "This is definitely a cross-hatching technique. Don't you agree?"

"Yes, definitely," I say. Why have we been adopted by some brush-stroke fanatic? Is this some sort of karma? *Please, no more.* I'm about to confess right now on my knees that I am not an artist.

No. I can do this. I'm a litigator. I can build up an expertise on any topic. "It appears to be building up the areas of light and shade."

"To show truth and deception?" the guy asks. "It's called *Lies and Other Truths I've Been Told.*"

What was I saying about karma?

"The deception seems to be dominating the truth," I say.

"I don't see it that way," Zeke says. "If we are interpreting the gray as the deception, I see the truth as peeking out. Don't you think that the pink is shining brighter than the gray?"

I glance at Zeke. For a finance guy, he's not bad at interpreting art. "It does. But I still feel sad."

"Let's find a happier painting, then," Zeke says.

We try to move away from the guy, but he is undeterred.

"Wow! Look at this! What an example of wet-on-wet cross-hatching. It gives a post-apocryphal feeling, like it can't be contained within the canvas."

Both Zeke and I nod very seriously.

"Definitely," I say. "Definitely post-conceptual."

"I thought it was post-apocryphal?" Zeke asks.

I'm not even sure what either of these terms mean. "I think it's both, don't you?"

The guy smiles. "I knew you guys would see it."

"Dystopian and bleak," Zeke says. "The end of painting as we know it."

"And I thought I had achieved that last time with my auction painting," I say.

Zeke grins at me.

"Let's go look at the Matisses. I love Matisse." I can tell him there. I grab Zeke's hand and pull him away from Mr. Brushwork. We hurry down the crowded hallway and up the escalator to the Matisse room. The woman in front of us puts her arm around her partner, leaning into him and kissing him.

We're standing right behind them on the escalator, not touching. It feels distant and awkward as the couple in front of us makes out. Zeke glances away. I look out over the railing at the people below. The couple manages to disentangle in time to get off the escalator. We follow.

"I'm sorry," I say. "That lecture was probably pretty boring for you."

"Not at all. Watching you try to stay awake kept me highly entertained."

I glance at him. I was that obvious. "You have to admit, the speaker spoke in a low monotone. He should create an app where he lulls people to sleep. He could make a lot of money."

We enter the Matisse gallery. It's also crowded. So much for my hope that it would be kind of empty and soothing and a good place to tell him the truth.

Next to us, a woman is explaining to her date that Matisse initially painted *Harmony in Red* in green and called it *Harmony in Green.* And then he changed the color to blue and called it *Harmony in Blue.* And then a collector bought it, but Matisse changed his mind again and painted it red. The collector still accepted it. The color of a painting seems like a pretty significant change to me. There's hope that Zeke will still accept me even if I'm a lawyer and not an artist. My hands feel clammy. I'm losing my courage to tell him. I was so ready to blurt it out on my way over to the museum.

My phone beeps. It's Ken.

"Oh sorry, it's work," I say.

"Work?"

"Volunteer work," I say. "Can you excuse me for a second?"

Ken tells me that our client came by and dropped off the documentation I'd requested, so he's sending it over. I hang up and turn back to Zeke.

"So, are you going to tell me your secret?" he asks.

I stare at him. *How does he know?*

"A childhood secret?" he asks.

I stutter. "O-oh yes. But only if you brought the picture of you acting like a CEO at your mom's desk."

"My mom emailed it to me. But only if you're sharing something embarrassing from your past." He opens his phone and shows me a childhood photo of a tiny him sitting at an enormous desk.

"That's hardly embarrassing," I say. "You're adorable. You definitely have to come up with something better than that." I show him a picture of me as a seven-year-old in a party dress scrunched up in the corner. "I saw this in the family photo albums and took a picture of it to remind me." *Unfortunately, it doesn't seem to be doing its job.*

"You're adorable too. How's that embarrassing?"

"This is embarrassing, but it's a distinct memory. I was around seven, and my birthday is in the summer, so my mom always threw a big birthday party for me. I was best friends with this boy next door. And he didn't show up. I remember waiting for him the whole party, upset that he wasn't there. At the end of the party, I realized that instead of enjoying my party, I'd wasted my birthday waiting for him. I'd resolved never to do that again."

"Wow." He's quiet. "I'm sorry he didn't show up." He touches me lightly on the arm.

"It turned out that his mother thought I was a bad influence. We'd been having a water fight the day before, and my T-shirt got wet. My mom brought out a dry T-shirt, and I changed in front of him. At seven, mind you. And his mom thought that was improper."

"Did you remain friends with him?"

"Yes. Apparently, I *was* a bad influence. He refused to listen to his mom and kept sneaking over."

"I can understand why." Zeke steps closer to me, and my heart skitters.

I have to tell him.

"Let's go down to the sculpture garden," I say. There is sure to be a private spot there. He can forgive me, and we can go out to dinner and have a good laugh about it. Or he can walk away. And we can ignore each other at our settlement celebration dinner he's hosting.

It's better I know now. Because I can't believe I just shared that memory with him.

We walk through the lobby toward the glass door at the back and step out onto the paved path of the sculpture garden. To the right is a Henry Moore sculpture of a couple embracing. A nice breeze is blowing. A few people are scattered about. I wipe my sweaty hands on my skirt.

I just need to tell him quickly. I rehearse my speech in my head again: I said I was an artist because I was pretending to be an artist to pick up a guy scamming artists. And then you said you hate lawyers and I was afraid to tell you I was a lawyer. *It doesn't sound compelling.*

"I have to confess something," I say.

"Another childhood story?"

"No. Much more recent. And I want to apologize in advance."

His brow furrows, and then he freezes, his gaze trained over my left shoulder.

"Zeke," says a woman's voice behind me.

"Paisley." His voice is cold.

I turn around. She's pretty and very polished in a skirt suit, high heels, even nylons. Blow-dried hair. She puts out her hand. Long, manicured nails.

"I'm Paisley, Zeke's ex."

I give her my nail-bitten, paint-stained hand in return. She takes it graciously. We shake hands, sizing each other up.

"I'm Tessa," I say.

"Out a bit early?" Zeke says.

"I could say the same for you," she says. "But I'm glad you're getting out and not burying yourself in work. I'm relieved."

The currents between these two makes me feel like I'm swimming in murky waters against a riptide, and I'm in way over my head.

He scoffs. "Congratulations on your promotion."

"I have to say, I expected at least an email or a text saying congratulations. Given ..." She shakes her head. "But at least you're out and about." She stares pointedly at me.

Zeke looks pale.

I reach for Zeke's hand and clasp it, gripping it tightly and rubbing my thumb against his fingers.

"I hope you and Matt are doing well," he says.

"We broke up. I told you he was a mistake."

Zeke drops my hand and puts his hand on the small of my back. "We're going to be late. We'd better go. Goodbye."

That was a very final tone—not a *see you soon* inflection in sight.

"I'll see you at Dylan's wedding, I hope."

Zeke's jaw tightens. "See you then."

I nod goodbye and walk away with Zeke.

His face is shuttered. It's clear he's still thinking about that encounter. He looks so hurt. I want to give him a big hug and cheer him up. We walk through the museum lobby and out the exit onto the quiet ambiance of 54th Street with its elegant rowhouses.

"Should we go out for dinner?" I ask. "There's a good Thai place down the block."

"I'm sorry," he says. "That was my ex-girlfriend."

"I gathered." I wipe my hands down on my pants. *Do I tell him now?* This is worse than arguing in court.

He turns to face me. "She cheated on me. We dated for two years, and then I found out she was cheating on me." His jaw clenches.

"Oh," I say. I wasn't expecting this.

He looks away. "It was obvious, in retrospect. But she's a lawyer. She works late, so I didn't suspect anything when she said she had to work. And she's very good at lying. Comes with the trade."

I have to defend my profession. "I don't think being a lawyer is synonymous with lying." Even though that's the least important of what he said. I take a breath. "I don't think you can beat yourself up over that. You can't live your life expecting that someone is lying to you. Especially someone you're dating."

He glances at me. His eyes look pained, his shoulders slumped. This is a different Zeke than the confident man at the bar, or the other night when we were playing pool. He takes a deep breath.

And I'm lying to him. *Do I tell him now?* I can't tell him now. Not when he looks so hurt. But the longer I wait to tell him, the worse it is. This could be the worst time to tell him, though. Given that he looks so defeated, and now he's all focused on lawyers and lying.

Chapter Sixteen

Zeke

I FEEL COLD. I'M over her. But every time I see Paisley, I can't help it. It's like a ghost walks through me. The girlfriend I thought I knew versus the woman she turned out to be. Like this alien took over my girlfriend's body.

Not because I'm still in love with her.

Because I still feel betrayed. That I could be fooled so deeply. That I wasn't enough. I'm not over that.

And it doesn't help when she says he didn't matter. That only makes it worse. Her whole excuse that she would be monogamous once we got engaged, so she wanted one last fling, only makes it worse. It would never have been the last fling.

If he didn't matter, our relationship didn't matter. She cheated on me with someone who didn't matter. Someone who wasn't going to last.

And her blaming me—that I was too busy. It's true. I was busy. I was trying to prove myself to Charles.

She was also busy. She was trying to get promoted. I thought we'd both understood that our relationship was briefly taking a back seat as we pursued our career ambitions.

And our breakup torpedoed all that work. Never again. I have one more chance at the venture capital side now. And one senior ally, Charles, whom I can't disappoint again.

We're outside the MoMA. I didn't even pay attention to how we got here. Tessa is standing silently by my side. Well, that's a great impression. She's clearly going to think I'm not over Paisley. *Dude goes green at sight of ex.*

I can show her I'm over Paisley.

We walk toward Sixth Avenue.

I stop and turn to her. "I'm over Paisley, but I'd prefer never to see her again."

Tessa bites her lip. She looks pretty tortured, come to think of it.

"I get it," she says. "Wyatt dumped me and immediately started dating someone new. He swore that he'd ended it with me before they kissed, but I suspect he met her and moved on while he was still dating me. That betrayal still hurts. Especially because I thought we were pretty serious. When he stopped pressuring me to get together all the time, I thought he was being understanding about my work schedule. In retrospect, I guess he was moving on. At first, it seemed like we had similar life goals, but in the end, we had completely different methods. I want to be in the trenches, and he wants to be the distant benefactor, attending charity benefits."

I wasn't moving on. I was preparing to propose. I shake my head. "I'm sorry. That's the first time I've seen Paisley without warning since we broke up. I'm not good company right now."

"Do you want to call it an evening?" She faces me as we stand next to a very large sculpture in the form of a metal egg. Yellow taxis race up Sixth Avenue. The wind blows her blonde hair onto her face, and she holds it back, looking at me earnestly.

I shake my head. Forget Paisley. Tessa is right here, and I'm going to lose her if I freak out over seeing Paisley. Again.

"No, let's go check out that Thai place you mentioned. I'm fine."

We walk up Sixth Avenue and then turn onto 58th Street as she leads us to the restaurant. *Get a grip, Zeke. That was good. Good that Paisley saw you with someone else. Good that you could converse with Paisley like a normal person.*

It was good.

A bright-yellow awning with TOPAZ THAI AUTHENTIC announces the restaurant. Authentic. That's what I'm looking for now.

And that's what I need to be too. So, I can't be accused of not talking about my feelings and putting work above everything else.

The waitress greets Tessa warmly. Tessa must come here often. The wooden-walled restaurant is fairly crowded, with a low hum of conversation. It feels comfortable and welcoming. The waitress gives us the prime table by the window.

"What's good to order?"

"It's all good." Tessa tilts her head and looks at me, like she's searching for answers. "Should we share some dishes?"

"Definitely." Paisley hated sharing dishes. She only wanted to eat what she'd ordered. When we first dated, when she was the one pursuing me and I was not sure—ironic, really—I hated that.

"Chicken curry?" Tessa asks.

"We definitely need a curry dish. And a noodle dish."

"Drunken Noodle?" she asks.

"But I'm tempted by the Dancing Chicken." The menu is filled with catchy names for dishes, like Roaring Tiger, Lovely in the Golden Nest, and Swimming Duck.

"It sounds like Dancing Chicken ate a few too many Drunken Noodles," she says.

I smile. "Have you tried it?"

She nods. "It's good if you want to eat that instead of the chicken curry."

"No, next time."

She looks up, her glance catching mine. And she raises an eyebrow and then signals the waitress to give our order.

There's silence after the waitress leaves. I take a sip of the ice-cold water.

"Do you want to talk about it?" she asks tentatively. "Not that you have to. It's ... you look conflicted."

Yeah. I've always been pretty easy to read. A frickin' open book.

I let out a short, harsh laugh. "I don't want to hash it out again. It makes me feel like an idiot. That I didn't suspect a thing."

She rests her chin on her hand. "That's interesting. So, you're less upset that you lost her and more upset that you didn't suspect anything?"

"Once I found out she cheated, that pretty much put an end to any feelings I had for her. It was pretty decisive." I guess that's a positive.

Tessa's forehead crinkles. "I think it speaks well for you that you didn't suspect anything. You don't want to be some crazy, suspicious person."

But I am now. I even suspect that you're not an artist. I push the tea light more into the center of the table.

"But if that's the first time you saw her since you broke up, you handled it well," she says.

"It's not the first time. We have mutual friends," I say. "It helped that you were there."

"Well, at least now we've met the exes. Isn't that usually sixth date stuff?"

"If not never. But I'm lucky I don't run into her on a daily basis. We used to work together. She was the in-house lawyer for my fund. Luckily, she'd changed jobs right before I found out she was cheating. I'll never do that again—date a work colleague."

Tessa's eyes widen.

Does she think dating a work colleague is a good idea?

The waitress pours us each our beers, and I take a sip of the frothy, golden liquid.

"Have you ever been to Thailand?" she asks.

That's an abrupt change of topic. Interesting.

"No. You?"

"It's on my bucket list."

"I've been to Vietnam and Bali."

"I went with some girlfriends to Bali. We thought we'd be living in a hut right on the beach, but the time when that was an affordable option was gone. Still, it was great."

We talk about our travels. A safe topic. All her trips seem to be with girlfriends. Except for a trip to Paris with her ex.

The waitress serves us the dumplings and spring rolls. On the side of the plates are vegetables cut out in a flower decoration, including a carrot rose garnish.

"Now that's art," she says. She calls back our server. "This is amazing. Who did this?"

"Malee. She was in Thailand for June and took a course."

"Chaba must be so proud," she says and then turns to me. "Chaba is the owner, and Malee is her daughter. Malee is going to Fordham, but she helps out on weekends."

The waitress nods. "Chaba is proud of everything."

"You know the owner?" I ask.

"Miranda and I have closed down this restaurant enough times that we met the family who owns it. Lot of nights hanging out at the MoMA," she says. "Occupational hazard."

I'm impressed. Definitely different from Paisley.

"So did you ever date a work colleague?" I ask.

She holds her drink in midair and pauses, just as she was about to take a sip. Then she carefully places it back down.

There's definitely something there. There's that moment when you're investigating an investment, and there's a slight pause before the person you're interviewing answers. And then you know … that the answer you're about to get isn't the whole truth. And that somehow you have to win this person over to get the real story.

She stares at her glass.

"Define a work colleague for an artist," she says.

"That's such a lawyer answer," I say. *Paisley saying, "Define what happily ever after is." And me responding, "It's not you sleeping with another guy."*

She blushes. "It is, isn't it?"

"So is answering questions with questions."

"What about interrogating the person you're dining with?" She sips her beer.

"That too." I raise my beer to her.

"Could you be considered a work colleague?" she asks. "You did buy my painting, so you're a client, so to speak."

"Other than me," I say.

"No."

That's a definite no. No hesitation. No pause.

Maybe she was just changing the topic away from Paisley.

I have to stop being a suspicious bastard who reads too much into things.

She smiles at me and tilts her head. And I want to kiss her again. *Her swollen lips after we kissed at Lincoln Center. Her soft skin.*

"Would you like to come with me to my friend's wedding in July?" I ask. "It's up in the Catskills."

"The one Paisley mentioned?"

"Yes."

She looks down at the table and then glances back up. "That's kind of far in the future. Maybe we should see how this goes. But if we're still dating, then yes."

I'm rushing things. She's right.

The waitress sets down our curry chicken and Drunken Noodle. The food is delicious. We discuss some of our favorite books. It's funny. Paisley and I always talked about work, but Tessa seems to make a concerted effort not to mention work. Our waitress clears our empty plates.

A young woman in an apron comes up to our table.

"Malee," Tessa says. "Your carrot rose was fantastic. How was Thailand? I want to go."

Malee shows us how to cut the rose out of a carrot. As she slices away at the carrot, forming each petal separately, a rose shape emerges. It's cool.

She hands it to Tessa.

"Clever, isn't it?" she asks.

"It's amazing." Tessa smiles. "Thank you for showing us."

The bells on the door chime as a group of new customers enter.

"I've gotta go," Malee says.

Our waitress places the check in a fake, black, leather folder on our table. I grab it.

"My treat."

"Are you sure?"

"I'm sure," I say.

Our glances meet. Time to ask her to come back to my place for a drink. I'm so rusty.

The waitress taps my credit card right at the table and hands me the pad to sign.

We walk outside to Sixth Avenue. Yellow cabs race uptown, competing with black sedans for the most direct route.

"Thank you. I had a great time, despite the lecture," Tessa says. "I have to work tomorrow, so I should go straight home. Should we grab Citi Bikes? I didn't bring helmets, but we can go straight up the bike path on Central Park West."

She's rambling.

She must think I'm not over Paisley. *Good going*.

I need more than one dinner to show her I am.

"Sounds good," I say. "I've purchased a Citi Bike membership now."

"I have to confess something." She faces me, but she's looking down, biting her lip. Her shoulders are curved, slumping. She looks miserable.

If she's going to say that she doesn't think this works because I'm not over Paisley, I don't want to hear it. I want to have another chance.

"You can tell me next time," I say.

"No. I can't," she says.

Chapter Seventeen

Zeke

"I'M A LAWYER." SHE doesn't break eye contact. "I was dressed as a struggling artist when we met because we suspect Jurgen is scamming artists, and I was hoping he would try to scam me. He was in earshot when you asked me what I did, so I lied to you and said I was an artist. I'm so sorry."

I step back. *She lied?* She lied.

"But why not tell me later?" *Do I have a sign on my forehead that says sucker?*

She swallows. "I was about to tell you when we were on the swing, but then you said you hated lawyers. So I ran away. I got flustered. That's why I jumped into a cab and left you behind. And then the next day, I read your email correspondence. I was the White & Gilman lawyer on the North American litigation who settled it. I read your email to Ben about not dating a lawyer and saying you wanted to date an artist. And then I looked up your picture and was horrified to realize you were the same guy I'd really liked the night before."

She continues, "And also, we saw you talk to Jurgen at the reception, and we were not sure if you were friends. And I also kept lying because I wanted a chance. I thought it was crazy to dismiss people because of their occupation. But I'm sorry. I didn't mean to hurt you. I didn't know how to tell you once it started. Because I was afraid"—she takes a big breath—"I was afraid you wouldn't give me a chance."

My stomach roils, and not in a good way. "I can't ... You read my email correspondence and took advantage of that? But did you know who I was when we were at the bar?"

Her face pales even further.

"No. I thought you were cute. I was horrified to find out you were Zeger van der Zee."

"Horrified? So horrified that you then decided to deceive me?"

"No. Horrified because I thought you'd reject me. It seemed you had a pretty strong aversion to dating lawyers."

She lied to me. "You were right. I'm not dating someone who lies to me. Especially not from the beginning. I've learned my lesson."

"But I wasn't lying about my feelings for you," she says.

I shake my head and turn away. I need to get the hell out of here. Tessa's face is white.

"I'm so sorry," she says again. She stands aside as I walk past her.

I just make the light to cross over to the next street. I don't turn around, but I suspect she's still standing where I left her.

Was she mocking me by pretending to paint?

What is real, and what is fake?

I pass by Columbus Circle, skirting the groups of people hanging out on the plaza, and stride up Central Park West, as if I'm trying to outrun my thoughts. One look at my face, and people walking toward me give wide berth.

My lawyer.

Lied to once again. When we were discussing careers on the walk to the Pier. When we were eating dinner on the roof-deck. When we were biking around Wall Street.

I'm a fricking idiot. Why do I keep falling for women like this? I think about calling Jasmine, my college girlfriend. *Did you cheat on me too?*

Central Park is murky in the night, the leaves of the trees rustling in the slight breeze. No one else haunts the street, except the lone doorman standing by an apartment building entrance under the awning. I reach the crosswalk and look for cars turning and then forge forth, against the red light, my hands shoved deep in my pockets. A scratching, scampering sound reveals a solitary rat foraging in the black garbage bags piled up to be collected tomorrow. I take a deep breath but inhale only the pungent smell of rotting refuse.

My phone beeps. Is she texting me? I pull my phone out of my pocket.

It's Paisley. Of course.

> Paisley: *Can't we talk? We're going to see each other at Lindsay and Dylan's wedding. Let's not make it awkward for them.*

I click off. We just need to *not* talk to each other and leave the focus on the happy couple.

I keep walking.

I feel cold. I really liked Tessa.

I button up my jacket. A bitter chill seeps into me.

And I didn't trust my instincts. Again. I suspected something was off. My gut was right.

Chapter Eighteen

Tessa

I FEEL NAUSEATED. HIS face went gray. *No.* Ashen.

My eyes feel sore, as if I've been crying. But I haven't. My stomach roils, and my legs feel weak. I lean against the wall of our hallway, my eyes closed.

I let myself into our apartment. Only the dining room lamp is on. The rest of the living room is shrouded in darkness, the easels looking like bare stick figures that have nowhere to go.

"Did you tell him?" Miranda asks. Her laptop is open in front of her on the dining table. Probably working on art show applications.

"Yes." I sink into a chair at our oak table. "I told him. It didn't go well. He walked away."

"He walked away?" Miranda asks. She stares at me in disbelief.

"Yes," I say.

"Didn't he understand about Scammer Guy?" she asks. "And that you just wanted a chance to be liked for yourself? Are you okay?" She comes over and hugs me. "I'm so sorry. It's my fault. We should have given up on Scammer Guy."

I cling to her.

Miranda looks like she is going to cry. "What are you going to do?"

"I don't know. I really like him. I wish I'd never lied to him. And the thing is, he'll never forgive me. He said his feelings for his ex-girlfriend were immediately gone when he found out she'd cheated." I take a deep breath.

Miranda hugs me tighter.

"Cheating is a lot worse than lying," Miranda says. "And it's not like you knew him personally when you said you were an artist. He shouldn't take it personally. He should understand that you were trying to catch a guy scamming struggling artists. And then you wanted a chance to have a fun date without any labels. It's not a huge deal."

She sounds like she is getting angry on my behalf, but she doesn't understand.

"You and I think that. But he's been betrayed before," I say. "And I'm like his kryptonite—not only a lying lawyer, but also a work colleague. Everything he's sworn to not date again. And I've sworn not to date someone who hates workaholic lawyers. So, I should stay far away from him too. And he's clearly not over his ex."

"But what about the client dinner?"

"I'll get food poisoning and miss it." I walk into our kitchen to pour myself a cold glass of water. My throat is dry. "Do you want some?" I drink it greedily.

"No. Won't that look bad for the bonus?"

I sit next to Miranda at the table. "That's why I thought it had to be food poisoning. Because then I really can't suck it up and come."

"You should go. What if Stuffed Shirt scores points with the Capital team?"

"Brooke and Zeke are savvy enough to see through him."

We sit in silence.

"I'm sorry, Tessa," Miranda says, rubbing my back.

"It's okay." It's not, but I have to believe it will be okay. "How was your day?"

"Fine." Miranda shuts down her laptop. "I sent Officer Johnson the photo of your painting and told him what Scammer Guy said about your having potential. He laughed so hard when he saw the image. He said we made his day."

"It was so bad," I say.

"But *Dalmations Gone Wild* shows potential, so it's in there—somewhere—under that corporate lawyer facade." Miranda pokes me. "It's just that working at a law firm doesn't give you any time to explore other creative outlets."

"That's for sure. Except cooking. And whatever schemes we come up with." The tears well up in my eyes. *Usually my schemes don't hurt the good guys.* "Officer Johnson believed us ... that Jurgen might be trying to scam artists?"

"Officer Johnson definitely believed that the guy was trying to scam struggling artists if he said your painting had potential. But we still need actual proof."

At least that was a small success. I hope the cost isn't Zeke. I hope he thinks it over and changes his mind.

"Are you crying?" Miranda asks.

"Tearing," I say and rub my eyes. I hold my head in my hands.

Miranda hugs me. She rubs my back. "It's my fault. I shouldn't have asked you to do this."

"No. It's my fault." I take a deep breath.

"Once he thinks about it, he should come around," Miranda says.

"I hope so."

"If he's smart, he will," Miranda says. "And you can give it a few days, and then you can call him and ask for a second chance."

"I'm not going to pursue him if he's not interested," I say.

"He sounds like he's worth pursuing, though."

"No. I learned my lesson early," I say. At age seven.

Miranda looks like she wants to argue the point, but instead she sighs. "Do you want to try painting something?"

"No." I snort. "Definitely not."

"It can help to get your emotions out," Miranda says. "Try it for a little bit. Maybe it will make you feel better."

"I should paint another one to show Jurgen," I say.

"You're still in?" Miranda asks.

"I don't want this to have been for nothing."

She turns on the overhead lights and sets up an easel for me.

I get up and pick up the brush. The thought of trying to paint another disaster ... Let's just say, I respected Miranda before, but now I think she may be a goddess in human form able to conjure emotions out of paint and canvas.

I dab a blob on the canvas. A big, gray splat. I add more gray paint and make it even larger. I really hoped he'd understand. I change to violet paint and mush that color in. And then I add some red for anger. Anger at myself for being the idiot who lied and kept on lying. And anger for letting myself fall for him. The strokes seethe and churn under my brush.

He actually complimented my pathetic painting. How did Paisley ever cheat on him? Has she met some of the jerks out there?

But then again, Paisley had this very put-together, sophisticated look. We're probably fishing in different pools. I can dress up like a lawyer, but my vibe is still less sophisticated society and more scrappy shark.

I make a gray sliver fin emerge from the roiling colors below. Now it looks like someone died in the waters below. I paint a long, horizontal line—a line I shouldn't have crossed.

I put my brush in the can of water, which is no longer clear but a murky brown. This isn't helping. A wave of exhaustion overtakes me.

"This piece looks good. Angry. Confused. Distraught," Miranda says.

"I'm going to bed." I pick up the can.

Miranda takes it from me. "I'll wash the brushes. You go sleep."

The next morning, at 7:30 a.m., I meet with my FLAFL client, Taylor, before I have to go into the office. I'm relieved I can focus on this and stop thinking about what I should have done—how I should have told him the truth when he picked me up at our apartment. How I wish I'd told him at the swing.

Taylor looks exhausted as we meet at a small café in Harlem, near where she's staying on a friend's couch. I order two coffees with milk and two quiches for us at the counter in the back while she grabs one of the small, round tables in the corner. The woman working the counter says she'll call us up when the order is ready. One other person with a dog sits near the front, reading something on their phone. I join Taylor. Taylor is slender and muscular, but shadows linger under her brown eyes.

"Are you okay?" I ask.

"I'm worried. I'm afraid he's selling or getting rid of all my grandma's stuff while he's in possession of the apartment. Mrs. Humming, the neighbor, said she saw him throwing out some stuff. It may not have value to him, but it means a lot to me."

"I can file for a temporary restraining order. Then he can't change the contents of the apartment until the case is decided."

"Oh, can you? That would be great," she says. "And then her possessions stay there, right? It's not like I have anywhere to put them right now. My friend is being generous enough to lend me her couch."

The barista waves that our order is ready. I pick it up and hand Taylor her coffee and quiche. I go grab some sugar packets, napkins, and utensils. Taylor sips her coffee, holding it with both hands, as I add sugar to mine and stir.

"But staying at a friend's is okay?" I ask. She looks so tired. I had offered her my couch, but she said no.

Several construction workers come in and order. And then two women with strollers join the line. The café is filling up. There's the hiss of the cappuccino machine and the low murmur of conversations.

"Sure. I've slept in far worse conditions in the army. It's the worry. And I feel bad I wasn't there with Grandma at the end. She always said she was fine and was going to live long enough to be a great-grandma. And I'm looking for jobs, and that's tough. Anyway, I invited Mrs. Humming to join us because I want you to hear what she has to say. She's willing to testify on my behalf." Taylor checks her watch.

"Thank you for organizing that," I say. "Should I order a coffee for her too?" Taylor nods, and I order another coffee.

Upon my return, Taylor says, "You look like you haven't slept well either."

And here I thought I didn't look that bad for a sleepless night after a breakup.

"A guy I just started seeing broke up with me," I say. *He was more than a guy.* A pressure builds in my chest, but I push it back down.

"I'm sorry," Taylor says.

"It's okay. It won't affect my work," I say.

Taylor frowns. "I'm not worried about that. You should take some time for yourself too."

A bell at the café door tinkles.

Taylor says, "Here she comes."

A tiny woman opens the glass door of the café. Taylor waves, and she comes slowly toward us. I introduce myself and grab an extra chair. After she is comfortably seated and I've picked up her coffee, I ask her for her thoughts on the case.

Mrs. Humming crinkles up her face. "No way were they having a relationship. He was the caretaker, nothing more."

"But she gave him power of attorney? And he submitted proof that he deposited his checks into her account," I say. "How would he have that account information?"

Mrs. Humming shakes her head. "Her mind was going a bit there at the end. And her eyesight. She might not have known what she was signing. She did trust him. He was very attentive and polite. He was very professional. I was shocked myself to hear that he was claiming to be a common law spouse." She harrumphs. "He's not that fine. Now, her grandmother was fine. But she was never interested in anybody else after your grandpa died. It's disrespectful to her memory and to Taylor's grandpa's memory that he's saying this."

Taylor smiles wryly. "My grandmother wrote down all her passwords in a book so it would be easy to find. How many checks did he deposit?"

"All of his checks for the last year." I study my notes. "Obviously, we can argue that he was only living there because the caretaking contract obligated him to live there. And I think that's a good argument. He's said that even though they were in a relationship, they kept the contract going for the extra income. I'm arguing that he can't have it both ways. But he did terminate the contract in March, saying he felt it wasn't right."

"He never told me he terminated the contract," Taylor says. "I would have worried that my grandma wasn't being taken care of. Especially in March, when she fell and broke her hip."

"His contract says he was only a Monday through Friday live-in. Did he stay for the weekend?" I ask. "He claims he did."

"He used to leave every weekend when she was alive," Mrs. Humming says. "I would look in on her and check that she was okay. Lately, I think he's been staying weekends. But I'm sure he only lived there during the week until she died."

"Even during this past year, and in March and April, he was leaving on weekends?"

"Yes." Mrs. Humming nods with extra emphasis. Her hoop earrings bob up and down.

"Okay. I'll ask your apartment building for the security footage to see if it recorded him leaving and returning. If he was gone for the weekend during this time they were supposedly together, that would definitely weaken his case. Is there anything else you can think of that might help our case?"

Mrs. Humming drinks her coffee and considers this. "I can't think of anything else."

"It would definitely be helpful for you to testify," I say. "If he still appears to be leaving on weekends, let us know. He must have some other place he stays. We should check out the address he gave on this contract. I'll do that."

This is good. And somehow, sitting in this small café, talking with these two women, makes me feel better. It's not the imposing conference room of White & Gilman, but I'd rather be in this café working together to save Taylor's home.

Is it enough to do pro bono on the side? *I don't know.*

We discuss the rest of our strategy, and then I go to the office.

My To-Do list seems overwhelming. And now I have to file a temporary restraining order on top of that.

I draft the temporary restraining order first and send that off to Ken for his comments. That's the most time-sensitive. Mr. Howard's former address is on the healthcare assistant contract. I also call Taylor's grandmother's building and ask if they have any security camera footage from the past year. The employee at the other end sheepishly tells me that the camera is broken in that lobby, but they plan to repair it. A dead end.

I email Jurgen with a photo of last night's painting and try to make the email sound all gushy, like I'm thrilled he might help me. I shudder and turn to writing my brief for a securities litigation case.

As I wait for my third cup of coffee to fill at the canteen dispenser, thoughts of Zeke gallop through my mind. I don't know what to do.

Should I call him and say I'm sorry again? *I want to call him.* Should I give him space to think about it?

Yes, I lied. And waited to reveal the truth.

But if he doesn't give second chances and doesn't date workaholic lawyers, then I should be the one saying "no thanks" and walking away. I click on that photo of me in the corner, crying at seven years old because my best friend, the boy next door, didn't come to my party. *Remember. Don't miss out on your life because of some guy who can't be bothered to show up.* If he doesn't put in the effort to be with me, then he's not worth my time.

Chapter Nineteen

Zeke

Ben was right. Going out for dinner was a good idea. Much better than sitting at home alone on a Friday night, thoughts wildly spinning about what an idiot I am. And I appreciate that Ben could be hanging out with Brooke but is instead here in this small Italian bistro trying to cheer me up.

We pick up our menus and tell the waiter we're still waiting for a third. Sebastian, another office colleague and friend, is supposed to join us. He got caught up in a deal, so he couldn't take the subway down with us to the West Village.

"Sebastian just texted that he is walking fast," I say.

"From midtown?" Ben asks. "He might want to jog."

"From Christopher Street," I say. "He just got off the subway."

I don't have much of an appetite.

"You look like crap," Sebastian says as he joins us at the table. "Is Arthur still on your case?"

"He just broke up with somebody," Ben says.

"I don't need you to broadcast that," I say. Seriously. Ben.

"*You* broke up with her? Why?" Sebastian waves at my face. "Given that you appear sorry. Can you get back together?"

"No," I say, as Ben says "Yes."

Sebastian says, "And here I thought you subscribed to my philosophy that being single has a lot to recommend it."

After the spectacular catastrophe with Paisley. He doesn't need to say it. It's implied. That's the drill when you have a well-known office relationship that ends badly.

"I've renewed my subscription," I say.

Ben shakes his head. "I'm looking forward to watching you fall hard, Sebastian. And Zeke, you should man up and call her and say you freaked out, but you've thought about it and you're back on board."

"Zeke freaked out?" Sebastian says. "This gets more interesting."

"He means I broke up with her," I say. "I found out that she was lying to me."

"She told you," Ben says. "It wasn't like you were doing some undercover investigation."

"No. She was."

"She's an undercover investigator? That's pretty cool," Sebastian says. "Maybe I should take up dating again."

"She's not for you," I practically growl.

Sebastian and Ben both look at each other. *Great.*

I wave my hand. "I don't want to talk about it."

"Do any of you play squash?" Sebastian asks. "My usual partner is less available now that he has a serious girlfriend."

Sebastian's a good guy. The change of subject is appreciated.

"I play," I say.

"There's a good bar around here if you want to go for a drink," Sebastian says. Ben has already peeled off to head home to Brooke.

"Sounds good," I say.

As we reach the corner of brownstone-lined Perry Street, we pass by a glass-fronted restaurant. Couples sit at tables outside.

"This café has excellent coffee," Sebastian says.

I glance inside. And there is Tessa. Framed in the window. With that Jurgen guy. She's leaning forward, almost as if she's beseeching him. He reaches out and puts his hand on hers.

She doesn't pull away.

I want to rip his hand off hers.

Why isn't she pulling away? She agreed that he was a pretentious prick and she didn't need him for her artist career.

I practically slap my forehead.

She's not an artist.

That must be the scammer guy she's trying to hook. I hadn't focused on that.

"Is something wrong?" Sebastian asks, looking back. I've stopped in the middle of the sidewalk.

I step back, out of view, and wave him over to the brick wall I've moved to stand against.

"Are we now undercover?" Sebastian asks, a laugh in his voice.

"Yes," I say. "That's Tessa, the woman I was dating, and that's the guy who she thinks is a scammer. She's a lawyer pretending to be an artist to see if he will scam her."

"Of course," he says sarcastically. "*What?*"

"I'll explain it later."

"She sounds cool—not like someone you should break up with," Sebastian says.

I narrow my eyes. "Do you want to help or give commentary?"

"Both," Sebastian says.

"Go make yourself useful and tell me what they're doing now. And warn me if they come out."

Sebastian shakes his head but walks by the café window and glances inside. More like stares inside. *Great undercover work, my friend.* My phone beeps.

> Sebastian: *Served mugs, and she has a plate of cake. She's eating. He's drinking. A table near them opened up. Should I grab it?*

What am I doing? What do I care if that guy seems like bad news? She knows what she's doing. *Maybe.* And she's hardly defenseless. She's out in public.

Still, I dislike that guy. And she should have backup.

I need to get a costume.

> Me: *Grab it. Thanks. I'm off to Screaming Mimi's for a wig.*

"What the heck look is that?" Sebastian whispers as I slide into the seat next to him. He's smartly placed them so that our chairs are

together, our backs to the table with Tessa and Jurgen. There are about four other small tables here in the front of the café.

"Seventies Heartthrob Hair. They don't have a lot of choices for men. This was way better than the mullet wig and mustache." The brown hair frames my face and reaches down to curl at my shoulders.

Sebastian gestures to the two coffees he ordered us. I drink mine.

"What's the title of this painting?" Jurgen asks. We can hear them really well.

Well done, Sebastian.

There's a pause, and then Tessa's voice says, "*Regret.*"

I've missed the sound of her voice. But not when its timbre deepens with sadness. What does she regret? If only I could see the painting.

"I'll tell Misty Morano that it's a yes," Jurgen says. "I'm sure they will want *Regret* too. They seemed very keen to have your paintings in their show."

"That's great. Thank you so much. This is such a dream come true. I can't believe I'm going to be in a show," she says.

"Would you like to come back to my studio? I can give you a few pointers," Jurgen says.

No. My whole body tightens. Sebastian gives me a warning look.

"I can't," Tessa says. "I have to get back to my boyfriend."

She has a boyfriend? Or is this part of the pretense?

No good ever comes of eavesdropping.

"That guy from the art show?"

"Yes."

At least I'm still fictionally in this picture.

"Here you go, guys. No rush." The waitress's voice. She must be handing them the check.

"I'll get it," Tessa says. "Thanks again. Let me know when I should deliver the paintings to the show. I can't believe I'm going to be in a show."

"I'll text you."

The chair behind me scrapes back.

"Okay, uh ... bye," Jurgen says.

Sebastian shifts his chair so that he faces them and me.

Sebastian whispers, "She's gone. The guy is still putting on his coat, and she's out the door."

"Would you like a refill?" The waitress comes over to our table.

I nod as Sebastian says yes. Jurgen might recognize me, so it's best to stay put until he leaves too.

Much as I'm tempted to run after Tessa and *coincidentally* bump into her.

"He's gone," Sebastian says. "Maybe we shouldn't have listened in. Are you okay?"

"I don't think she has a new boyfriend," I say.

Sebastian's giving me a look, like poor, misguided sod.

"I'm that guy from the art show."

"Okay," Sebastian says, but then winces and adds, "there could be more than one art show, though."

"I'm the guy from the art show. We met Jurgen at the Dumbo Arts Center," I say.

Sebastian doesn't look convinced.

"I'm going with that anyway," I say.

"Whatever works for you," Sebastian says.

"It's only been three days since we broke up."

"Not that you're counting," Sebastian says.

"I'm not counting," I say.

I scratch my neck. This wig is itchy. But I should keep it on.

"I hope we don't run into anybody I know while you're sporting that thing," Sebastian says.

"It can only help your image. Not everyone is friends with a 70s rock star. I'm definitely coming to your next party with this wig on."

"That's one way to stay in the singles club," Sebastian says.

Not for Tessa. She'd love it.

We're over. Stop thinking about her.

"You still seem to like her," Sebastian says. "Was her lie unforgivable?"

"No," I say. "But my reaction to it made me realize that I'm not ready for another relationship. I know I hurt her when I walked away."

But I couldn't stop myself. I couldn't breathe. I had to get away. And yet, her face, pale.

"And subterfuge seems to be her middle name," I say. "I'd never know if she cheated on me."

Even if I liked her. There are other women. Women who do not lie as part of their extracurricular activities.

But she is trying to build a case against this guy. She had to lie at that moment.

"You're not doing so bad at subterfuge yourself," Sebastian says.

I sigh. That's not exactly reassuring.

"How do you know when you'll be ready?" he asks.

"That is the question," I say.

Chapter Twenty

Tessa

Time to update everyone on our Jurgen case at Banter & Books.

When I arrive, late, Lily is soliciting volunteers for an Oasis Garden summer event. I sit down next to her at the back table and glance at her list. Miranda is performing with her band in the evening and has agreed to run a face-painting booth during the day.

Fairy lights are strung under the glass panes of the conservatory, giving it a very festive atmosphere. It's warm out, so only a screen door separates us from the rear garden. A comforting breeze brushes in, carrying the scent of fresh air.

Iris says, "Patrick is on tour this summer, so he can't perform."

"I hope my next-door neighbor goes on tour. That would be so amazing. Quiet at last. No guitar strumming. No singing at midnight." Maddie looks blissful at the thought of her rock-star neighbor leaving for the summer. The wall between their apartments is apparently paper-thin.

"Excuse me," says a tall guy. "Are you lovely women holding a book club? I'd love to join."

Because it's not like he needs to read the novel first or even know what book it is.

"No," Lily says with a kind smile. "I think the book club finished at eight."

He reaches to pull out a chair next to Iris, but she plops her backpack on it in one smooth motion.

"I can give a presentation on self-defense," Iris says, glancing up at him.

He backs up quickly and leaves.

Maddie snorts.

"Or computer safety," Iris says without missing a beat. "That's very important."

"Oh," Lily says, looking like she's trying to hide her doubt that people will be interested.

"It will be perfect for the teenagers and the seniors," Iris says. "You look totally dubious, but I can make it exciting. I can demonstrate how AI can take your voice from social media posts and use it for voice phishing."

"Self-defense sounds good, but don't scare everyone," Lily says.

"I volunteer for the face-painting booth," I say. "I should be able to do that."

"I can also help with face painting," Yvette says.

"Here's the Jurgen update. He's following the exact same playbook he followed with you, Yvette," I say. "At our last meeting, he said Misty Morano was interested in my work. He didn't even change the name."

"Jurgen set up that Misty Morano 'dealer' website," Iris says. "He didn't pay for privacy protections, so it's easy to determine that he's the owner. He probably doesn't want the hassle of setting up another website."

"I knew it! We are definitely building our case," Miranda says.

"We still need more before we go back to Officer Johnson," I say. "Jurgen pretending it's a third-party gallery is not enough. We want to see if he's doing the fake-check scam."

So many awful people out there taking advantage of someone's passion and desire for success. It's so cruel to promise them their dream and take advantage of all their hard work and give nothing in return.

"Did he offer painting lessons?" Yvette asks, fiddling with the packets of sugar in the white mug on the table.

"Yes, but painting lessons would definitely reveal that I've never taken any art classes, so I said no."

"You'll have to pay him some money for the check scam. I'm willing to contribute five hundred dollars," Yvette says. "I really want to catch him in the act."

"I'll contribute five hundred dollars," Miranda says.

"Thank you," I say. "So now we wait to see whether the Morano show falls through, as it did with you, and whether he then reaches out with a Brazilian buyer."

"I'll do some searching on the other artists featured on his Instagram," Iris says.

"I can direct-message them, but we also don't want to reveal our suspicions to them if their loyalty is to Jurgen," Miranda says.

"So Iris will research them, but let's hold off on contacting them for now," I say. "We've got our plan of action."

"If we catch him, I can write an article and warn other artists of these types of scams," Maddie says.

My phone rings. It's Ken. I excuse myself to take it and step outside into the Banter & Books garden. A few couples occupy the various tables amid the leafy vegetation.

"Sorry to call you so late, but I wanted to let you know that we chose you as our Law Firm Associate of the Year in recognition of your provision of legal services to indigent clients," Ken says. "And White & Gilman was awarded Law Firm of the Year as a result of your efforts."

"Are you serious? Wow." My eyes tear. "I'm so touched. Thank you."

"Thank you," Ken says. "I'll let you go. The award will be given at the FLAFL dinner in July."

I can't believe it. I cover my mouth with my hands as I let out a little scream of joy. Shivers race down my spine.

Yvette comes outside, her jacket on, mouths *Thank you so much*, and then waves goodbye. Her bartending shift starts soon, so she'd said she could come for only a half hour.

The FLAFL Award. Wow. I text my family the news. I pull up Zeke's number, and my finger hovers. *No. It's over.* My eyes feel wet again. I'm so emotional lately. I slip back into Banter & Books.

"FLAFL chose as me as the Firm Associate of the Year," I announce to my friends.

"Yes!"

"Congratulations! Can we go to the FLAFL dinner?" Iris asks.

"I'm sure my law firm will buy a table and allow me to bring some guests," I say. "But I can't afford to buy my own table, unfortunately."

They all stand to hug me, and Lily orders a round of fresh chocolate chip cookies to celebrate.

"This will help you get the bonus, right?" Miranda asks.

"It should," I say. "White & Gilman gets recognition as a law firm encouraging pro bono too."

We all sit back down at the table as the cookies arrive. Everyone takes one, and we clink our mugs.

"I still wish this investigation hadn't cost you Zeke," Miranda says.

"It's his loss," Lily says.

"I know," I say. It's my loss too. "And I know if he's not interested, I need to forget him. But I still think about him."

And I even thought for a second that this guy was Zeke when I was at the café with Jurgen. Not that I'd admit that to my friends. His back reminded me of Zeke's. I'm going insane. Especially since that guy was rocking some crazy 70s-style hair.

"I was so stupid to keep holding on to this total fantasy about Aiden and me when he was so clearly not interested," Lily says. "Don't worry. Someone better will come along. Someone who loves you for who you are. Don't settle for anything less."

It's easy for Lily to say that now that she's dating Rupert. Aidan was an idiot. But Zeke isn't. He definitely liked me, and my actions killed it.

But Zeke didn't like me enough. Like Wyatt didn't like me enough. Two encounters with Marla, and Wyatt said goodbye to me—even though we'd dated for eight months.

Chapter Twenty-One

Tessa

I STARE AT THE calendar on my office wall as my computer powers down. "Team Dinner with Zeke" in bright red colors marks today's date. I can't wait to see him, but my stomach has been tied in knots all day. *Is our relationship over?* He hasn't called in the past week and a half. I've tried to forget him. *Don't wait for a guy who doesn't want you and all that.* But I like him.

This work dinner is a chance to see him. Maybe he's had second thoughts, but he's still not sure. This could be an easy way for him to acknowledge that it wasn't all bad and that we should try again. How can he walk away like that? But I also don't want to be the crazy ex who doesn't take no for an answer.

My phone rings. I'm about to let it go to voicemail so I'm not late for the dinner when I see it is Taylor calling. I pick up. My assistant waves good-bye in the doorway as she leaves for the day.

"Mrs. Humming says Howard seems to be living in the apartment on weekends," Taylor says.

"Oh no," I say. "Because I visited that apartment building that Howard previously listed as his address, and his name is still on the mailbox, along with the name of a woman, Angel Morris. *Together.*

I'm really hoping they're still in a relationship. Wouldn't she have removed his name if they broke up?"

Or she could be like me, hoping he'll come back. I sigh.

The restaurant is in Chelsea but several long blocks west from the subway station. I stride past a locked and empty playground. Lakshmi went straight from another client's office, so I don't even get to enter with her as my shield.

My phone beeps.

Lakshmi: *Just arrived. I can see Zeke's appeal.*

Ahead of me is the restaurant, its name in gold lettering on the glass windows, giving off a sophisticated, modern vibe.

The door closes behind me as the maître d' asks for my reservation. I scan the diners and immediately find our party. And Zeke. Tom has claimed one of the seats next to him. That's fine. I want to sit far away. Sitting next to him is too intimate, too close, too raw. I prefer to ease in.

I hand my coat and bag to the coat check person.

When I get to the table, there's only one seat left. Next to Zeke.

Paul says, "And here's Tessa. She's the one you should thank for getting your case settled so quickly and fortuitously."

Zeke stands up and says hello. "We've met before."

I put out my hand. "It's good to see you again."

There's a moment when we assess each other. His face looks thinner, like he's been working hard lately. He shakes my hand. I glance at our clasped hands. We both pause, holding hands a second longer than necessary. And then both pull away.

I scoot into my chair, trying to pull it a slight distance away from his. Luckily, Brooke is on my other side.

Zeke turns toward Tom.

I turn to Brooke.

Tom is happy to completely dominate the conversation with Zeke; he's very keen on making that business connection, even if in-house counsel usually decides the law firm.

It's like there's an electrified wall between me and Zeke. I'm very aware of his every move. His arm brushes mine—shocking me—as we reach for the bread basket at the same time. I pull back awkwardly.

He gestures for me to take it first.

I gather we're going to pass the whole dinner without exchanging another word. *Fine.* If he wants to play it like that, I can out-silence anyone.

Should I even try to apologize again? What's the point? He's not interested. And I'm not interested in dating some unforgiving dude who wants to date artists.

The butter has been carved into a rose. I glance over at Zeke—as he looks at me. I smile. His lips curve up but then stop. He turns away.

Yeah. I still want the chance to apologize again. I didn't act with malicious intent.

Our main dishes are served. Brooke and I discuss a recent litigation in the news and discover we have some mutual friends in common. I can't tell if Zeke is listening in. It's so clear I'm a lawyer. My stomach plunges, and my peas taste like sawdust, impossible to swallow. It feels more final now. Is he really going to ignore me the whole time?

I ask Brooke what she does for fun and thankfully lead our conversation from any law-related discussion.

Tom is going on and on about his last cases, extolling the abilities of the firm. Zeke shifts next to me. It's like the brushstroke lecture—but legal.

When Tom pauses to take a breath, I break in and say, "The waiter wants to know if we want dessert or coffee."

We all give our dessert orders to the waiter, and Paul engages Tom in conversation.

Zeke glances at me and whispers, "We should introduce your colleague to Mr. Brushwork."

But then his face shutters closed, as if he regrets making that overture.

The dessert and coffee are served. Brooke and I share a fallen chocolate cake. We both mmm about how good it is. Zeke shifts next to me.

His phone buzzes, and he excuses himself to take a call outside. I go to the bathroom to reassess. As I stare in the mirror, I remind myself that I'd planned to use this dinner to make my case.

This is my opportunity. He's outside alone.

Fine.

It's a challenge.

I don't step back from challenges. And we did have something good. I'm worth the risk.

And he did whisper to me.

I walk outside. He's still on the phone, his back to me.

I keep my distance so as not to intrude or overhear his call, but seeing his back and tall, lean legs ... I miss him. A couple is standing near a streetlamp, smoking and discussing something on their phones. A lone cab races uptown on 10th Avenue.

He turns around, and a flash of surprise crosses his face.

"I wanted to apologize again—in person," I say. "And to say that I was lying about being an artist, but I was still being me. You still know me. I was about to tell you that first night, but then you said you hated lawyers. And my plan was to tell you at MoMA, but then you looked destroyed when you saw your ex. I felt I should wait until you recovered your equilibrium at dinner and then tell you."

"I get it."

"You get it?" I ask slowly. What does that mean?

"I get it," he says.

But I don't. "What do you mean by that?"

"I understand how it all happened—that you had to say you're an artist when the scammer guy could overhear you, and then I said I hate lawyers and you didn't want to tell me you're a lawyer. And I reread that email, and it was kind of obnoxious. If I read someone's email and they said, 'Don't date a finance guy,' I'd also be tempted to prove them wrong. So I get it."

He does get it. "But so, there's no chance of trying again?" I can't help it.

"I don't think I'd trust you. And that's not fair to you." He glances down. "Paisley left me with some major trust issues. To quote my sister." He shrugs.

A short, harsh laugh escapes me. "It's ironic. I'm usually pretty up front and honest. To my detriment. But okay." I step closer. "What about friends? I can earn your trust."

He swallows. "My feelings toward you are not just friends."

"Tessa!"

Not Wyatt.

He must have some radar for me with Zeke.

Oh no. Now Zeke will tell him we're not dating anymore.

And Wyatt will think another guy dumped me because I'm a workaholic.

Maybe that is the real reason Zeke doesn't want to date me.

I turn around. "Wyatt."

"Surprised to see you out on a weeknight," Wyatt says. "Impressive that you're here. This is the new hot restaurant. I didn't think you cared about such things."

"It's a work dinner," I say, annoyed that I have to admit that. What did I see in him? Note to self: Don't fall for a pretty face. The even hotter face of Zeke glances at me, his eyebrow arched.

"She must really like you if she's bringing you as her date to a work dinner," Wyatt says.

Don't say you're my client. Wyatt will have a field day with that. I can hear him now: How else would Tessa meet someone?

Zeke slides his arm around me. "We'll have to come back another time when we can actually talk to each other. The food is amazing. Although I prefer a little more privacy." He nuzzles my neck.

Nuzzles.

My stomach is doing full cartwheels.

I am utterly still.

Thank you for not telling Wyatt we broke up.

But what fresh torture is this?

The heat from his hand against my waist is burning. I want to sink into his arm.

And then he whispers in my ear, "You could look a little more devoted."

I turn my head to face his.

Big. Mistake.

He's like an inch away. His eyes have a teasing light in them. And his lips are open and so close. His breath smells of red wine.

I reach up my hand to run it through his wavy hair. "We should make our escape soon."

Zeke puts his other hand on my waist. I think he's trying to hold me in place so I can't come any closer.

I leave my hand resting against the back of his neck and slide my fingers through his hair at the base of his scalp, rubbing it. Like I'm trying to tame a wild cat.

Wyatt clears his throat. "Well, glad to see all is still well. I'll see you around."

It seems like he will.

We stand there, staring at each other.

"See." He removes his hands and steps away. "Not just friends."

My hand falls back by my side. I look down. *No.* Not just friends. But really, this chemistry. He can step away?

"We should go back in," he says.

"Yes, before they wonder. We've done such a good job of not talking, they might suspect we're actually dating." I turn to head in. But then I look back at Zeke. "Thanks for not telling Wyatt that we're not dating. I really appreciate it. If you still need that date for that wedding, I'd be happy to be your fake date."

He smiles wryly. "I can handle it."

As we go back in, the rest are preparing to leave. I grab my bag and walk out with Lakshmi.

"Any luck?" she asks.

"No," I say.

"I think he was looking for you at the beginning when you didn't show up immediately."

We say goodbye to the others, and I walk her back to her apartment, which is down by 15th Street. I'll take the express subway up from there.

I shouldn't want someone who doesn't want me. I can understand his reluctance to trust me. I don't believe in easily trusting either. But I trust him. I think he's a good guy. *Why?* Because he shows his emotions? He looked so sad after seeing his ex-girlfriend, even though he was trying to hide it. Because he was so up front about his feelings for me. Did I lose him by not sharing more of my feelings for him? I don't want to give up on us. But what can I do to show him that I am trustworthy and I really do like him?

I scoff. How ironic that I've met distrustful me in male form.

My phone beeps.

Wyatt: *Just received email about FLAFL dinner honoring you. Congrats! Bought a table. Business deduction. And great networking opportunity. I'd like to meet Rupert. Can you invite your friends to fill the table?*

I should've known Wyatt would know that Lily and Rupert were dating. Rupert would be a great connection for Wyatt.

Me: *Are you sure you want me to fill it?*

Wyatt: *Yes. Already filling another table that week.*

Me: *Thank you. My friends would love to go. I'll confirm Lily and Rupert can attend first.*

My phone rings, and I answer. It's an associate with a question about an assignment. It's best to focus on work and the bonus—and not on guys who are not interested.

Chapter Twenty-Two

Zeke

I HOLD THE PHONE close to my ear. There's a frenzy of activity in one corner of the trading floor with people shouting. I can barely hear Dylan over the noise. Plus, he's traveling, and I caught him when he's in a cab. There's a lot of honking in the background.

"What do you mean you're not coming for the whole wedding?" Dylan asks. "You're one of my best friends. First, you don't want to be a groomsman because you'd be paired with Paisley, and now this. At least you agreed to do the toast."

The toast has been a nightmare to write. Complying with Lindsay's instructions to make it sincere rather than funny (Lindsay was very clear that no jokes were allowed) was fine, but the beginning of Lindsay and Dylan involved Paisley and me. And referencing Paisley and me is not an option. And the fact that we didn't last is not a good omen.

"You don't need me around for the dancing," I say. *Lame. I know.*

There's only one woman I want to dance with, and she's not going to be there.

Ben looks over from his desk next to mine and shakes his head. Easy enough for him to say I should ignore Paisley. There is no privacy here. Invigorating as the buzz of trading activity around me is, I do miss the ability to have private conversations.

I slide closer toward my monitors and speak in a low voice so the guys around me can't hear. "I think Paisley is going to try to get me back, and that is not happening. And you don't need that drama at your wedding. I'll come to the rehearsal dinner and attend the wedding, but I'll bow out early at the reception."

"Look, you guys set us up. Paisley is Lindsay's friend. We couldn't *not* invite her. You're seated at separate tables at opposite ends of the room. She's coming with some guy. She's also really sorry. Haven't you seen her since?"

"Yes. With Tessa. Whom she thinks I'm dating." But doesn't see as competition? More fool her. I'd much rather go with Tessa. That devil voice inside me says, "And you could, dude. You're the idiot who shut that down." It's been two and a half weeks since I broke it off and a week since I last saw her. Not that I'm counting.

And she did apologize. Unlike Paisley blaming me.

"Look, it's no shame to you if you're not dating Tessa. And you have your friends. We have your back. Sebastian is coming alone."

Sebastian likes being single. Paisley said that she'd made a play for him first before falling for me. Clearly, he has a better rubbish radar than me.

My phone rings. It's Brooke on the other line.

"I have to get that," I say.

"We're not done. You're staying until the end." Dylan hangs up.

I pick up Brooke's line. "Did you call the wrong number? You're off by one number."

"No. I called you. I received an anonymous email that there's fraudulent activity at Comidas en Canasta. I think you should come to my office so we can discuss."

"What? I'll be right there."

Ben looks over from his desk next to mine. I shake my head but don't explain. This can't get out. I rush to Brooke's office.

"But how?" I ask as I enter her office, closing the door behind me. Today, paper stacks are piled high on her desk, and a large cup of coffee is next to her keyboard. A box tray from the cafeteria peeks out of her garbage can. Ben said she's been really busy.

"Probably when I handed out my business card. I translated it roughly from Spanish. Here's the email and the translation." She moves a stack of paper to the credenza behind her and places two pieces of paper in front of me on her desk.

> *Dear Lawyer B. Smith:*
> *I am writing to inform you of money being stolen.*
> *Fraud will hurt the company. Invoices have been paid*
> *for services that were never rendered. But we cannot*
> *speak up. We need our jobs. I want to confirm that*
> *this email address is valid before I send proof. Also*
> *kickbacks. We ask you to investigate as someone outside*
> *the company.*

I just persuaded Capital Management to include Comidas en Canasta in the portfolio and invest millions in a scam. I'm screwed. That's it. That's my whole career. I might as well hand in my resignation right now. I lean over Brooke's desk, reading the email. "Is there any way to find out who sent it?"

"I can ask IT, but it looks like a generic email address."

I sink into the chair in front of her desk. "The financials looked legit. There were no red flags. And we had them audited by a reputable firm."

I don't believe this.

Don't panic.

It's not like it hasn't happened to Charles before. There was that time a year ago when Charles advocated for an investment in a company in Costa Rica. We discovered the fraud and remediated. It wasn't the end of Charles's career, and he was matter-of-fact about it. But he's also the boss with a lot of years under his belt. Still, I might be able to save this.

Brooke says. "It's hard to catch kickbacks and fraudulent services. Maybe there's a second set of books. It sounds like it's someone senior, if they feel the need to go outside the company and not use the ethics hotline. I put in a call to Tessa Jackowski. She's the one who settled your last case. She's done a fair amount of internal investigations, so we should hire her again."

"No."

"What?"

"No." The last thing I need is a liar as counsel to uncover the truth about another bunch of liars. Although they do say it takes one to know one.

No.

I don't want to see her again. I can't be distracted. I need to focus on securing this transfer.

This is my career on the line.

Look what happened at that thank-you dinner. I used her ex as an excuse to pull her close to me.

Working together will be a nightmare. I'll never be able to keep my resolution that we shouldn't date. *This is about self-preservation.*

"But she has experience." Brooke turns her screen to face me and starts reading out Tessa's experience.

Indeed, Tessa has a long list of impressive accomplishments. And there's her picture. She has her arms crossed in that typical lawyer "I'm-all-business" picture. I huff. Far cry from the paint-stained woman who swooped down Wall Street with me. If only I'd checked her picture when Brooke had first mentioned hiring her. I'd never have approached her at that bar. Or probably, I would've introduced myself to her as her client.

I feel a pang.

And it would've been a different story.

Although then, I would've missed out on what a truly terrible painter she is. My lips curl up slightly in a wry smile.

And maybe it wouldn't have been a different story. We'd have dated, and then she'd break my heart out of the blue. I wouldn't be what she wanted. I wouldn't be enough.

"Shouldn't we bid this out?" I ask. "I don't think we should hand it over to her just because she did a good job on the last one."

"I thought you would want to move quickly." Brooke's eyes narrow. "And as confidentially as possible."

Point taken. I'll have to tell Charles, but I definitely don't want Arthur to find out. He'll bandy it about and use it as ammunition against my full-time transfer to venture capital.

"Can't she at least prepare a presentation that shows she's the right person?" Let her do some work for this. "This is my career on the line. You said you thought it was a bit risky to settle. I'm worried about placing my career in the hands of some aggressive, reckless lawyer."

"She has a perfect resume for this. She speaks Spanish. And we already know she's smart."

"I thought all the lawyers at White & Gilman were smart," I say.

"Are all the managers here smart?"

I smile slowly at her. "That's the least impolitic thing you've ever said. I thought you were always careful to tread the line."

Brooke and Sebastian are the smartest lawyers here. Brooke's diplomas from Howard University and Harvard Law School are framed and hanging on the wall of her office. Deal toys decorate the credenza next to me.

Brooke huffs. "She's good. It's your investment. But it's ultimately my decision."

"Why are you so invested in hiring her? Do you know her outside the office?" Was Brooke in on the whole artist deception?

"No. I was super impressed she settled that case so quickly. It saved me time and budget."

"What about that Tim guy from Howard, Parker & Smith? He seemed good."

Brooke puts her hands on her hips. "I'm not going to waste his time asking him to pitch when I'm going to choose Tessa. He doesn't speak Spanish."

"You're going to hire her, no questions asked?"

"Fine. I'll ask her to prepare a presentation listing her strengths and her suggested approach."

"We dated," I blurt out. "Isn't that a conflict of interest?"

"You dated?"

"Yes." I cross my arms.

"You dated Tessa? Our *lawyer*?"

"Yes."

She tilts her head, her brow furrowed. "How did you meet? Wait. Did you take her out for a private dinner to congratulate her? I didn't mean to suggest you date her. I know you have women throwing themselves at you, but I wouldn't have thought ... I thought you didn't date lawyers." Brooke moves a pile of papers to the side of her desk—the better to pin me with her icy, lawyer glare.

"So, it's a conflict of interest and we can't hire her?"

Brooke's eyes narrow. "Are you still dating her?"

"No."

"No conflict of interest." Brooke leans back and crosses her arms.

"I don't think we can work cooperatively together now that we've broken up." It sounds lame, but it's also true. I could never have worked with Paisley after we broke up.

"You didn't sleep with our lawyer and then ghost her? I didn't think *you* would do that."

"No. What kind of guy do you take me for?" I'm offended.

"I don't take you for that kind of guy. You're Ben's best friend." Her voice softens. "Who told Ben not to date me because I'm a lawyer." She glares at me.

Guy friends. It's amazing any CIA agents are men.

"How did you guys meet?" she asks.

"I picked her up at an art gallery."

"So, you're saying you can't work with Tessa because you dated for ... How many dates did you have?"

"Three." Brooke is going full-cross-examination on me. *Great.*

"You're saying that after three dates, you can no longer work cooperatively with our outside lawyer? Are you in kindergarten? Did she dump you?"

"No. I ended it."

She throws her hands up in the air. "I finally find some cost-conscious, brilliant outside counsel, and you screw it up. I'm not sympathetic. I'm not happy. For future reference, outside counsel are off-limits to you."

"I'm sorry. I definitely won't date any other outside counsel. I've learned my lesson." I don't say Tessa lied to me. I don't want to trash her to Brooke. Brooke should feel free to hire her for her other cases. Just not mine.

"Given how hard a time you gave Ben, I can't believe you dated a lawyer—and our outside counsel to boot."

"Can I tell Ben my 'no lawyers' dating rule now has your seal of approval?" I ask.

"No." Brooke glares at me.

"I didn't realize she was our outside counsel at first. We met at an art reception, purely coincidentally."

"Oh." Brooke's tone is somewhat mollified. "But it didn't work out, and now you definitely think you can't work together?"

"I'd prefer not to." My phone rings. It's Tessa. My finger shifts to press off. But I hesitate. I don't want to ever talk to her again. *But I do.* I still want to hear her voice. Her laugh. That look of glee when she shot that billiard shot right in the pocket.

She definitely isn't your typical lawyer.

"It's Tessa. I'll discuss it with her." I leave Brooke's office.

"Hi," Tessa says.

"Can I call you back? I need to get to somewhere more private." I walk down the hallway past the open office doors and take the elevator to the roof terrace.

Up on the firm's roof terrace, a few other employees are hanging out, smoking or enjoying a coffee in peace. I call Tessa back.

"I'm calling because Brooke left me a message about a potential internal investigation with you, and I wasn't sure," she says. "Well, I thought you probably don't want to work together, so I should tell her that I'm too busy."

I stare at the towering buildings of midtown, all clustered together, and the open, blue sky. So many buildings crowd the city, but it also feels empty up here because so few people are visible. It's such a different view from my brownstone rooftop. There, it's all the flat, horizontal roofs of buildings at the same height as mine—some with terraces or chairs. There are so many facets to this city. So many different viewpoints. And if not for my history with Paisley, I might have been able to brush off the artist lie.

"Do you think we can work together as work colleagues?" I ask.

"Of course," she says.

Huh. She's kidding herself. She leaned in for a kiss when I held her. And I wanted to pull her in and kiss her senseless. And feel her melt against me again.

"You're not too busy?" I ask. "Bartending?"

Tessa clears her throat. "No. Although I do sometimes bartend when Miranda can't pick up her shift if I have time. And now that I'm only working on one litigation other than my pro bono case, I am seeking work. And it will look bad for me if I don't get your next case, if the partnership finds out."

It will look bad for her. I should definitely tell Brooke we can't use her.

But that's also a big admission. She's basically telling me, "Here's your chance for revenge."

"I understand if you don't want to work together," I say. "Brooke seems to think you have some expertise in this area. You have to make a presentation, obviously, but I think we're grown-ups." There's no way I'm going to come off as the weak, hurt party in this. I mean, I am the hurt party. But for sure, I can act like we're strangers. If she thinks we can be work colleagues. I'm over her.

Or I'm not over her, and I'm a fool who wants to spend more time with her. In a safe, protected setting.

I'm a fool, aren't I?

I better tell Brooke we also need some other firms to pitch. It would be much better if I worked with someone else.

Chapter Twenty-Three

Tessa

I smooth down my skirt as Paul and I wait to pitch for the Comidas en Canasta investigation in the Capital Management conference room. The room is small, with a white table, brown, modern chairs, and a view of midtown buildings. On the wall is a photo of the Brooklyn Bridge. But a very different view from what we saw on our date biking across it.

Please, Zeke, don't be setting me up for failure as some sort of revenge.

What a stupid move to admit that it would look bad for me.

Way to fail Life Lesson #1: Don't reveal your vulnerabilities to guys, especially those who may wish you harm.

It's not like I *want* to work with Zeke. *I'm not over him.* I'm afraid I'll reveal that. I still want us to get back together. It's silly because it was only three dates. And I know, more than anyone, not to date someone who doesn't like lawyers or respect the hours I work.

But I do love internal investigations. Uncovering corruption makes me feel like I'm on the side of the good guy.

Zeke enters the room with Brooke, and my stomach flutters. He looks good in a suit. It's been so long since I've seen him in person. And my memory didn't do him justice. I was hoping my memory was exaggerating—that I wouldn't find him as attractive as I remembered. He doesn't look at me. I can't stop staring at him. Hungrily. And my stomach is doing those little flips. I shake my head and shuffle my papers.

He's a client.

Focus. This is critical.

Paul stands, as do I.

"Great to see you again. We were very impressed with your work on our last case together," Brooke says. Her glance is close, more inquisitive than normal. As if she knows.

No way. Zeke would never confess to her that we dated.

They take their seats across the table. My PowerPoint is already up on the screen on the wall. I pick up the clicker and flash a glance at Zeke. Please let this be a real chance. Please don't screw me over in front of Paul.

I walk through my experience on internal investigations and then click on the slide describing my plan for the investigation based on what we've received so far. Zeke is staring at me, stone-faced. Not a good sign.

"I think that when you do an internal investigation, you should keep as close to the truth as possible." I don't look at Zeke as I say that. "And in this case, we don't want to alert senior management that we're doing an investigation. My understanding from Brooke is that you have to write a midyear disclosure update to portfolio investors. Let's tie the rationale for our visit to that. And not just use that as an excuse—but also start crafting the midyear disclosure for this investment so that you're killing two birds with one stone, so to speak. And you can do whatever due diligence you need for that report at the same time."

I click to the next slide, showing my preliminary document requests and the employees we should question for the investigation. I turn to face Zeke.

"Your presence would also be helpful because you can research what you need for the midyear disclosure and help with understanding any financial improprieties we find. I can read financial documents, but I wouldn't call myself an expert. Of course, we do have an in-house expert on staff if you can't come." I look away from Zeke, back to the slide with the qualifications of our in-house expert.

Brooke nods and smiles encouragingly. Zeke's mouth is still in a straight line. I'm so used to seeing him smiling. It's throwing me off. I can't read him at all. Or maybe I can. Given how open his face usually is, he's trying hard not to show any emotion.

But suddenly, he leans forward. "You're suggesting we both go to Mexico?"

"Yes. Because although I minored in finance, your financial expertise would be invaluable, and it gives you a chance to get what you need for the disclosure."

He winces. *Winces.*

Great. Now he thinks I want to travel with him to Mexico.

"Your going would be cheaper in terms of our costs. And it would probably be worth your time—unless you're going to sell the investment."

He nods.

"But to me, this looks like an opportunity to improve your investment and make the figures even better. I handled a case in Texas. Here are the returns the year after we finished our investigation and ousted the guy siphoning off funds." I show a slide with a 20 percent earnings improvement from the year before. "That's not all due to getting rid of that corrupt CFO. He was stealing about 10 percent. It was mostly due to an improvement in morale. The workers felt like they had been listened to." I get a chill as I say that. I'll never forget the whistleblower clasping my hands and saying, *I thought I was going to be fired. Thank you for believing me.*

"I'd give this investment a second chance," I say.

Zeke's glance meets mine at that moment. We stare at each other. *Like you should have given us a second chance.*

"But if not, here's what we'd suggest for disposition of this asset. Our corporate team would handle that." My slide shows the preliminary advice from the corporate team at White & Gilman.

Brooke nods. I sneak a glance at Zeke. He tilts his head.

"Additionally, I looked at the records you sent over from the due diligence that we requested. I reviewed the ethics line calls because the note suggests that the whistleblower can't call the hotline because they're afraid of being fired. One of the finance personnel called the hotline a few months ago saying Mr. Stone, the CFO, was harassing employees. It was 'investigated' and found to be without merit. But that name is not on the list of current employees. If this allegation was legitimate and the caller was fired, then we, as the investigators, are going to have a higher hurdle to get employees to open up because past experience indicates that termination is the end outcome. We'll need to earn their trust."

This is a bit risky, given that he doesn't think I'm trustworthy. But I'm willing to prove to him that I can be trusted.

Do I have to show the next slide? He is so distant. Maybe I should stop here.

What am I doing? I steel my jaw. I feel like I'm a dog rolling over and showing its belly. Not to mention I'm mixing White & Gilman work and my personal life. That's an F for Life Lesson #2: Don't mix business and personal.

And I know not to show any vulnerabilities to a guy who can take advantage of them.

I hesitate. This seemed like a great idea late at night when I was preparing my slides.

Paul glances at me, his brow creased. If only I could skip over the next slide.

Zeke was open with me. I need to be open back. *Relatively*. It's a risk I'm willing to take.

I click on my last slide. It has two paintings side by side. One is my terrible painting from the art auction. The other is a Matisse cutout with the word "verve."

"I know you have choices when you hire lawyers. We've worked on three cases for Capital Management, the most recent one being the North American Fund that involved you. Each time, we've brought them to a successful conclusion. We pride ourselves on our cost efficiency. We have the legal expertise, the internal investigation acumen, the financial knowledge, and the language skill. This is my wheelhouse. If you asked me to paint, my painting would probably look like this." I point at the photograph of my Dumbo Arts Center cityscape painting on the PowerPoint slide, and I face Zeke directly. I'm pleading, yes, but I also mean every word.

Have his eyes softened? Or is that just what I want to see?

"But I can paint with words." I point at "verve." "I'm a good investigator. I can instill that confidence that they can trust me because I will do the right thing. Ultimately, whether the employees open up is going to come down to whether they trust the person interviewing them. They're risking their jobs—and possibly the livelihood for

their families. I understand that. And my track record proves that."
I click to the slide showing my past investigations, and then I click
to the final "Any Questions?" slide.

Zeke is looking down at the papers on the table. No way to read
his reaction.

I did my best. He was so much colder than the last two times we
talked. Maybe he was afraid of revealing any warmer emotions in a
professional context.

To find out if certain management personnel are requiring kickbacks or bribes, we might even have to create a fake competing
company and interview recent restaurant vendors. But I fear if I
suggest that, he'll think my whole modus operandi is lies and deceit.
It's not something for the pitch, so at least I didn't have to present
that. Maybe we can avoid doing it. But if it's the best thing for the
client, even if not great for me ... Let's focus on winning the business
first. I can make that decision later.

Brooke asks some penetrating questions—questions that seem
designed to showcase my strengths. Brooke is solidly in my corner.
Then she says, "We have to discuss, and then we'll let you know."

Chapter Twenty-Four

Zeke

ARTHUR HAS GIVEN ME one assignment after another, as if he needs to get as much work out of me as he can before I escape his clutches, and now I have a meeting with Tessa at 5 p.m. in our conference room. Because I might as well get all of this over in one day. I'm not looking forward to "working" with Tessa. But objectively, it made sense to hire her.

I need to maintain my cold front and not allow any personal lines to be crossed.

Thankfully, I'm meeting Sebastian afterward for a squash game. I'll need that decompression.

Tessa has her back to me as I quietly enter. She's wearing a dark-blue pantsuit and standing at the windows, looking out, her phone to her ear.

"Mrs. Humming thinks he was away last weekend? So, he might have gone to his former apartment and former girlfriend. That would be good." She pauses. "Let me follow him. He doesn't know who I am yet." She laughs. It's so joyful. I still like how she laughs wholeheartedly. My gut twists. "I wish we had the funds to hire a private investigator."

I harrumph loudly to indicate I'm here.

Tessa whips around. "I've gotta go. But I'll call you back later."

"I didn't realize your firm handled divorce cases," I say.

"Hasn't anyone told you to knock before entering?"

"I didn't realize I had to knock when I'm entering my company's conference room. But trailing someone? I'm not far off when I say lawyers are practiced in the arts of deception."

She winces. "I think we've pretty much proved that I'm not practiced in any arts." Her gaze is level and open, meeting mine squarely. "But let's get it all out so we can work together. Thanks again for choosing my firm. I appreciate it."

I place my laptop and papers on the conference table at the spot across from her.

"I didn't have much choice. The other firm was going to bring along a Spanish-speaking paralegal, which was immediately going to increase the cost. Plus, your pitch was better. And Brooke wanted you." I shrug. I can get through this. I pour two glasses of water from the pitcher on the credenza and add ice cubes.

Cold front, Zeke.

Two seconds alone, and I've already crossed the line. I set the glasses on the table and sit down across from her.

She takes a deep breath and ducks her head. "To your other question, my firm doesn't handle divorce cases. That's a pro bono case I'm handling. So don't worry, I billed the five minutes you were late to my pro bono matter and not you. If there is anything personal you want to discuss, I won't start the clock running yet."

I stare at her. She takes a deep breath and seems to steel her body, waiting.

No personal discussions. I'm not going there. I don't believe in rehashing things anyway, and I'm definitely not going to share all my *emotions* with her.

Because that worked so well with Paisley. I can still hear Paisley saying, "If you feel that betrayed and that hurt, doesn't that mean you still have strong feelings for me and we should stay together?"

I shake my head. "I'm good. Let's go."

She turns on her laptop. "Here you go. I've analyzed what we have so far. As you know, Comidas en Canasta has a pretty small team. And senior management is the CEO, CFO, the HR VP, the Marketing VP, and the VP of Information Technology and Security. Given that it's the books that are being cooked, the most likely suspect is the CFO, Cameron Stone."

"He's Roberto's right-hand man. I also can't imagine it's the CEO, Roberto. This is Roberto's baby. Unless it really is a fake front company being used to launder funds. In which case, I'm screwed. Because if it's him, there goes the company. But then, it doesn't make sense to get venture capital funding with its additional oversight."

I should have reserved a bigger conference room. This fits four people. It would have been better if I'd reserved the one for twelve people and we'd been able to sit at either end of the long table.

"Given the email, it appears that the whistleblowers believe in the company and want to save it," she says. "But let's say it's the CFO. They clearly don't feel comfortable telling Roberto directly."

"For good reason. Cameron and Roberto went to business school together in the States," I say. "They're very close. Which also makes it unlikely that Cameron would screw Roberto over."

"Let's hope the whistleblower contacts us again when we go down there. Presumably, she has support for her allegations in the email."

"She?"

"I suspect it's a woman. Two women report to Cameron in the finance department, so it seems like a safe bet. Plus, a woman was the caller in that hotline report I referenced in the pitch."

I nod. "That's one of the things that impressed me about your pitch. That you asked for past hotline call records. The other firm didn't."

"I've done a fair amount of compliance work. I like it."

"Because you like to do undercover investigations?" I ask.

"Miranda and I do joke around that when we're old ladies, we should open up our own detective agency, although maybe we've already started with the Jurgen case. But no. I like compliance work—in part because it's like solving a mystery, but also because you're on the right side. You're trying to do the right thing."

"And that's why you also do a lot of pro bono work?"

"You checked out my profile."

"I had to do my due diligence." And I was definitely curious. "Did you consider *not* working for a corporate law firm?"

"I did, but I wanted to pay off my law school loans. And working at a law firm is valuable experience."

"So maybe one day?" I ask. "I'm also being careful to save as much as possible for the venture capital partnership buy-in." If Charles picks me, and if I prove myself worthy of being invited into the partnership.

"Maybe." She shrugs. "We're supposed to be discussing the case—not me."

"It's weird that there is so much I don't know about you," I say slowly.

She huffs. "You know me better than you think you do."

I'm off track. *Again.* I need to stay out of this personal territory.

"Here's the marketing folder you requested." I hand it to Tessa. "It's called Comidas en Canasta—or Food in a Straw Basket or Strawbundle—because each delivery comes in a reusable, woven plastic bag to give the feeling of a picnic and to be eco-conscious. But for every hundredth order, the customer receives a handwoven, vinyl, Oaxacan mercado bag made from artisans in Oaxaco to support those artists."

"That's cool. This seems like a great company—in theory." She taps her pen against her legal pad. "Anyway, first up is what reason we're giving for our visit and our deep dive into their books. Can you explain more about this midyear disclosure?"

"We see ourselves as a partner in helping that company reach its full potential. In general, I monitor the performance of the company to ensure that we make our money and that the money we've invested is being spent wisely. Trust but verify."

Our glances meet, and there's that pause. I should've verified Tessa was an artist. But I don't usually Google my dates.

A shadow flickers across her face, and she looks down.

"And in July, we issue a more in-depth report to investors on our portfolio."

"Okay, that's good." She opens the folder and hands me an annotated checklist. "I looked at the checklist you sent over for the midyear disclosure report. I've annotated it with additional documents we need for the investigation."

I flip through it. "These should be easy to add—and unlikely to raise questions." I pull up the PowerPoint on my laptop that she sent in advance.

Doing better. Let's keep it all on the investigation.

"I looked through the financial statements you sent. There are not so many areas for kickbacks among the expenditures for outside services." She points to her PowerPoint slide with the topics listed: software developers, talent scouting, office location scouting, office decoration, and outside legal services, among others.

"That's what I thought." I sip my water. "Office decoration is the only area where maybe there's some latitude, but their offices were nicely decorated."

"I agree. Office decoration is a gray area, where there could easily be kickbacks or overbilling. The few software developers' contracts are probably legit. You said that they were doing most in-house, and you met with them and they knew their stuff. I'd hope, anyway; otherwise, you're compromising the essence of your platform. Same with the talent scouting."

"Let's hope, but office location is pretty key too. That's going to affect talent scouting, although maybe less nowadays with so many people working from home. And they have a central location—in Roma—which is a very hip neighborhood. Their office was impressive. It felt both high end and comfortable. It's not big, though."

"Okay, good to know." She bites her nail. "At least we can bring up both topics pretty easily, and we'll ask for any documents related to those areas."

"I still asked to meet with the software designers again. I want your take."

We discuss what else we need to do and what its disclosure would mean—good or bad—for the investigation.

All right, so we have our plan of attack. Tessa stands and moves to the credenza, where the tea and coffee thermoses are set up. "Do you want a tea or a coffee?"

"Coffee. I'll make mine." I stand and join her there. I watch as she makes her tea. No paint on her nails now. She's so close, and yet we're strangers.

"Should we send the document list now?" I ask.

"No. That will give them time to think about it and possibly doctor documents," Tessa says. "Let's give it to them when we get there."

We take our hot drinks back to the table and sit down.

I pull up another document for her to view. "Here's my research on what the services should cost. We can compare these numbers to whatever Comidas en Canasta is paying to see if the rates are legitimate or if there are any kickbacks or padding of the contracts."

Tessa reads it, her hair falling down slightly. She pushes those strands back behind her ear and keeps reading. She finishes the document and puts it in her folder.

"Let's brainstorm where else you could get kickbacks if you have a food app." She pulls out a pad and stares at the photographs of New York on the conference rooms walls. "What about the restaurants ... asking for an extra kickback to be featured on the app?"

"That seems kind of self-defeating. And I interviewed a sample of restaurants."

"Did Comidas en Canasta provide the sample?"

"No." I look at her. "I'm not a complete idiot. I looked on the app, found some, and went to speak to them directly."

"Hmm." She tilts her head. "I don't think you would ask for kickbacks to be featured initially—before the app has proven itself. But based on these returns, the app is now #1, so if you're not featured, then you're at a disadvantage. So now there's an incentive."

"Good point. All right, I'll run a comparison and see what new restaurants have been added. And we can go interview some of those. But I don't see them admitting it if we ask outright."

"They might. But do you have the pitch deck Comidas en Canasta used initially?"

"Yes." I pull it up on my laptop. I connect my laptop to the screen and flash it up there. We flip through it.

"Okay, let's make a pitch deck for a fictional competing company. And ask what they like and don't like about Comidas en Canasta so we can make our new service better. Do you have any suggestions for a name?"

I glance at her sharply.

She holds my gaze. "Like you said, it's unlikely that they're going to come out and admit it if we say we're there on behalf of Comidas en Canasta."

We write down the names of the American company equivalents.

"Something with traveling and quick delivery? I doubt thinking of a name is going to be my strong point," I say.

"Don't sell yourself short. You didn't think you could paint, either, and then *Dalmations Gone Wild* inspired a bidding war."

Our glances meet, and we share a smile. I still can't believe *Dalmations Gone Wild* inspired a bidding war. That was a crazy moment. And painting together was ... different.

"I hope you didn't throw it out," she says.

"No." I shake my head. "I was impressed that you included your painting in your slide deck. That was a daring move. Weren't you worried that it would backfire and remind me that you lied to me?"

"I didn't think you'd forgotten, so I thought I might as well face it head-on."

I nod. That move had impressed me. "Did you tell Paul you actually painted that?"

"Paul didn't ask. Thankfully. I highly doubt that possibility would even occur to him. He did like the concept of that slide, though. He wants to use it in another pitch. I'm not sure how I feel about that."

We're both silent. I look at the framed photograph of people boating on the Central Park Lake. I've never done that, and I'd actually thought—before we broke up—that was something we could do as a couple during the summer.

She taps her pen against her pad. "I'll start us off. Dinner Delivered. Or, No Dishwashing Necessary."

"Don't tell me you thought of that off the top of your head."

She grins. "Picnic Express. Picnic *Expresso*. Your own personal picnic?"

"Are you stealing my client's idea?" I ask.

"Since we're trying to steal their clients, it fits the bill."

"Let's not go there. I'm still hoping to save this investment, per your persuasive pitch that this might increase revenue," I say. "Food for thought?"

"I want to eat my food, not think about it," she says. "How about *Vámonos*?"

"Let's Go. I like that. Let's go with that." I lift my eyebrow at her.

"That's such a lame joke," she says. "I can go by myself if you're not comfortable pretending to be another company."

"No. I'm coming with you. I'm not about to let you do some undercover operation on your own that involves my investment." Not because I'm worried about her alone on the streets of Mexico City. It seemed safe enough when I was there, but everyone I talked to said to be careful.

"I think we're ready." She stands and packs up her laptop and notebook. I throw out our used cups and hold the door open for her as she exits.

We stare at each other for a moment in the hallway. Being work colleagues doesn't feel quite right.

She clears her throat. "I'll be off, then."

I watch her walk down the hallway to the elevator bank. I take the stairs back to my desk.

That was fun. Her PowerPoint was straight to the point—no slides with complicated legal concepts to impress me. Maybe because this is an investigation. But still. Tessa is very comfortable with herself. I was right to be surprised she was such a bad artist.

I had wanted to spend more time at Comidas en Canasta to ensure it succeeded, so this is an opportunity to get back down there and learn as much as I can—after we figure out if there is any fraudulent behavior. That's the focus of this trip. I take a deep breath. It's doable. And okay, I kept straying into personal territory, but I survived. There's no more personal stuff to discuss.

First meeting together as work colleagues done. A week to go. *Together.* In Mexico City.

Chapter Twenty-Five

Zeke

Unfortunately, our corporate policy that precludes certain senior executives from traveling together in case the airplane crashes does *not* prohibit my traveling with Tessa on the same Monday morning flight down to Mexico City. And not only that, but my assistant booked our seats together. I tried to suggest we *not* sit together: "She probably doesn't want to sit next to her client for the whole flight, as that's not very relaxing," but my assistant laughed and said, "Give yourself some credit."

I find Tessa immediately at the gate. She's staring at her phone, wearing a tailored, black, skirt suit, a worn, orange backpack resting on a small carry-on, wheeled suitcase. It's hard for me to square this crisp and professional image of her with the paint-splattered, lip-biting, frustrated artist. Which one is the real Tessa?

The lawyer one is the real Tessa, but maybe she's right and she's just her—not to be defined by her career.

Her hair is up in a bun, but a few tendrils have escaped and rest against the nape of her neck. I say her name as I approach her. She looks up.

"All right, let's get this done as quickly as possible," I say.

She tilts her head, and a slight smile teases at her lips. "From a career perspective, of course, that's my goal. Especially since I suspect that's why Brooke supported my pitch. But personally ..." She glances at the ticket agent, who just announced that people on standby can now come up to be assigned a seat. "But personally, I'm hoping that the added time together will make you want to give me a second chance."

She's not dating anyone else.

Not that that matters.

"Normally, I do think honesty is the best policy." She smiles, that mischievous glint back in her eyes. "Although that's also not the policy we're employing in this case. So don't count that against me." She gestures toward some empty seats in the nearby gate area that doesn't have a flight listed. "Do you want to sit over there and discuss any last thoughts on the case? Do you have any edits on the fake pitch?"

I blink at the change in subjects. If she's trying to keep me off balance, she's succeeding.

It's fine. I'm not going to change my mind. I've learned my lesson. We're going to stay professional.

"We're working together," I say. "And I'm definitely not disclosing that I'm dating a coworker to the powers that be—*again*." I don't wait to see her reaction but set out for the empty row of seats, wheeling my luggage behind me.

She sits down next to me, opens up her laptop, and pulls up the fake pitch document she created. Her apple hair shampoo scent wafts over. Triggering memories. *Kissing her, her body pressed against mine, her soft chest* ... The balance sheet liquidity was good, earnings growth on the income statement, return on assets, and operating cash flow is adequate. I'm back in control.

Especially because she seems totally unaffected.

The flight staff announces that it's time for boarding.

Tessa packs up her laptop and stands. "I'll see you in Mexico City."

"We're seated next to each other."

She stills.

Not so unaffected, then.

"My assistant booked us together. We can work, if need be." Because work is what's important here.

We get in the boarding line.

"It's too confidential to discuss on the plane," she says. "We can find a romantic comedy to watch together since you're not completely averse to watching them."

I'm definitely not watching a romantic comedy with Tessa.

"As the client, don't I get to pick?"

"There's no such thing as client privilege, only attorney-client privilege. But okay. But I can't watch anything scary. And I'll cry if we watch something sad, so we basically have to watch a comedy because I don't want to arrive at the clients looking like I've cried."

"That would not be a good look." I show the boarding pass on my phone to the gate agent, and we stroll down the jetway and enter the plane. As we walk through the aisle to find our seats, I ask, "Have you been to Mexico City before?"

"No. Did you see any of it the last time you were here?"

"Not really," I say. "I worked the whole time. But the office is in a cool location. I saw that one neighborhood a little bit—Roma." I put our bags up in the overhead storage bin. "Do you mind if I take a nap? The 3 a.m. wakeup for this flight was brutal."

"I'm all for that."

I wake up to find her head on my shoulder, my head leaning against hers. I stare down at her sleeping face. She looks so unguarded—and beautiful, although I miss her eyes laughing up at me. I want to brush that tendril of hair that lies against her cheek.

The plane lights switch on, and she is up, lifting her head. Her eyes blink into mine as she wakes up. Her eyes swallow up her face. They're so vividly blue and make me want to swim in them forever.

That's how I got into trouble in the first place.

"Well, at least we both napped," she says.

She doesn't appear embarrassed or flummoxed.

"I'm going to run to the bathroom before the seatbelts sign comes on." She grabs a small makeup bag and makes her way down the aisle. I follow her. Roberto, the CEO, is picking us up from the airport to mitigate any kidnapping risk—although I can't help thinking, doesn't that worsen the kidnapping risk? They'll probably want the CEO more than us.

"Wow. These offices are great." Tessa stops to take in the reception area of Comidas en Canasta. "I love the full-height windows and the restored, wood floors and all the art." The reception area has one red wall and one white wall with a red couch against it. A towering, green plant is next to the couch. A bamboo screen separates the reception from the back canteen area. Several pieces of modern art decorate the deep-red wall, whereas the white wall has a very colorful piece of art made out of what looks like dyed, straw fibers.

"We had a lot of fun. My wife helped too. We wanted to go with the straw theme, so we found some Popotillo art and ordered those rattan screens. My wife knows a lot of emerging artists, so we bought some of their pieces to give it a more modern flair," Roberto says. Roberto is in his early forties, fit, with a dynamic presence. "And the location is perfect for our business. There are so many up-and-coming bistros and restaurants in Roma. As soon as I discussed founding this company with Cameron, I knew exactly where I wanted our offices to be."

"Oh. Did you know it was this office building, or did you have a few choices?" Tessa asks.

"I knew it was this building. If the price worked. And it did," Roberto says. "This was pretty much the only easy thing about setting up the business. I suggested this building, and Cameron agreed."

Tessa doesn't look at me. Point One for Tessa. She is good at subterfuge. But I already know that. And that's why we'll never get back together. *Never.*

"I love the décor," Tessa says.

"It turned out well. My wife and I pulled it together with our Head of Human Resources, Pamela. You will meet her later," Roberto says. "We're working pretty hard, so we're not taking long lunches right now, but we made a reservation for dinner. We've set you up in our main conference room down the hall, and later, Ana, our all-around executive assistant, will come by, and you can choose to order lunch via our app. She keeps our office running."

"That sounds great," I say.

We enter a conference room. A long, white table sits in the middle with ten office chairs around it. Modern art is interspersed with Popotillo art on the walls. A woman follows us in to ask us what we'd like to drink. We both say coffee. It was an early flight.

"Are you Ana?" Tessa asks. When she nods, Tessa says something in Spanish and then translates for me, "I thanked her for her help with the hotel reservations."

Ana smiles and leaves.

Tessa turns on her laptop. I take a seat several chairs down. We need some space between us. Roberto sits across from me.

"I have to say, I'm a bit surprised by this visit," Cameron says as he strides into the room. Cameron is older, in his late fifties, with a full head of white hair. He worked in corporate for hotels for years before deciding to switch careers and go to business school. "It's not that I have any problem with it, but I thought we covered everything pretty extensively last time."

"We're writing up a midyear update on our investments," I say. "In general, we take an active role with our investments since we're still a junior player in the venture capital market." And I'm a junior player on our team, so I need my picks to succeed.

"I'm sure they will be happy with our returns." Roberto smiles and leans back in his chair. "We've already acquired an impressive market share due to our marketing and business model. Your capital infusion allowed us to ramp up quickly, and then some immediate viral successes put our name out there."

Ana returns with our coffees and then hands out our schedule.

"Here's our list of the documents we'd like to look at," Tessa says.

"That's quite an extensive list." Roberto frowns. "That may take us some hours to compile."

"Yes. It will take us some time to review," Tessa says. "That's why we'd like to meet with you, Cameron, on Wednesday. But maybe we can talk to Valeria if we have any basic questions. She reports to you in finance, right?"

"I'd like to be there if you talk to Valeria," Cameron says. "She's quite busy as well."

Both men leave, and the head of marketing enters. Liliana radiates competence as she flips through the marketing contracts and shows us the sell-through. The rates are consistent with the comparables I researched. Tessa glances at me and nods.

Next up is software development. The developers are equally impressive. There is a reason why I invested in this company. I'm feeling better about my decision.

Ana drops off a box of documents in response to our requests, and we order lunch from the app. Tessa commends its ease of use.

After Ana leaves the room, I stand and stretch. Tessa stretches, too, and then walks over to look closely at one of the paintings on the wall. It's an abstract painting of two blue, amorphous shapes layered on top of each other. Tessa snaps a picture of the painting and writes down the artist: Gabriel Rosas Alemán. She also takes a picture of the photograph of a plastic cup of a white drink with letters scrambled like an alphabet soup. "The artist is Ana Bidart. Hopefully, even though this case looks like a jumble now, the answer will reveal itself soon."

"Are you familiar with these artists?" I ask.

She shakes her head. "No. But their work is provocative and playful. Miranda and my sister will like them. I do love art. Thankfully, given that both Miranda and my sister are artists. I just can't do it."

I don't answer. *Keep the focus on business.*

We pull out the folders of documents to review, and keep working through lunch. In the late afternoon, we meet with Pamela, the HR VP. She's an American woman, probably in her mid-fifties, very professionally put together. It turns out that she worked with Cameron before, and he suggested she move down here as an affordable alternative after she got divorced.

Pamela explains their recruiting and hiring practices. Tessa reviews the organizational chart with her.

"Who meets with the restaurants to see if they want to be included on the app?" Tessa asks.

"There's an application on the app, and then I meet with them in person to finalize the contracts."

Not Cameron.

"Is that step needed?" I ask.

Pamela shrugs. "We do want to make sure we're offering quality choices. Roberto also sometimes meets with them. And Roberto definitely orders from the restaurants listed. We're all asked to do that. We give each employee a certain monthly budget to order off the app."

"That's smart," Tessa says.

"Employees appreciate it. It's an employee benefit that has been lauded in recent online forums."

"I bet the office atmosphere is also lauded. The way you guys decorated it gives such a comfortable vibe," Tessa says.

That was a smooth transition.

"Did you hire an outside company for help?" Tessa asks.

"It was mostly Roberto and me, but I consulted with an outside company because, obviously, neither of us has any design expertise. Still, we didn't want to outsource, given our limited funds."

I feel like my eyebrows raise, but I have to hand it to Tessa because she looks completely unfazed.

She's good at hiding her emotions. So I won't be able to read her.

Get your mind back in the interview. Pamela contradicting Roberto is a frickin smoking gun, and you're thinking about Tessa. Roberto was adamant they did it themselves.

"That totally makes sense," Tessa is saying. "And I love what you did. It has an amazing, inviting vibe but still conveys sophistication."

Pamela smiles and leans back in her chair. "I'm pretty proud of how it came out."

Tessa looks down at her notes. "Are there any other vendors or outside services you use, other than the outside recruiter?"

"I also consult an HR lawyer at our local law firm."

"Of course." Tessa nods. "That's good to hear. On a related topic, how do you handle hotline cases?"

"They go to me—unless I'm implicated. If I'm implicated, then the call is referred to this employment law firm we've hired."

"Why not send all the calls to outside counsel?"

"That would be ideal, but we're worried about cost."

"Have you had many? Before the investment, it looked like you only had one."

"Yes." Pamela winces.

"What happened there?"

Pamela tilts her head. "I interviewed the hotline caller. She alleged that Cameron was harassing her. He kept requiring her to stay late with him in the office and sometimes sit in his office to watch as he took calls. She thought he was abusing his authority and it felt inappropriate. Cameron said that he suggested that she watch him take calls as a training opportunity. He asked her to stay late because she was helping him with projects that had time-sensitive deadlines."

"Did he ask only her to stay late? Not the other two women?" Tessa asks.

"The other two women in his department are working on their own projects. And they have families, so he didn't ask them to stay late. They did not find his behavior harassing but said he can be very brusque. I counseled him on that. It was clear she felt uncomfortable, so then I asked him not to request her to stay late alone with him. But that situation wasn't really tenable because they have to be able to work together. We offered her a severance package if she wanted to leave. And she took it."

"And you haven't hired a replacement?" Tessa asks.

"Not yet. Cameron said he could handle it. That it was easier to do it himself than train someone. He was understandably upset to be accused of harassment."

"You told him?" Tessa asks the question in a flat manner, but it still sounds accusatory.

Pamela straightens. "Not in the beginning. But once I didn't think it was actual harassment, yes, then I told him so he could understand how his behavior was being perceived and improve."

Tessa asks her if she uses any other outside services, and Pamela confirms that there are no others.

Roberto knocks on the door. "Time for dinner. I'm sure it's been a long day for you, and we want to make sure you also eat. We have made a reservation at Neuve Neuve at Casa Lamm. It's within walking distance. We can drop your luggage off at your hotel on the way there."

Ana comes in with another armful of documents. We agree to meet Roberto and Cameron in a few minutes in the reception area after we pack up. They leave, and Tessa flips through the folders.

"These documents relate to the office decoration and location. Let's review them after dinner." She puts the folders into her backpack. "It didn't appear as though they needed to pay for any location scouting."

The hotline call didn't seem like the opening Tessa expected. But did we get anything with the inconsistency between what Roberto and Patricia said about the office decoration? That is a good lead.

Tessa is smart, and it's a thrill when we're on the same page.

This investigating together is definitely a problem.

Chapter Twenty-Six

Tessa

I'm EXHAUSTED. I'm DEFINITELY feeling that 3 a.m. wake-up call.

Dinner at Casa Lamm was delicious, the inner courtyard and the views from the glass-walled Neuve Neuve gorgeous. No more business travel is definitely something to consider before I make my final decision about leaving White & Gilman.

Still, it's a relief to say goodbye to Roberto and Cameron, check into our hotel, wheel our bags into the elevator, and relax. It's just the two of us. I lean against the elevator wall.

"I can't wait to take these shoes off." I let my high heel dangle off one foot as I shift my weight to the other.

Zeke stares at my foot and stills. His gaze meets mine, and all the air disappears out of the elevator. I flush.

He loosens his tie.

And my mind goes there. Pulling off that tie. Unbuttoning his shirt. Being held tightly by him. That kiss.

He looks down.

I feel my cheek. It's hot. *Think about the case, all the documents we still have to review.*

That attraction is still there.

If anything, it's increasing. It's fun to work with him. I think of something and look over at him, and it's clear the same idea occurred to him.

Zeke clears his throat and says, "Cameron was in fine form tonight. Very funny and charming."

"But he definitely asked you a lot of questions, as if to confirm that you were really here to do the disclosure," I say.

Zeke glances at me and nods. "And to confirm the parameters of what we were investigating for that mid-year report. I thought he was checking to see if his activities might be implicated."

"I thought the same." I nod. "But he and Roberto seem tight."

"We're going to need some strong evidence to accuse Cameron of any misconduct," he says. "Do you still want to meet in your room and go over some of the documents after we've had a chance to shower and change?"

"Yes. We should." *No.* I definitely don't want to be alone with him in a hotel room, being tortured by his presence. I want to study the documents by myself because we still don't have anything. I'm worried. I don't want to fail Zeke. I know how important this is to him. And to me for the bonus.

"Shall we meet in about thirty minutes?" he asks.

I nod.

The elevator door opens.

Zeke waves for me to go first. I pull my suitcase down the hallway to my room.

It's good that our dating ended when it did. Before I fell any further.

Anyway, I'm not interested in a man who doesn't want to date a workaholic.

Do you hear that, heart?

I am not interested. Stop buzzing whenever his green-blue eyes glance at you.

Only men who love workaholic lawyers need apply here.

I press my plastic key card against the door. As it flashes green, I push it open.

A half hour until I meet Zeke to discuss the investigation and where we go from here.

We don't have anything that shows that Cameron is corrupt.

Sure, it appears as though Roberto was unaware that Pamela consulted an outside party for decorating advice, but it's not completely unreasonable to do so. And Pamela was open about it. Maybe that was within her purview.

Our bedrooms are connected by an adjoining door.

There's only one chair.

The double bed takes up most of the room. But we can't meet in the reception area. That's hardly private.

And this is too private.

I should take a shower and get my second or third wind.

Ring. I open my eyes and roll over. My phone is ringing. Ugh. I fell asleep. I thought I'd rest my eyes while waiting for Zeke. I answer it.

"I'm outside your door. Are you in there?" Zeke asks.

"Um ... yes," I say, still a bit groggy. "I fell asleep. Hold on a minute. I'll let you in."

I open the door to a fresh-faced Zeke with wet hair. That definite-ly wakes me up. His laptop tucked under his arm is pulling up his white T-shirt, revealing his worn jeans hanging low on his hips.

This is torture.

Then again, I'm wearing a black tank top and shorts, so I'm not exactly playing fair either.

I point at the chair and the bed. "There is only one chair." *Way to point out the obvious, Tessa.*

"I brought tea." Zeke hands me one of the hotel mugs I hadn't even noticed, since I'd been too busy trying not to stare at that sliver of toned abs, but failing, to see what else he was carrying. "Careful, it's hot."

I'm definitely hot.

I stare at the steam rising from the cup. "Did you make this tea in your room?"

He nods and adds with a wry smile, "Only the finest for you."

Oh, so sweet.

Shush. It's to make sure I'm awake enough that he's getting his money's worth.

I sip my tea. "It's exactly the way I like it."

"It's nothing. I watched you make your tea when we did our planning meeting."

"It's hardly nothing." I gesture toward the pile of papers on the desk. "Anyway, we should get started. Let's do the folders from the office—location scouting and the interior design—first, since those are the biggest leads we have so far."

"Or the only leads?"

"It's early yet," I say.

"But we can't even talk to Valeria without Cameron."

"I interpreted that as a good sign," I say. "That he was worried about her meeting us alone."

"Or he doesn't want her to feel like she's alone when being interrogated by an American lawyer," he says.

"I wouldn't interrogate her."

"It's still intimidating to speak with a lawyer."

"I'm intimidating?" I ask.

Our glances meet, and he smiles. "Yes. You're smart. So for someone who didn't meet you in a paint-stained shirt, yes."

I blush, but my whole body hums under his gaze. *I'm smart.*

Zeke sits in the chair, and I take the bed. We pore through the documents.

I find an invoice for location scouting with a report in Spanish accompanying it.

"Look! An invoice, and here's the report." I show it to Zeke. The smell of his freshly shampooed hair wafts over as he leans closer to me to study the document.

"Should we ask Roberto again?" I ask. "Maybe they did this as an extra measure and he forgot?"

"Roberto is very sharp. That's one of the reasons I was so impressed and eager to invest. He wouldn't forget. Let's make a copy of this but not raise it until we have more evidence. As you saw at dinner, Roberto and Cameron are very close." Zeke pulls out the accounting records. "There's no separate line for interior decoration consulting in the accounting records. It must be lumped in with something else, which makes it harder to find. It's suspicious, but again, it's not enough."

I study the furniture bills. "Some of these furniture bills appear to be exorbitant, but I have no idea. But they seem high, given that they were proud that they didn't spend a lot of money on decorating. It makes sense to buy top quality, and it definitely gives a great impression." I compare two bills. "How many couches were in the reception area—only two, right?"

"Yes."

"But here, they are billed for another two couches. The same bill but a different date. Are there couches anywhere else?"

"No. They don't have couches in their offices. Their offices are pretty small, as befits a start-up." Zeke leans over to study the two bills. Mmm. He smells like ivory soap.

"Genius," he says. The way he's looking at me ... I'm sure he can hear my heart pounding. His eyes soften. I want to reach out and touch his cheek, push back that errant lock of hair that's almost in his eyes.

He scrutinizes the two bills I'm holding in my hand. "Wait. The banking information is different."

A chill sneaks through me.

We both stare at each other, inches apart.

I look down. "Well, that's definitely something. I'm not sure how to trace the bank account, but I can call the furniture company tomorrow and ask them if this is an alternate bank account they provide for payment."

"That's a good idea." He pulls away, leaning completely back against the chair.

"And I'll try to talk to Valeria or Ana—maybe in the bathroom or in the coffee break room."

I shift. It's uncomfortable on the bed. I'm either leaning over the documents or seated on the edge with nothing to lean against.

"Do you want the chair?" he asks.

"No." I stretch out on the bed so that I'm lying on my stomach, propped up on my elbows.

"Don't tip off Cameron," he says.

"I can be subtle."

"I'm not sure subtlety is your strong point."

I snort. "It's definitely not. I should have said, I can be devious."

"That I'll give you. Obviously."

"So I keep showing you—to my detriment." I pout.

His hand brushes mine. "You're an evil genius."

"But *I'm* not evil. I'm fighting the forces of evil. And while I'm confessing, I also want to confess that I'm the one who picked you up."

"No, you didn't. I saw that guy cut in front of you, and I spoke to you first." He leans back in his chair.

"Yes. But I set that up. Have you ever seen the movie *The Lady Eve*?"

"The 1940s Barbara Stanwyck movie?"

"You know your movies." I'm impressed.

"It's a classic. Friday was family movie night, and we rotated who picked. My mom always chose a romantic comedy or those old screwball comedies."

His mom raised such a good son.

"I saw you across the room and thought you were attractive. But I also saw you reject three women before me. Similar to *The Lady Eve*."

"But she trips him."

"Well, that seems a bit extreme, as a first approach anyway. Instead, I asked William, Miranda's boyfriend, to cut in front of me so it would give you an opening if you were interested."

Zeke stares at me, his mouth slightly open. "You knew the guy who cut in front of you? You arranged all of that?"

I nod. That's a look of horror. I shouldn't have brought this up. I knew this wouldn't go well, but I definitely wanted to get it out before he somehow meets William. Given our luck so far, that's only a matter of time. And better now while he has to continue working with me. "But I mean, I guess you did have to take the initiative to start a conversation. I take back that I picked you up. You did pick me up."

He shakes his head. "I don't even know what to say. Do all women do this?"

"I can't speak for all women, but I would say that for sure, some of my friends can come up with quite intricate plots to 'coincidentally bump' into the guy they like. My college roommate memorized her crush's class schedule so she could randomly run into him. Another friend pretended that the coffee shop was having a two-for-one sale so she had an extra coffee that she gave him. And I actually first joined the sailing club because I'd met this guy at a party, and he mentioned that he was a member. I joined, hoping to run into him. But at least I could sail."

"Yeah." The corners of his mouth tip up. "Did that work? Did you run into him?"

"Not once. But there were a lot of other hot men sailing, so all was not lost." Did he growl? I think Zeke may have growled. He looks away.

Outside the hotel room door, some guests converse in Spanish as they pass our room.

"I had to actually call that guy to see him," I say. "But I don't think he was looking for a long-term relationship. He seemed like more of a free spirit. He was the guy I liked before Wyatt. Wyatt was definitely looking for a serious relationship—that was probably part of his appeal." I shouldn't feel the need to defend my dating Wyatt, but I do. Although frankly, Paisley was not someone I'd want to date.

"Having your friend cut in front of you is quite elaborate. But I guess I'm kind of flattered that you went to all that trouble."

I smile. "You should be. I don't do that for everybody."

His eyes narrow. "You've done it for other guys too? Gosh, I feel so commonplace." He makes this adorable pout.

I cough. Damn. I stuck my foot in my mouth again. "I've done it twice before," I admit softly. "But once, it didn't work. There has to be a certain spark for it to work."

"And what happened with the previous guy with whom it worked?"

"He was the sailing guy. Nothing. And now you. I guess I should retire it as a method, given its track record."

"You should definitely retire it." And the way he says it, it's like there's an underlying, frustrated, possessive growl, and I feel this shiver deep in my gut. Like he's saying I need to retire it because he is the guy for me.

And I think he may be.

But until we're back together, he's not. I stick my chin up. "You're right. I definitely need to come up with a better method."

He stares at me, and there's something in his gaze I can't read.

"Let's focus on the case. I'm relieved we have some leads," he says dryly. "I've highlighted the most recent restaurants that joined the app that are all close together. Let's meet them tomorrow at lunch. They're in an area called Romita."

"That sounds good," I say.

We look at each other. Suddenly, I am very conscious that it is late at night, and we are in a hotel room with one bed.

Zeke breaks first, busying himself with gathering up the mugs and closing down his laptop, not looking at me.

"I think we've done what we can for tonight. I'm going to bed," he says. "My hotel room, I mean." He practically runs out of the room.

I can't help smiling as I get ready for bed.

My phone beeps.

> Taylor: *Mrs. Humming saw him come back tonight. We must have missed him leave on Saturday.*

> Me: *Okay. Let's try to follow him again this week-end.*

And then another text pops up, this one from Jurgen.

> Jurgen: *The funding for the Misty Morano gallery show fell through. But don't worry. I'm talking to another dealer I know. Can you meet this week?*

Just like what happened with Yvette. Jurgen follows his script closely.

> Me: *Oh no! I'm so sad to hear that. Is there any chance still for the Misty Morano show? Thank you*

for talking to another dealer. Thank you! Thank you! Next week? I'm working overtime this week.

I text Miranda.

> Me: *Jurgen just texted that the Misty Morano show folded.*

> Miranda: *Next up should be a Brazilian interested in your work!*

> Me: *Let's hope.*

> Miranda: *What's happening with Zeke? Is he being friendly?*

> Me: *Yes.*

> Miranda: *Are there sparks?*

> Me: *Yes.*

That flare of electricity in the elevator. Just now when he ran out of the room.
I might have a second chance. I'm afraid to get my hopes up.

> Miranda: *Are you being held hostage and can't answer?*

Me: *I like him even more. Investigating together is fun.*

Miranda: *He should be so grateful to date someone like you. I have no patience if he holds our scammer investigation against you.*

I send her a heart emoji back.

I turn off my phone and sink into the bed. The attraction is still there. And Zeke is not being cold and distant, so there's progress.

More importantly, there's progress on the investigation. Because if I don't figure out if there's fraud, that's both of our career hopes dashed. Mine for the bonus. His for the transfer.

Chapter Twenty-Seven

Zeke

WE SPEND THE MORNING buried in piles of paper, reviewing the rest of the documents. I also start writing up the investment disclosure report, working with White & Gilman's corporate team via email. All of the vendor services look legitimate, except for the interior decoration consulting and the location scouting. The scouting memo is basic and definitely not worth the price paid.

Tessa calls the couch company. She's so cute when she speaks Spanish. The treasurer says that's not their bank account number.

Yes. We have a definite lead.

I pull out the interior decoration services consulting invoice. "Can you try calling this vendor's number? Let's see if this is legit."

"Good idea."

No one answers.

We stare at each other.

"They could be out for a long lunch," she says.

"Let's try again at three," I say. "Speaking of which, we should go for our own lunch."

We put all the documents back in the boxes and take our notes with us in our backpacks. She pulls up a map on her phone and shows me.

"If we go down Avenida Álvaro Obregón to Avenida Cuauhtémoc and then up that until we turn here to find the first restaurant, that's probably the easiest," she says.

I peer over her shoulder. She smells of fresh laundry and roses. I don't turn my head because she's so close.

"But if we walk up Calle Jalapa, we'll hit the Plaza Rio de Janeiro, so we'd get to see that," I say. "And then we can take Calle Durango. That's a more scenic route."

Roberto comes out as we leave the conference room. "I'm sorry I can't take you to lunch today. I scheduled this meeting with these government officials a while ago."

"*Está bien*," she says. "We wanted to walk around Roma and check out some of the restaurants on the app, so we're fine. Thank you anyway."

"Dinner last night was delicious," I say.

"Roma is pretty safe, but be careful," Roberto says. "Watch out for pickpockets."

The sun is hot, but the trees provide lots of shade as we walk down Calle Jalapa to Plaza Rio de Janeiro. Plaza Rio de Janeiro lives up to its picturesque reputation.

In the center is a fountain with a bronze replica of Michelangelo's *David*. Mansions surround the plaza, and we take our picture in front of the most famous one. It is called The Witch's House because its top looks like a witch's hat.

As we keep walking through Roma at a brisk pace, there's so much to check out: murals, the Porfirian architecture, bustling cafés. Tessa keeps pointing out street art.

We pass by a mural of an older couple hugging. LOVE IS AN ART is written in block, capital letters around the elderly couple.

She stops and walks back to take a photo.

That might be my favorite piece we've seen so far. I want to be that couple who makes it.

We pass by the Plaza de Romita with all its lush, green trees, a fountain in the center, and a small church built in 1503. The streets are narrower here, but there are so many murals to see.

The first restaurant has a cheerful, orange-and-yellow-painted storefront. Tessa asks to speak to the owner about our new app. A middle-aged man comes out from the kitchen and joins us at the table outside. Tessa quickly goes through our fake pitch PowerPoint. She's nervous, not that it's obvious. Maybe I'm learning to read her. Still, her Spanish sounds impressively fluent.

He nods and responds in Spanish. Tessa translates that he doesn't see a downside, so he's willing to join, but he wants to confirm that there's no up-front fee.

I shake my head. "No. Why would there be an up-front fee? It's to our benefit to have as many restaurants as possible."

Tessa translates my response and his reply back, which he says with some disgust, "Some other apps say that they only want the 'best' restaurants included, but being the best is so subjective that maybe a little payment under the table can help persuade them that you're one of the 'best.'"

"Like Comidas en Canasta?" I ask.

He nods and says in English, "But not from me." He shakes his index finger.

Tessa pulls out a picture of Pamela and asks, "Did she ask you for that 'extra' payment?"

He nods.

It's Pamela. Pamela is the one asking for kickbacks.

But then his face closes down. *"Tengo que ir."* He stands abruptly.

"Gracias," Tessa says. "Do you have a card in case we get funding?"

He shakes his head and backs up into his restaurant, but then he turns and asks, "Do you have a card?"

Does she? I glance at her.

"I'm out, but we'll come back here if we get funding," Tessa says. Smooth.

We move to the next restaurant, an old-fashioned taqueria, and the next. The scenario repeats over and over again. All of these restaurant vendors—except one—have been asked by Pamela for kickbacks in order to join the app. The one exception appears to be the most popular café.

At the last one, we order lunch and sit at the tables outside. The spices in my taco are so good. I scoop up some bits that fell out.

"I didn't expect it to be Pamela," she admits. "Maybe I should have, since they couldn't call the hotline. Even though we have the restaurant vendors saying it's happening, I don't know how we prove it is Pamela. It's not like we can bring in all these shop owners. Especially if they don't want to be on record admitting it."

"Why would Pamela even do this?" I ask. "What's the motivation?"

She leans forward. "Would the motivation excuse it?"

"No. It would help to understand it." Like it helped me to understand why you lied to me.

She sighs. "I'm a lawyer, not a mind reader. Let's finish up our lunch. We need to get back to the office within a reasonable amount of time. Let's go through the rest of the documents, and then we can discuss it back at the hotel."

We spend the afternoon working on the disclosure, and we finish reviewing all the documentation. Tessa leaves to linger around the bathroom and canteen, but neither Ana nor Valeria ever appear. It's probably too risky in the office. She calls the number again for the interior design service, but no one answers. It's definitely suspicious.

We order dinner in so we can keep working. I definitely want to minimize our time in her bedroom. Last night, that black tank top with her bare shoulders and then her long, shapely legs ...

Focus on work.

At eight, we wrap up and leave the office. Frankly, we still don't have much solid evidence. We may need to provoke Pamela to admit it but also not anger her because we are in a business relationship—especially given that I have to continue working with this company.

And don't share an elevator alone with Tessa again.

Chapter Twenty-Eight

Tessa

Zeke mutters he has to talk to the hotel receptionist at the front desk, and I go up in the elevator alone.

Investigations are not easy, especially when conclusive proof is needed. I shift my backpack and wave my card at the door sensor. The green light flashes.

The door slides over a manila envelope addressed to me. A little early for my checkout receipt. I pick up the envelope and throw it on the desk. I slip off my heels. Finally. Then I collapse on the bed and close my eyes.

What can we still do? Ask to speak to Valeria alone? Confront Pamela and pretend we have more solid proof than we do about the kickbacks at the restaurants? That seems too risky. Tomorrow, we can show Roberto the fraudulent invoices and explain the kickback requests we discovered at the restaurants. That's all we have so far.

I should change before Zeke comes over.

Dressed in comfy pants and a T-shirt, I pick up the envelope. It's taped tight, like it's a secret missive.

Like it's a secret missive.

I pull off the duct tape. Out slides a printed sheet of what was obviously an email exchange.

To: Cameron Stone
From Gian

Here's the memo you requested. I did a google search
and populated it.

To: Gian
From: Cameron Stone

I will call you. I told you to CALL for all communi-
cation.

The memo attached is the location scouting report.
Cameron is involved.

And that's why if you want to commit fraud, you need to hire a
smart accomplice. And not someone who emails and creates a paper
record trail.

A typed letter explains that Pamela was paid money for services
that were never provided via the fake interior decoration consultation invoice, while Cameron created the fake location scouting
invoice. And Cameron signed all the invoices without any further
investigation. When a previous employee questioned the interior

decoration consultation invoice, Cameron made her sit and watch him work.

Pamela was the one who wrote up the investigation of that hotline call. And she didn't include that.

But how did they know my hotel room?

Should I be worried?

At least Zeke is with me, and I'm not alone in Mexico City receiving incriminating envelopes in my hotel room.

Is Ana the anonymous emailer? She helped with the hotel arrangements. But would she know the finance issues?

There's a knock on my door. I peek through the keyhole to confirm it's Zeke.

I open the door and let him in. He's also changed into more casual clothes. Wow. The tight, waffle shirt gets me every time.

"I got a secret missive filled with incriminating documents under my door."

Zeke's eyes widen. "Of course you did."

I hand him the packet, and we sit next to each other on the bed.

"Both Cameron and Pamela are involved," I say.

"Even if we didn't have this email, he's not doing his job as CFO if he's not catching the double invoicing for the couches and a fake invoice for interior consulting when they didn't hire a consultant. Roberto couldn't have been more open that he and Pamela came up with the design." He flips through it. "But how did they know your room number? Ana? Do you think you're safe here?"

"I don't think they're pissed at me. I still think it's one of the women. You should leave me alone at some point tomorrow with Valeria."

"Because she reviews the invoices?"

"Yes. Ana and Valeria were smiling and chatting near the coffee station. They rushed away as soon as I approached."

"Maybe they just didn't want to talk to you."

"I'm hurt." I pout.

"I like talking to you." He bumps my shoulder.

"Even though I'm a lawyer?" I ask.

"You're not like any lawyer I've ever met. Maybe because you're a litigator? Paisley was a corporate lawyer. I had no idea being a lawyer involved so much detective work."

"It does because you have to build a case. Especially with my pro bono work. Last weekend, I tried to figure out if this guy is still together with his girlfriend. I staked out the address of his former apartment, where she lives, but I never saw him arrive. There were two entrances, so maybe he used the back one. I'm going to try again when we get back."

"That doesn't seem safe."

"He's never seen me, so I think it's okay." I should have sat on the chair. He's sitting way too close to me on this bed.

"I can come with you."

"It's okay. Trailing is actually pretty boring. And I really don't need help. I'm quite capable of doing it on my own."

"I'm not saying you're not capable. You're more than capable. Or I wouldn't keep hiring you to save my career. But police officers and detectives always work in teams because two are better than one."

He has a point.

"I thought we couldn't be friends," I say.

"We seem to make an excellent professional investigation team," he says.

That's not the direction I want this relationship to go in.

But spending a day together out of the office—even if it is trailing someone—might take this relationship in the direction that I do want it to go in.

"Great," I say. "I'll text you the details."

"I think we have enough now to meet Roberto. I'll text Roberto and ask if we can meet with him tomorrow before anyone arrives at the office." He pulls out his phone and types quickly. Almost immediately, his phone beeps. "He said fine." He glances at the manila envelope on the desk. "Are you sure you're safe here? Maybe we should keep the adjoining door open."

I move to the desk and open up my laptop to add these last revelations to our talking points for our meeting with Roberto. "I'm sure I'm safe tonight. If we don't nail Pamela and Cameron tomorrow, then maybe not."

His eyes widen.

"I'm kidding," I say. "But we can keep the door open. And I *am* relieved that you're with me and that I'm not here by myself."

He takes a moment to absorb this. "I'm glad you suggested I come as well. I'll knock before I open the door."

Zeke disappears back into his room through the front door. I get ready for bed. I'm relieved we have some evidence now.

I unlock my side of the adjoining door, turn off the lights, and slide into bed.

There's a click on his side, and then the door slightly opens. "Can I open it?"

"Yes."

Zeke rustles about in his room, and then his lights go off.

"Good night," he says, the deep timbre of his voice reaching out to me through the darkness. I turn onto my side. The sheets are crisp, like they've been starched. They smell of vanilla. His sheets rustle. My face flushes as I remember feeling the hard muscles of his back and the way he chuckled into my mouth and then said that tickles as my one hand moved to his back. And the way he tasted of peppermint. I hug my extra pillow. It's going to be a long night. And we both need to be absolutely in top form tomorrow when we tell Roberto that Cameron and Pamela are stealing money from Comidas en Canasta.

Chapter Twenty-Nine

Zeke

We meet Roberto at 7 a.m. in the morning in his office. Behind his desk is a framed, red-and-blue painting. Along the side walls are pictures of him and his wife with two smiling boys. We sit in the two chairs in front of his desk. No couch.

I explain that we received an email alleging fraud, so we came down to investigate and write the investment status report at the same time. Tessa gives him a short memo outlining what we think Pamela and Cameron are doing: the fabricated invoices, the unknown bank account payment, the duplicate invoices for the couches, and the kickbacks from the restaurant vendors. It doesn't look like much, but frauds generally start small to avoid detection.

"We didn't hire anyone to do location scouting or provide design services," Roberto says. He frowns.

I hand him the invoices for the office scouting and the design services.

"And what do you mean by kickbacks?" Roberto points at the last bullet point.

We explain further about our conversations with restaurant vendors. He looks horrified.

"*No. No. Eso es terrible.* That is not what Comidas en Canasta is supposed to be about. That ruins our reputation. Do you have the names of the vendors? I must reimburse them and apologize."

We hand him the list we've compiled and then give Roberto the fake couch invoice.

"I can't believe this of Pamela. Cameron recommended her." He stares at the documents. "And Cameron didn't catch it? That's not acceptable. We've been friends since B-school in the US. I know he is dating Pamela, but I thought he believed in this."

He stands and paces back and forth, running his hand through his thick, black hair. *"No es posible."* He faces us. "But how do you know he approved these?"

"Isn't that his signature to process them?" I ask.

"And here's the email exchange that was included in the packet that has Cameron requesting a location scouting memo," Tessa says. "We can ask your IT vendor to confirm it's real, but it looks real to us."

Roberto takes the printout and reads it. His face falls. *"Qué carajo! No entiendo."*

Tessa translates that Roberto said he didn't understand, but I don't need a translation. It's obvious Roberto is angry and upset.

Both of us avert our eyes as he takes a moment to collect himself.

"If you have local employment counsel, this is more their jurisdiction than ours as to next steps," Tessa says.

Roberto nods and emits a deep sigh. "Does anyone else know? How did you find these documents?" He sits back down at his desk. He's pale but looks resolved.

We explain our process. He asks us for a recommendation for local employment counsel to avoid using the one hired by Pamela. Tessa emails her law firm and Brooke for suggestions and gives Roberto the name of the recommended firm.

There's a knock on the door, and Cameron sticks his head in. "You guys are starting early. All going okay? I thought you might need me at some point today to review the disclosure language."

I stand, blocking the view of Roberto. "We do. We were giving an update to Roberto." I check my watch. "Are you available at 9:30? We have a few things to finish up here. Should we come to your office, or do you want to meet us in the conference room?"

"My office is good." Cameron closes the door behind him.

"We do have disclosure to discuss with him," I say.

Roberto nods. "*Está bien.* I'll call the lawyers and let you know. They'll probably want to speak directly with you as well. I'll try to arrange that for lunchtime."

We spend the morning reviewing the financial disclosure with Cameron. And then we discuss our findings and strategy at the offices of the local employment lawyer during the afternoon. We return to Comidas en Canasta with the local lawyer. While we're sequestered in the conference room, finalizing the disclosure, Roberto and the local HR lawyer confront Pamela and Cameron separately, and fire them.

The office is eerily quiet.

"Should we have pushed harder to attend those meetings?" I ask. It feels so anticlimactic.

Tessa shakes her head. "No. I don't like attending those meetings where people are fired. And this is the company's internal business—to be conducted consistent with Mexican law."

"You're right." I turn back to the midyear report. We reschedule our flight for late this evening, as we're done here.

Later, Roberto joins us in the conference room to give us an update. He says, "Cameron asked for a second chance. He and Pamela had gambling debts and needed to tide themselves over. They were planning to reimburse the money. I said no."

Roberto shakes his head. "How can he repair the damage to our reputation from what she did with the vendors? How could he? He wanted to know how you figured it out, so I told him discrepancies surfaced while you were doing your due diligence. I didn't want him to know about Ana or Valeria. Valeria has been following up with restaurant vendors, and we've reimbursed the twenty who were required to pay this kickback."

Roberto looks down at his desk.

"I've promoted Valeria as the new CFO, and she plans to rehire the woman who filed the first hotline report. I'll use our new employment counsel for HR matters—at least for now. Ana and Valeria told me that they'd contacted Brooke. They'd felt more comfortable approaching her as a woman and trusted her integrity. They also left the envelope for you. I've thanked them both. I'm sorry they didn't feel they could come to me directly, and I've asked them what I can do to make them trust me."

"I think your actions now have probably given them that trust in you," Tessa says.

Roberto smiles faintly. "That's what they said."

He looks tired but more hopeful than he had earlier.

"*Muchas gracias.*" He clasps both of our hands warmly. "You shouldn't mix business and friendship. I know that. It's my mistake too."

Yes. Dating Paisley publicly in the office was most definitely a mistake for me. If Tessa and I are going to continue to work together, it's better not to date. But …

I nudge Tessa and tell her to show Roberto the increased returns from her prior investigation experiences to give him hope. She pulls that slide up on her pitch PowerPoint and explains again how increased morale led to an increase in revenue.

"That makes me feel better. We will see," Roberto says. "I hope you're right. Thank you again."

Tessa shakes his hand and smiles brightly at him. That huge, warm smile. As much as this case was a reminder that business and friendship don't mix, my resolve to not date Tessa again is slipping. I should give her a second chance. The way we work together, I'm not imagining this connection. I can trust her. I think.

Roberto sits back down heavily and shudders as if it's too much. Betrayed by a close friend and colleague—and about his dream company.

My brain flashes back to my memory of that moment of betrayal when I'd realized Paisley had cheated on me.

Paisley came over to my apartment, her hair wet. It wasn't raining outside. She was supposedly coming from her new job at the office.

"I was at the gym, and I took a shower," she said.

But I'd been at our gym.

She had not been there.

But I still couldn't believe it.

"Our gym on 79th Street?" I asked.

And then she told me that she'd slept with someone else. She'd just showered at his place. I couldn't breathe. I've never had that feeling before. When I could breathe again, I asked her to leave. I broke it off right then and there. It was over.

Chapter Thirty

Tessa

As I WALK UP to the 72nd Street subway entrance in the island in the middle of Broadway, Zeke is there, holding a closed umbrella. At 6 a.m. on a gray Saturday, the streets are empty, except for one lone jogger and a man sleeping on cardboard under scaffolding. Zeke sips from an aluminum thermos. I didn't dare have coffee to make sure I wouldn't have to pee during this stakeout. We might be out all day.

I wave and cross the street. "Early enough for you?"

I'm still surprised he wanted to come. I wouldn't be caught dead getting up this early unless I *really* liked the guy. Or I was helping a client. I shake my head. *We're just friends.* We make a good team. That's what he'd said. And this is my chance to show him that I'm a fundamentally good person.

He's not ready to date, but he's here. Spending the day with me, trailing some scammer guy. So that says a lot.

Zeke is wearing a worn T-shirt and jeans. He looks so good. Frickin' butterflies as I gaze at him. Is he trying to torture me?

He holds the green, wooden door open for me as we enter the subway station. Inside, black-and-white signs direct passengers to go left or right for uptown or downtown trains.

"This is him?" He holds up his phone to show the picture I forwarded yesterday.

"Yes. Taylor took that photo last Sunday when she tried tailing him."

"You think he has another girlfriend and was using Taylor's grandmother to get her apartment? That's a hell of a long game."

I glance sharply at him. I wasn't expecting Zeke to come along to be the voice of reason.

"The rent is three hundred dollars a month. A rent-controlled two bedroom in West Harlem."

"That's incentive enough," Zeke says. "Is this usual? I didn't realize lawyers were trailing people around."

I shrug. "It's not. But I honestly don't know what else to do. He's managed to tick all the boxes to show he's a common-law spouse. It's too neatly wrapped up." *I really hope I'm right.*

"You're really suspicious."

I continue, ignoring that commentary. "And lawyers will definitely search through any of your social media posts and hire private investigators. But I can't afford to employ one, so it's up to Taylor and me to do the legwork. It's actually great that you're coming along because we can switch trailing at 59th Street—if he is going to this address in Queens. I'll text you what subway car we're in so you can wait at 59th Street and pick him up and trail him from there. I'll drop back and meet you in Queens—if he does go there."

I tap my card and pass through the turnstile. He follows.

"Clever plan." He slides his mug into his backpack.

"I know this isn't helping me to convince you that I'm not a master of deception—"

He snorts. "I already know you're not a master of deception."

I shoot him a stern "be quiet" look. "I'll see you at 59th Street."

I jog down the steps to the platform for the uptown No. 1 train. Across the tracks, Zeke waves at me from the downtown platform right before a subway pulls into the station and blocks him from view.

At 125th Street, I text Taylor that I'm on my way to the building.

Taylor: *My friend is at the back exit.*

Me: *I'm at the front exit.*

Taylor: *He just left the apartment. Mrs. Humming called.*

And we're on.

Mr. Howard exits the front entrance of the building, a short, muscular figure hunched over, wearing a heavy raincoat to shield himself from the drizzle. I follow him, using my umbrella to hide my face.

Luckily, he is a slow walker. I cross the street and walk up the metal stairs on the other side so that I'm not directly behind him. The 125th Street Station is outside on an elevated platform. Once he passes through the turnstile, I follow. A few other people wait on the downtown track platform. I stand on the open platform under my umbrella as he takes shelter under the iron awning.

The subway approaches, the station platform shaking slightly, even though the train reduces speed. I get in the same subway car as Howard but enter at the other end. I take the two-person seat near the door and pull out a newspaper to hide my face. He's seated at the opposite end. I text Zeke my approximate subway car location.

If the subway car fills up, I won't be able to see Howard. I bite my lip.

The hearing is this week. This is our one chance to determine where he's going on weekends. If we lose him, our last option is to stake out the potential girlfriend's apartment.

The subway fills up as we proceed downtown. I stand and move to the middle so I can see him. The train gets absolutely packed at 72nd Street, and I'm smooshed between three people, with no visibility at all. At 66th Street, as some passengers get off, I use that opportunity to move closer to him.

As we approach 59th Street, I text Zeke. My text doesn't go through.

Howard's not getting up. Maybe he's not leaving. But Zeke will then join us on the train.

The doors open on the 59th Street platform, and Howard slips out the door. I follow him but let him get ahead of me. Zeke texts me that he's picked Howard up and they are on the B train. I drop back and also get on the B train but at the other end. Zeke texts that they've switched to the E, so it does appear he's on his way to this apartment in Queens. I also switch to the E. Howard gets off at the stop closest to his "former" address.

Me: *Will run ahead and see if I can get to that apartment floor.*

I didn't tell Zeke this part of the plan in case he objected.

Zeke: *Be careful.*

As soon as I'm out of the subway, I run ahead to the apartment building. I tell security I'm there to meet a client and show my law firm ID. The guard nods and tells me to sign in. I scrawl some illegible signature. I'll be on the security cameras, but that's okay. This guard is glued to his phone instead of the video footage on the screens in front of him.

If Howard does show up, I'll ask for the security camera footage. Maybe it will show a persistent pattern of living here over the weekend.

A minute from entrance to elevator.

I get off the elevator on his floor.

Zeke: *He entered building.*

No time to check out where the security cameras are situated. It sounds like a family is about to exit the apartment across from his. I slip into the garbage room. I use tacky wax to stick a mirror at head height to the garbage room door and prop the door open. And then I stand just inside and catch my breath. The hallway is visible in the reflection. If he comes to shut the door, it's game over, unless he believes I'm some new neighbor throwing out garbage. I wait.

A grinding sound comes from the elevator bank.

He walks out. *Yes.* Heavy, plodding footsteps. Howard inserts a key into the keyhole. *He still has keys.* And then a woman opens the door, talking excitedly, and she hugs him. *And they kiss.*

Yes! My hunch was correct.

His deep voice responds in an unintelligible murmur.

The family that was getting ready emerges into the hallway, and the high pitch of the excited kids' voices echoes in the hallway.

"You need to share your marinade recipe before you move," the neighbor says.

Bingo. The neighbor just confirmed he lives there and is only now "moving." Maybe I can interview this neighbor.

"I tell you it's easy," he responds. "And we definitely need your picadillo recipe."

Nobody is carrying any garbage, thankfully. I text Zeke.

> Me: *Neighbor woman with 3 kids coming out. She has red shirt. Kids wearing blue shirts. Can you follow?*

> Zeke: *On it.*

It's a good lead. Although neighbors will usually be reluctant to testify.

The family takes the elevator, and Howard's door closes.

The hallway is now quiet. I remove my mirror and look around for the placement of the security cameras, then hurry back to the stairwell.

Me: *Coming down. He kissed woman!*

I get into the elevator on the next floor.

On the ground floor, I approach the security guard.

"I'm a lawyer investigating a housing court case, and I'd like to see your security camera footage. Is there someone I can talk to about that?"

"Sure." The guard scribbles a number down on a piece of paper and hands it to me. "Try him."

"Thank you." I leave the building.

Zeke: *At playground around north corner.*

I find Zeke by the CVS next to the playground. I tell him what I saw and what the neighbor said.

"But maybe they got back together after the grandmother died?" he asks.

"Still. Show a bit of respect for your last girlfriend and have some waiting time. It's only been a few months. If you really cared for someone, how can you immediately jump into another relationship? Even if it's returning to a former flame." I huff. "But I get your point."

I stare at the window display of suntan lotion in the CVS window. "I'm still going to argue he and Mrs. Robinson were not in a relationship. But if he insists that they were, he was not faithful. My argument is that he was also in a relationship with Ms. Morris that preceded his 'relationship' with Mrs. Robinson and that he was just using Mrs. Robinson for her apartment. I need to show him romantically involved with Ms. Morris during the time in question."

I bite my lip. "We'll see what the video footage shows. If they even have any. Maybe the neighbor will be willing to talk to us. And then I think we should hang around and see if they leave together. If we could get a photo of them physically together, that might at least spark some doubt in his picture of devotion to Taylor's grandmother."

"Won't the security company want a subpoena?"

"Not always."

I call the number the security guard gave me. I explain that I'm a lawyer on a housing court case requesting permission to see any security camera footage for a specific hallway for any weekends that they still have. The guy says sure and that they retain the footage for sixty days. He gives me the central office address. I make an appointment for Monday.

"Okay, let's go talk to the neighbor," I say.

"What? How are we going to talk to her?"

"We're newly engaged and looking for an apartment in that building." I came up with that on the fly, but it definitely fits my goal of getting us closer.

Zeke blinks. "We're engaged?"

Chapter Thirty-One

Zeke

Tessa winks at me. "Keep up with the program."

She grabs my hand and pulls me along to the playground entrance. I grip her hand back. It's so small, and yet, she's such a force. She unhooks the playground gate and swings it open. The small playground has a slide, a swing set off in the corner behind another gated enclosure, a colorful, yellow-and-blue, metal structure for climbing, and a square sandlot.

"I don't think this is a good idea," I say, following her inside the playground.

She hooks the gate closed. "That's great. You should look reluctant. That will make this seem more credible."

"I'm not acting."

"Excellent. You should also not think of this as acting."

She's definitely not listening to me.

She pulls me over to where the neighbor is sitting on a bench, watching her children play in a sandlot.

"Excuse me. I know this is extremely forward and random, but we're looking for apartments in this neighborhood, and I thought we should ask some people who might live around here for advice.

We just got engaged." Tessa waves at the playground. "I thought you might live nearby."

"I do," the woman says slowly, cautiously, as one should when approached by a stranger in New York City asking personal information.

"Great." Tessa sits next to her and pats the bench for me to join her. I stay standing.

"He's a little shy," Tessa says. "Anyway, we're looking at Garden Towers. Do you know anything about that building? I'm hoping most tenants are long term. It seems like a stable building with a lot of families and married couples. How is the super? Is he responsive? Any issues with heat or noise?"

"Give her a chance to talk," I mutter.

"Sorry," Tessa says. "I wanted to make sure she knew I had legitimate questions."

"I do live there. It's a good building. The super has been there many years and feels like family. Our neighbors have lived across from us for about ten years. They're planning to move, so maybe their apartment will open up."

"A couple lives in the apartment? Is it a one bedroom?" Tessa asks.

"Yes, a couple lives there," she says. "It's a one bedroom."

"Why are they moving? Not because of the building, I hope?"

"They found a new apartment in the city, closer to her job."

"That's the dream. We can't afford that yet," Tessa says. "He's a photographer, and I'm going to be working for FLAFL."

My head whips toward hers. *I'm a what?* Way to invent on the fly.

"FLAFL? Are you a lawyer?" the neighbor asks.

"Yes."

"That's great. My friend needs a lawyer." She pulls out her phone. "And you're a photographer?"

I nod. Reluctantly.

"Can you take a picture of my kids for me?"

"Uh ... I didn't bring my equipment." I shoot a concerned look at Tessa. She's supposed to be the artist, not me. "But I'm happy to take one of you with your kids."

"Hold on." She dials a number on her phone. "My friend. Her landlord won't fix her toilet. It's been a month. I told her she needs to talk to a lawyer. I'm calling her now."

"If you want, I can take a photograph, and then we can mail you a print if you give me your address," I say. That will confirm her address.

Tessa stares at me, and I wink at her.

"Yes, great idea." The woman tells her friend that a FLAFL lawyer is at the playground and to hurry down.

"Ms. Peres." She recites her address and phone number while I note it in my phone.

The three children sit next to her on the bench while I take a photo with my iPhone. Let's hope I'm a better photographer than Tessa was a painter. My sister gifted me a photography class once because I take the annual photograph of her family for her Christmas card so I have some experience.

Tessa peeks over my shoulder at the photo, the apple smell of her hair wafting over, and says it looks great. I take a whole bunch. The mom smiles at the snapshots.

I can see why Tessa likes doing this detective work. It feels good.

Another mom comes over. The neighbor introduces us by profession to this mom, and that mom asks me to photograph her and her children. I agree, and she hands me her phone. Tessa jumps up and down behind me to get the kids to smile. I glance back, at one point, and miss the shot because I laugh at the face she's making.

"So how did you guys meet?" the neighbor woman asks as I return her phone.

"We met at an art opening," Tessa says. "How did you meet your husband?"

"Block party. He was a friend of a friend."

The woman turns to me. "You must have had a romantic proposal as a photographer. How did you propose?"

I blink. I'm so out of my league.

"I proposed to him," Tessa says.

I smile. "You should tell them the story of how you proposed, snookums. It's a good one." *You're the one responsible for this cha-rade.*

"I'm sure they don't want to hear it. Not if they were expecting something romantic," Tessa says.

"I love proposal stories," both women say.

"It really wasn't romantic." She is totally stalling for time. But I'm also relieved that she doesn't have a ready-to-go fantasy in her head of how she wants to be proposed to. Wyatt was her first serious boyfriend. Had she wanted him to propose? Why hasn't she dated anyone seriously since?

"It was romantic to me." I can't help teasing her. This is definitely fun.

"I made a PowerPoint presentation," she says.

Our glances meet. *Is she referring to her PowerPoint pitch to give her a second chance?*

"A PowerPoint?" Both of the women appear horrified. They look back and forth between us.

I've clearly lost all credence as a romantic guy.

"I was over at his apartment working late. And I asked him if he could review my PowerPoint to see if it made sense. And I'd put a whole bunch of pictures of our relationship in there—meeting at this art opening, biking over the Brooklyn Bridge, dancing late at night, helping each other at work." She holds my glance. "And he said yes."

My lips curve. I was impressed by Tessa's presentation even if I tried hard not to show it.

"Aww. That is romantic."

"Were you surprised?" the second mom asks.

I glance at Tessa. "She always surprises me."

"Well, I can tell that you're going to last. I have a good sense for that."

Her friend laughs and affectionately punches her arm. "She always says that. But she does have a good sense for that. And I agree." She turns to Tessa. "The way he gazes at you. That's the way mine looks at me. That's the way you want a man to look at you."

Do I look at her like that?

I can't. I thought I was keeping it all hidden.

"Like that?" Tessa asks.

The friend waves her hand. "Not like that. That's the way they look when they've been caught."

I school my face.

At that moment, her other friend arrives and explains that the landlord keeps saying he's going to fix the toilet, but he doesn't. They're using a bucket of water to flush the toilet. She and Tessa sit on the bench together. Tessa leans forward, totally immersed in this woman's plight, her desire to help palpable. I snap a quick shot.

"I have a contact in the Queens FLAFL office. I can put you guys in touch. But you should also contact your council member since you live in New York City housing. I used to help with these types of cases when I was a legislative assistant for a council member. Here, let me write some emails for you," Tessa says. "But I also recommend this YouTube video. It shows how to fix a toilet."

The two other moms are swiping through the photos, looking delighted and showing them to each other.

"Which one do you like best?" I ask.

They each show me the one they like best, and I tell them I'll send them a print.

Tessa stands, having sent the emails. "It was great to meet you."

"We have to go," I say.

We walk away, back to the apartment entrance.

"You didn't ask them much about Howard," I say.

"No, not yet," she says. "They seemed too close. I wasn't sure if I could trust them. But I still got useful information that corroborates my hunch, and hopefully, the video footage will be conclusive. Do you want to watch the entrance? If we can get some videos of him with this other woman, that would be great."

"Sure. And you didn't think I'd be helpful?"

"I didn't realize that this was a multi-person operation. I'm glad you came." She smiles at me. She has such a mischievous grin, like we're kids up to no good.

It's hard to be inconspicuous on this block. There are no stores. We move a bit down the block and lean against a brick wall of a building.

"Why was I a photographer?" I ask.

"I didn't think I should say you work on Wall Street. And I definitely don't want to say you're a doctor or anything that might require immediate services. I didn't realize that they'd all want you to take pictures. What do you want to be next time?"

"Is there going to be a next time?"

She looks up at me. "That depends on you. I still think we should give this a try."

The attraction is still there.

I look at her like I like her.

I do like her.

Even more now that I know her better.

I swallow. I avoid eye contact for a moment and then turn back to her. "You know you're a little crazy."

"Only a little? In a good way or a bad way?"

"Is there a good way or a bad way?"

"You're the one who wanted to date a 'creative artist,' my dear." She makes air quotes with my hands. "You don't think artists are a little crazy? Lawyers also have license to be crazy, although I prefer to call it creative."

I shake my head. "Touché."

She pulls a book out of her bag.

"You're reading my dad's book?" I ask.

"I thought I should."

"I'm touched."

"It's gripping. I might finish it today. Except I'm afraid that I'll get so involved, I'll forget to look up and check if Howard has emerged. But your dad must also have a lot of creativity because these plot twists are clever."

I smile. "You're right. He's a good crazy too." I pull out my book, and we lean there, reading, looking up periodically to check the building entrance. It's a comfortable feeling—to read side by side.

An hour passes. No Mr. Howard.

She bites her nail. "If you send me the photos, I'll get them developed and mail them to Ms. Peres."

"No, I'll do it. It's my reputation on the line. You're lucky my sister made me take a photography class."

"I'll pay you back."

"It was fun." Our glances meet, and we both can't help grinning at each other. I look away first.

"Would you like some peanut M&Ms? I brought you your own pack." She opens up her backpack.

"I was expecting a bit more exciting grub in your backpack than peanut M&Ms."

"Peanut M&Ms are actually filling. I often rely on them when I have to work through a meal." She steps away from the wall and stretches. "I'm thinking that even if we snapped a picture of them together, it might not be so useful compared to the other stuff we have. And as you said, he could have just restarted this relationship. Should we get lunch? My treat. There's a deli on the corner. I can pick up sandwiches while you watch the building entrance."

"Sure." I give her my order. She waves goodbye and walks down the street toward the deli. Once she's out of sight, I return to watching the building.

There's Mr. Howard, leaving. I text Tessa.

Me: *He left the building. Alone. I'm following.*

Chapter Thirty-Two

Zeke

Mr. Howard enters the deli—the same one Tessa disappeared into. The front window is plastered with sale signs, so I can't see in. Ice cream is two-for-one. Huge posters announce reduced prices on rice, pasta, and beer. Another handwritten banner says: "Grab Your Goya Beans! On Sale Now."

Do I follow? Tessa is already in there. We don't need both of us. If I go in and he leaves immediately, it will look obvious if I follow him out. I bite my lip.

I should stay outside. Tessa can handle it. I retreat to wait for him or Tessa to emerge.

> Me: *He entered deli.*

As if she doesn't know.

> Me: *Are you ok?*

No answer. We should have used those walkie-talkie earpieces. Maybe she can't respond if she's ordering or paying.

Still, that guy was muscular. And I came along because I didn't like the thought of her being alone, trailing some scammer. He might get violent if he feels threatened.

And now we know he is involved with Ms. Morris.

I jog back to the deli.

I'm sure she can take care of herself. She can probably talk herself out of any situation.

Better safe than sorry.

I push the door open. The bell jingles. Every inch of space has been used to showcase products. Stacks of cans are lined up on the rows of shelves in front of me. Behind a clear, plastic barrier, the deli guy mans the front counter, bright packets of candy in the shallow bay shelving underneath.

I look down the aisle for Tessa.

Howard has backed her up in the corner.

I move slowly down the narrow corridor toward the two of them.

"You're following me. I know you," Mr. Howard says. "You're Robinson's lawyer. I looked you up."

"I am Ms. Robinson's lawyer," Tessa says. "I can't speak to you without your lawyer present."

"Two turkey sandwiches ready," the counter guy calls out.

Tessa moves to get them, but Howard blocks her. He has a broad chest like a bull.

"You can't talk to me?" Mr. Howard gets in her face. "You can follow me, but you can't talk to me?"

Tessa stands straighter, holding her ground.

"Come get two turkey sandwiches," counter guy repeats. He's trying.

"Sir," I say. I think I'm allowed to talk to him.

He turns slightly. I can't get between him and Tessa. There's not enough space.

"You appear to be threatening my fiancée," I say.

"Two turkey sandwiches," deli guy calls again.

Mr. Howard turns toward me. "I wasn't threatening. I don't like being followed, and I don't like someone claiming they can't talk to me."

"Let's go," Tessa says. "Let me pick up our sandwiches. I already paid for them. And you can tell Mr. Howard that this rule exists to protect him." Tessa scoots from behind Mr. Howard toward the counter, pulling me with her. I hold her hand but face Howard, walking backward, so I can watch him. She grabs the two sandwiches.

He stays where he is. Tessa tugs me out the front door.

"What were you doing? He could have hurt you," she says as soon as we're outside.

"He could have hurt *you*," I say.

"It's not going to go well for him if he punches the opposing lawyer," she says. "He could've punched you."

"That's all very rational, but what if he is angry and irrational?" I ask.

"Point taken." She holds me by the hand and quickens her pace. "Let's get out of his vicinity. I have no idea where we can eat our sandwiches, though. We need to find another playground or park."

I like Tessa pulling me by the arm and being concerned about me.

Google Maps shows another playground nearby, and we walk there. The sprinklers are on, and kids are running in and out of the water, shrieking. We unlock the gate and slip inside to sit on a bench shaded by a tree.

"I feel like I need a child to be here." I unwrap my sandwich and take a bite.

"Maybe for our next escapade, I can arrange that."

"I wouldn't be surprised if you did."

"I don't think my sister is going to lend me her baby for one of my escapades. But I'm glad you're still in for another one." Tessa drinks some water. "We should have left immediately. It was silly to wait around, especially because a photo from today won't prove much."

Tessa's phone beeps and she checks it and exclaims.

"Something good?" I ask.

"Iris just texted me that Scammer Guy is showcasing my paintings on his Instagram account. Look." She shows me his account on her phone, and indeed, there is her painting of what I think was supposed to be a tree in rain.

"I was wondering what was happening with him." It's a question I've wanted to ask ever since we started talking again, but I also didn't want to raise what broke us up.

"Not much yet. I've been so busy with work that I've had to put him off, but he seems to think I'm an artist. He's following the same course of action that he followed with the artist who alerted us about him. He should try his check fraud next."

"I saw you guys once, meeting at a café in the village. I was out with some friends for dinner."

"Really? That's the last time I saw him. I pretended we were still together so he would think I had a boyfriend. Were you in the café?"

"Yes, behind you."

"That was you?" she asks. "Were you wearing a wig?"

"Yes," I say sheepishly. "I didn't want either of you to recognize me."

"I thought that was you. I thought I was going crazy, hoping to see you."

"Hoping to see me?" I ask.

She holds my glance.

"Yes," she says.

I look away first.

"That wig." She laughs.

"You're definitely seeing that wig again," I say. "I've told Sebastian I'm wearing it to his next party because he was so embarrassed by it." I pause, realizing what I've just said. "You were good at helping out that woman with her plumbing problem."

"It's frustrating. When I worked on these types of cases as a legislative assistant for a New York City council member right after college, I thought it probably would be faster if I learned how to fix that kind of stuff, and they sent me out. Faster than my calling this city agency every day to see if they can send a plumber over. I finally did just that in a previous FLAFL case. I watched a YouTube video, and I fixed the running toilet."

I finish my sandwich. Tessa calls Taylor to warn her and some neighbor woman that Howard saw her in his neighborhood. She'll check the security footage on Monday. She practically does a little hop as she says that he *kissed* the woman at the apartment. She hangs up.

"I can certainly cross-examine him now and ask him about this apartment and this woman. It will buttress Mrs. Humming's testimony," she says. "I wasn't sure I had much of a case. Can I make dinner for you tonight as a thank-you?"

I want to say yes. Her lying about being an artist is not comparable to Paisley's cheating.

It's also clear that she's absolutely devoted to getting justice for her pro bono client. We've just spent seven hours seeing if we can get some evidence for this case. And it doesn't even count toward the bonus she wants. She goes all out for her clients. Even that fake pitch document. I'm not sure we would have discovered the kickbacks without it. And if we hadn't discovered that Pamela was asking for kickbacks, we wouldn't have been able to rectify the damage to Comidas en Canasta's name. I was half-surprised Tessa didn't pull out business cards when that manager asked for one.

It's only 1 p.m. now. The sky darkens.

"We need to pick a recipe and go food shopping," she says. "I think it's about to rain, though."

"Can you cook?" I do appreciate a home-cooked meal.

She sighs dramatically. "Yes. I take food very seriously. And to be fair, when I said I was an artist, I didn't expect to have to demonstrate my artistic ability."

"Okay." I'm having fun. I like being with her. Maybe we can just be friends.

She grins at me, the whole smile lighting up her face, and I want to kiss her. *Maybe not.*

"Great," she says. "I promise not to poison you. Do you have any allergies?"

"No."

Drops of water fall. We both run to the subway entrance as the rain pelts down. Her upturned face glistens with water.

She taps her card and pushes through the turnstile. We jog down the steps to the platform. The next train is in five minutes.

"Do you mind if we read on the way home?" she asks. "I'm in a really good part, and I want to finish."

"I'll tell my dad that you chose to read his book over talking to me. It's a compliment to him."

She glances at me. "It's also a compliment to you. I think one of the most important characteristics in a mate is that they give you the freedom to do your own thing. I see that with my parents. Of course, it's great if you enjoy the same things. But if you don't, and you each allow the other person to pursue their own interests, that helps to give a relationship breathing room. It definitely involves a bit of trust too—that that passion won't take them away from you."

I stare at her. There's a lot to unpack in what she just said. *Mate. What makes a relationship last. Pursuing passions. Trust.*

I don't even know where to begin.

"Don't look so scared. I'm only saying it's a compliment to you too." She opens her book, her shoulder brushing mine, and ignores me, turning the page.

Fine. I pull my book out of my backpack. "Can we stop by my apartment on the way back and walk my dog?"

We decide we'll stop by Tessa's apartment, pick out some recipes, and then cook them at my place after food shopping. Then my dog, Brit, isn't alone for the evening.

Tessa pulls out five cookbooks and lays them on her kitchen counter. Her kitchen is in a long hallway that connects the front living room with the back two bedrooms.

"What's your preference? And what can I get you to drink? We have white wine, water..." She looks in the refrigerator. "And water."

"Water is good."

The cookbooks are definitely well loved, with wrinkled pages, recipes tabbed. I open them up, but I'm not someone who cooks anything beyond the basics.

"How do you have time to cook?" I ask.

"I usually only cook on the weekends. I find it kind of relaxing and yet productive. It takes my mind off work because I have to concentrate on the recipe. And I like feeding my friends."

"What do you recommend? I'll put myself in your hands."

"Will you?" She tilts her head, exposing her neck. "Here's your water. In my favorite mug." She hands me a mug that says: I'M A LAWYER LET'S ASSUME I'M ALWAYS RIGHT.

I snort. "That's pretty much the perfect gift for you."

"Miranda gave it to me." She flips through one cookbook. "Let's try one new recipe and one tried-and-true recipe. Let's prepare this braised fennel with radicchio and parmesan. That looks yummy, and then I can make a turkey meatball curry with leeks and rice. Can you make a list of the ingredients so we can go shopping?" She hands me a pad that was sitting next to the stove.

"Sure. But both recipes say they make enough for six."

"Don't worry. We love leftovers, and I can give some to my downstairs neighbors." She leans close to me to read the recipe over my shoulder. I breathe in the apple scent of her shampoo. She moves away again and grabs an opened bottle of white wine and lemon juice out of the refrigerator and puts them in her backpack, along with some other stuff. I finish writing out the list of ingredients and read them aloud to her to confirm what we need to buy.

She grabs two Fresh Direct shopping bags, and we head outside. The sun peeking out casts a golden glaze over the buildings, although the street and trees are still slicked wet.

We walk down the brownstone-lined side street, and I'm very conscious of her presence. I want to hold her hand.

We're friends.

I can't date her.

I may not have seen any red flags when I first dated Paisley, but here, red-flag bunting marks the start line. Beware! Danger ahead!

We wander around the aisles of Fairway and pick up food like a couple. In a good way. In a way that I'd like to continue.

It's a bevy of colors in the produce and fruit departments. Orange, green, yellow, and red peppers are all lined up on top of each other to create blocks of color. Like a work of art.

Can she really cook?

She glances over at me. "You're looking at me very suspiciously."

"I am?" She can read me well. "It's true. I'm wondering if this is another one of your plots, following the old adage that the way to a man's heart is through his stomach."

She shakes her head. "This is honestly what it looks like. I'm thanking you by making you a meal. And I will say that the way to my heart ... well, someone who can cook is definitely a keeper."

"I can't cook," I blurt out. Like an idiot.

She pats me on the arm. "Sometimes it's all about the effort."

As we pass by the spice shelves, I suggest we pick up whatever spices we need.

"You must have some spices."

"Curry, salt, and pepper," I say. "If we need anything else, we should get them."

We buy the rest of what we need.

After checking out, we walk back, each carrying a huge Fresh Direct bag. She stops by Levain Bakery to pick up a chocolate chip cookie for dessert. The late-afternoon sun glints off the buildings.

Brit greets us excitedly as I open the door to my one-bedroom apartment. "And this is Brit."

My boxer wags her tail excitedly. Tessa kneels down, and Brit licks her face. She sits on the floor and pets Brit.

And I swear, my heart melts a little bit. She's a dog person. Paisley didn't want any pets, so Brit was my breakup gift to myself.

"I need to walk her after dinner," I say. "My neighbor's teenager walked her around noon, so she's okay for a bit."

My kitchen is an open concept in the back of the living room with my bedroom off to the side. I show her where everything is. She hands me a cutting board, the onions to dice, and an apple to peel and shred.

She ties her hair up into a ponytail and chops the fennel. Then she sets about combining the various ingredients in a bowl to make the meatballs. She unearths a hand mixer from her backpack.

"You brought a hand mixer?" I ask.

"You said to come prepared," she says. "Do you have one?"

"No." I peer over her shoulder to see what else is in the backpack. "Is that like the Mary Poppins' bag?"

She tilts her head and looks at me. We're so close. Her lips part, and I hesitate. I want to kiss her. I pull back.

"Did you ever want to be a public interest lawyer?" I busy myself at the counter.

"Yes. That's why I went to law school. I summered my first year at FLAFL as an intern. Another lawyer recommended I practice at a law firm first to earn money to pay off my loans and because it's valuable legal experience. And I do enjoy it."

"Why'd you want to work for FLAFL?" I ask.

She pauses as she's pouring milk into the mixing bowl, and it's like she's thinking about what to say. Or rather what to tell me.

Finally, she says, "To do good."

I divide my chopped onions into two separate bowls per her directions and shred the apple. She hesitated too long when answering. I didn't pass whatever test she has for deciding whether to give the short or long answer. The real reason.

"But there must have been something specific that made you want to become a public interest lawyer," I say.

"Must there?"

"Yes." I nod. "Because otherwise, you'd be happy with working as a corporate lawyer and doing some pro bono on the side."

She glances at me sharply. "Yes. You're right." She blinks.

"But I didn't pass the test for you to tell me?"

"It's not a test per se. But it's not something I'm sharing willy-nilly."

She checks the recipe page and hands me some leeks to cut up. Bowls of chopped-up onions, fennel, radicchio, and shredded apple cluster all over the counter. I wash the broccoli in the colander. As the leeks boil in a pot of water, she puts on a pot of rice.

"Can't you tell me?" I ask.

"If I recall correctly, you never did tell me something embarrassing about yourself."

"I thought my telling you that my ex cheated on me for three months, and I didn't suspect a thing, was pretty embarrassing. And I didn't believe my best friend, Ben, when he told me he'd seen her with another guy."

"What made you believe it, then?"

I look away and grip the counter. I was so stupid. So naïve.

"I caught her in the lie. And then she told me. She saw Ben when he saw her, and she wanted to admit it before Ben told me—in case that helped make her appear less guilty. And there were clues. I felt so stupid that I'd missed them." Like scented candles by her bed in her apartment. We didn't use them when we made love.

She hugs me from behind, resting her head against my back. That warmth. Offering solace. No judgment. Leaving me my privacy. My hands clasp hers.

"I don't think you see the clues when you're the party in love," Tessa says. "I was devastated when Wyatt dumped me out of the blue. But like I said, in retrospect, there were clues."

"There are always clues afterward," I say.

I turn around to face her as she drops her arms and looks up at me. I add, "And now I'm paranoid. I feel like my office is bugged. I have this boss who doesn't like me, I'm up for this transfer, and he seems to know everything about me—before I even know it myself."

"Well, we can go in and search for bugs." She removes the leeks from the boiling water and starts forming the meatballs and plopping them into the water.

I love that she says that like it's totally normal.

"Do you know how to do that?" I ask.

"No. But I saw *Crash Landing on You* on Netflix. The main character searches for bugs planted by the North Korean government, and we can look at YouTube videos. I studied YouTube videos to learn how to paint."

"That doesn't give me a lot of confidence."

She snorts. Then she sets me to making the fennel dish in a saucepan next to her. I stir the fennel.

"I know he's not bugging me," I say. "There's always a good reason for how he finds out before me. But since discovering that Paisley was cheating on me—and that I had no idea—I feel like I have a hard time trusting people. And I feel bad about that."

"You can't always trust people," she says.

"No. But you can't live your life not trusting people either." At least that's what I keep telling myself.

She takes the meatballs out and combines them with the curry leek sauce she's been making. The dish turns this yellow-green color.

I set the table as Tessa finishes up the last of the dinner preparations. It feels like a long time since I've sat across the table from someone. Despite all my joking around with Sebastian about the benefits of being single, I've missed this. Among other things. She sets the dishes down. I pour us some wine as we each take a seat. Brit curls up at my feet.

"Bon appétit," I say, and we each take a bite. It's good.

"I guess I decided to become a lawyer in high school," she says. "My best friend came to me one day in tears because she and her mom were going to lose their apartment. Her dad had died a few years before. They had a rent-controlled apartment, and the landlord was trying to kick them out by not providing heat. Then the mom fell for this guy, and he told her to move out because he didn't like to see her without heat. But moving out almost lost them their apartment. FLAFL stepped in and saved it for them. It turned out the man had been paid off by the landlord. That's when I wanted to work for FLAFL. I wanted to be a lawyer so I knew how to protect myself. And others. Because you can't always trust people."

Tessa would not cheat on someone.

Tessa would not play around with someone's heart.

"That's why this case is so important to you." I sip my wine.

"Exactly."

"Did your friend become a lawyer?"

"No. She became a doctor. Because maybe better medical care would have saved her dad." She eats some more. "Do you like the curry leek meatballs?"

"They're delicious."

"Even though they look a strange green?"

"Healthy."

She chuckles. "The fennel with radicchio is more bitter than I expected."

"I thought it would have more of a licorice flavor. Maybe I messed it up."

She takes another bite. "Hmm. It still tastes good."

We finish dinner, and then I suggest we eat dessert after we walk Brit.

The minute "walk" leaves my mouth, Brit barks and spins around excitedly. She barks again, her front paws forward, her body down, as if to say hurry up.

Brit leads us down the stairs and out. The night air is warm and balmy as we amble along in comfortable silence with Brit on Central

Park West. Brit sniffs all her favorite spots. *I don't want the day to end.*

Tessa says, "I plan to eventually get a job working for FLAFL, once I pay off my law school loans. I think."

"But you're a really good corporate lawyer."

"And I'll be good at that too." She leans in. "You have to promise not to mention that I'm considering quitting White & Gilman for FLAFL. That's top secret. I don't want that to get out and scuttle my chances of getting the extra bonus because they think I'm leaving."

"My lips are sealed." I turn around to return to my apartment. I almost reach for her hand but stop.

Tessa carries the rest of the dishes to my kitchen sink. I barely recognize my kitchen with all the pots and bowls we used to make dinner piled up—a sharp contrast to its usual pristine, unlived-in condition.

"I'll do them," I say. "Since you wanted to name our fake app No Dishwashing Required."

"Good memory." Tessa grins at me. "I'll dry."

We stand side by side, and I focus on cleaning the plates with the soapy dishcloth.

I'm done resisting.

I hand her the last dish. She dries it and places it back on the shelf. And then I wash my hands and flick her with soapy water.

"Hey."

I take a step closer. "I want to give us another chance."

She holds my gaze and steps closer to me. "Yes."

I reach out and caress her neck, my thumb lightly outlining her chin, and then as I fan my hand through her hair, I lean in to kiss her. She meets me, her lips parted.

Chapter Thirty-Three

Tessa

HE PULLS ME IN close as he leans against the brick side wall of his kitchen. I fall into him, one hand against the wall above his shoulder, the other on his chest. The brick wall feels uneven, hard, and gritty. He trails kisses down my neck as I close my eyes, tilting to allow him access. I shiver.

I'm scared by the depth of my feelings. He was able to turn his back on us before. *Am I making a mistake?*

He looks at me like he likes me.

He cradles my face tenderly, gazing at me with such intensity and care.

"Are you okay?" he asks, his warm, blue eyes looking concerned into mine.

"Better than okay." I run my hand along his jaw, a little scratchy with his five-o'clock shadow, and then into his silky hair. He watches me.

"Why? What is making you give us a second chance?" I ask.

"Because I can't get over you. I like you. And I don't want to get over you. I know I have these trust issues from Paisley cheating on me, but I can do better. I trust you." He kisses me firmly on the lips. "Tell me what you want."

I want more. I press against his lean, firm body as I give myself into his kiss, reaching my arms around to hold him. His warm hand is against my neck and my face, caressing me. He slants his mouth, nipping at my lips. He tastes of wine and chocolate. My hand grips his flexed bicep, and he pulls me closer against his hard chest. There's a small *mmm*, and I realize that's me. I pull his shirt out of his jeans so I can rub his back muscles. He chuckles, this deep, hoarse laugh against my mouth. His lips brush firmly against mine as we take our time exploring. I lose myself in him, as everything narrows to the two of us together.

When we finally take a moment to breathe, my eyes flutter open to find his, dark and intent, gazing into mine.

"I really like you," I say. "I usually try hard to hold some piece of my heart back, but I don't want to here." But I should guard my heart a bit. I can't fall completely until I know for sure. But usually, it's not this difficult.

"I tried very hard to forget you and move on, but I couldn't," he says, his voice deep, as he holds me tight against him.

"Even though I'm a workaholic lawyer?"

"Especially because you're a workaholic lawyer." He rubs my back. "But more—because you're you."

"I was right." I grin wickedly at him.

"And now I'm yours." The muscles of his chest strain against the blue button-down. His pupils are dilated, and his eyes are hungry.

"Can I unbutton your shirt?" I ask.

He nods, his gaze not leaving mine.

I slip open the top button. I have to use both my hands. And then another and another.

"You're too far away," he says, sweeping his arms down and clasping me to him. He kisses me again, hungrily, and I kiss him back. With one hand, he unbuttons his shirt. "I want to feel you against me." He removes his shirt and throws it to one side. I pull off my shirt—only my black, lacy bra between us now. He takes a deep breath as he gazes at me. Goose bumps. I kiss him again as he massages my back. Shivers of desire cascade through my body.

"Should we go to my bedroom?" His voice is low and gravelly and is definitely doing things to my stomach.

"Lead the way."

Holding my hand, he pulls me out of the kitchen. But then we stop and kiss again, his body against the wall. He lifts me up so my legs are around his waist.

And then we're in his room, and he kisses me again, pulling me tight against him. He pulls back and cups my face with his hands.

"You're so beautiful." His hand caresses my collarbone, tracing, teasing, igniting a trail of fiery embers. And he grins at me like he knows exactly what he's doing. His blue eyes are completely focused on me. I step back. Two can play at this game. He pulls me back toward him and kisses me again, harder, with desire.

The next morning, Brit's wet nose wakes me up. She barks, wagging her tail vigorously.

"I have to walk her." Zeke sits up, and the sheets slide down, revealing his muscular chest. He kisses me quickly on the lips. "You stay here. I'll be right back."

I stretch out and smile. The sun peeks through his shades. Last night was amazing. I'm so happy we're back together. He was so focused on making sure that I was enjoying myself, and the fact that I was clearly turned him on as well. Bubbles of happiness rise in my chest, and I hold the sheets up to my chin, clamping down on my desire to squeal with delight. *I like him so much.* I jump out to go to the bathroom. I have a chance to freshen up before he gets back.

In what seems like seconds, I hear Brit barking. I jump back into the bed and snuggle under the covers. Zeke comes in and joins me in the bed, pulling me against him. I smell peppermint. He's also brushed his teeth. He nuzzles my neck, and I kiss him back.

"Will you come to my friend's wedding with me?" he asks.

"Yes." Yes! This isn't just a fling. I didn't think so, but dating in New York can be a minefield.

"Where are our paintings?" I ask.

"In the closet. I didn't want to throw them out, but I didn't want the reminder. But let's hang *Dalmatians Gone Wild* on that wall today."

"Why did you want to date an artist?" I ask. "You don't actually seem that interested in art." He has a poster with a black-and-white photo of the Brooklyn Bridge on his bedroom wall, but no paintings.

"I wanted someone creative," he says. "Because it seems to work well with my parents' marriage. My dad is creative and constantly thinks of things outside the box. And my mom loves that. But my mom is the one who keeps it all on track. I had no idea that lawyers could be so creative." He kisses my shoulder.

"You're pretty creative too." I kiss him back.

Breakfast can wait.

Chapter Thirty-Four

Tessa

I AM STILL BUBBLING over with giddiness as I enter the small office of the building security company located in Queens. Yesterday was a perfect first day as a couple: a late, leisurely brunch, a walk with Brit around Central Park holding hands, cooking dinner together, and staring into each other's eyes as we made love, being open and vulnerable and giving. I blush and wave my hand at my suddenly heated face.

I school my expression to be more sober. *Focus.*

Two guys who look like ex-cops occupy desks near me. An American flag hangs in the corner. I sit in front of an old, brown desk and explain my request to Mr. O'Brien, an elderly man with a buzz cut.

They have footage from the past thirty days. He pulls it up on his monitor. Mr. Howard shows up several weekends on Saturday morning and doesn't leave until Sunday. They even have footage of Mr. Howard and Ms. Morris kissing hello in the hallway when he arrives and going out together holding hands. But as Zeke pointed out, they could have gotten back together after Ms. Robinson died. It's not conclusive.

I bite my lip. There's Ms. Peres who said Mr. Howard lived there and was only now moving. But she probably won't want to testify against her neighbor.

"Do you have any CCTV footage from earlier this year—say January through May?" I ask.

"We might have some old footage around. We're supposed to record over them, but we're not always diligent about it. And we have some files that we were holding for another case, I think during that time period." He clicks on some folders on his computer. "Let's try these. They're from March."

He plays it back for me. *And there it is.* Mr. Howard came consistently every March weekend. And he is kissing Ms. Morris in the hallway and going out holding hands when Taylor's grandmother was alive and he's alleging he was in a loving relationship with her.

Yes. There's nothing like that thrill when your case comes together.

But also, how dare he? How dare he try to take away Taylor's apartment?

"This is great," I say. "This is such a tremendous help. I can't thank you enough. This CCTV footage is the smoking gun in this case."

"Like *Law & Order*? That's my favorite TV show."

"Well, you have a starring role in this one. Would you be willing to testify in court about how this footage is kept? I might need to establish custody."

"Yes. Wait until I tell my wife."

I text Taylor that we have the footage. I can't wait to cross-examine Mr. Howard. And I text Zeke.

As I walk into my office building, through the imposing, marble reception area, past the guards at the reception desk, Stuffed Shirt is ahead of me, a cup of Starbucks coffee in hand. He looks back, sees me, and stops. I catch up.

"You missed the litigation department lunch," Stuffed Shirt says.

"I had to do something for a pro bono case."

We turn and join the queue waiting at the bank of elevators.

He shakes his head. "I keep telling you. Pro bono is not going to get you partnership."

I smile at him, so happy that I can't be bothered by his petty remarks. "You're right. But it does give me a very satisfied feeling and courtroom experience, so it has its benefits."

He sips his coffee. No response.

Shouldn't I stay at the firm? The Comidas en Canasta case was fun. I'd helped Roberto, Ana, Valeria, and the woman who'd lost her job. And Zeke. There is still a personal element in corporate law. Isn't pro bono on the side enough?

I don't know.

"Why did you become a lawyer?" I ask.

"It seemed intellectually challenging and paid well."

The elevator arrives. We get in and each press our floor. He stands stiffly next to me as the elevator fills up with associates.

"I was commended for having the most billable hours this past month." He turns, looking down at me. "Maybe you were second?"

"Maybe." So my trip to Mexico City did not produce enough bill-ables. Tom worked more. If only I didn't need sleep. And this month is going to be even less with all the time I'm spending on Taylor's case. And then there's catching Jurgen. I hope that case turns out like this one, and we're not only right that Jurgen is scamming artists, but we get the evidence to prove it.

It's fine. I relax my face muscles so Tom can't see he's getting me stressed.

My floor is first, so I get off and walk down the hallway to my office. *Shake it off.* I was so happy about my case, and then Tom succeeded in riling me. He definitely knows how to do that.

I text Jurgen and suggest we meet soon.

But now I can pull together my list of witnesses and prepare my direct and my cross-examination. That's always exciting. And if I get done quickly enough, maybe Zeke will be free for dinner.

I submit my affidavit of my client's evidence showing that she lived there prior to her military service (all her mail, her school records, her voting record showing this apartment as her primary residence) and then her military service. We can definitely prove this part of the case. Without any other evidence, it's up to the judge whether to grant it to the "spouse" or the child, and usually the legal spouse would win.

We'll find out at the hearing this week.

I meet Taylor, Mrs. Humming, and Mr. O'Brien outside 111 Centre Street, where the Manhattan housing court is located.

As we walk into the courtroom, Mr. Howard is there, chatting up the transcribing typist. His lawyer calls him over. Ken is at our table, already conferring with a clerk about technology. I nod hello to opposing counsel. I take my seat at our table, Taylor next to me.

Mr. Howard comes over and says to my client, "I'm sorry about your grandma's death. And I want you to know that I'm happy to have you come by and pick up whatever keepsakes you want. Other than this afghan she knitted for me. Once this is over. No hard feelings about your contesting this."

Taylor raises an eyebrow. "We'll see how this plays out. But if Grandma knitted an afghan for you, I'm willing to give that to you."

Stalemate.

Their side presents their evidence first. Mr. Howard takes the stand and swears to tell the truth. He explains how they commingled financial accounts with his depositing his work check into her bank account. He produces a cable bill in his name for the apartment. The utilities had all remained in her name.

He comes across as earnest and likable. Not the man I met in the deli. But he's someone who relies on his charm, so I'm not surprised.

Still, it means I have to be gentle at first in case the judge likes him.

Now it's my turn for cross. Taylor tenses.

I stand and cross over to him, my clipboard with my questions on it in hand.

"You testified that you deposited your checks in Ms. Robinson's account," I say.

"I did. And the bank account shows that."

"But you also withdrew all of that money?"

"To pay expenses."

"You testified that you and Ms. Robinson were in a romantic relationship?"

"Yes."

"A monogamous romantic relationship?" I ask.

"Yes."

"And you met because you were her home care attendant?"

"Yes."

"Where did you live before you moved in with Ms. Robinson as a caretaker?"

"Garden Towers."

"In apartment 3C with a Ms. Morris?"

"Yes."

I walk up to the judge and submit the rental lease as evidence. I then hand a copy to opposing counsel.

"Were you in a relationship with Ms. Morris?"

"Yes. But we broke up when I met Angelique Robinson. I'm not on the lease anymore." And there's that slight smile—like he's proud of himself that he outwitted me. Body language doesn't lie.

"You broke up. So, you're not in a romantic relationship anymore with Mrs. Morris?"

"No. Not since I met Angelique."

"But you still get your mail there?"

"I don't think so." He looks at the judge. "I may have forgotten to file a change of address, but nothing important goes there."

I submit the USPS record of address of Mr. Howard as Apartment 3C in Garden Towers.

"You don't visit her every weekend—even weekends when you were allegedly romantically involved with Mrs. Robinson?"

"What?" His tone is confrontational. His eyes narrow, but then he visibly relaxes his face. "I'm allowed to be friends with my ex, aren't I?" He turns to face the judge. "I see her every now and then. Sometimes she asks me to fix something. I'd feel bad saying no. She's a single woman, and we have a history. But that doesn't mean I cheated on Angelique." He pats his heart.

"I'd like to submit this security camera footage of the hallway outside apartment 3C from March—when Mr. Howard is alleging he was in a monogamous romantic relationship with Ms. Robinson. I also submit the affidavit of Mr. Dean, who is willing to testify as to the custody of these files."

"Objection," says his counsel.

The judge raises his eyebrow. "Overruled. Please show us the footage."

Ken presses play. The clips of Mr. Howard hugging and kissing Ms. Morris, the footage time-stamped, fill the courtroom. It stops, and the silence echoes.

"We'd like to take a recess so I can confer with my client," the opposing lawyer says. "And I'd like a bench conference."

The judge calls us both up to the bench.

"This should have been disclosed in discovery," the opposing lawyer says.

"You didn't ask for this in discovery." I hand over his discovery request. "You only asked for what proof my client had that she lived in the apartment. You didn't request what proof we had that your client didn't solely live in that apartment or have a romantic relationship with another woman."

"She's right," the judge says.

We are dismissed from the bench conference, and the opposing lawyer whispers earnestly with his client. The judge reconvenes the courtroom.

"Do you have any further questions for the witness?" the judge asks.

"No further questions," I say.

I call Mrs. Humming to the stand. She testifies that Mr. Howard left nearly every Saturday morning and returned Sunday night or Monday morning during the time period he was supposedly in a monogamous relationship with Mrs. Robinson. She also testifies that she never saw them display any romantic affection toward each other. And that Mrs. Robinson was not entirely with it that last year, so she wasn't sure if Mrs. Robinson was checking her accounts or would have known if he'd added his work check to her account. Mrs. Robinson also referred to him as Mr. Howard or her attendant. She never used his first name.

Opposing counsel objects that this is hearsay.

I counter that the grandmother is now deceased, so it's allowed as an exception.

The judge overrules opposing counsel.

Mr. Howard's attorney cross-examines Mrs. Humming, but he makes her look even more like an upright citizen.

She is unflappable. "I've lived a long time, and I call it the way I see it."

I call Mr. O'Brien to the stand, and he testifies as to the chain of custody for the footage. Mr. O'Brien frankly looks a little bit disappointed when Mr. Howard's lawyer says, "No questions."

The judge asks if I have any other witnesses to call, and when I answer in the negative, he says, "Let's take a five-minute recess while I weigh both sides of the case."

Those five minutes feel like forever. We presented a strong case, so I have to be confident that the judge will see it our way. When he steps back into the courtroom, I feel Taylor freeze.

Once seated, the judge steeples his fingers, looks long and hard at Howard, and then glances quickly at Taylor before straightening. "After careful deliberation, the court rules in favor of the plaintiff, Ms. Taylor Robinson."

Taylor turns to me with the hugest grin.

And this is what makes it all worthwhile.

Tears come to my eyes at the joy in hers. I don't cry easily, but I'm so relieved and happy. I hug Taylor and Mrs. Humming. *We did it.*

I'm wiped out from the tension of the hearing. Frankly, I'd like nothing better than to go home, order in, and take a nap. But I have to go to the office and put in a few billable hours. I've spent the whole day on this.

I enter the marble building entrance as Jack Miller, my mentor and favorite partner, is leaving.

"Tessa, good to see you," he says. "Great work with the Capital Management Comidas en Canasta investigation. The corporate team appreciated the business referral, and it was clever to wrap that work into this investigation."

"The client told me that's one of the reasons they'd hired us, so thank you for putting me in touch with the right team so fast. He liked that we were solving two problems with one action. And it gave our investigation a great cover."

Behind Jack, a courier arrives and hands a package off to the guards at the reception desk. We stand off to the corner in the vast, marble hallway.

"What happened with your pro bono case? Did you win?" Jack asks.

"Yes." I grin. "It was great."

"Way to go." He shakes my hand. "And congratulations on winning FLAFL Associate of the Year. That's fabulous. And the firm is thrilled to be honored as well. That accolade is already up on our corporate website."

"Do you think pro bono work can be counted toward the mid-year bonus?" I ask. "As you know, I try to always have a pro bono case. I wasn't going to take on this housing case, but I couldn't say no. I'm obviously asking because it will help me, but it will also benefit the firm. It would reflect better on White & Gilman if those hours were counted as well."

"That's true. The Management Committee meeting is next week. I'll coordinate with the pro bono coordinator to bring it up. It may be difficult to persuade the partners that it should count for the extraordinary bonus. The regular bonus may be easier, but I'll persuade them." He pats me on the shoulder. I can see why people pay big bucks to have him represent them. He radiates assurance but also trustworthiness.

"I appreciate whatever you can do," I say.

We chat about my other case for a few minutes, and then I take my leave. I've done what I could. He's the one who told me that you should always ask for what you want, because if you don't ask, then you already have the no. He's such a giving mentor.

I take the elevator up. It's empty, and I lean against the wall and text Zeke.

Me: *We won the case!*

Zeke: *Yes! Can I take you out for dinner to celebrate?*

Me: *I have to put in a few hours here.*

Zeke: *8?*

Me: *Sounds perfect.*

Zeke: *And we can continue celebrating this weekend in the Catskills.*

Would Mr. Howard have fooled me if I had just met him? Would I have taken him for a nice guy? I don't think so. And not because I'm suspicious. I've learned to read body language. I can trust my instincts as to who is a good guy and who isn't. Zeke is a good guy. Whereas Wyatt was not without an ulterior motive—he wanted a partner who reflected well on him. And I knew that from the beginning. Maybe that's why I never opened up that much to Wyatt. I don't think I need to worry that Zeke isn't sincere.

I should let myself fall completely for Zeke.

Chapter Thirty-Five

Zeke

THE SMOOTH VOICE OF the GPS says, "Turn right in half a mile."

We're on our way to Dylan's wedding. This road dips into a valley between the mountains that frame the landscape. Tessa volunteered to drive so I could practice my toast for the rehearsal dinner at eight.

"I still can't believe I'm getting a FLAFL award this Thursday," Tessa says, her eyes on the road ahead. "I'm so honored. You can come with me as my guest to the dinner, right?"

"Wouldn't miss it," I say. "It's the turn after that blinking *Rooms Free* sign up ahead."

Tessa pulls into a parking space in front of the reception building. We're staying at a motel off the main road. Little, wooden cabins dot the landscape. Fairy lights decorate the office door.

"It's cute," Tessa says. "Are other guests staying here?"

"I'm not sure," I say. "But the bed is solid, it has good water pressure, and there's no moldy smell."

"Did the other option have a moldy smell, no shower pressure, and sinking beds?"

I laugh. "I usually stay here when I ski. The cabins are cozy, and the young couple who runs it is very nice. They bought this place a few years ago, and I like supporting them. The other option was the hotel where the wedding is being held. I didn't want to stay there."

"Is Paisley staying there?"

"Yes."

She shakes her head. "Zeke. You can't stay at the same hotel as her?" Disappointment tinges her voice.

I hug her close. "Maybe I wanted you all to myself."

She kisses me lightly on the lips. "Okay. Points for that. Keep talking."

"C'mon. I'll get the key, and then we can get ready for the rehearsal dinner."

I open the door to our motel room. It's your basic huge bed in the middle of the room, a small kitchen and bathroom in the back. The room smells of freshly washed sheets. On the desk is a big, white wedding basket with water bottles and snacks. Typical Lindsay. To even send a basket here. She runs a tight ship. Above the bed is a photograph of the mountains around us. It's much better than the usual motel art and décor.

My phone beeps.

Arthur: *Need memo on the investment potential of Peekaboo by Sunday. Due date changed.*

"Arthur strikes again." That was supposed to be due next Friday.

But I'm ahead of him. I did it earlier this week because I didn't want that hanging over my head on a weekend with Tessa.

Tessa slips off her shoes at the entrance, pulls in her suitcase, and hangs up her garment bag in the closet.

"What's wrong?" she asks.

"My boss moved up some memo to Sunday, as if he knows I'm away this weekend."

"Hmm." She sits on the bed and puts her hands back. Which has the effect of pushing her chest forward. And I'm no longer thinking of Arthur. I sit next to her. She's so cute. We have some time before dinner.

"Should you be working now? Am I leading you astray?" she asks.

"How far astray can we go?" I hug her and tumble back onto the bed, with her falling on top of me.

She kisses me, her hair cascading over my face. I kiss her in return, rubbing her back down to her cushy butt, her soft body melding against mine.

She raises her head, putting both hands on the bed. "Zeke. We have an hour to get ready before the dinner. We don't have time."

"I know. I know."

She rolls off me and stands. She grabs a water bottle from the wedding favor basket, then picks up the card attached to the basket and hands it to me.

Thanks for coming, Zeke!

"They do know I'm coming?" she asks.

"Yes."

"Are Lindsay and Paisley best friends?"

"Not best friends. But they are close. I knew Paisley would be here, so I told Dylan I didn't want to stay for the dancing."

Tessa raises her eyebrow. "Why are you so worried about seeing Paisley?"

That is the question.

"Does she want you back?" she asks.

"I don't know. I haven't talked to her in months, other than running into her at the MoMA. She definitely didn't want to break up initially. I also booked this room before you and I started dating."

"Looks like she has an ally in Lindsay."

"Yes. Lindsay always credits her with setting her up with Dylan."

"This will be interesting." Tessa smiles.

My money is on Tessa.

"I should have done a better job of warning you. But I don't think Lindsay's going to actively help her. I mean, she knows Paisley cheated on me."

"Is there anything else I should know?" Tessa asks. "I feel like we should have a debrief session like we did before Mexico City and Garden Towers."

"Like the debrief session where you told me I was going to be a photographer? We're not acting here. It's not like we're fake dating. We are dating."

Tessa steps close to me. I want to slide down the spaghetti straps of that dress ...

If we take quick showers, we might have time before the rehearsal dinner.

"But why are you so worried about seeing her? Are you afraid you'll want to go back?"

We don't need an hour to get dressed. I can feel my cheeks heat up.

"You still like her?" She steps back, and that flash of hurt in her eyes kills me.

"No. I was thinking maybe we had time to fool around." I reach out and touch her arm. "These spaghetti straps have been driving me wild."

"I figured if I had to wear a strapless bra for the rehearsal dinner dress, I might as well wear it for the car ride too." She winks at me.

I slide my hand down her arm to grasp her hand. "I have no interest in getting back together with Paisley. But I don't want to see her. She's a reminder of what a fool I was. And I don't trust her at all. I don't want to talk to her. Why would I want to talk to her? To exchange pleasantries about the weather when I thought we'd get married?"

"You thought you'd get married?" Tessa plops down on the bed. She looks stunned.

I wince.

Okay. I didn't want to admit that.

"So ..." But she stops there and doesn't say anything. I've never seen Tessa at a loss for words.

"Not in the near future. But I wasn't dating just to have a fling." I sit next to her on the bed. "Like I'm not dating you to have a fling." I'm going to lose Tessa with this stupid wedding. I probably should have sucked it up and gone by myself. Why didn't Lindsay include Tessa on the card? Thanks, Lindsay. What am I supposed to say now?

"Okay." She places her hand on mine. "That must have been even more devastating than I thought. I'm impressed you're out there dating again at all. And at this wedding." She threads her fingers through mine and holds my hand.

I look at her. "That's what I thought when my friends said to get back out there. And when Dylan wanted me to come to this wedding." This wedding weekend is clearly some sort of relationship test that should not be happening when you're first dating.

I'm lucky I found Tessa. I pull her in for a hug.

Chapter Thirty-Six

Tessa

Zeke thought he'd marry Paisley.

That thought pops into my mind. And being at a wedding does not help. Especially one with a setting as idyllic as this—a mountaintop view behind the dais, just the right amount of warmth, and a light breeze with the scent of honeysuckle.

Zeke keeps saying he's over Paisley, but I'm not so sure. He's actively avoiding her. That meeting at the MoMA had so much tension, as if to prove that old adage that there's a thin line between love and hate.

It's also that he didn't want to tell me that. He looked horrified that he'd let that slip. I've admitted I was devastated when Wyatt broke up with me. Does he feel like we're not close enough to share that?

It's not like he's ever said he loves me. But it is too early still for that.

We take our seats in the middle on the groom's side. At least Paisley will sit on the bride's side.

But no.

There's a rustle behind us, and then Paisley's voice slices through.

"Zeke, Tessa, I'd like to introduce Tom."

I turn, and there's Stuffed Shirt.

"Tom?" I ask in astonishment.

"You're dating the client?" Tom asks.

"He's not the client," I say. "And I wasn't dating him during either of our recent representations."

"I was suspicious when you weren't trying to schmooze him during that dinner," Tom says.

"When do I ever schmooze clients?" I ask.

"Whatever," Tom says. "You usually try to talk to them. You definitely don't let me monopolize them. You knew you had the inside track."

"Easy there," Zeke says. "I don't like what you're implying. The only inside track advantage she had was that she settled the North American Trust Fund case quickly and on very favorable terms. If anything, after dating Paisley, I definitely didn't want to date another lawyer. And certainly not one I might work with."

"Thanks." Paisley grimaces.

"Your loss is my gain." Tom puts his arm around Paisley.

Tom and Paisley are dating?

"How do you guys know each other?" I ask.

Paisley moves away from Tom. "We met recently through a friend."

Not dating.

Paisley leans back in the chair and crosses her legs, her miniskirt revealing most of her super long and thin legs. I glance at Zeke. He doesn't seem bothered. The vibe is less murky waters than last time. More melting arctic zone. I can't believe Stuffed Shirt is here with Paisley.

"Shouldn't you be sitting on the bride's side?" Zeke asks.

She waves over at the crowded left side and then smiles at Zeke. "This seat has a better view."

She definitely wants him back.

"You're My Everything" plays, and the groom comes out with his parents, followed by the groomsmen. He takes his place at the front, smiling, and looks straight ahead, waiting.

The "Wedding March" swells up, and we all stand and turn to see the bride. She pats her dad's hand and then, holding Dylan's gaze, floats down the aisle. She reaches Dylan, kisses her father, and then faces her soon-to-be husband.

I do love weddings. And my favorite line is the vow.

"I, Dylan, take thee, Lindsay, to have and hold, from this day forward, for better or worse, in sickness and health, to love and cherish, 'til death do us part."

Because that's what love is all about. It's going through the ups and downs together and getting stronger. I've seen it with my parents. And with my friendships.

But not yet with a guy.

Zeke reaches for my hand. Could Zeke be that guy?

And then the pastor says, "Should anyone present know of any reason that this couple should not be joined in holy matrimony, speak now or forever hold your peace."

I hope I'm not being used in some game between him and Paisley. He admitted he didn't want to come unless he had a date. And he couldn't stay at the same hotel. And she wants him back.

Please speak now if I'm a rebound.

Thankfully, we're seated far away from Paisley and Stuffed Shirt. The MC announces the competition to catch the boutonniere. Dylan comes over and insists that the guys join. Zeke, Ben, and Sebastian stand.

Sebastian says, "I can't believe Dylan is making me do this. Ben, you have to stand in front of me. It'd be just like Dylan to aim for me."

The single men stand in a row, and Dylan tosses it. It's straight to Zeke, who catches it at the last minute.

The MC announces the bridal flower toss. And Paisley is first up on the floor, hugging Lindsay and giggling.

Zeke walks past her, straight toward me, frowning as he stares down at the boutonniere.

I have to catch the bouquet. If he didn't want to be in the same hotel, he definitely doesn't want to slow dance with her. And if I don't try really hard, is that going to give some signal that we're not serious and give Paisley an opening? I didn't think this whole wedding appearance thing through.

Zeke comes up. "I definitely didn't mean to catch this. Good luck."

"Are you sure you want to wish me that?" I ask. He looks so grim.

Zeke's glance catches mine and his face relaxes. "Maybe I should wish your competitors good luck. They'll probably need it more." He grins.

I laugh. "Probably."

Zeke massages my shoulders as if I'm about to enter into a wrestling match. "I'm counting on you. You can do it."

Great. No pressure.

I gather in a huddle with the rest of the single women.

Paisley stands in front of me. "No offense, but there's no way I'm going to let you get it."

Lindsay looks over and frowns. She gestures at me—or Paisley?—to move up to the front. The DJ plays "Man! I Feel Like a Woman!" I'm all for competition, but not for women competing against each other for a man.

I smile stiffly and move up to the front row, Paisley by my side. She steps a little forward, her shoulder in front of mine.

Lindsay turns around, her back facing us, and tosses the bouquet over her shoulder.

In our direction.

I jump for it, but Paisley blocks me out and grabs it.

Paisley holds the flowers high, grinning triumphantly at me.

I nod, conceding her victory, and return to our table. Where there is no Zeke.

The DJ calls up the winners of the bouquet and boutonniere toss and asks them to take the dance floor as he plays "I've Found Love (Now That I've Found You)."

I watch them. Zeke is stiff. Not the Zeke who danced the salsa with me. But he's also so tight that it's clear he's not comfortable. Because he still has feelings for her?

Paisley leans in, resting her head against his shoulder. They fit together.

I don't consider myself a jealous person, but seeing them in an embrace ...

It's because he wanted to marry her. And I'm so different from Paisley. What if he doesn't feel the same way about me that I do about him?

I turn away. I don't want to watch Zeke holding Paisley and torture myself with these questions.

I can disappear to the bathroom. But when I get inside the main building, a server says the bathroom is being cleaned, and there's another one at the back of the second building near the gazebo.

Stuffed Shirt waylays me. "Would you like to dance?"

"Not particularly. I don't think we have that kind of relationship." I keep walking.

"What kind of relationship do you have with Zeke? Is it serious?" He keeps pace beside me.

I sigh. "That's none of your business. And I'm on my way to the ladies' room."

"There's a bathroom over there that's probably not as crowded." He points to an entrance around the corner of the second building. I thought they said the back, but maybe that's what they meant. I change course, but he follows.

"Paisley said she saw you guys together at the MoMA. Before that investigation."

I stop and face him. "She did. We had a few dates, and then we decided not to pursue a relationship."

"Is this smart of you to date right before the end of the bonus period?" he asks. "You didn't quite seem your usual competitive self when you and that last guy broke up. You let me get the Menmal case. What was his name ... Wyatt?"

I was a disaster after our breakup and not completely my same competitive self. But I didn't volunteer for the Menmal case because it was going to be a hot mess. "I didn't realize you were so interested in my personal life."

"And didn't you break up because you worked too much?" he continues.

Ugh. I have a dim memory of saying that over drinks with summer associates last summer to console a junior associate who had been dumped.

"What if I told the partnership that you were dating Zeke and didn't disclose it?" He taps his chin. "I think that might hurt your chances for the bonus."

That's more in line with the Stuffed Shirt I know.

"But I wasn't dating Zeke when I did that case." I shrug. "I think we've exchanged enough pleasantries for now. Don't you?" I turn to leave, and Stuffed Shirt grabs my arm.

"I'm serious."

I pull my arm away. "It's not true."

There's no way he'd do that. Right?

I walk away toward the restroom. Not only Paisley, but Stuffed Shirt too? So much for a fun, relaxing weekend.

As I turn around the corner, Paisley and Zeke are standing off in a gazebo by the woods. She steps closer. They look good together. Zeke is especially attractive in that dark-blue jacket, his white shirt open at the collar. She puts her hand on his chest. He stands still. He doesn't push her hand away.

My chest hurts.

And there's a solid back wall of a building here. No door to a bathroom.

Well played, Stuffed Shirt. Well played.

What is Tom's game here? *He wants me to lose my focus at work.* Tom is committed to getting this bonus. And he's more of a foe than I realized.

But I'm done with this drama. I'm not going to just stand by. I walk over to Paisley and Zeke. Zeke has stepped back.

But something clever to say escapes me.

"They're serving the appetizer. Salad. Dressed," I say.

"I do hate soggy lettuce," Zeke says and steps past Paisley. As we walk away, he says, "Thanks for rescuing me."

"It wasn't on purpose. Tom sent me here, but I think his plan was for me to see you two together and lose heart."

Zeke turns to face me. "I'm sorry about all this. I didn't want to catch that flower. But to let it drop in front of me ... I told Paisley how happy I am with you."

That's not what it looked like. He didn't push her hand away. But jealousy is never a good look.

Should I say I'm jealous? Wyatt did say I should be more open about my feelings. But I think he meant my positive feelings. Not my "I'm worried I can't trust you," and "I'm jealous and insecure" feelings. It's not Zeke's fault that I feel this way. *Thanks, Wyatt.* I need to figure this out on my own.

"I understand," I say. "I actually have to go to the ladies' room, but I'll see you back at the table."

"She apologized. She never apologized before. She also said to warn you ... that Tom is really out to get this bonus and undermine you. But she didn't say how."

"He threatened to disclose my relationship with you to the partnership so that they think I didn't disclose a conflict."

Zeke's face hardens. "That—"

"But you're not the client. I checked the ethics rules again when we started dating this time. I'm not representing you. Capital Management is the client. It's not an issue, and it's only going to reflect poorly on him if he brings it up. Don't worry."

As I take my seat at the table, Paisley and Tom walk over.

"We noticed that there are two empty chairs here, and it's been so long since I've caught up with all of you—the Capital work gang." Paisley waves at Brooke and Ben. "This is Tom. He works at White & Gilman with Tessa, coincidentally."

Both Ben and Zeke straighten on either side of me like guard dogs. It's touching.

Tom pulls out Paisley's chair and takes the seat next to her. Paisley introduces Ben, Brooke, and Sebastian.

There is silence.

Paisley does have guts. But why did she join us? I can understand if she wants Zeke back, but I don't see Zeke going back to her. Except *I was planning to propose to her.* Was something more said when they met? Something that made her think she has a chance with him?

"Maybe you can flag the waiter and get a salad." I'm not going to appear concerned. "Since they served our table already."

"It's fine." Paisley shrugs. "I don't need a salad. I'm interested in the main course." She looks straight at Zeke. Like I'm not here as his date.

Am I salad? Soggy salad?

Tom clears his throat and turns to Brooke, who is next to him. "I enjoyed talking to you at the dinner the other night. I know you have Tessa on speed dial, but if you ever need a second lawyer from our firm, I'd love to have that opportunity. I speak French and Chinese, so I may be helpful in certain international deals. I admit I don't speak French as well as Paisley. She sounded like a native the other night at dinner at Le Ciel."

Does Tom want me to realize that Paisley is stiff competition? His reminder that I lost my last boyfriend because I was working all the time was not subtle. Or does he want Paisley to realize Zeke is truly no longer available?

Paisley blushes. "That's very kind of you. French is the language of love, so I wanted to make sure I sounded like a native. I lived in Paris after college."

"You went to Paris with your last boyfriend, didn't you?" Tom asks, smiling at me.

"For a week." I look down. That trip was one of the reasons I'd thought Wyatt and I were in a serious relationship.

Tom is trying to rattle me.

"Do you speak French, Sebastian?" Paisley asks.

Sebastian raises an eyebrow. "Yes." He turns to his salad. At least he likes salad.

"What inspired you to learn to speak Spanish?" Brooke asks me.

"There was a lot of Spanish spoken in my neighborhood growing up, and I wanted to know what everyone was saying," I say. "What inspired you to learn Spanish?"

"Same," Brooke says.

Brooke and I share a smile. When Brooke and I first met, we'd learned that we had grown up pretty close to each other—in Morningside Heights in Manhattan.

"Zeke is fluent in Dutch," Ben says.

"I spent summers in Holland, so if I wanted to play with the other kids, I had to learn," Zeke says. "And my dad always extolled it as some secret language that nobody else knew. Other than Dutch people."

"Aren't Lindsay and Dylan going to Paris and Amsterdam on their honeymoon?" Ben asks.

"That's what I heard," Paisley says. Then she asks me, "Where would you pick to go for a honeymoon?"

"I'm not sure," I say.

"Not Mexico?" Zeke grins at me.

"We should go back and actually see Mexico City," I say. "There's some cool bed and breakfast where they have a king-size bed on tracks that allow you to roll it out onto the rooftop terrace and spend the night sleeping under the stars."

"That does sound cool, as long as there are no mosquitoes," Paisley says.

"We worked on a case together in Mexico City, but we didn't see much," Zeke says. "Just the office, a few restaurants, and the hotel. It was a short turnaround time."

"Mexico City is very different from Paris." Paisley turns to me. "We always planned to go to Paris. I wanted to share with Zeke all my favorite places."

They discussed where they'd honeymoon?

The whole table suddenly busies themselves with their drinks, napkins, finishing the salad—anything but watching this car wreck.

"I honestly don't think we got around to jointly discussing honeymoon destinations," Zeke says to Paisley. "That's where *you* always said you'd like to go."

Paisley was confident enough in their relationship to mention where she wanted to honeymoon.

"Is your weekend basketball team looking for new players, Zeke?" Sebastian asks. "It sounded fun last time you mentioned it."

"We play in Riverside Park around eleven. It would be great to have you."

The waiters remove our salad plates and serve dinner. Tom leaves to pick up their dinner plates from the other table.

"Dylan tells me you two are dating." Paisley turns to Brooke and Ben. "Another couple at Capital. I definitely didn't have you on my bingo card, especially after Zeke and I didn't work out."

Brooke puts down her bread.

Ben says, "I never had you and Zeke on my bingo card."

Paisley laughs. "You were so surprised."

Ben blushes.

"Ah, well, I'm sure you and Brooke are more well-behaved in the office." Paisley smiles saucily at Zeke.

They were fooling around at the office?

I put down my fork. I've lost my appetite.

"Ben and Brooke are perfect together," Zeke says. "They both make each other very happy."

"How is working at Red Can?" Ben asks.

"It's definitely different," Paisley says. "I like finance, but I also like working for a food product company. And I wanted to work in a start-up. And one benefit so far is more women in upper management."

Tom returns with their dinners. The food is good, and now we have an excuse not to talk.

Paisley says, "And you guys met on a deal too."

"We didn't meet on a deal. We met at an art gallery," I say. Again.

Ben mutters to Zeke, "Never a dull moment with you."

"We ended up dating after a deal." Paisley glances at Zeke. "You do have a habit of dating the lawyers you work with on deals. All those late nights, I guess. But how's that working for you?"

Zeke reaches for my hand under the table and squeezes it. "You learn a lot about a person in those late nights under deadlines."

A waiter comes around to refresh our water glasses.

Ben whispers to me, "He actually didn't want to date another lawyer. You overcame that bias."

Ben is such a sweet wingman. It's a good sign when a guy has good friends.

The music starts up again.

"Shall we dance?" Zeke asks.

It's a slow song, and he pulls me in close. He smells of fresh air. Yummy. I want to be here in this moment with Zeke. The air smells of roses and orchids, mixed with the scent of some citronella candles, and Zeke. He kisses me quickly on the lips.

We dance to a few more songs and then take a break to get refreshments. Sebastian pulls Zeke aside for a moment, so I suggest I'll pick up the drinks.

As I wait at the bar for the bartender to pour our two glasses of wine, Paisley comes over.

"Zeke looks very happy with you," she says. "He's a good guy, so I hope you guys work out. I wanted to apologize to him and see that he was okay."

I busy myself grabbing an extra paper napkin. That intimate discussion in the gazebo did not look that innocent. And both of them feel the need to tell me that it was?

I'm not sure what to say in response. It's Zeke's place to tell her his feelings. And I definitely don't want to appear worried. "Thanks for telling me. Maybe Tom and you?"

She shrugs. "It's too early to tell. He's very focused on work—and competing with you. It seems like you will have to maintain those billable hours to keep up with him."

And Zeke doesn't want to date a workaholic is her unspoken reminder.

I pick up the two glasses of wine.

"I certainly hope Zeke is more open with you," she says.

"He seems pretty open," I say. She raises an eyebrow.

We walk back to our respective tables with our drinks. Tom and Paisley have returned to their assigned table.

I don't believe Paisley hopes we work out.

I place our glasses on the table and look for Zeke. Lindsay has claimed him on the dance floor for a slow song. They look like they are having an intense conversation. Dylan comes over and asks me to dance. I say yes, of course.

He pulls me over next to Lindsay and Zeke. Dylan takes me in his arms, holding me very loosely. As we dance, I hear snatches of their conversation—"But Paisley is really sorry," "You guys were so great together"—until Dylan suddenly seems to overhear Lindsay's remarks. He steers us across the room, away from Lindsay and Zeke. *This doesn't make me feel better.*

I shouldn't feel so threatened by Paisley. Zeke said he was serious about me. He looks at me like I'm the only one. That passion at night. That's not fake.

But. He planned to *propose* to Paisley.

I'm the girl whose childhood best friend had to sneak around his mom to see her. And maybe Wyatt wants me back now, but he was quick to dump me when he met Marla.

I have to trust Zeke and my feelings for him. But it's not my usual modus operandi.

Chapter Thirty-Seven

Zeke

THE LIGHTS IN THE other cabins are off as we drive up to park in front of ours. It's late. We let ourselves into our motel room.

I want to focus on the night ahead with Tessa, but I also need to respond to Arthur. Just thinking of him dampers any other thoughts.

I reluctantly pull out my laptop. "I have to check in and do a bit of work. I'm sorry. Just so I keep Arthur satisfied."

"I have to ask," Tessa says. "At the office?"

Paisley and her innuendos. I knew that was going to come up, but I like that Tessa asks me directly. "Paisley kissed me, and Ben walked in. It was a lot tamer than she made it seem, although Ben was surprised."

An emotion flickers in her eyes, but I'm not sure what.

She nods slowly. "It's horrible when your boss is a nightmare. Is this the guy who wants you to fail? I'm afraid I read that correspondence too with Ben."

I like that we've already moved past Paisley's remark. Like when Tessa didn't even blink an eye when she found Paisley and me in the gazebo. She's not the jealous type, I guess. She's totally cool.

Then I focus on what Tessa said.

"Oh no. I hope Arthur hasn't read it," I say. "I should be more careful what I put in emails."

"You should. For sure. And don't use your work account for any personal emails. I'm going to change." She takes some clothes and disappears into the bathroom.

I don't get to slowly slip off the strapless dress.

Maybe.

No. I can't give Arthur any ammunition against me.

I stare at the email Arthur sent. Okay, it's not that bad. It's make-work. Obviously, he's trying to hassle me but couldn't think of anything substantive for me to do.

She comes back out in a soft-gray T-shirt and baggy, blue pajama pants—still cute—and plops on the bed next to me. No bra. *I'm not going to get any work done.*

"No black lingerie?"

"I was saving that for tomorrow night." She pulls out a book. "Is Arthur the difficult partner?"

"You also have an amazing memory." I kiss her quickly on the lips. And then I close my laptop and put it on the side table.

"Are you done?" she asks.

"No," I growl. "But that's not what I want to be doing right now." I caress her face. "You're so cute."

"I'm not cute."

"And sweet." My fingers thread through the back of her soft hair, massaging her head, and I can feel her melting. Her eyes flutter closed. I trail light kisses on her nose and her cheek.

"I'm not sweet," she says but without any heat.

She's too sweet. She has no idea what others are like.

I nuzzle her neck, then plant more light kisses down to her collarbone.

She *mm*s. What that sound *does* to me. I growl.

I trace her collarbone under her T-shirt, my hand lightly brushing her silky skin. The temptation. She strains forward.

But no. Not yet. Slow down. Stay in this moment.

My hands frame her face again. She opens her eyes. Our glances meet. I really like her. I'm falling so hard.

Tonight, seeing her next to Paisley, there was no comparison.

There was that one point when Ben told that funny story. And Paisley chuckled. But Tessa laughed so hard, she was practically crying. She gives everything.

I feel so lucky.

And her eyes say the same. And her open smile. The way she looks at me—like she can't get enough of me, like she can't believe I'm hers.

I can't believe she's mine.

Something loosens in my chest, opening up and breathing again. That pain from Paisley is lessening.

Chapter Thirty-Eight

Tessa

I PUT MY CUP of coffee down on my office desk and turn on my computer. I didn't get much sleep again last night, but it was for a very good cause. My lips curve up in a smile. Lakshmi's bag is by her chair, so she must be in the office already but at a meeting.

Jack: *Come to my office immediately.*

That's weird. Jack has never texted me before. I rush downstairs and walk into his office. He's reading a document at the round table. He takes off his glasses and puts them down slowly on the table.

"I thought you should know that Tom told his mentor that you were in a relationship with an associate at Capital Management when you were representing them and hadn't disclosed it," Jack says.

A chill ices me. An accusation of ethical misconduct. I know it's not true, but still ...

An ethics investigation could torpedo my whole career.

"He's not the client. I have no conflict of interest with the client," I say.

"You are dating Zeger van der Zee?"

Is my legal analysis wrong? My stomach plunges.

"Yes. I am now. I was not dating him when I represented Capital Management. I met him at an art reception, and we didn't realize our connection. But we only dated when I was not representing Capital Management. But in any event, he's not the client. Capital Management is the client."

My legs feel like rubber. I grip the back of the chair.

"That's what I told his mentor, and his mentor agreed," Jack says. "But I wanted to warn you that Tom is gunning for you. I wasn't sure if he'd made up the whole thing."

I sink into the chair at the round table.

"Well, he wants that bonus too," I say calmly, even though I feel queasy. My legs are still shaky. I take a deep breath. My heart is pounding.

It's okay. He didn't succeed. I'm not going to be brought up on ethical charges.

I clasp my trembling hands together under the table. "But it's still concerning that he went that far."

Tom must hate me.

"It's a very serious accusation—but completely false. I wouldn't worry too much about it. We have made it very clear to Tom that we do not tolerate false accusations. In good news, I was also able to get pro bono to count," Jack says. "And now your hours are higher than his."

If Tom is willing to accuse me of ethical violations, I'm not sure that is good news.

"Which is going to piss him off." I've discounted Tom too much. Last year, when I won the bonus, he was angry. He'd turned and walked out of the room.

"He's only demonstrating that he does not have the collaborative and collegial skills we're looking for in a partner," Jack says.

"Do you think it will go further than his mentor?" I ask. "I don't want an ethics violation allegation being bandied around with my name on it."

"His mentor warned him that that would go poorly for him in terms of his chance for partnership, so I think not." Jack's gaze is reassuring and calm.

Jack's assistant interrupts with a call from a client, and I leave his office.

I walk slowly to my office. My legs are still shaky.

Tom actually accused me of an ethics violation. He wasn't bluffing.

I close my office door and sink into my chair. This is crazy.

A knock sounds on my office door.

"Come in," I say.

In walks Tom. I grip my armchair rests. *Don't let him see that he got to you.*

He puts his hands on his hips. "You could have told me it wasn't an ethics violation. I warned you I was going to do it."

"I didn't think you were actually going to report me for an ethics violation to the partnership." I stand and step toward him.

He backs up.

He's an underhanded coward.

"I can't believe you got pro bono to count toward the bonus hours." He shakes his head. "You're living a charmed life. But you're not going to beat me this year."

He storms out as Lakshmi enters, practically knocking her over.

"What was that all about?"

"Tom accused me of an ethical violation to the management. That I didn't disclose I was dating Zeke. He's pissed that pro bono hours are counting toward the bonus."

"That's despicable." She glares at our empty doorframe. "They are?" She high-fives me. "Though I shouldn't be rooting for the bonus. What am I going to do without you?"

"Shh."

"Don't worry. My lips are sealed."

I call Zeke and tell him. He's outraged.

"That's screwed up," Zeke says. I feel better as he gets indignant on my behalf, saying he's going to tell Brooke to blacklist Tom as outside counsel, and in fact, he'll tell his other lawyer friends to do that too.

"Dinner at my apartment tonight at 8:30?" I ask. "We can order in because I have to work late."

"See you there."

My assistant walks in. "Taylor dropped this off as a thank-you."

I smile and take the basket, opening up the note:

> *Thank you so much for everything. I sit in my grandma's apartment, and I can feel her comforting embrace all around me. I don't have the words to express my gratitude. But I'm hoping you and Zeke can come over for a dinner with Mrs. Humming on a Friday or Saturday. And please enjoy these oatmeal cookies (Grandma's recipe).*

I'm excited for Zeke to meet them.

I catch a glimpse of the *Wall Street Journal* clipping framed on my wall. These cookies mean a lot more to me than that recognition. I'm tired of competing against Tom for this bonus. *But what else will Tom do?*

Chapter Thirty-Nine

Zeke

My assistant buzzes to tell me that Arthur would like to see me in his office. *Now.*

I take the elevator up to Arthur's office. He motions for me to enter but continues staring at his computer monitor, ignoring me. I sit in front of his desk and wait.

He turns to face me. "We heard whispers that Red Can may be looking for investors. As I recall, you and Paisley, their associate general counsel, dated. I thought you might have an in."

It makes my skin crawl that he knows I dated Paisley.

And even worse that he probably knows I fell apart after we broke up and missed my flight to the venture capital conference in California, missing the morning pitch sessions. I tried to make up for it by listening to their pitches that night. But if I hadn't found that unicorn at that conference, I might have been fired. I shudder.

"*Dated* would be the operative word," I say.

Arthur raises his eyebrows. "You can't ask her facts about the company? I guess I can ask Winthrop to reach out to her."

"No. We're still on friendly terms." *Relatively.* "I can ask her." But I don't want to.

"I was thinking today." Arthur leans forward.

I'm not ready to see Paisley today. Tessa has her FLAFL award dinner tonight, and I'm swamped.

But Red Can might be a good investment opportunity, and it fits within our portfolio criteria. The irony.

He smiles slightly, but it's more like a shark showing its teeth.

He knows how torturous this is for me.

"I'll see what I can do," I say.

"Maybe play on her sympathy that you need to bring in business to transfer," Arthur says.

No way am I making some pity plea. The last thing I want is to be beholden to Paisley for transferring.

"This doesn't seem to be in your interest," I say. "I thought you didn't want me to transfer out of your department."

He shrugs. "The firm's interest comes first." He waves his hand at me. I'm dismissed. Abrupt as always.

I walk down the hallway back to the elevator. The Red Can intelligence is useful. Even if I don't want to work with Paisley in any context.

I get back to my desk and sit next to Ben. "Arthur told me Red Can is looking for venture capital."

"*Arthur* gave you that tip?"

"Another way to torture me."

"Are you going to call Paisley?" Ben asks.

"I thought Ming could call Paisley."

"She's not going to want to hear from him," Ben says. "And he's kind of junior."

"I'm not calling her." I sound like a five-year-old.

"Why can't you call her and be totally up front? That you heard this and wondered if you could discuss?"

"Okay." I was fine at the wedding. More annoyed, really. I reach over to the handset.

"But probably for this first call, you should call her in private," Ben says quickly. "Because you may have some more personal things to discuss …"

"That's exactly what I don't want. But you're right. As always." I pick up my cell phone and go up to the roof deck.

Paisley picks up on the first ring.

"Zeke?" Her voice is surprised and yet hopeful.

"Hey, Paisley." I stop. Now that I hear that hope, how can I say that I called for a business deal?

There's silence on the other end. That's Paisley. She can wait out a lull.

"I need to talk to you for business reasons," I blurt out. "Arthur told me that Red Can is looking for venture capital investors."

"Oh." She sighs. "Arthur's spies at work again. He knows we're looking for investors?"

"Yes."

"I'll email you our pitch," she says. "But are you sure you can work with me?"

No.

"We're a small team, so I'm not just the general counsel sitting off in some ivory tower," she says. "I help out with everything I can."

"It also won't be me alone. Ming takes the lead on some investments. He can spearhead this one."

"Maybe I'll request your input," she says.

"We're adults, and I'm in a serious relationship with Tessa. I'm sure we can work together," I say.

Maybe their fundamentals will be lacking such that I won't want to recommend them as an investment to the partnership. That would be best. But Paisley wouldn't have taken the job if Red Can didn't have a promising future. She did want the associate general counsel title, though.

"I saw Tessa is being honored at the FLAFL dinner tonight," she says. "I guess I'll see you there."

Let's hope it's from a distance.

It's not. The first person I see when I arrive at the check-in for the FLAFL dinner in the corridor outside the Aqua Hotel ballroom is Paisley. And Tessa has just texted that she's running late.

So far, Red Can looks like a solid investment.

And now I have to pretend that I have no issue working with Paisley.

"Hi," I say. My smile is probably more of a grimace, but I'm trying.

"Zeke."

Paisley looks genuinely delighted to see me.

"You know, I think this could be a great opportunity to recover our relationship," she says.

I still.

"I mean our friendship. You never looked at me the way you look at Tessa, so I accept there's no going back. But we were also good friends as well as lovers, weren't we?"

"Yes," I say cautiously. This is like a fricking minefield.

She hooks her arm through mine and pulls me off to the side next to one of the posterboards listing the names of the benefactors. "I've decided to help you. I've learned so much about the beverage industry since coming on board. It's fascinating."

As she shares her insights, I am impressed. This is the Paisley I fell in love with. This smart go-getter. I'd forgotten. I thought I was an idiot for not suspecting she was cheating. I'd questioned why I'd fallen for her, wondering if it was *all* fake and false. But it wasn't. That gives me some comfort. I wasn't a complete fool.

But she's missing Tessa's moral compass.

She reminds me of that one deal we did where we had to scramble to fix the mess Winthrop had created. That was such a crazy time. We both laugh.

This is good. Maybe we *can* work together. Maybe I'm finally over Paisley's betrayal.

"I just want to say one thing. I know I'm the bad guy here, but I think I knew deep down that something was missing. Probably once you said you didn't want to move in together," Paisley says. "Anyway, I'm sorry I hurt you and I'm glad you're happy now. I'll see you at the pitch." She pats me on the arm and pivots away.

I stare at her retreating back.

Maybe I never proposed because something was missing.

Something I've now found with Tessa.

Chapter Forty

Tessa

THAT WAS DEFINITELY ZEKE and Paisley laughing together.

None of that tortured vibe. So that's good. Less tension. And good for Zeke if he's over her betrayal.

But is he over her? They seemed so comfortable together. And totally absorbed with each other.

I was about to walk over, but then they laughed and Paisley put her hand on his arm.

He's been very up front that he's not over her cheating. There must be a good reason for their meeting. I'm being unnecessarily insecure. Again. He told me he liked me.

I don't want to be that girl constantly claiming her man.

I pin my name tag to my blazer as I check in at the FLAFL Dinner reception table.

My parents text that they, my sister, Kiara, and her husband are running late because the babysitter hasn't shown up yet, but they are leaving now. Kiara's husband will wait for the sitter. White & Gilman invited them to join us at the firm table.

I step away, and there's Ken.

He shakes my hand. "Congratulations!"

"Thank you."

"I have to talk to you privately." He looks around and then gestures to an empty corner. We walk over to stand behind the posterboards announcing the main speaker.

Ken says, "We listed the position. Tamara gave notice earlier than I expected. I know I told you she would give notice in October. You have to apply now if you want it."

"Now?" My heart sinks.

"You know these positions don't come around that often. If you want it—"

"I do."

"Then this is your shot," he says. "Let me know when you submit, and I'll send in my recommendation. I wanted to let you know as soon as possible, and what better place than at this FLAFL dinner?"

"What better place?" I repeat. *I can't apply now.* Not before I get the bonus. My stomach roils.

"Someone's trying to get your attention," Ken says.

Wyatt waves at me from across the room, holding a huge bouquet of flowers.

"Your boyfriend?" Ken asks.

"My ex. He bought a table and invited all my friends."

"And he's your ex?" Ken asks. "Sounds like he wants you back. I'll leave you, then. Let me know when you apply."

Ken walks away as Wyatt and my friends make their way through the crowd.

When I apply. Not if. Ken will doubt my commitment if I don't apply now. This position is perfect for me.

Do I give up the bonus? I bite my lip. I could apply and not tell the firm. *Not ask for a recommendation from Jack.* It's not like you usually tell your boss that you're applying for new jobs before you actually secure the position.

But Jack has been such an important mentor for me. I want to tell him and ask for his recommendation. I'd feel better being open about it. But that would mean giving up the bonus. They're not going to give me a bonus if I'm leaving.

Why did Tamara have to resign now and not in October—three months after the bonus was awarded?

If I don't tell Jack, he'll be using up his political capital to advocate for me to be awarded the bonus, and then he'll look like a fool when I up and leave the next week.

But people quit jobs.

I bite my lip.

This is business. I have to focus on what's best for me.

And I'm just applying for the job. I may not even get it. I shouldn't sacrifice the bonus before I even know if I've secured a different job.

I'll tell Jack if I get the job.

My friends join me, and we exchange hugs. Wyatt hands me the bouquet of flowers. *Awkward.*

And there's Zeke, looking so handsome in his crisp, blue suit with his shirt open at the collar. My heart does a little flip. He comes up to me and kisses me.

"Let me introduce you to my friends," I say. "Wyatt bought his usual table and invited some of my friends."

Zeke's eyes widen. I didn't mention it before because I didn't want Zeke to feel pressured to do the same when he's saving money for the venture capital partnership buy-in.

I should have told him.

Zeke looks at Wyatt. "That's very generous of you."

"It's not every day that my girl wins an award," Wyatt says.

"Ex-girl," I say.

"We're still friends," Wyatt says.

Zeke raises an eyebrow.

I introduce everyone to Zeke. He's met Miranda. Miranda introduces her boyfriend, William.

Zeke says, "You."

William blushes. "Don't hold it against me. But welcome to the world of Miranda and Tessa. I'm glad to meet you."

Lily introduces her boyfriend, Rupert.

"Good to meet you," Rupert says. "Lily says you work at Capital Management. My friend Sebastian works there. Do you know him?

"Yes," Zeke says. "He's a good friend. Incredible squash player."

"I know. I used to play regularly with him, but I've slacked off lately." Rupert gazes warmly at Lily and then smiles at us. "It looks like you may be otherwise occupied too."

"We really have to find him someone," Zeke says.

"Lily's on it." Rupert rubs her back. "And she's got the guy who helped matchmake us working on it."

"My friend Ben is also working on it," Zeke says.

"I'll grab drinks. What are your orders?" Rupert asks.

"I'll go with you," Wyatt says. "We'll find you by the tables."

As Wyatt and Rupert leave, Zeke and I step off to the side for a moment to catch up.

I say to Zeke, "That's why Wyatt bought the table. He wants to connect with Rupert. Rupert is the co-CEO of Strive Developers, and you know, Wyatt is very ambitious."

"Give yourself some credit," Zeke says. "I should have thought to buy a table."

"That's not necessary," I say. "That's why I didn't tell you. I know you need to save up your money to buy into the VC partnership."

"I still think Wyatt wants you back," he says. "Where's Marla?"

"Are you jealous?" I ask.

"No," he says quickly.

I think he might be jealous.

"Paisley is here," I say. "Did you know she was coming?"

"Yes. She told me when we talked this morning. And I now assume I will see her at any lawyer function." He squeezes my hand. "I definitely have the feeling Wyatt will join us at any event."

"You called her?" I ask. I hate that I sound jealous.

"For business reasons. Red Can is looking for venture capital funds."

"So you might have to work together?"

Paisley's remarks from the wedding about all those fun nights working together and how they fell in love ping pong in my head. That's how Zeke and I fell in love too.

My stomach feels queasy. But I can't let it ruin my night.

Forget it, Tessa. This is your night. This award is a huge deal. Don't get sad about this like when you missed your birthday party.

And I was beginning to think Zeke might be *The One*.

And the FLAFL job. I want to apply now, but how can I not tell Jack? It's like a huge weight is pushing me down. I'm trying to find my way out of this fog, but there is no flashing beam from a lighthouse, guiding the way to a safe harbor.

Zeke glances at me. "Are you okay? Are you nervous?" He clasps my hand, lacing his fingers with mine.

I look into his warm, blue eyes and get a grip on myself. "Definitely nervous."

He rubs my hand. We enter the festively decorated ballroom and join my friends. The hum of conversation buzzes in the background. People stand, chatting and catching up with others in the spaces between the round tables decorated with purple tablecloths and white flower arrangements.

"I looked up the artists' names on Scammer Guy's Instagram, and I found the contact information for two of them, so I'll send that to you," Iris says.

"Jurgen called me last night to tell me that someone from Latvia was interested in purchasing my *Regret* painting," I say.

"He's changed countries?" Lily asks. "Now he has to find someone who speaks Latvian."

"I was a bit surprised by that," I say. "Anyway, given that he's supposedly been scammed like this before, you'd think he'd mention that. But no. He was incredibly enthusiastic. I think he's definitely in on the scam."

"Yvette also sent her bank statement showing the fraudulent check, so hopefully the handwriting will match that of the check he gives you this time," Miranda says.

"Are you going to have to give Jurgen money, then?" Zeke asks.

"Some," I say. "Hopefully, I can get my money back if he gets arrested."

"Officer Johnson said he'd be willing to follow Jurgen to see if he goes immediately to a shipping store, but if he doesn't, it'll hardly be conclusive," Miranda says. "Still, it's pretty damning that Jurgen is running the same scam again. But a fraudulent check is key."

"Let's hope we get him. One more meeting, and then I hope I'm done." I shudder. "He's so slimy."

Rupert and Wyatt return. Wyatt hands Zeke and me our drinks as he stands between us and the cluster of my friends.

"Where's Marla?" I ask.

"She thought it sounded boring," Wyatt says. "Hanging out with a whole bunch of lawyers didn't interest her."

"Oh," I say.

Zeke says, "I admit I'm a recent convert myself."

Wyatt smiles at me, with a glance at Zeke. "The thing about lawyers is that they're very bright and pose a challenge. You don't find that everywhere so easily."

I meet Wyatt's glance. *Is he hitting on me?* In front of Zeke?

"That's why you should definitely appreciate lawyers and treat them accordingly," Zeke says.

Exactly.

Zeke puts his arm around me and pulls me closer. I kiss Zeke on the cheek.

Wyatt raises his eyebrows.

Has he recast my "not revealing all my emotions" as a challenge? That's one way to put it.

A server asks us if we'd like some shrimp appetizers. We all pass.

"Anyway, John thought Maddie was cute at our last party. Remember our Happy Spring party, Tessa?" Wyatt turns to me.

I nod. *So not subtle to mention our party, Wyatt.*

"He was happy to take Marla's place and try his luck again," Wyatt says. "I hope he makes it. He's running late because of work."

Lakshmi comes up. "Ugh. Tom is here."

I introduce her as my friend and officemate to Wyatt and Zeke.

"You know he is," I say. "He's afraid that I'll score some points if I'm left alone with the partners."

"I didn't think he could stomach seeing you win an award," Lakshmi says.

"I think he discounts it because it's a FLAFL award."

A few friends from law school who are in public interest law come up, and I chat with them while Zeke joins my group of friends. Zeke fits in well, so that's good. Wyatt is monopolizing Rupert.

Mrs. Humming and Taylor arrive, and I introduce them to my friends. Zeke regales everyone with the story of our tailing Mr. Howard.

"Do you still remember all the jujitsu moves we learned in that self-defense class?" Iris asks. "Maybe we should do a refresher."

"I still remember. Don't worry. He was bluffing," I say. Iris still looks worried. She's definitely going to make us all take that jujitsu class again. My body feels sore just thinking about it.

There is an announcement that dinner is about to be served and everyone should take their seats. I tell Zeke I'm going to run to the bathroom first. He squeezes my hand. Lily takes my bouquet. My parents text that they have arrived and will meet me at the table.

As I exit into the hallway, I run straight into Tom. He wasn't invited to the firm's table, so he must be at a friend's.

Ugh.

Tom says, "You certainly look very cozy with all those FLAFL lawyers. Almost like you're one of them."

"But I'm not," I say.

"Yeah. You're too good at being a corporate lawyer," he says. "You'd be wasted as a FLAFL lawyer."

"Hardly wasted," I say. "They need top legal advice more than a corporation."

"That was so nice of your ex to buy a table," he says. "Paisley brought me as her date."

"You still have a chance there," I say. "I'm rooting for you."

More than you know.

Paisley then comes out of the bathroom and walks over.

"Zeke called me today. It was like old times," she says. "I'm looking forward to working together."

"So he said," I say. I slip quickly into the restroom and into a stall and sag against the wall.

This is your night, Tessa. Don't let a guy throw you off your game. Just because Wyatt dumped you precipitously doesn't mean Zeke will.

He's not going to go back to Paisley, even if they work together. She cheated on him. He's over her. But I should stop pretending I'm not jealous. I can't be afraid to be honest—and *maybe* share that vulnerability.

Chapter Forty-One

Zeke

I hold Tessa's hand as Brit sniffs the tree trunk next to us on this pathway just inside Central Park. We wait under a canopy of whispering leaves for Brit to finish her extremely thorough investigation. We're spending the night at my place so Brit isn't alone. Two women jogging together pass us.

"Taylor gave a great speech about you. She captured you as a lawyer and as a person," I say, squeezing her hand. I was proud to say Tessa is my girlfriend. "I can see why you were so determined to catch Howard."

She glances at me. "Don't make me tear up again."

"I enjoyed meeting your friends," I say. "But you seemed off when I first arrived. Did something happen?"

We sit down at one of the benches as Brit barks at a squirrel. The night air is balmy. The wood of the bench feels smooth and worn. The green grass looks particularly bright in the circle of luminescence around the lamppost. Beyond that is murky darkness, with patches illuminated here and there by the hazy, white light from the luminaires' glowing orbs.

"Ken said that a FLAFL position opened up and I have to apply now—before I get the bonus," she says. "It's a senior position, and they don't open up that often. But I wanted the bonus first."

"Can you still afford to take the job without it?"

"I've thought about that. I have my mortgage payments, law school debt payments, and my living expenses. And my food expenses will increase because I'm not eating on the client's tab. As a last resort, I could rent out my room in my apartment and live with my parents for a year. But that's not so great for Miranda."

She leans against my shoulder. "I'm not sure that's a real possibility, though. I haven't lived at home since high school. I love my parents, but I don't want to live with them. We end up annoying each other after two weeks. I now limit family vacations to a week."

"You could move in with me," I say, surprising even myself.

She glances at me and then gives me a hug. "I worry that might put too much pressure on our relationship because we just started dating. But staying over at your place will be a welcome respite from my parents. And I'm not telling you all this to ask for your financial help. It's more the job. I'm scared to give up my corporate job and my substantial paycheck—as bad as that makes me sound. Because I do get to do pro bono at White & Gilman. And I like the cases and the partners."

Brit comes back over and puts her snout on Tessa's leg. Tessa definitely has Brit's seal of approval. Tessa pats Brit. A warm breeze with the scent of grass and leaves and flowers brushes over us.

"But I hate the system they've set up where we compete against each other. Tom is such a jerk, and yet he's doing well at the firm. Plus, I can't always do the cases I want. The firm refused to allow me to represent Lily's garden when it was threatened with eviction."

"What makes you want to go?" I hold her hand.

She stares off into the distance. "It means more to me. When I succeed in one of my FLAFL cases, it means so much to me." She taps her chest. "I feel it here. When I win a motion for a corporate client—other than you—I'm happy and relieved, but it's not like I get that feeling of deep satisfaction that I've changed someone's life for the better."

"There's your answer," I say.

"Is it that simple? I've been agonizing over this," she says.

"Then maybe it's not that simple," I say. "What's holding you back?"

The sound of a plane flying overhead thrums in the background.

"The decline in income and the security that income brings. And the fact that working for White & Gilman immediately commands respect. But saying I'm a FLAFL attorney ..."

"Ms. Peres was definitely impressed," I say.

"But people like Tom ... not that I want to impress people like Tom," she says.

"I thought you were the one who told me that being a lawyer doesn't define you."

She stares at me. Her eyes blink. She looks a bit stunned.

"You're right. You're so right." She shakes her head. "I can't believe you had to point that out to me."

"And you command respect just by being you."

"Thank you." She kisses me, and when I pull back, her eyes are glazed over. She rests her head on my shoulder. The only sound is Brit sniffing around our bench, searching for a squirrel that's been smart enough to scamper up a tree.

"Let's head back to my apartment," I say. We stand.

"I'll apply tomorrow." She smiles and hooks her arm into mine. I love how affectionate Tessa is.

Then she pouts. "I'll miss business travel."

"We didn't even get to see Mexico City, except for a few blocks and restaurants."

"That's true." She kisses me. "All right. I'll definitely submit my application. It's not a foregone conclusion it will be accepted anyway."

"After Ken's speech about you tonight, you should accept it as a foregone conclusion," I say.

"Maybe, but that's Ken. He's not the sole decision-maker. I don't want to get my hopes up and then have them dashed."

A German Shepherd comes up to Brit, and they sniff each other. The leashes tangle, and I exchange pleasantries with the older man walking that dog. They meander off, and we walk up the slight incline toward the park exit.

She stops and turns to me. "Will you have to work with Paisley a lot if you invest in their company?"

"Potentially. Sort of. But there are a lot of variables before that's a possibility. We'd have to decide to present Red Can to the investment committee, and the committee would have to approve it. And even then, I'd make my junior be the prime contact. And she's the lawyer, so she wouldn't be our first point of contact either."

"That's quite a detailed explanation." Tessa looks down. "I know it's stupid, but I feel insecure about it. I think it's because Wyatt dumped me so suddenly. And you guys were going to get married—if she hadn't cheated. You clearly loved her very much."

"But she did cheat," I say. I hold Tessa's hands and stare into her eyes, willing her to believe me. "I like you. I'm not in love with Paisley anymore."

"How did you guys end up in the gazebo at the wedding?"

"She apologized during the dance and looked like she was about to cry. The last thing I wanted was some scene, so I hurried us off the dance floor. And then she pulled me into that freaking, flower-filled gazebo. And she apologized again, and I said I accepted it. Then she put her hand on my chest and asked something like, 'Even in your heart?'"

I wince. That was cheesy.

"And I said yes and that I'd moved past it because I was happy with you. I should have explained. I thought you weren't jealous."

"Apparently, I am the jealous type." Tessa looks forlorn about this. She scuffs her foot. I kiss her quickly. She looks so cute.

"You don't have to be jealous," I say. "I have no interest in anyone but you."

Does she still feel anything for Wyatt? He was her first serious relationship.

"It was impressive that Wyatt bought a table," I say. Rationally, it's great that Wyatt bought a table. More funds for FLAFL. It's not like she should have told him not to. I should have bought a table. I understand her rationale for not telling me, but it still rankles. "I wish you had told me."

She faces me. "I didn't want you to feel any pressure to do the same. And it wasn't about me."

"Wyatt was definitely flirting with you," I say.

"I thought so too." Tessa shakes her head.

"Maybe he wants you back," I say. "If he did—"

"I don't think he means it. Remember, he dumped me. I hate to break it to you, but not everyone finds me that appealing or irresistible. Which is why I have to hold on to you." She hugs me. "You can't get rid of me."

Did she answer my question of whether she wants him back?

She hugs me even tighter and nuzzles her face into my neck. "I'm keeping you."

I hug her firmly against me. "I'm keeping you too."

"You better be."

If I ask her again about Wyatt, I'll look like I haven't recovered from my Paisley trust issues. But I have. I'm good.

Chapter Forty-Two

Tessa

I say "thank you" again to Ken and put my phone down on my desk. *FLAFL offered me the job.*

I got the job!

I stare at the framed *Wall Street Journal* clipping on my wall and then at the thank-you note from the grandparents.

I leave a message for Zeke on his voice mail that FLAFL offered me the job. One week to decide. And in four days, I'll hear about the bonus, unless I tell White & Gilman now.

Am I going to actually accept the job? My stomach feels queasy.

My assistant knocks on my doorframe.

I look up.

She comes into my office. "Jack asked if you were free to go to his office. Immediately."

"A new case?"

"I couldn't tell. He was very abrupt. Not like him at all."

A crazy M&A case? That's one of the few reasons he'd need a litigator.

I take the elevator down to his office. A new case right now is not exactly perfect timing, if I'm going to quit. *If.* I need to tell Jack if I'm going to quit.

I walk into his office. He swivels around to face me.

His face is stern and unsmiling. "Please close the door behind you."

This must be a hot mess of a case. I pull back the chair in front of his table.

"Are you leaving us for FLAFL?" he asks.

I drop into the chair. My mouth opens. But nothing comes out.

His eyes are hard. This is the man who negotiates billion-dollar contracts.

"Are you?"

"I haven't accepted yet," I manage to get out. "I was only offered the position today."

His eyes flicker.

"I'm so sorry I didn't tell you." My whole body flushes with cold. "I just applied. It's a position that would be perfect for me ... one that rarely opens up." Please understand. *I didn't want to not tell you.*

"You plan to accept it?" His voice is still cold. Distant. Not the voice of my mentor.

I nod. I wasn't absolutely sure a few minutes ago, but I know, deep down, I'm going to accept it. My stomach clenches.

"I can't support you for the bonus if you're about to leave."

I look down at the floor and take a deep breath. My hands feel shaky. "I understand that."

"I'm also personally disappointed that you didn't tell me. I've been telling my partners that you deserve it—that you're the type of lawyer we want to keep at this firm, that we want to make partner. And then you would have received the bonus and left."

I played this wrong. He's looking down at the desk. His shoulders curve a little down. He's getting older. For five years, he's been the guy I've gone to whenever I had a question or wanted to discuss a legal point, and he has always taken off his reading glasses and made time for me. I justified not telling him by lying to myself that this was business. But it's not.

"I'm sorry." My voice cracks. "I made the wrong choice. I've worked hard, and that bonus would pay off my law school debt so I could go debt-free to FLAFL. But you've been a tremendous mentor to me. I should have valued our relationship more than the bonus. I'm sorry. I wanted to tell you that I was applying. And I guess that makes it worse—that I thought about telling you but didn't. But I planned to tell you if I accepted the offer."

His lips compress into a thin line. "Even without the bonus?"

No bonus. All that hard work. *And* I've hurt Jack.

The shelf above his desk is filled with all the deal toys. A miniature Delta airplane. A crystal triangle. A globe with some movie characters. To the right is a framed newspaper clipping—his first case reported in *The New York Times* and *The Wall Street Journal*. He was the one who'd inspired me to frame mine.

I meet his glance. "Yes. If I turn this down, I'm not sure I'll get another opportunity that's as perfect for me. I'll tell the partnership today so no one else advocates for me. Unless you want to tell them ... so you protect your position."

He rubs his brow. "Thank you for thinking of me. I do think you should tell them today. *You* should tell them—not me."

He's still protecting me.

"I'm so sorry." My voice breaks. "I keep making the wrong decisions. I should have told you." When will I ever learn? I need to be open with my people. I know who my people are, and I need to trust them. "I'll tell them immediately."

He sighs and looks up. "It's understandable. And if you don't make mistakes, how do you learn? If you haven't accepted yet, can I convince you to stay?"

"I don't think so. I've learned so much here, but this is my passion. And I'm afraid that if I stay, I'll get swept up in making partner, and I'll get used to the money. I'll convince myself that it's enough to do pro bono as part of my law firm practice. And that's not to say that it isn't. But it's not enough for me. For why I became a lawyer."

He nods and smiles, lines creasing around his eyes. "You're wise to go now. It does get harder to give up the money and the prestige. I'm sorry about the bonus."

"I'm sorry if I undercut you."

"I'm a big guy. I can play politics with the best of them. I'll survive." He leans back in his chair. "I hope we can work together on a case for FLAFL."

"That would mean a lot to me. I'd like that—and to stay in touch. Thank you for being such an giving mentor."

"I'm sure we will stay in touch," Jack says. "I'll ask my assistant to add you to my quarterly lunch with associates who have left."

"There are so many?"

"I have a tendency to adopt those who are going to leave. I thought you were actually going to break my streak." He shrugs.

"It wasn't an easy decision. I'm looking forward to meeting the others."

"It's a lively bunch, that's for sure. And some good connections for you."

I stand. "I'll tell the managing partner now."

Jack nods. "That would be for the best."

"If I may ask, how did you find out?"

"Tom told me."

"Of course," I say. *How did Tom find out?*

As I enter the rarely used, interior fire exit stairwell, silence greets me. I pause and sink down onto the hard concrete step. *No bonus.* The cold of the concrete seeps through my cotton pants. I stare blindly at the green EXIT poster on the wall ahead.

Should I give all this up?

No bonus. It won't be easy financially.

I could go back and tell Jack I've decided to stay.

No.

I hold on to the metal stair rail and pull myself back up.

It is what it is. It'll take me another year to pay off my debt.

I can't lose this opportunity to pursue my dream.

And it's better for me to leave the law firm on this note—as opposed to taking the bonus and then quitting the next week.

I go straight to the managing partner's office and tell him I've been offered a job at FLAFL and I'm planning to take it.

"Have you accepted yet?" he asks.

"Not yet."

He asks me to think it over for one more night—to consider of all the pro bono I can do here with the resources of the firm, including the opportunities to train younger associates. Granted, it would not be full-time, but by encouraging younger associates to take on pro bono cases to obtain that additional legal experience in courtrooms and with clients, it's as if I'm cloning myself. He repeats how valuable I am to the firm—especially with the amount of business I am bringing in from Capital Management. He lets it slip that the bonus was basically mine.

It definitely hurts.

I can feel myself wavering. The cloning argument is a good one. I tell him I will think over what he said.

As soon as I close the door to his office, though, I know I'm still going to FLAFL. Those are the cases I want to spend my time on. I can still recruit younger associates from here to help. Jack would help me.

But how did Tom find out?

I take the elevator back to my floor. As I walk down the hallway, Tom is outside my office, waiting.

"You're going to FLAFL, aren't you?" he says as I approach. A printer grumbles in the background as it spews out sheets of paper.

"They made the offer today. How'd you find out?" And Zeke was worried his office was bugged. It seems my office is.

"From your boyfriend." His smile is sly.

"My boyfriend?" I snort. "Nice try. There's no way Zeke would tell you."

"Not that boyfriend."

I stare at him. "Wyatt?"

"Bingo. Wyatt told me at the FLAFL dinner that you were always planning to go to FLAFL. And then I spoke to some FLAFL lawyer who was talking about how a position just opened up. And that it's a rare opportunity for a mid-level lawyer. I put two and two together, and I made a very good guess."

Wyatt. I can't believe it. His indiscretion has cost me the bonus. He knows I can't stand Tom and the feeling is mutual.

He asks, "You're really going to FLAFL?"

"Yes," I say.

"I wasn't sure you would go even if you got the job," Tom says.

"At least you'll get the bonus."

"No, I won't. My accusing you of a 'fake' ethical violation torpedoed that. I thought it was real." He looks off to the side like a petulant child.

Tom is not getting the bonus either. The firm did address his behavior.

"But you should keep Zeke on a tighter leash. Paisley may say that she doesn't want him back, but don't believe her. She's just using me so she looks like she has a date. The minute she saw him at that function yesterday, she made a beeline right over to him. And she said he was all puppy eyes around her when they were dating." He smiles slyly and walks away.

I walk into my office and sink into my chair.

How could Wyatt?

I can't think about his betrayal right now. I have to focus on my career.

I call Ken to accept the job. I'm actually quitting White & Gilman. It's hard to believe. I inform the managing partner.

Zeke's line goes straight to voice mail. He has a key presentation today—the one that decides whether Charles will back him for a transfer. I can't bother him. I don't leave a message.

I still feel bad about Jack.

I call Wyatt. That jerk. He doesn't pick up either. I leave a very angry voice mail telling him I never want to speak to him again, and I can't believe he betrayed me like that. He knew my desire to work for FLAFL was confidential. This is my career. How dare he treat that like some bit of gossip good for sharing at a cocktail party?

I saw the disaster that happened when my best friend's mom trusted her new boyfriend. And yet I never learn the lesson.

And Tom knows exactly how to push my buttons—*Zeke's puppy eyes around Paisley.*

Stop already with the doubts about my relationship with Zeke.

Zeke won't betray me.

I have to trust my people. That's the lesson from the Jack debacle.

New Lesson #1: Trust your people.

I trust Zeke. There's no relationship without that trust. What Zeke and I have is solid.

Zeke's puppy eyes are now for me.

My phone buzzes. It's Wyatt.

Chapter Forty-Three

Zeke

I POWERED THROUGH THE presentation to the venture capital partners, and Charles nodded at the end. One nod. But it's enough. Goodbye, Arthur.

I made the cut.

My career is finally back on track. I can't wait to tell Tessa, to hold her in my arms, and spend the night celebrating.

I cradle the box of Levain Bakery chocolate chip cookies I bought to celebrate her job offer.

As I walk up her block, the streetlamps glowing in the dark, a brisk breeze crosses over from the Hudson. The bow windows of Tessa's apartment are lit up.

A man stands there.

Miranda's boyfriend?

I increase my pace.

The man turns to face the street. It's Wyatt. Laughing.

Then Tessa.

Tessa reaches over him to pull the drapes shut, but he holds her arms. It looks like he walks her back. Both are out of sight.

The curtain closes.

I stand there.

I can't breathe.

It could be nothing. She's celebrating with her ex. The one she said was all wrong for her.

He *is* all wrong for her.

But that body language in the window was not saying that.

Is Tessa cheating on me? She seemed normal last night. Except for when I first joined her and Wyatt.

I can't lose Tessa because of my paranoia. But I'm not paranoid. I was right that Tessa did not seem like an artist.

It could be nothing. She's with her ex. She's allowed to be with her ex. Paisley and I danced at the wedding.

But she did worry that I might still have feelings for Paisley.

Because she still has feelings for Wyatt?

Wyatt made it clear yesterday that he wants her back. He bought a fricking table and invited all her friends, as if to say he's the man for her.

Tessa would never cheat on me. I know that.

I race down the street. *I'm the man for her, and she's the only woman for me.*

A whoosh of air signals a summer thunderstorm, and then the rain torrents down in a straight line. The guy in front of me starts running. I look like I'm chasing him, and indeed, he looks back.

He stops short under an awning, and I almost bump into him. He jumps.

"Sorry," I say. I run through the torrential downpour. My button-down shirt is drenched and sticking to my body.

I reach Tessa's door and ring the doorbell. She buzzes me in, and I hear her calling my name in the stairwell.

Tessa is up there on the landing, looking over, like our first date. *Right.*

I reach her floor. I want to hug her, but I'm soaked.

"Why are you so wet? Did you run over in that thunderstorm?" she asks.

"I saw you and Wyatt in the window," I say. *Stupidly.*

I glance in the room. Wyatt is sitting at the table, sprawled out, a huge, fresh bouquet of flowers in a vase next to him. A small ice cream cake is on the table.

"He's leaving," Tessa says.

He puts his hands up. "All friends here. I came to clear my name. Tom said I told him that she wanted to work for FLAFL, and that's how it got leaked to Jack, so she lost the bonus."

I turn to her. "What? What happened?"

Wyatt talks again. "What I said to Tom was that Tessa always wanted to work for FLAFL, but it seemed like she was able to have her cake and eat it too because here she could work for White & Gilman and still do pro bono work. I admit I shouldn't have said that, but I didn't realize that Tom would immediately figure out that she'd applied for the open FLAFL job and tell Jack."

She lost her bonus?

"I told you Tom is not a friend," she says and opens the door. "You've said what you had to say, and I accept your apology. Now please go."

"I'm going," Wyatt says, slipping out the door.

Tessa is standing there, and her face is pale. "Did you think I was cheating with Wyatt here?"

"You lost the bonus?" I ask. "Not really." But I know she can see on my face that the thought crossed my mind. Because I'm messed up.

She sinks into a seat. "This day can't get any worse."

"It doesn't look like you were having a bad day here," I say and regret it immediately. "I'm sorry."

Her eyes fill with tears. "You thinking I'm cheating on you says a lot."

"Look. I pulled an all-nighter last night. My thoughts aren't entirely rational. I haven't slept. I know you wouldn't cheat on me."

She stares at the table—at the ice cream cake melting and spilling over the plate.

"But the thought crossed your mind?" She stares at me.

"For a minute." I can't lie to her.

Her shoulders slump.

"You're never going to get past my lie about being an artist," Tessa says. "I'm not Paisley. I'm tired. I've lost my bonus. I hope your presentation went well today. I don't want to do this anymore."

"Tessa."

"Can you please go?" She opens the door.

"It was a mistake," I say. "I know you would never cheat on me."

"Please go. I'm tired. I want to be alone. And tomorrow, I'm meeting yet another crappy guy, and I need to be in top shape."

"Tessa, please."

But there's a tear rolling down her cheek, and I can't say no to her.

I walk out the door and down the steps. *I really messed that up.*

Chapter Forty-Four

Tessa

I'M NOT GOING TO cry. I don't cry. Not over men. My insides feel like a windowpane cracked into a million shards of sharp glass, now piercing me. A tear escapes. I brush it away with the back of my hand. Fool. Stupid fool. I knew I shouldn't fall for him. He couldn't have been clearer that he didn't want to date a workaholic lawyer. He couldn't have been clearer that he had trust issues—that he was messed up from his ex.

My eyes squeeze shut to stop the tears falling. I lean my head back against the stone-cold, metal door of our apartment.

If anyone knows not to date someone who isn't all in, it's me. I deserve someone who is all in. Someone who knows I would never cheat. *It's not who I am.* If he doesn't trust me or know that fundamentally, there's no relationship.

My phone rings. It's Iris. I pick up.

"Can I stay with you guys tonight?" Iris asks. "Patrick and I had another fight, and I don't want to be in the same apartment as him."

"Sure. Zeke and I broke up. We can commiserate," I say. "Miranda is over at William's. You can have her bed."

"Oh, Tessa, I'm so sorry. And he seemed like such a good guy too," Iris says. "I'll bring ice cream."

"What happened with Patrick?" I ask as Iris plunks three pints of ice cream on the table between us. I open the mint chocolate chip and spoon out a hefty bite.

"You go first," Iris says.

"Wyatt came over, and Zeke saw us in the window and actually thought I might be getting back together with him."

"Does he know that Wyatt dumped you?"

"Thanks," I say.

"Sorry." Iris picks up the pint of New York Super Fudge Chunk and takes a big spoonful. "I mean, does he know that you would *never ever* get back together with Wyatt?"

"Apparently not," I say. "Case in point: Wyatt was over here apologizing because he's the idiot who told Tom I was always planning to go to FLAFL. And Tom told Jack. So that was a mess. And then, to have Zeke believe that I would cheat on him ... As if I would ever cheat on anybody. I feel like he's never going to forget that I lied to him. Or recover from his ex-girlfriend cheating on him."

Iris wrinkles up her brow. "But then, what did he see in the window?"

"I don't know." I stare at our closed blue drapes. "I guess I went to close the curtains, and Wyatt followed me. He reminded me of the time we'd hidden behind them while playing hide-and-seek with some friends' kids visiting. He was trying to charm me out of being pissed off with him. And then I think Wyatt wrestled with me to close the curtain. Maybe that looked really bad from the street? I don't know." I take another huge bite of ice cream. I feel so sad, and the coldness of the mint chocolate chip ice cream doesn't help. *How can he not know that I would never cheat on him?*

"I mean, the guy was cheated on, and then he sees you wrestling with your ex in the window—which might have looked amorous from the street view. It's not entirely implausible," Iris says. "We are all a bit insecure. What's good is that he came right over here to figure out the truth. He didn't disappear to stew about it."

"He did say it was only for a minute, that he knows I wouldn't cheat on him."

"There, see? Intellectually, he knows. But sometimes what we know intellectually doesn't always translate into emotions." She comes over and hugs me.

"What happened with you and Patrick?" I ask.

Iris's shoulders slump. "He's touring this summer, so he made me this schedule of where he'll be every weekend so I can fly out to see him, saying he'd pay half. He even researched flights." She looks at me, her eyes sad. "But I can't do that. I often have to work weekends. And then he was upset that I always put my work first."

"But this is his work. That's like Wyatt."

"It's not that I don't want to see him for three months. It's a long time," Iris says. "But he's also right that I accepted that he'd be gone for three months. I didn't even think to research flights home for him in between tour stops."

I put my arm around Iris. "I'm sorry."

"I'm sorry too."

We hug each other. Iris says that we should get a good night of sleep, and everything will look better in the morning. I make Miranda's bed for Iris and then retire to my own room.

I feel a bit better about Zeke. I was too abrupt to break it off. But I'm still not sure about someone who doubts me. I understand rationally what Iris said, but emotionally ... I'm still upset. I toss and turn. It's lucky tomorrow is Saturday, even if I do have to snare Jurgen.

I can't get out of bed. Some more sleep, and then I'll rally to meet Scammer Guy.

Miranda knocks and opens the sliding door.

"Are you okay?" she asks.

"I had a hard time falling asleep last night. I'll get up soon and get ready to meet Jurgen."

"You don't have to meet him. I talked to those two other women Iris found, and he pulled the same scam on one of them so she will look for her copy of the check. But it would be cool to get a video of Jurgen handing you the fraudulent check and to confirm the handwriting matches. If you're up for it. But no pressure." Miranda sits on my bed. "Do you want to talk about what happened with Zeke?"

I pull my comforter up to my chin. "No." But then I sit up. "You can't begin a relationship based on a lie. It was never going to work."

"That's absurd, and you know it," Miranda says. "Nothing is predetermined. People make mistakes all the time. What matters is what happens next. You admitted you made a mistake and vowed to do better. You're usually up front, so he should be able to move past this."

"He can't. Maybe if his ex hadn't lied to him. But he actually thought I was cheating with Wyatt."

"That's ridiculous."

"But I also made a mistake." My voice chokes up. "I shouldn't have said we were done because he had a second of doubt. I had a second of doubt about him with Paisley, also because of Wyatt leaving me."

Then again, should either of us have even a second of doubt?

Miranda sits on the bed and pulls me into a big hug. "You have to give yourself some leeway too. Yesterday was a rough day for you."

"It was certainly a lot. But I know love means giving second chances ... and third chances. It's a constant work in progress." I push back my hair. "In a way, Tom did me a favor. It's better I told the partnership before the bonus, anyway."

"But the bonus is for past work."

"Fundamentally, it's a retention incentive. And it's better I leave the law firm on good terms. Especially because I want to keep the door open so I can recruit lawyers to help me on pro bono cases. I can live with my parents. I'll survive."

"We'll figure something out so you don't have to live with your parents," Miranda says. "And I don't have to live with a different roommate. I did look for studio space near William's apartment."

I hug Miranda. I feel weepy.

"I have to tell Zeke I don't want to break up. But he left like he accepted it," I say.

The tears flow. Miranda pats my back.

"I really liked him," I whisper.

More than that ... I love him.

I take a deep breath. I wish I'd realized that before I kicked him out yesterday. More tears slide down my cheeks.

"And he adores you. You should see the way he looks at you. Don't give up yet. At least see him in person and tell him. You could prepare an investment report like how I prepared that accounting report for William."

I chuckle weakly and wipe the wetness away from under my eyes. "I'm definitely a start-up in terms of relationships, but I want a long-term investment."

"That's good. You should put that in."

"I'd actually like to paint. It did help me last time to get my feelings out. I'm going to take a leaf from your playbook and share more of my vulnerability."

"That's great." Miranda bounces on the bed. "I'll get the stuff. And you should take a shower."

I chuckle weakly. "And don't worry. I'll meet Jurgen."

Chapter Forty-Five

Zeke

I PACE BACK AND forth in my apartment living room, Brit following behind me.

Crumpled pieces of paper dot my dining table. I tried last night to write an apology or an explanation. To express my feelings for her.

Outside, a garbage truck rumbles through the streets. I watch out the window as the trash bags disappear, the sidewalk now clear, ready for a new day and a new start.

It all happened so quickly. But does Tessa really mean we're over? That she's done? How could she say that?

I'm sure Tessa didn't mean our relationship was over. I have to think that she didn't.

I can fix it.

I should have never intimated that she was cheating.

Tessa wouldn't cheat. Sure, she lied about being an artist, and she's not above using some creative schemes, but the purpose of them is to excavate the truth underneath. She's fundamentally honest. Like when she said, *I really like you. I usually try hard to hold some piece of my heart back, but I don't want to here.*

And she HATES cheating. She had no patience for the thought of Mr. Howard dating another woman immediately after Ms. Robinson died.

I have to apologize again.

Tessa would never cheat on me.

I don't want to break up.

My phone rings and I pick up. It's Ben.

"Congratulations! I just saw the email announcing you're reporting solely to Charles," Ben says. "Thrilled for you. Well-deserved."

"Thank you," I say. My voice comes out hoarse.

"Is everything okay? You sound rough. You saw the announcement, right? Did you think it didn't go well?"

"No. I knew it went well."

"Did I wake you up?" he asks. "Did you spend the night celebrating?"

"No." My throat closes up. I take a second. "I messed up with Tessa. I think, maybe, we broke up."

"What? Well, do your best to convince her to take you back. Apologize and tell her you'll do better."

"I will do better."

"Don't tell me. Tell her. What are you doing on the phone with me? Go fix whatever you messed up. Don't lose her. She's great for you."

"You're right. I'll talk to you later." I hang up.

I have to do better.

I've been holding back. I've been afraid to say how much I care about her. That was my fear talking. My fear of getting hurt again.

I sit at the table and pull over another piece of paper. Simple is best.

I write, *I love you.*

I love her. I lean back, my body hitting the chairback. *I love Tessa.* It's true. I thought I loved Paisley, but it doesn't compare to what I feel for Tessa. I run my hand through my hair again.

Brit whines.

"I'm trying," I say.

Brit brings me her ball and lies down at my feet, the much-loved ball between her paws. She looks up at me with that beseeching expression. If only I could bottle that look and bring Tessa an "I love you" note.

Would it work? Probably not after yesterday. But how to tell her?

What she'd probably like is for me to catch a scammer and present him all tied up with a big bow tie on top, but that's not exactly doable. And I don't want to confess my feelings in front of some crappy guy.

She's meeting Jurgen today. *Alone?* I don't like the thought of her going alone. Wasn't Officer Johnson supposed to be tailing them? Maybe I can meet her at her apartment and go with her as backup.

But I definitely messed up yesterday. I can't just run over to her apartment without a plan.

All right. Head in the game.

What kind of proposal would Tessa like?

I could try to cook her dinner, but I'd probably poison both of us. *A PowerPoint.*

A PowerPoint about us. Like she told that mom in the playground. Only from my point of view. When I first saw her trying to order a beer at that bar. When I wanted to spend more time with her. When I didn't want the night to end.

I have to tell her what I feel.

Chapter Forty-Six

Tessa

So far, so good. I was able to get the table in full view of the café's security camera. My eyes are puffy, but that should help with the suffering artist depiction. I also feel like I'm operating in slow motion, with the majority of my brain cells arguing that I made a huge mistake last night. *What if Zeke doesn't take me back because I didn't listen to him?* Why did I have to say, *I don't want to do this anymore?* And most importantly, *what if Zeke doesn't fundamentally know that I would never cheat on someone and we really are over?*

It's the same café downtown where we met before. The place is not overly crowded, and Jurgen seems pleased with *Regret*. He retapes the bubble wrap around it.

I don't like handing *Regret* over. I'm proud of my painting. And it's part of my relationship with Zeke, even if it's what I painted when I regretted that I lied to him. Isn't it a bad omen to give it to Jurgen?

Jurgen hands me an envelope. I open it up and pull out a check. The check is for two thousand more than the sale price.

The scam is on.

I look up at him. "This check is for four thousand."

"It is?" He scans the check that I've pulled out of the envelope. "Wow. That's a lot more. Let me call him."

"I have free international calls," I say. "Do you want to use my phone?" Then we could trace who he calls.

He pauses, glancing at me. *Is he suspicious?*

"It's okay," he says. "I'm calling him via WhatsApp."

He picks up his phone, clicks on an app, and holds his phone to his ear.

"Hello," Jurgen speaks in very slow English. "The check is for four thousand. We agreed on two thousand. Why more?"

He repeats his sentence again as he looks at me, shrugging.

He's a really good actor.

"Oh. For shipping? And me? My commission?" Jurgen says. "You were supposed to send separately. Separate checks."

He shakes his head and says to me, "He doesn't understand. I told him to send separate checks."

He listens intently to the caller again.

"Okay," Jurgen says. "She can deposit and pay me back. Okay."

I shake my head.

"Do you want to talk to him?" Jurgen hands me the phone.

A stream of what sounds like Latvian comes out of the phone. Jurgen definitely sets up his scam well. I'll give him that as one subterfuge master to another.

The guy on the other end says, "I want painting." Some more words I don't understand. "For wife." More unknown words. "Sent one check for all." And a fervent string of something that could be Latvian.

I have no idea what he's saying, but he sounds absolutely desperate for my painting.

I hand the phone back to Jurgen. "Okay."

"You'll pay me the difference?" Jurgen asks.

I nod.

He says "thank you" into the phone and then hangs up. "He wants a photo of the proof of shipping before we deposit the check. Do you have cash?"

"I have only one thousand," I say. "I can Venmo or PayPal you. Or pay you by check."

"I don't have either. Should we go to a bank? A check will take too long if he wants me to ship it today. The shipping is fifteen hundred dollars. If you give me that in cash, then I'll ship it, take a picture, send that to both of you, and you can pay me my commission later after you deposit the check."

"Okay." I place the check in my pocket and zipper it closed. *I have the check.* "I'm not sure where the nearest Citibank is."

"It's only a few blocks away." Jurgen hefts my painting up. "The Misty Morano show might be back in play."

"Really?" My brow creases in a frown. That's new. I follow him out the door. He turns left.

"They wanted to know how you would describe your brush-work."

Be more ecstatic about the Misty Morano show. I'm slow today.

"My brushwork?" I ask. "That's so great about the show. They got funding?"

Jurgen faces me. "Yes. How would you describe your brush-work?"

Um. If only I had paid attention to that lecture.

"Definitely not a cross-hatching technique," I say. Wasn't that guy fixated on that one afterward?

I didn't sleep at all last night. I'm definitely not up for some brushwork cross-examination.

His eyes narrow.

Think.

"I would say that with *Regret*, I definitely used a heavier stroke to convey my emotions."

He nods.

Leaving the café and walking with Jurgen feels weird. I can't explain how.

But it is the middle of the afternoon.

What I want to do is check that Officer Johnson is trailing us.

That was the plan: Officer Johnson will trail him when he leaves to see if he actually ships the painting or if he pockets the money.

But I don't dare look around.

We walk out the door and down a side street, then pivot into another narrow street, Jurgen talking a mile a minute about this last art show he's seen. We make a few more turns. I've lost my sense of where we are amid the crisscrossing streets of the West Village. I'm trying to respond to his questions about my artistic process and hoping that I make sense.

I'm off today. My body still feels sluggish, and my eyes are so puffed from the crying, they hurt.

This feels like an interrogation. I must just be tired.

And then he turns into a narrow alleyway between two buildings. I stop.

"You're not an artist, are you?" he asks. He puts down my painting.

"That Latvian deal isn't for real?" I ask stupidly.

He grabs my shirt collar with one hand. His face is mottled red.

I freeze, shocked.

Johnson must be nearby.

Jurgen's hand grabs for my pocket.

I clutch at my pocket so he can't unzip it, trying to push his hand away. He's stronger than he looks. It's like battling an octopus. His hand tightens on my collar.

"Are you wired? Are you an undercover cop?" he growls into my ear.

He grabs my hand. *That hurts.*

I knee him between his legs.

Jurgen doubles over.

Johnson runs up, Zeke behind him.

"You're under arrest," Johnson says, getting between Jurgen and me. I stand there in shock as Johnson gives a Miranda warning.

I can't stop shaking.

Johnson arrests him for assault. I hand Officer Johnson's partner the fake check.

We got him. We nailed Scammer Guy.

Zeke is here.

Zeke hugs me, and I turn gladly into his strength and warmth.

"What are you doing here?" I ask him.

"You said you wanted to be a lawyer to protect you and others," Zeke says. "But you keep forgetting to protect yourself. I got worried and thought I should come. But I tried to stay far behind so he wouldn't see me. That's why I was late. And because I thought you could handle him. As you did."

My body is still shaking.

"I don't want to break up," Zeke says.

"I don't want to either," I say.

Zeke holds me tight against him, and I can feel my body slumping as the adrenaline wears off.

Jurgen is hustled into a waiting patrol car. It speeds off.

Zeke releases me but still holds my hand as we turn to face Officer Johnson. Officer Johnson hands me my painting.

"I'm sorry about that," Officer Johnson says. "We didn't assess the risk as physically dangerous."

Neither had I. I didn't trust him, but I hadn't been paranoid enough.

"I think I failed all of his artist questions," I say and turn to Zeke. "Let's go home."

I grip Zeke's hand tighter. Zeke is the one for me. I need to tell him that so he isn't hurt by doubts about me.

"I'll drive you back to your apartment, and we can debrief on the way," Officer Johnson says.

Chapter Forty-Seven

Zeke

When that guy grabbed Tessa, my heart rate exploded. I grip the edge of Tessa's kitchen counter in her apartment.

I fill the electric kettle with water. She went to take a shower and change. She said she wanted a cup of tea. I remove the paper copy of my PowerPoint presentation from my backpack and place it on the table for later. I take a deep breath. *We're back together, but I still need to tell her how I feel.* I return to the kitchen and take down two mugs from the shelves. Is she okay? Should I check on her? I pace in the narrow kitchen hallway.

As Tessa enters the room, she still looks pale. The black shirt and yoga pants she's thrown on clearly don't help. She looks like she's going to a funeral.

"I'm sorry," she says. Tears glisten in her eyes. "I never should have said let's break up. I was so tired last night."

"I'm sorry again about thinking even for a moment that you were getting back together with Wyatt. I know that possibility isn't even in your DNA," I say immediately. "I'm a jealous fool, but I will try to be better."

"I'm also a jealous fool, so I understand."

"You shouldn't be. I will never get back together with Paisley. And I can hand off this Red Can investment opportunity to Ming or a more senior associate who can handle the whole thing."

"It's okay. You guys can work together. I trust you," she says. "I gave myself a stern talking-to last night, and I realized that we both have mirror situations with exes, although yours was much worse. You shouldn't be jealous of Wyatt. I have no desire to get back together with him. *Ever.* But I was upset that you even thought I could cheat."

"I know you wouldn't cheat. It was a momentary, stupid thought, and then I realized that I had to tell you that you are the only one for me. That's why I was running."

"So if I'd just let you explain, we wouldn't have gone through last night?" she asks.

"Maybe. But last night gave me some time to think about us."

"Is that good or bad?"

"That we're good together." I reach out to hug her. We stand there like that for a moment, drawing strength and comfort from each other.

Steam billows out of the kettle. I pull away to make the tea, but I keep hold of her hand. I don't want to let go of her. I take my mug while she grabs hers, and we make our way to the dining room table, hands still clasped. We lean against the table.

She updates me on everything that went on yesterday. "Did you get your transfer?"

"I got the transfer. No more Arthur. And it's in no small part due to all your work on my account."

We both put our empty cups down on the table.

I reach out to pull her close. I've missed holding her so much. As she fits within my arms and curls into my chest, a happy warmth fills me. I'm never letting her go again. I squeeze her tightly.

She looks up at me. I kiss her, trying to convey how much I love her. She kisses me back, and there's a desperate energy to our kiss—like we're both trying to reassure the other that we're back, that we're never going away again. I cradle her head, and my hand rubs under her soft hair. *I'll never get enough of her.* As we stumble slightly, I pick her up and put her on the table. But as I do, I push aside my PowerPoint. There's a slight rip of paper.

My PowerPoint.

She puts her hand down on the table. "What's this?"

"I made a PowerPoint to express how much I love you."

"Repeat that." She tilts her head.

"I know. A PowerPoint is kind of lame."

"No. Not that. The second part of that sentence."

I kiss her cheek. "I messed this up too. I love you."

She smiles, and it's as if she glows from within. "I love you too." She kisses me quickly on the lips. "And I don't think a PowerPoint is lame at all." She leans back in my arms. "I want to see it. I wrote a short 'legal brief' for you."

"You did?"

"Yes. With arguments as to why we worked. Although fundamentally, I want to say you have my head and my heart."

I place her hand over my heart. It's beating so fast. I'm sure she can feel it. "You have all of me too."

"But I still want to see your PowerPoint."

"All right." I take her hand and my PowerPoint and tug her over to the couch. I sit down and pull her into my lap. I'm not letting her go. I flip to the first page. It has a picture of the art gallery invitation and a photo of us. Ben snapped it secretly to show me how happy I looked talking to her. And it's true.

"I fell for you at that very first meeting," I say.

I show a picture of the swing and the café we visited on the next slide. "And I fell hard."

"How'd you get the picture of the swing?"

"I ran around this morning and went to every place we'd visited."

I turn the page. This slide has our text exchange with our two terrible drawings.

She laughs. "I put that in my brief too."

And then the next slide is a picture of the two paintings from the art auction.

"This is when I realized that you could be everything I was looking for. We had so much fun creating that painting. Both of us were terrible, basically, and yet combined, we actually succeeded," I say.

The next page has a photo of the painting from the MoMA called *Lies and Other Truths I've Been Told*. "The truth was always peeking out. And I got too hung up on the artist/lawyer thing."

"I'm still sorry I lied to you." She nuzzles my neck.

I turn to the next page with a picture of us in Mexico City. "You're an amazing lawyer, and we make an unbeatable team. I want to be there for you with your career, and you've already shown how much you're there for me with mine."

And finally, there's a picture of us at the wedding—first laughing, and then staring at each other, our hearts in our eyes. "Dylan sent these to me. I do think we'll be next."

She squeezes me tightly. "I love your PowerPoint. It's much better than my brief."

"You still have to share."

She gets up and goes to the closet, where she pulls out a garbage bag. A canvas peeks out. She stands in front of me.

"Are you sure you're okay after he grabbed you?" I ask. "My heart stopped when I saw that, and I was so far away."

"I'm okay. More shocked. I'm not hurt."

I pull her back into my lap. "You're too far away. It's good to have a warrior lawyer girlfriend. But I still want to see the brief. I made you business cards too." I hand her the Tessa Jackowski, Private Investigator business cards. She clutches them to her chest.

She pulls a piece of paper out of the bag while hiding the canvas.

> Argument #1: We're good for each another and we can work, as evidenced by our working together on *Dalmatians Gone Wild*, the Comidas en Canasta investigation, and the Howard investigation.
> Argument #2: I LOVE YOU, with a picture of our text exchange with the drawings of a stick figure couple holding hands and a Dalmatian.
> Argument #3: Also I LOVE YOU. Underneath it is the photograph of the LOVE IS AN ART mural we saw in Mexico City of a gray-haired, stooped couple holding hands.

"But in the end, I can't really make an argument about why we should be together," she says. "It's not about logic. It's about emotion. You have to feel it."

I kiss her. "I love you."

"Maybe you should reserve judgment until after you see this." She reveals the canvas.

Wow.

It is terrible.

Even worse than what she painted at the auction. There is a black blob, and then there are some red hearts and two stick figures holding hands, and another blob below that. Like a crawling snowman. And then lots of splatters of paint.

"I tried to paint another one to express how much I love you, but as you can see, I can't create it alone. We're better together."

"Why is there a crawling snowman?" I ask.

"That's Brit. And the splatters of paint represent *Dalmatians Gone Wild*."

"Oh."

"And the black represents my sadness apart."

"I see." I nod. "I love it." I kiss her again. We fall back on the couch, her body underneath me.

"I love you," I say.

"I love you," she says.

I brush back a strand of hair from her forehead as she gazes up at me, love shining in her eyes. Her face is now so dear.

Tessa is the one for me. I'm looking forward to a lifetime of adventures with her, although maybe a few less encounters with shady men like Scammer Guy and Howard can be negotiated.

But if not, I'm willing to ask Iris for the name of that self-defense class so I can brush up on my jujitsu skills.

She pulls down my head for another kiss, and I cease thinking about anything else—except for Tessa and me together.

Epilogue - Tessa - Three Weeks Later

WE WALK HAND IN hand up Amsterdam Avenue on our way to the Oasis Garden summer celebration. The street is relatively empty this early in the morning.

"How was the roommate interview this morning?" Zeke asks.

"A definite no." I shudder. Miranda and I realized that we could convert the living room of our apartment into a combination bedroom and studio for Miranda if we built a wall there. Then we could rent out her back bedroom to a third person for more income. Renting out the whole place and moving back home is still an option, but that would mean Miranda would have to find studio space—and I really don't want to live with my parents—so we're hoping this might work. But first, we have to find a suitable roommate.

"She didn't like Miranda's art," I say.

"She said that?" Zeke frowns.

"Yes. She also didn't like the smell of oil paint, so she wanted to know if that 'odor' would be there."

Zeke snorts.

We run into Maddie as we turn the corner. Just as we hug hello, her phone beeps. She checks it.

"It's Nick," Maddie says. "He's double-parked outside the garden and needs help unloading the band's equipment."

Contrary to Maddie's hopes, her rock-star neighbor, Nick, is not going away for the summer on tour. He is spending the summer playing in various New York venues. But that means his band is free to play here.

Ahead of us is a white van double-parked. Framed by the open van doors, a tall, dark-haired guy lifts something heavy, his muscles rippling under his shirt. He glances over his shoulder as we hurry over.

"He's hot," I say to Maddie. Maddie shrugs, but she definitely scoots ahead of us and reaches Nick first.

Zeke glances at me, an easy smile curving his lips.

"Not as hot as you," I say.

He laughs. "Only you think I'm as hot as a rock star."

The guy hands a guitar case down from the back of the truck to Maddie, as Maddie says, "I'm not going to drop it, Nick. Have a little faith."

Maddie walks over to me, carrying two guitar cases.

"These guitars are like his babies," she says. "He said he didn't trust me to carry them."

"I'd be worried, too, if I was him that you might sabotage him; you do complain a lot about his playing," I say. "But he should know you'd never do that."

"He should," Maddie says. "And he'd probably then take up drums—just to really torture me."

Zeke helps the drummer carry his equipment into the garden to set up on the makeshift stage.

Nick hops down from the truck. He is wearing this threadbare T-shirt, and as he lifts his arms up to grab the speakers from his bandmate in the truck, his shirt rises up to reveal sculpted abs. Maddie is transfixed. She blushes and huffs when I catch her staring.

"I might as well enjoy the view," Maddie says. "I need the extra kick of adrenaline after being kept up half the night listening to his latest musical attempt."

I raise my eyebrow.

Nick walks over, carrying a speaker.

"Nick, my friend Tessa," Maddie says.

Nick puts down the speaker and shakes my hand.

"Lily is thrilled you agreed to play," I say.

"It's not like he did it out of the kindness of his heart," Maddie says.

He tousles her brown hair. "Yes, I did."

"Then give me back my coupons."

"No," he says, grinning, and pulls out handwritten vouchers on slips of paper from his back pocket. "These are worth their weight in gold."

He reads the text out loud: "One night unlimited singing and guitar-playing by Nick. No complaining by Maddie. Redeemable August."

He carefully folds his coupons back up and tucks them into his pocket. "I especially like me as the stick figure with this circle mouth and some notes coming out of it," he says. "Why only August?"

"Because I can stay with Iris. Her boyfriend is on tour."

Nick clutches his chest. "You're so cruel." He picks up the speaker. "Nice meeting you. I need to help with the rest of the stuff. But we are thrilled about this opportunity." He disappears into the garden.

"Are you sure there's nothing between you because—"

"That's just him," Maddie says. "It's like flirting is in his rock-star genes."

"He wasn't flirting with me," I say.

"He's not an idiot," Maddie says. "The way you and Zeke look at each other … it's pretty obvious you guys are meant to be together. Anyway, let's get the rest of the stuff before the van gets a ticket for illegally parking."

We haul the band's gear into the garden.

It looks like the summer celebration is in full swing already. Tall, leafy trees shade the gravel pathway where compact tables are set out for the various activities. Behind the tables, purple flowers of the chaste trees envelop the viewer in a soft haze, contrasting beautifully with the red-pink rosebushes.

Lily and Rupert are running an activity where visitors can plant carrot or kale seeds in little cups to take home. Zeke's friends, Brooke and Ben, are helping out at the refreshments table. Miranda is painting a child's face, and no other children are lined up. William is seated next to her, tilted slightly toward her.

Taylor brought Mrs. Humming, and she's sitting with Mrs. Potter, the founder and co-director of the garden.

Taylor and Iris are giving a demonstration of self-defense techniques in another corner of the garden. About twenty people, ranging in all ages, are lined up in front of them. So far, that looks like the most popular offering here, despite Lily's doubts.

I feel such a sense of pride to be a part of this community created by this garden.

Zeke lets go of my hand to pour us each a cup of coffee from the thermos on the picnic table off to one side.

"I was thinking …" Zeke pauses.

He rubs the back of his neck. *Is he nervous? What could he be thinking that he would hesitate to tell me?*

He holds my glance and continues, "That I could be your third roommate, sharing your room and paying rent, if that worked. My apartment lease is up this September. If Miranda wouldn't mind. I'm not so sure you want to live with me all the time. You guys can discuss among yourselves. If your building accepts dogs too. Brit is part of the package."

I gaze at him, my heart melting. This could be perfect.

"Are you sure?" I ask.

"I am absolutely sure," Zeke says. "It's not even a question for me. But I do think it's a question for you and for Miranda."

He stares into my eyes, his own earnest, so much love and care shining out of them.

"Yes," I say softly. And then when it hits me what he's just suggested, I squeal "yes" and jump into his arms. He stumbles back. My body trembles with happiness. It feels like he's proposing.

"Well, that's a yes. I feel like I'm proposing," he says with a slight laugh, as he pulls me close. "I guess it's good practice for when I do."

I hug him tightly. I like that it's not even a question.

"But don't you have to ask Miranda?" He looks down at me, smoothing my hair back from my face tenderly.

"Yes, but Miranda and I already discussed last night that you would be the perfect roommate. Well, you and William, but William needs the extra space for an office that his apartment provides. Come!" I pull Zeke over to Miranda. "Miranda, Zeke suggested he room with us!"

Miranda looks up. "Yes!" She is holding a mirror to show the small girl that she now looks like a lion, but as soon as the little girl roars and runs happily to her mom, Miranda jumps up and puts out her hand. "Welcome, new roommate."

"Then we can keep the living room, and you can stay in your bedroom," I say. "Not that you're there that much since you spend so much time at William's apartment."

"I don't like to be separated." William embraces Miranda in a back hug.

Zeke reaches out to hold my hand, with a quick smile at me. *We're moving in together.* Just like that. It's so easy now.

"Should we join that jujitsu session if you're going to continue your private detective business?" Zeke asks.

"I'm still so happy that the handwriting on the checks matched," Miranda says. "You can go. We don't have any customers right now, and William and I can handle it. "

"Iris has promised us private lessons," I say, winking at Zeke.

The strains of the band warming up sound in the background as Zeke takes my hand and pulls me into a secluded enclave of the garden, where the towering trees create a nook of privacy.

"Can I have the first dance?" he asks.

I kiss him quickly on the lips. "You can have all my dances—except for the ones I dance with my girlfriends."

He pulls me into his arms, and I go willingly, feeling such a sense of rightness. The smell of honeysuckle combines with Zeke's pine- and fresh-air scent, and I relax into him. He holds me tightly.

"I love you," he says.

I look up at him. "I love you."

The guitar chords resonate across the park, followed by the drums, and then Nick's voice—clear and haunting—causes the crowd to hush. It's a slow ballad, and I rest my head against Zeke's chest as we sway to the music.

"They're good," Zeke says. "Do you think they take requests for salsa?"

I look up at him and grin. "We can always ask. Maddie said they were willing to play requests."

"I think I've already received everything I've requested this year: the transfer and, most importantly, you," Zeke says.

"I know I did," I say.

He nuzzles my neck.

Ticklish, I giggle. "You know when you do that, I can't concentrate on anything but you."

"Is that supposed to stop me?" Zeke asks, the corner of his mouth tipping up. He lowers his head to kiss my neck again, and I laugh, squeezing my shoulders up.

Then I quickly kiss him on the lips in a surprise move.

"You're right. That's a better idea," he says, and he kisses me, his hands framing my face.

I melt against him. I've found the love I was looking for. Our love is its own art—one that we have the rest of our lives to paint.

Epilogue - Tessa - Six-Month Anniversary

"Is it close?" I ask, removing my bike helmet and smoothing down my hair. We've biked down to the East Village to try out this new restaurant that Ben recommended.

"Around the corner," Zeke says, lacing his fingers through mine. "Come."

We walk down the narrow block and turn the corner to a rather familiar street.

I glance at Zeke. "Look! The gallery where we met. We should see if they're having a show."

"Sure," Zeke says.

Curtains block the front windows.

"It's closed," I say, a bit disappointed. It would have been so perfect to visit this gallery again on our six-month anniversary. But Zeke has moved away. *Is he checking the door to see if it's open?*

"What are you doing?" I ask, following him. He's pulled out an envelope—*and a key!*

"I rented it."

"You rented the whole gallery?" I ask.

"They're in between shows, so they gave me a discount," he says. "It was sitting empty, so they were glad for the business."

"But why?" I turn to face him.

Zeke pushes his wavy locks out of his eyes. His gaze on mine is so intent. That look of love gets me every time. I reach out to hold his hand. He clasps mine but then tightens his grip. I give him a reassuring squeeze back.

"To celebrate our six-month anniversary." He's biting his lip as he pushes the door open. Zeke flips on the light switch, and I let out an "Oh!"

A table for two sits in the middle of the gallery, with tea candles ready to be lit. And there are 8x10 photographs framed on the wall.

The ones nearest me are the ones that I included in my brief and that he included in his PowerPoint from that time we made up. But our most recent escapades have been caught as well. He put so much effort into this. My heart pings with little yips of delight. I made him breakfast in bed, and then we went for a walk in Central Park with Brit to celebrate our anniversary, but this is a whole other level of effort.

I stand in front of the photo of us having dinner with Taylor and Mrs. Humming. That's become a regular event now.

The photo of us from last month's Halloween party where we dressed up as pieces of modern art makes me smile. Our "art" was not particularly good because we created our own costumes. But we had so much fun painting each other. I blush.

There's the photograph of me on my first day as a FLAFL attorney and another one of Zeke his first day solely reporting to Charles, like those first day of school pictures.

One by one, these photos mark our relationship history.

I gravitate to the photo that is my favorite—Zeke and I staring at each other with so much love in our eyes. Miranda took it at a September weekend in Fire Island with all our friends.

Zeke is fiddling with the picnic basket next to the table-cloth-draped dining table. I bounce over to him and hug him from behind.

"What are you doing over here?" I ask.

"I'm just trying to get everything ready," Zeke says as he fumbles with the top button of his shirt and loosens his collar. He pulls out a whole bunch of take-out containers, including a prepared salad, my favorite balsamic vinegar dressing, and dumplings. Yummy.

"I can't believe you did this," I say. "It's perfect."

His head snaps up. "It is?"

I nod. "Perfect." I kiss him quickly on the lips. "Do you need help?"

"No." He swallows, and I watch his Adam's apple move. I want to kiss him again. But then he wipes his hands on his pants and takes a deep breath.

Why is he nervous?

His glance finally meets mine, and his blue eyes soften. "You know, Tessa, I don't think I'm going to be able to eat anything first."

He drops to one knee.

My mouth opens, but no sound emerges.

He holds my hand and looks up at me, with so much warmth and love.

"I love you," he says. "Will you make me very happy and do me the honor of being my wife? I want to share my life with you."

"Yes," I say. "Yes." I sort of jump, but it ends up being more of a fall, into his arms to hug him, knocking him over.

"Oops," I say as we lay entwined on the floor.

Zeke laughs and kisses me. "That pretty much sums up your effect on me. You bowled me over, but as long as we're tangled up together, I'm happy."

We're engaged! My heart floats with happiness.

"I love you," I say.

He smooths back the hair on my face and kisses me again, a deeper, more desiring kiss. I give myself over to these fluttery feelings.

"I love you," he says, giving me a quick, hard kiss again.

Trust Zeke to propose in the perfect place for us—with our love as art.

THE END

For Sebastian's story, read *My Secret Snowflake,* a holiday, workplace romantic comedy.

Sebastian has sworn to remain single, but he may have just met his match.

Available to Order here: https://books2read.com/MSS

FREE NEWSLETTER EXCLUSIVE BONUS EXCERPTS!

Find out what Tessa thought during the final Chapter 47! And read a deleted scene—Tessa and Zeke's plane ride from Mexico City with some more zippy shenanigans! Sign up for my newsletter at https://books.kathystrobos.com/LIAAmore

For Miranda's story, read *Caper Crush*, my opposites-attract rom-com caper! She's an emotional artist. He's a reserved accountant. When they team up to search for her stolen painting, will they find love? Available to read now: https://books2read.com/u/bp8wBg

For Lily's story, read *My Book Boyfriend*. She loves her community garden. He wants to bulldoze it to build housing. When feelings grow, will they blossom or turn to rubble? Order here: https://b ooks2read.com/MBB

For Kiara's story (the sister of Tessa), read *A Scavenger Hunt for Hearts*. Kiara is done with dating. But to win her favorite painting in an art scavenger hunt, she pairs up with a handsome stranger. Will deciphering the clues lead to love? Available wherever books are sold or for free when you sign up for my newsletter.

Acknowledgments

Thank you to all my readers.

It makes me so happy when readers tell me that they enjoyed my books.

Thank you also to my ARC team, my newsletter subscribers, the librarians, book bloggers, bookstagrammers, and booktokkers who recommend my books and help me find my audience. You make it possible for me to follow my dream of being an author.

Thank you also to the bloggers of Rachel's Random Resources for such heartwarming blog tours.

Thank you to Lauren Rochester (@coffeebooksandescape on Instagram) for suggesting Strawbundle Food for the name of the food delivery company in Mexico City. Such a great name! I had asked in my October 11, 2022 newsletter for suggestions. What a fantastic reference to Strawbundle Publishing! And I had so much fun with it. As Zeke explains, "It's called Comidas en Canasta—or Food in a Straw Basket or Strawbundle—because each delivery comes in a reusable, woven plastic bag to give the feeling of a picnic and to be eco-conscious. But every hundredth order, the customer receives a handwoven, vinyl Oaxacon mercado bag made from artisans in Oaxaco to support those artists." Comidas en Canasta also used a straw theme in its interior design scheme.

Also, thank you to Lin for thinking of the name *Vámonos!* for the fake food app.

I'm so grateful to my newsletter readers for helping me with names and ideas.

Thank you to my friend Charlita M. for the line: "He better jog." That was such a fun dinner. And to Joe T. for the inspiration for the envelope under the door moment.

Thank you also to my cover designer, Lucy Murphy, of *Cover Ever After*. I love my covers.

Thank you, as always, to my critique partners: Giulia Skye and Ellen Gilman. I am always in awe at how they pinpoint exactly how to improve my story. I'm also very grateful for their friendship. I really love being able to discuss the ups and downs of indie publishing. Ellen even read *Love Is an Art* twice, and both times, found even more ways to improve it.

Thank you also to my RWA-NYC critique group (Ursula Renee, Laurel Anne Raven, and Roma Cordon) for all your thoughtful insights and to Diana Georgelos, whom I met through a WFWA Donald Maass course, for critiquing the first ten chapters.

Thank you, as always, to Emily Poole of *Midnight Owl Editing* (my developmental editor), Sharon Coleman of *Twisted Metaphor* (my story editor), Brooke Crites (my alpha reader), Jenny Rarden of *Stormy Edits* (my line editor), and Joyce Mochrie of *One Last Look* (my copy editor and proofreader) for making my story the best it can be. This story went through so many revisions.

Thank you so much to my friend Annette Vazquez and her translation company, AV Translation Services, who came up with the correct translation of Strawbundle Food (or food in straw baskets) and who checked my Spanish.

Thank you also to my Romantic Novelists' Association reader who read my partial (the first one hundred pages) in August 2022 and gave me such encouraging feedback.

Thank you to Gail Chianese who critiqued the original first chapter of *Love Is an Art* after I had the winning bid on her Orange County Romance Writers critique auction donation. As a result of her constructive critique, I rewrote the first chapter completely.

Thank you to Parinyarat Cutone for the suggested names for my Thai-American mother and daughter.

Thank you also to my husband, who serves as my final copy editor.

Also, below contains SPOILERS as I talk about my writing process, so only read this after you've read the book.

Thank you also to the members of my two Gotham screenwriting classes in 2021 for all their helpful comments and critiques. I wrote a treatment for *Love Is an Art* in those classes. In that treatment, Tessa's revelation of her lie was the "dark moment of the soul" when they break up. But once I started writing the novel, I couldn't keep up the lie for that long, and I realized it might be better for her to tell the truth sooner and face the fallout. And indeed, last summer, in a Sarah MacLean conflict class, she discussed how many times it's better to reveal the lie sooner because the consequences give so much material to work with.

As I researched scams perpetrated on artists, I came across a March 17, 2023 *New York Times* article that described artists being scammed by a person seeking to buy a painting via email. The artist then received a large check, which included the cost of the painting plus the shipping fee. The artists were then asked to forward the shipping fee by money order to the person arranging the shipping, only to discover later that the first check was fraudulent. I used that as the basis for the scam in this book.

And don't forget to check out my website at www.kathystrobos .com for behind-the-scenes blog posts.

Thank you to all my friends who cheer me on. I am so touched by all your support.

And thank you to my family, who encourage me and put up with me disappearing to write at my computer.

About the Author

Kathy Strobos is a writer living in New York City with her husband and two children, amid a growing collection of books, toys, and dollhouses. She previously worked as a lawyer before switching careers to write romantic comedies and get in shape. Born and raised in Manhattan, she loves writing about New York City and the accomplished heroines who live and fall in love there, amidst its vibrant energy and the aroma of homemade chocolate chip cookies. She is still working on getting in shape.

Also by Kathy Strobos
A SCAVENGER HUNT FOR HEARTS
PARTNER PURSUIT
IS THIS FOR REAL?
CAPER CRUSH
MY BOOK BOYFRIEND
LOVE IS AN ART
MY SECRET SNOWFLAKE
MY ROCK STAR NEIGHBOR

www.ingramcontent.com/pod-product-compliance
Lightning Source LLC
Chambersburg PA
CBHW061351190726
48288CB00005B/1678